When It's Meant to Happen

A Teapot Cottage Tale (#3)

Annie Cook

ISBN: 978-1-917129-41-1

www.Anniecookwriter.com

For Yvonne Raymond, my long-time friend and spiritual mentor, who always puts everything gently and beautifully into perspective.

Chapter One

Darren Davies heaved a long sigh of relief as he finally stopped his truck outside the front door of Teapot Cottage. The sun had long-since set, but someone (presumably the owner, Mrs Raven?) had switched on a lamp in the one of the front windows and left the curtains half open. As he'd pulled up, an elegant wall-mounted sensor light had also come on, above the front door.

It was good to see some welcoming lights. Arriving late at night somewhere strange and remote wasn't much fun at the best of times, and this trip had been a real challenge. Sunset had quickly plunged the Lake District landscape into a pocket of pitch-black nothingness. The last half-hour had been particularly spooky and unnerving, driving through dark valleys flanked by fells that huddled almost oppressively around them, with their backs set solid against a starless sky. There hadn't been a single streetlight, on most of those roads. He'd wondered what might be crouching around the edges of the blackness, watching with beady eyes.

They'd set off from Devon as early as they could, after lunch. The drive to Torley should have taken around six and a half hours, according to the Google map. He'd hoped they would arrive well before dark, but trips like this always took a lot longer than planned. Extra time had been swallowed up by rest stops and a need to come off the M5, to try and find a fuel station that wouldn't ask him for an arm and both of his legs, as well as the contents of his wallet. Thanks to a couple of clutches of roadworks, tailbacks on the M6 had gobbled a fair chunk of time too.

Nightfall had coincided with Darren's satnav showing a truly torturous route after leaving the motorway, and he'd fretted about getting lost. He'd somehow managed to miss a turning at a slightly weird junction called Bracefield's Top, on the other side of Torley valley, and had quietly cursed to himself until he realised the mistake had actually done him a favour. The satnav had recalculated and shown a more straightforward way. It made him wonder, and not for the first time, who'd been responsible for setting up the satellites the satnav hooked into, and whether they knew that at least half of the digitally mapped-out routes they provided didn't make the blindest bit of sense.

He looked across at his wife, Debby. She was sound asleep. She had fastened one of those curved squidgy travel pillows back-to-front around the bottom of the passenger seat headrest, to make her neck more comfortable. It seemed to be working, and he was pleased about that, because she hadn't been sleeping well for a long time now. He was as grateful as she was herself, for any opportunity she could get, to bag a bit of shut-eye. She tended to snore like an idling tractor whenever she slept sitting up, but he accepted that as a small price to pay.

He watched her slumber for a full minute before she somehow sensed the truck was no longer moving, and woke up with a start. Badger, their border collie dog, was also awake now, and whimpering softly, excited to be in a new place. Unfortunately, the dog snored too; as loudly, in fact, as the average drunken lord who'd sunk nine pints of lager. Darren had driven pretty much the whole way from the Warrington turn-off listening to the percussion-heavy Dog and Debby Stereo Show, which had felt like a rather cruel and unusual test of mental fortitude.

Good job I love the bones of both of them!

'Wake up, Debs, we're here,' he said gently. Debby yawned and stretched, and blinked sleepily at him.

Darren was pleasantly surprised by Teapot Cottage. Probably thanks to its quirky name, he'd been expecting some higgledy-piggledy structure with a rickety doorstep, a buckled porch and a crooked chimney. He'd been prepared for finding the place to be as draughty as hell, with wonky windows that didn't properly close, and a thicket of unruly, bug-infested ivy wending its way around an ancient, warped front door.

This place was about as far removed from that as anything could ever be. It was a gorgeous, solid stone house, with clean lines and a perfectly sturdy door. A tall chimney at one end promised an open fire or wood burner, and the multi-paned windows were modern and nicely painted. A dense tub of yellow miniature roses sat squarely at each side of the front door, and there wasn't a scrap of straggly ivy to be seen. Paving stones were laid in a neat herringbone pattern in front of the doorstep, which made the place look clean and tidy. It all put paid to any misgivings Darren might have had, about staying somewhere so quaintly named.

He hadn't paid any real attention to the pictures on the website. He'd just been keen to book something, *anything*, that was available for an entire month at the start of summer, that would allow them to bring their dog. Suitable places were already thin on the ground by the time he'd got around to booking but he'd got lucky. As Mrs Raven had said in her email, she'd had couple of late, back-to-back cancellations, so her cottage was available for the full month they wanted, and a dog was fine as long as it slept downstairs.

Research about the cottage or the area wasn't even on his mind when he'd said yes. He'd just been relieved to have found somewhere for the three of them to relax in while they tried to figure out what – if anything – was next in their lives together.

As promised, the key was hidden under the left-hand rose bush pot. As Darren opened the front door, and allowed the ever-inquisitive Badger to push past him, he was met with a surprising sense of warmth. He was delighted to find that a fire had been lit, and a few embers were still alive and glowing gently, behind a pretty wrought iron screen.

Debby gave a small cry of pleasure. She picked a fresh chunk of wood from the log basket, and carefully placed it onto the fire to boost it up a bit. The flames licked around it straight away, and it quickly crackled into life. She looked around, and then grinned at him.

'Wow! What a place! It's gorgeous. It feels so homely already, don't you think? Good choice!'

Darren gave her a wink, and went back to the truck to start hauling their bags in. They'd brought lot of stuff, but being here for a month meant they'd need a decent amount of clothes and personal things. Also, because it was the Lake District, where the weather could change in the blink of an eye, they'd been advised by Mrs Raven to pack for four seasons. Random bouts of rain were common, even through the summer, and it could still be chilly at night.

One of the heavier bags contained enough books and jigsaw puzzles to keep them both absorbed for probably twice the length of time they'd be here. The paperbacks would only be read once, and Darren figured they could then be given to a local charity shop, or even left at the cottage for other guests to enjoy. He didn't intend to drag them back to Devon, but he *would* be keeping the two new John Grisham hardbacks his mum Barbara had given him for his thirty-ninth birthday, a month ago. He was looking forward to reading those, before they joined the already impressive Grisham collection that had its own full bookshelf, back at home.

He'd discovered his joy in reading many years before, in a past life, on one of his longer holidays at His Majesty's pleasure (or *Hers*, as it was back then). A prison cell was the ideal place to sit and read a good book, especially when you were lucky enough to have a pad-mate who wasn't a drama king or a crack-head, and who also liked a quiet life. Darren had come to love escaping into different worlds, whenever he had the chance, but finding the time to sit and enjoy a bit of escapist 'downtime' was pretty hard to do these days. Balancing careers and their relationship, meeting the needs of a boisterous dog, keeping fit, and catching up with friends and family didn't leave a lot of time for him and Debby to relax and unwind.

It was hard to know where the time went, sometimes. You got up in a morning, with an entire day in front of you, but by the time you rolled back into bed at night it was all you could do to account for the time in between. Reading in bed never worked; he was usually asleep within two minutes. Curling up with a book was a luxury he couldn't wait to indulge in again, in the coming weeks, here in this lovely little cottage.

He set their bags down by the foot of the stairs, and wandered into the compact but well-appointed kitchen. It was brick-lined, with a flagstone floor. A small Welsh dresser occupied one wall, loaded with cups and plates, and a good-sized table and chairs sat squarely in front of it. Debby was staring anxiously at a fire-engine-red Aga cooker with two chrome lids on the top, that dominated the opposite wall. An old-style rope-and-pulley drying rack hung above it, and two tartan-patterned tea towels were neatly folded over the rack-handles in front of the hotplates. The little beast was switched on, lending more warmth and a great deal of character to the rustic but charming space.

Darren remembered hearing somewhere that cooking in an Aga was a practised affair. He wondered if Debby would take it on, or decide to give it a swerve and use the small electric bench-top oven sitting next to it, instead. She was so tired, so burned out, he wasn't sure if she'd be up to any kind of challenge, however small. Maybe a month here would bring the sparkle, that he missed so much, back to her lovely blue eyes. It had been a long time since he'd even heard her laugh.

Debby Cameron had walked into his consultation room one morning, eight years ago, with her little tortoiseshell cat, 'Lindy-Lou.' The poor thing had been vomiting for two days and Debby was at her wit's end. He'd vaguely remembered her from school as a quiet, almost timid girl, who'd kept very much to herself. She'd had very few friends, and wouldn't have said boo to a goose. She hadn't seemed to be the kind of girl who would ever let a boy get to second base, either, so she'd held no interest whatsoever for a teenage boy looking to score.

But that day in the surgery, as she'd confessed her anxiety about Lindy-Lou, Darren had looked at her with fresh eyes. No longer was he looking for an easy score. He wasn't actually looking for *anything*, being more focussed on establishing his career as a newly qualified vet. But Debby had spoken to him with real respect, and when she remembered too that they'd known one another at school, their conversation had become more animated and informal. They recalled a few classmates in common, and talked about the ones who'd gone on to achieve big things.

He'd been too embarrassed to tell her about his own life journey, peppered with petty crime and a few short stretches in prison. But he'd guessed that she already knew about it, because she hadn't asked him anything at all about what he'd been up to since school, and he didn't think it was because she had no interest. She was intelligent enough to read the court reports in the local papers. She probably knew other ex-classmates too, who wouldn't hesitate to indulge in a bit of gleeful gossip about the school's biggest 'bad egg,' and the sorry state he'd got himself into.

Luckily for Darren, life had thrown him the kind of curveball chance most people in the doldrums only ever dream of getting. He'd been incredibly lucky, to get a rare opportunity to turn his screwed-up life around, and he'd never failed for one single second to be profoundly grateful for his good fortune.

Sadly, that didn't matter much to a handful of local people, who still thought of him as a common thief, long after he'd made a fresh start. He'd dreaded the prospect of being confronted by someone he'd robbed, waltzing in with their pet and learning that he was the one who'd be treating it. But you had to expect that at some point, didn't you, if you'd made a new nest in exactly the same place where you'd fouled the first one? People had long memories. It was going to take time, for the new leaf to turn.

But, slowly but surely, it was turning. Most people *were* taking him seriously now, and Debby Cameron had been one of them. She'd stood beside the sterile stainless-steel table, in her faded black jeans, scuffed boots, and a fluffy mohair jumper that matched the colour of her lovely blue eyes, with her once-mousy brown hair gleaming richly with blonde and caramel highlights, and she'd treated him like a vet.

To her, he was intelligent and competent, and she trusted him to heal her little cat. He had done exactly that, and she'd shyly said yes to meeting for a coffee. And, even after he'd hung his head in shame and confessed everything to her about his previous life, how he used to be, what he'd been through, telling her what she doubtless already knew but had been kind enough not to ask about or pass judgement on, she still said yes to going out for a meal. After that, she said yes to another one, and spending a night with him, then to a weekend away, and eventually she even said yes to his hesitant, stuttering proposal of marriage.

They'd been married for seven years now and it was something *else* he gave thanks for, every single day of his life. To a man who once thought his future would amount to a big fat zero, and that no worthwhile woman would ever give him the time of day, Debby was about as perfect a partner in life as he ever could have hoped for.

He grabbed the last little holdall from the truck now, and brought it into the cottage. He was surprised by how light it was. Did it even have anything in it? Then he remembered.

Oh, shit. Oh no! What the hell is this doing here?

It was the bag full of baby things; wool, needles and knitting projects, a few of which were only half finished. Debby had taken up knitting around the time they'd decided to start a family. She'd started making bootees, matinee jackets, hats and blankets, enough for ten babies. But no baby had materialised, and with every IVF treatment that crushingly failed, and every unwanted period that showed up, month after month after month, her interest in making baby clothes had shrivelled to the point where she simply couldn't bear to even look at any of what she'd started, let alone finish it.

Darren's heart broke afresh, thinking about the last five years. After their wedding they'd both been keen to start a family, but they'd put it off for the first two years, to spend time just together. He was thankful for that, because those first couple of years had cemented their relationship, providing good grounding for a union that – so far at least – had managed to withstand a further five gruelling years on a soul-stripping merry-go-round of failed attempts at getting (or staying) pregnant. The last three years had been particularly brutal, dealing with the endless, eviscerating pain of no less than seven unsuccessful attempts at IVF, six of which they'd had to fund privately.

The emotional toll was heavy enough. Financially, it was now more or less untenable too. They just couldn't find any more money for more treatment. The first round of IVF had been free, and their savings had comfortably covered the three after that, but the last three had cleaned them out. They'd drawn the line at re-mortgaging their house, but they now had to face the fact that they were at the end of their reserves. They were tapped out. To add to their anguish, they'd been advised that Debby's chance of conceiving through IVF, now that she was in her late thirties, was reducing with every round of treatment.

The worst of it was that nobody could even explain why she couldn't conceive! She was normal and healthy, and according to the doctors there were no clinical reasons why she wouldn't be able to have as many babies as she wanted. All tests had indicated that Darren was functioning properly too. It was baffling, and when one of their doctors had ventured to suggest that maybe the problem was more psychological than biological, Debby's response had been astonishingly hostile.

Her reaction had been so extreme, Darren knew there had to be more to it. So he'd dug into her, despite massive resistance, and he eventually managed to break through her wall of stubborn silence. She'd finally admitted that she'd fallen pregnant when she was sixteen and had been forced by her parents into having a termination she didn't want. She knew it had been the most practical decision at the time; she'd known she wasn't emotionally or physically equipped to raise a baby, but the termination still haunted her. She'd never told Darren, in fear of being judged and rejected.

He had a less-than-spotless past of his own, so he knew exactly what that particular fear felt like, and he fully understood why she hadn't told him. It was something that happened a long time before they'd got together. He wasn't angry that she hadn't said anything, but he was sad that she'd felt forced to keep it all to herself for far too long, and that it still preyed on her mind so much. Her hostile, uptight parents (who had about as much emotional awareness as a pair of concrete slabs), had flatly refused to ever discuss it with her too, which only made her feel more isolated.

An unwanted termination was a lot for someone to carry all alone. It was no surprise that Debby was tearing herself apart over it now, constantly worrying if that was the reason why she couldn't get pregnant. Every hurt was larger than life now, even potential 'causes,' however big or small they might have been.

Every single medical professional involved had done everything they could to reassure Debby that it wasn't the case; everything was still intact, and working exactly as it should. One had tentatively mentioned the possibility that the early termination might have created a psychological block that was having some kind of biological impact, but Debby stubbornly kept refusing to even consider that. Darren was no psychologist, and with his wife angrily refusing to see one, or even talk to a counsellor, there was no way of knowing for sure. All he knew was that her misplaced guilt over the termination certainly couldn't be helping.

He felt so inadequate, and at such a loss, for how to help her, or cope with her increasingly fragile mental state. On top of that, he had pain of his own. He was grieving too, in his own way, at the prospect of never becoming a father. But Debby hadn't seemed to consider his feelings, or if she had, she never asked him about them. She was too wrapped up in her own anguish. Generously, he wondered if maybe acknowledging his too would simply be more than she could cope with.

He was surprised though, at just how unexpectedly lonely he felt. He had friends he talked to, from time to time, and he had been able to confide in his mum. It did help a little, to offload some of how he was feeling to people who cared about him, but talking about something so deeply personal wasn't easy, even with his best friend Paul, who he'd gone through vet training with, and who probably knew him as well as anyone did. Darren could never bring himself to go into much detail, so his isolation was often profound.

He and Debby were friendly with a handful of couples, including Paul and his lovely wife Pam, but there were two who had quietly and unexpectedly drifted away without a word, and that had really hurt. One of the couples had young kids, and maybe they thought that talking about them wouldn't help Darren and Debby feel any better about their own situation. The other couple had got pregnant very quickly, after deciding to try, and maybe they felt too cruel in expressing their joy and excitement. But he missed those friendships, and he knew Debby did too. She'd also lost other friends, who had let her down when she needed them. It made him angry, that when she was at her most vulnerable, and most in need of support, certain women who'd once declared what a great friend she was to them hadn't managed to find it within themselves to be one to *her*. Hypocrites, one and all. It was such a painful way to find out who cared and who didn't.

What also made him angry was the fact that, of the friends who'd fallen silent or disappeared, not a single one had asked beforehand; 'what do you need from me?' or 'what can I do for you?' If they'd asked those simple questions, perhaps they wouldn't have felt so awkward that severing contact had ended up being the more comfortable option for them. The truth was, if any of them *had* asked him, he'd have told them honestly that they didn't need to do or say *anything*. They just needed to be there, with a kind word or a listening ear, or even just with as something as simple as a cup of coffee, now and then.

That's a really big part of the misery of infertility that most people don't understand, he mused to himself now. The inability of some friends and family, to know what to say or do, meant that some of them drifted away instead. All it did was make a isolating situation even more lonely and difficult to bear.

Darren didn't know where he and Debby would be now, without the friendship, trust, love and belief in one another, that had cemented them so firmly in that first two years they were married. Without that, would they have been able to survive this kind of stress? He doubted it. They hadn't been prepared for how powerless being unable to conceive had made them feel. Now their marriage *was* unravelling, and he really wasn't sure if they even had the strength to stop it from happening.

He wasn't sure why she'd brought the bag of knitting, and he didn't want to ask.

'I really don't know, about this thing,' Debby was still looking dubiously at the Aga, while Badger sniffed intently at the bottom of the back door. Darren set out the dog's big metal water bowl, and the smaller one for his biscuits, but the curious dog was less interested in eating or drinking, and more intent on sniffing around and getting to know his new surroundings.

'Maybe I can give it a go. There's an instruction book, here on the bench, with a recipe for fail-safe fruit scones. Might not be a bad place to start?'

Darren grinned, glad that she was at least considering the prospect of tackling the red oven. It was quite intimidating. He wasn't too keen to get up-close and personal with it, himself!

'Yeah? Go on then, babe. I guess we could live with the worst that could happen, like busting a tooth on a raisin rock or spitting out something half raw. I reckon you should give it a go. You might surprise us both.'

On the old, scrubbed pine table was what looked like a fairly decent bottle of red wine, a loaf of home-made bread wrapped in a tea towel, a small bag of dog treats, and a note from Mrs Raven, welcoming them to Teapot Cottage. It said that she'd be down to see them briefly in the morning, but if they needed anything in the meantime, all they had to do was go up the driveway to the farmhouse, and ask.

Darren opened the fridge door to find a litre of milk, half a dozen eggs, a pack of bacon, and a small slab each of cheddar cheese and butter. Glass containers next to the bench-top oven held teabags and sugar, and a new packet of ground coffee sat next to a plunger on the bench. They'd be absolutely fine for tonight, he decided. They had already stopped for some overpriced and underwhelming food at a motorway services on the M6, near Preston, so they only needed something light. Grilled cheese on toast and a glass of wine seemed perfect. They could explore the town tomorrow, and pick up some groceries.

Teapot Cottage had an unusually warm and welcoming feel, unlike the typical sterile, characterless holiday houses he'd stayed in before, where people passed through without getting or leaving much of an impression. This little place was very different. It was beautifully decorated, with gentle warm, muted colours, and furnished very simply with a comfy sofa and matching armchair, a coffee table with a lamp on it, and an elegant sideboard that held another lamp, a TV, and a small stereo with a docking station portal at the front. A bookshelf tucked behind the front door was loaded with books and board games. A pair of generous custom-built, curve-fronted windows seats with deep-filled pads and pretty cushions offered cosy places to sit, where you could hunker down and while away an entire day, lost in a good book or daydream.

The cottage felt like a real home, where you could easily settle and feel like you belonged, at least for a little while. Darren felt more at peace here than he did in his own house in Devon, which seemed a tad strange, but he shrugged it off. Tiredness did trick the mind sometimes.

Upstairs, the cottage was just as comfy and cosy, with two bedrooms of similar size, and a well-equipped bathroom with a stand-alone shower and a generous roll-top bath. On the top landing, the space had been neatly filled with a small but comfortable armchair and a little bookcase holding books of various genres. It was clearly a morning suntrap, if the skylight window above it was anything to judge by. Whoever had designed or remodelled this place had made the most of every available space and feature. It was lovely, and Darren was sure they'd be happy here. Badger's tail was wagging nineteen to the dozen. He was certainly happy enough. It was almost as if the house were actually hugging them all, from the moment they walked into it. *Extraordinary energy*, some would have said.

The master bedroom had a king-sized bed, which had been covered with a cheerful old-fashioned crocheted blanket made up of various multi-coloured squares. It wasn't the kind of thing Darren would ever consider for his own house, but it was exactly the sort of home-made comfort his mum would have at her place, so it made him feel at home. The plump pillows looked comfy and enticing, and he realised how tired he was, after working an intense half day then driving what had turned out to be a full eight and a half hours to get here from their home in Exeter.

Debby was tired too, after pulling a night shift at the hospital. Her job as a theatre nurse could be intense and demanding. There was rarely a dull moment in an operating theatre, and sometimes the job could be heart-breaking. Last night had been routine for her, without any drama, but she was completely exhausted, and the relentless disappointment she'd been battling with for far too long now was starting to etch lines into her face that hadn't been there before.

He checked his watch. It was just after ten thirty. Normally they didn't get to bed much before midnight, with one thing or another, and for Debby the rotation of different shifts often made it hard for her to drop off quickly, however tired she might be. A quick bite to eat and an 'early' night would be just the ticket for them both.

He saw that his wife had found a corkscrew and was opening the bottle of wine.

'Debs, d'you fancy cheese on toast?'

She nodded. 'I was just thinking the same thing, but I'll do it in that little bench-top oven. I'm not sure yet, about the Aga. It's probably straightforward but I know where I am with the little one. It's got a grill element, so it'll be perfect.'

She set about preparing their supper and fished a can of tomato soup from the small box of supplies they'd brought with them.

'I can heat this on the Aga's hotplate though, because that's ready to use.' She rummaged in the cupboard for a suitable pan.

The log Debby had put on the fire when they first came in was now blazing brightly and throwing out enough warmth to extend the upstairs. He'd felt the heat in every room when he'd gone up there. There were central heating radiators too, in all the rooms, and he suspected the Aga would be the source of the heat that powered them. Currently they were turned off but it didn't matter. They weren't needed right now. Clearly, being cold wasn't going to be a problem here, no matter what the weather might choose to do.

He started lugging their bags upstairs and put them in the second bedroom. There was no need to clutter up their sleeping space when they had the choice to spread out.

He decided to take a quick shower and came back down the stairs to let Debby know, so she wouldn't run any taps while he was in there. He found her standing at the bottom, with her arms firmly folded, glaring at the knitting bag.

'Why is that here? Did you pack that, Darren?' she demanded.

He shook his head vehemently. 'Nope, I thought you must have.'

A shadow passed across her face. 'Well I bloody didn't.'

'I dunno, babe. I must have grabbed it by mistake then. I'm sorry. I don't even remember picking it up, to be honest. D'you want it upstairs?'

'No.' Debby snapped. 'I don't want it here at all. Please put it back in the truck or, better still, dump the damn thing in the nearest bin.' She turned on her heel and went back to the kitchen.

Mystified, Darren picked up the bag and headed for the front door. He was absolutely certain he had not picked up this bag to bring with them. Even if he'd even *considered* bringing something so sensitive, he would definitely have run it by Debby first. She said she hadn't included it, and he believed her. How it had come to be here was a complete mystery. All he could think was that he'd somehow grabbed it with other bags without realising, even though he knew it generally just lived under the stairs, out of sight and mind. It probably hadn't seen the light of day for more than a year. Had he gone under the stairs for something else? He really couldn't remember.

In any case, the bag was going back into the truck, and there it would probably stay. The last thing either of them needed in here were reminders of all that was wrong in their lives. A bag full of baby clothes would do nothing but torment them at precisely the time they needed to relax. Darren didn't even want it in the truck, and Debby didn't either. He was tempted to just throw it away, as she'd suggested, but that somehow felt like the wrong thing to do, as if disposing of it would be a direct acceptance that they were never to have any children. He couldn't bring himself to do that. Not yet. Even if it was what Debby *really* wanted, he doubted if he could say goodbye yet, if push came to shove, to that little bagful of white, lemon and mint-green hopes and dreams.

He ate the light supper Debby had put together, saving the crusts for the dog to polish off. As they washed and dried the dishes together, he felt another wave of exhaustion come over him. He didn't even bother to stifle his yawn. Debby touched his arm lightly.

'Let's get Badger sorted with his bedtime wee, and get away to bed, shall we? It's been a long day. The unpacking can wait. All I need tonight is my p.j's and my toothbrush, and I know which bag they're in.'

He slipped an arm around her and pulled her close, burying his face in her hair. It always smelled beautiful.

'I love you,' he mumbled.

She hugged him back. 'I love you too. Always and forever.'

Darren took Badger outside for ten minutes, then settled him into his bed by the dwindling fire, and climbed the stairs. To his delight, the big bed was every bit as blissful to lie in as it looked. He managed to stay awake until Debby had finished in the bathroom and joined him. He felt himself drifting away as she snuggled close, and the next thing he knew, it was morning.

Chapter Two

Debby woke with a start. For the first few seconds, she struggled to remember where she was, then realised she was at Teapot Cottage, having woken up in the most comfortable bed she'd ever slept in, in her entire life. She didn't want to move. Darren was gently snoring beside her, clearly comfortable too. She gently slid her feet across to touch his, and he grunted lightly to acknowledge her, but didn't wake up. She planted a kiss on his shoulder, and he grunted again. It was a lovely peaceful start to the morning.

Predictably though, as soon as she was fully awake, she felt the familiar heavy feeling of failure and despair settling into her chest. Every day, waking up was pretty much the same, no matter what the circumstances. It begged a couple of questions – was coming all this way to take a break really the answer they needed? Or were they really just trying to outrun their problems? Time would tell, she supposed, but she knew it would take a lot more than a simple change of scenery and a different bed to dispel the wretched heaviness, and the grief that was tearing her apart. The only thing that would ever get rid of this crushing, all-encompassing misery she woke up with every morning was a baby. She needed to be pregnant, and soon.

She glanced at her watch. It was still early, only just gone seven, but it was Saturday morning, and there was nothing important to get up for. No more work for a full month. Getting so much time off had been tricky, but Debby's wonderful supervisor Karim had fully understood how strung out, stressed and sad she was. Seven unsuccessful IVF treatments had taken their toll on her mind as well as her body. Karim had juggled everything he could, including bringing in a couple of agency nurses, to be able to give Debby the time off that she needed, and he sent her on her way with a warm hug and reassurances that a bit of time out would help her feel better.

She listened to Darren as he lightly snored. She envied how he could always sleep virtually anywhere, and for as long as he wanted. He didn't lie awake much, ruminating for hours, like she did, but it would have been unfairly dismissive if not downright cruel, to suggest that he wasn't affected by their inability to conceive. She knew he was upset about it too. But, unlike her, he didn't let his anguish get in the way of whatever else he had to do. He was able to neatly compartmentalize his feelings when required and direct his full focus to what needed it, at any given time.

It was part of what made him such an excellent vet. His devotion to diagnosis and healing was second to none because, as he'd said himself more than once, he owed it to every single animal he treated, to give it his undivided attention. That could often make the difference between whether or not it survived, and he never wanted to live with wondering if he could have done more if he'd been less distracted by something else. His passion for animals meant that he really could leave his troubles in a jar by the door, so to speak, at least while he was at work.

It was an admirable trait, but sometimes Debby felt frustrated by the fact that she seemed to be largely alone in her suffering, most of the time. It wasn't fair to expect Darren to be spending all his spare time grieving too, and railing against the brutal unfairness of life, just to keep her company in her misery, but this kind of grief was deeply profound and lonely. Self-pity wasn't the most appealing quality, she knew, but she really couldn't help herself at times.

Karim had suggested that maybe Debby could find a support group of other women in the same or a similar situation, but she couldn't face the prospect of sitting around in a circle with a bunch of other struggling women, and having to bear witness to their suffering as well as continually fighting to avoid being completely submerged by her own. Catching some silly 'talking-pillow' and being expected to offload her own anguish to a bunch of total strangers was more than she could confront right now.

On one level, she knew how selfish that was, and she did appreciate that there probably *was* great comfort to be derived from connecting with people who were going through a similar agony to her own, but she simply couldn't bring herself to take that step. She may be ready at some future point, but not yet. The rawness of failure was something she felt she needed to work through on her own, right now. But it certainly would have helped a bit more to have had Darren more engaged with it, as the only person she *did* want to share it with.

He was doing his best, and she knew it. He just had a different way of dealing with life's difficulties, and she had to accept that. And sometimes, to be fair, the tenderness in his eyes when he looked at her made her want to cry even harder, because nobody else 'got' her the way he did. He understood how she felt, but he wasn't going to turn her into a raving basket-case by colluding with her whenever she wallowed for too long.

Nor would he keep trying to reinforce to her that she wasn't the abject failure she saw herself to be. He'd said, many times, that she was being too hard on herself, that she was a 'roaring success' in every other area of her life. Wife, nurse, sister, daughter, friend, runner, knitter! He'd told her, over and over, that in everything else she was and did, she was amazing. And he meant it. But he wasn't going to play like a cracked record. That just wasn't his way.

It was so ironic though, that the one thing that mattered above all else, the one role she wanted more than all of the others put together, was the one she was biologically programmed for but somehow couldn't manage to achieve. That, so far, could categorically be classed as a 'roaring failure.'

Mother. Will I ever hear a child call me that? Will my biggest lifetime regret be shuffling off the mortal coil at the end of my meaningless life, having never had anyone call me 'Mummy'?

Debby felt herself sinking once again into the depression that so often overwhelmed her, these days. Darren mumbled something in his sleep, which indicated that he would be properly awake soon, so she decided she'd get up and make them both a cup of tea. Reluctantly she hauled herself out of bed.

Thanks to the Aga, it was still warm downstairs, even though the fire had long since gone out. Badger was still curled up in his bed, in front of it. He wagged his tail half-heartedly, lifted one eye, and promptly closed it again.

She walked across and gave him a loving scratch behind the ears. As a surrogate child, this shaggy, affectionate collie was truly lovely. She adored him. He let out a massive sigh and wagged his tail again, but that was the extent of his enthusiasm. Clearly, he was too comfortable to move.

'So, you're not ready to get up either, you lazy old lump! Well, I don't blame you, really, but I think it's high time I trained you to make a pot of tea in a morning!'

She lifted one of the Aga's lids, then filled the kettle and set it on the hotplate. She looked out of the small bay window in the kitchen and saw a group of brown and white hens scratching about on a small, almost bald patch of lawn. She unlatched and opened the window and saw a slim, middle-aged woman wearing fitted blue jeans and a light grey knitted jumper. She was scattering some seeds around for the hungry hens. She caught sight of Debby at the window and waved, before wandering over.

'Hi! You must be Mrs Davies. I'm Adrienne Raven, cottage owner and hen-chaser.' She proffered a hand, and Debby widened the window, reached out, and warmly shook it.

'Oh, please come in, Mrs Raven. I'm just making a cup of tea. Would you like one?' Debby was rewarded with a wide, generous smile.

'Well, I'll pop in for a minute, but I won't say yes to a drink, if you don't mind. I've been up since half past five, baking shortbread, and I'm already awash with coffee. I was going to pop down a bit later, but since you're up…'

She came around to the back door, as Debby unlocked it from the inside. Badger was immediately up on his feet and bounding towards the newly arrived guest.

'Oh, hello, lovely dog! Gosh, aren't you spectacular?' Badger ran around her legs and placed his nose into the palm of her left hand. She laughed and bent to give him a quick hug.

'He's gorgeous! Collies are such good fun, aren't they? I'm Adrienne, so please call me that. This 'Mrs Raven' malarkey just makes me feel old!'

She had twinkly eyes, and a youthful complexion. Debby decided she was probably in her mid-fifties.

She must have been a real stunner in her youth. The lines around her eyes don't age her much at all! They only show that she smiles a lot.

'The gorgeous one is Badger. And you must call me Debby. All this 'Mrs Davies' malarkey just makes *me* feel old!'

Adrienne laughed again. 'I think it was your husband I dealt with, Darren, is it?' She smiled as Debby nodded.

'Yes, the lazy one, the one who's still in bed, snoring his head off. And I'm still in my pyjamas too, as you can see.'

'Well, why wouldn't you be?' Adie waved her hand. 'It's still pretty early, and you're on holiday. I wouldn't have expected anything else. Did you have an easy journey up from Devon? It's a long way.'

Debby nodded again. 'Yeah, it was easy enough, but long, as you say. We left early afternoon, as soon as Darren could get away from the surgery. We had a few hold-ups, and finally got here about half past ten last night. Thank you so much for the wine and food, by the way, and for lighting the fire for us. That was so nice to walk into.'

'Yes, a fire does make a difference. As I told your husband, it can get quite cold way up here at night, even through the summertime. We're fairly high above the valley, so it's a little more exposed, and I think the air's a bit thinner up here. When I lived here myself, I used to light the fire even in the middle of July, some nights. I'm glad it was still going when you got here.'

'What a gorgeous place this is, so warm and welcoming. And I haven't even seen the view from the living room windows yet. I bet that is just stunning!'

'Well, it's not bad,' Adie laughed. 'Oh, and of course there's the hot tub out the back. It's ready to use, and it's nice and private out there, with the hedges all around it. Please feel free to use it. Being out there with a glass of wine under the stars is rather lovely, especially on a chilly night.' She looked at Debby intently. 'Did you say surgery? Is your husband a doctor?'

Debby shook her head. 'No, he's a vet.'

'Ah, okay,' Adie said sagely. She shook herself a bit. 'Anyway, so, info about the area… there's a Farmer's Market in Torley town on Saturday mornings. It's in the church hall. Easy to find, on the High Street, and it runs from ten until one-thirty.

If you need any fresh produce, fruit, veg, meat, home-baked bread, that kind of thing, the market's a nice place to get it, and it's all local stuff.'

'We do need some groceries, so that sounds great.'

'Torley isn't a big town, but there's all the usual shops that cater to most needs. You'd probably have to head over to Carlisle if you wanted anything more specialized, or a department store, or something,' Adie explained. 'Maybe I'll see you down at the market. I sell eggs, shortbread and preserves – jams and jellies, that sort of thing. I'm the organiser, so I'm down there most Saturday mornings. Best come early, if you can. The good stuff never lasts long.'

She pinched her bottom lip with her thumb and forefinger, clearly thinking.

'Erm... what else? Oh, yes – you'll find a sheaf of takeaway menus in the little basket on the bookshelf behind the front door. Most places do deliver up here. There's a couple of good pubs in the town too, The Feathers, and the Bull and Royal. Both do decent food, and both are dog-friendly. There's an excellent chip shop called Cat's Fish, and a nice little Indian restaurant in town called the Kashmir Garden, if you fancy a curry. The Beeches Hotel on the main road between here and Carlisle offers very nice a la carte dinners, if you want something a bit more upmarket.

'There's also a traditional little café in town, on Amble Walk, just off the High Street. It's called Ye Olde Torley Tea Shoppe, and you could probably take Badger in there. It's run by a good friend of mine. Her name's Peg. She does great coffee and all-day breakfasts and the like, and she makes *very* yummy pies. They're the talk of the town.'

'Ooh, Darren loves a good pie! I'll definitely have to take a look at that. I thought I might tackle the Aga at some stage too. Maybe make those idiot-proof scones in the instruction book.'

Adie laughed, looked over at the bright red Aga fondly, and shook her head. 'I was scared to death of that old thing, once. But I love it now. Once you get the hang of using an Aga, if you do have a go, you might not want to go back to using a conventional oven again. We have a really big Aga up at the farmhouse, and it's all I'd ever use now. There's something quite special about these old girls.'

It was Debby's turn to laugh. 'I'll take your word for it. I'll see how I get on.'

Adie nodded and turned to go, giving Badger's nose a light squeeze before she left.

'You won't let him chase the chickens, will you?'

'No, I won't,' Debby promised. 'He'll probably be scared of them anyway. I don't think he's even seen chickens before.'

After her hostess departed, the kettle started to whistle and Debby quickly whipped it off the hotplate before it could get into full swing. If Darren was still sleeping, she didn't want to wake him with a shrieking noise like that.

He wasn't asleep though. As she took up the two cups of tea, she found him sitting up in bed, watching a video on his mobile phone. He looked up and grinned as she approached.

'Morning, sexy! Phone reception's alright up here!'

She handed him a mug and he winked at her. 'Did I hear voices downstairs, or were you just rattling away at the dog?'

'No, it was our landlady, or whatever you'd call her. Adrienne. She was feeding her chickens out the back. She seems nice.'

'Ah, I'm sorry I missed meeting her! I'd have come down if I'd known.'

'Don't worry, you'll meet her later this morning, at the Farmer's Market in town. She runs it, apparently. She also has a stall there herself; selling eggs, predictably.'

Darren chuckled. 'Right. So, I'm guessing those in the fridge are free range.'

'I imagine so, with hens running around outside, and all.'

'Sounds like an omelette in the offing then. There's still some cheese, is there? Not a lot else, I guess.'

'Well, I did pack some cereal, but Adrienne mentioned a good cafe in the town that does all-day breakfasts. Maybe we could do that this morning instead, then go to the Farmer's Market. We do need groceries, and perhaps we can have a general mooch about, after that.'

Debby remembered what Adrienne had said about the hot tub, but was dismayed at the sudden realisation that she hadn't packed a swimsuit.

‘Why didn’t you tell me there was a hot tub here, you noodle-head? I’d have brought some bloody swimwear if I’d known!’

Darren had evidently failed to notice that particular detail about the place. He shrugged apologetically and pulled a face. ‘Skinny-dipping, then?’ he offered.

‘Hmm… maybe I can find a swimsuit in the town, or at least on a trip to Carlisle, which I’m sure we’ll do in the next few days?’

‘Yeah, I don’t see why not,’ Darren conceded.

Until then, Debby decided, if she wanted to take a dip during the day it would have to be in her birthday suit, or in the oldest bra and knickers she’d brought with her. Darren would probably just go ‘commando.’ He wasn’t bothered about what anyone else might think, not that she expected they’d be having much company at all, and certainly not after dark. It didn’t seem to be the sort of place where people just turned up unannounced, and who did they know that would do that, anyway?

After taking Badger for a quick run across the field next to the cottage, they drove into Torley and were delighted to discover that the parking was free for two hours. It took a while to find a vacant space, but not long at all to find Ye Olde Torley Tea Shoppe. In record time they were tucking into massive plates of eggs, bacon, sausage, beans, mushrooms and tomatoes, with a stack of hot-buttered toast, and massive mugs of coffee. Adrienne Raven had been right. Everything tasted amazing, and the pies in the glass cabinet up by the counter looked heavily filled and gorgeous. Debby could see Darren’s eyes constantly straying to the selection, and she decided she would buy one, as a treat, to take home.

They were served by a young woman in her early twenties, and Debby wasn’t sure if she was the proprietor – Adrienne’s friend Peg. Later, however, an older woman came out and spoke to the younger one with some authority, and Debby decided that this lady was far more likely to be the owner of the cafe. As she came by, Debby spoke up.

‘Excuse me! Are you Peg, the café owner?’

The woman looked slightly startled, as if she was waiting for Debby to start complaining about something. She wiped her hands on her apron.

'Yes, I'm Peg Tripper. How can I help?'

'You're a friend of Adrienne Raven's? She recommended this café. We're staying at Teapot Cottage. I just wanted to say; your food is lovely, and the coffee is great, just like she promised.'

Peg smiled broadly and stuck out her hand.

'Pleased to meet you both. Adie's a great champion for this place. I don't think she's had a single guest she hasn't shepherded into here.'

Debby beamed back at her.

'Well, it's not hard to see why! I'm Debby, and this is my husband, Darren. I think we'll be coming again, and I also think we need to have one of your pies. Apparently, they're the talk of Torley?'

Peg grinned again. 'They're popular, I'll grant you that. They'll all be gone by eleven.'

Darren cleared his throat. 'Well, I guess we should choose one now, shouldn't we?'

'I've steak and onion, minced beef and cheese, chicken and mushroom, lamb and mint, or creamy veg,' Peg replied.

Darren looked baffled, clearly spoilt for choice. Debby grinned at him and turned her attention back to Peg.

'We'll take a steak and onion, and a chicken and mushroom please, if that's ok.'

'Course it is, love. I'll wrap them for you, and you can pay at the counter.'

Darren clapped his hands. His eyes were dancing. 'Two pies! Two!'

'Alright, calm down!' Debby said, grinning.

'Calm down? No chance, babe! You don't normally let me have *one* little pie, and now you're getting *two big ones*? That's a proper cause for celebration. You can't blame me for being this happy! I think we need to alert the media, or at least order another pot of coffee'

She laughed at his pleasure. He was like a little kid who'd been told he could have sweets *and* ice cream.

'Well, how could I not get two? You've been virtually foaming at the mouth with longing, and they look so damn good I want to just bury my *own* face in them!'

It was Darren's turn to laugh. 'In a million years, I never thought I'd ever hear you say *that* about a pie!'

Debby waved a hand at him. 'Well, they'd better be as good as they look, or there won't be any more. And if they are good, you'll have to step up and do more running. One of us has to watch your waistline.'

Darren pulled a face at her, and she poked her tongue out at him. She knew how much he hated the fact that his weight ballooned if he ate too many carbs. He played squash twice a week with a couple of mates, which provided a much-needed outlet for the stress that sometimes came with his job, and no doubt diffused a lot of the anxiety they were both dealing with over their continuing inability to conceive. He also went for a run most mornings before work, which all helped him stay trim and fit.

But Darren loved his food, especially pies, burgers, fish and chips, pasta, and any other carb-laden dishes. That was what he'd been raised on, reportedly without any issues, but somewhere along the line he'd simply started packing on the weight. Medical checks had thrown up nothing significant; he just had to start limiting his intake of carbohydrates if he didn't want to run the risk of developing diabetes. Debby took it more seriously than he did, and it was a good job too. Left to his own devices, he'd likely be the size of a small office block.

Changing his diet had been like waving a red rag at a bull. Debby had locked horns with him, many times, about the changes she tried to introduce. They eventually got into a workable dietary routine that he mostly complied with, albeit with regular rounds of grumbling and the occasional indulgence, to make him more inclined to stay on the straight and narrow for the rest of the time.

Debby wasn't about to watch all her hard work and commitment go to waste, but what the hell. They were on holiday, and she acknowledged that her hardworking hubby did deserve a few treats. He *would* have to work them off, but that was going to be a whole lot easier to do up here, while he wasn't tied up with gruelling work schedules. He could run cross-country with Badger, they could all take long walks across the fells, and everything would be just fine as long as he did – for the most part – eat more healthily than not.

So, it looked very much as if pie would be on the menu tonight, and she'd bet her bottom dollar that Darren would pick the steak one. Debby planned to put it in the Aga to heat through. As long as she kept an eye on it and didn't let it burn, they'd have a nice, easy hot supper in fairly quick time. She'd have a look at the fresh veggies on offer at the Farmer's Market and pick something nice to have with it.

As they paid for their pies and breakfast, Peg asked them what their plans were for the day. She nodded in approval, at their intention to go to the market. She also suggested they take the signposted walk along the back of the town on the stream side, which opened into a pretty park and picnic area at one end, and wound its way up the west side of the valley at the other. There were car-parks at either end, she said. Darren told her they'd probably wait until they had their dog with them. She nodded.

'Oh, it's a great walk for dogs! It's been properly geared up for them, with poo bins all the way along and everything, and you'll find lots of sticks to throw. The weather's good at the moment, which helps, if you do want a picnic or two. It's not usually so stable up here, but they've predicted a fortnight of warm weather. You've come at the right time, but I hope you've packed a couple of raincoats too, for when it breaks, which it usually does with a bang, after a hot spell.'

She invited them to bring Badger next time they came down to the cafe.

Debby was pleasantly surprised. 'I'm glad you're dog friendly. Adrienne said you might be.'

Peg winked at her. 'We're not *officially* dog-friendly. It's invitation only. To be honest though, some of the dogs that come in here are better behaved than some of the people! I'd have most of the dogs back at the drop of a hat, but without their bloody owners!'

Darren threw back his head and laughed.

'A woman after my own heart, Peg!' he exclaimed. 'Most dogs *are* nicer than most people, in my humble opinion.'

Debby jerked a thumb at her husband and grinned at Peg.

'Spot the vet!'

Peg handed them their two pies, traditionally wrapped in brown greaseproof paper and tied with string. They said a cheerful goodbye and left the shop.

The Farmer's Market also wasn't hard to find. A big sign hung from a hook on the lamppost at the corner of Amble Walk and the High Street, with an arrow that pointed them in the right direction. As they walked into the church hall, Debby was surprised by how big and busy the market actually was.

'Wow! Look at this! I was expecting half a dozen stands, with a tower or two of limp lettuces and a few manky old bags of bird nuts!'

The market was a feast for the eyes. There must have been twenty stalls, if not more, offering everything from home-made sweets and locally produced sausages and sides of organic beef, to trays of lush lemons and limes, ripe juicy apples, and almost every vegetable it was possible to grow. The assortment of different cheeses, pickles, salamis and patés on one stand would rival most large supermarket delis. Strings of garlic and red onions were hung alongside free-range chickens, and Debby was amused to see that even Peg's café had a stand, with a simple sign that read 'Peg's Pies and Pastries.'

One stand offered a variety of practical craft items, made in patchworked and cheerful printed cottons. There were pot-holders and oven gloves, pin cushions and washbags, tea-towels with bands of pretty floral prints across the edges, and hot-mats. Unlike many craft stands that were more about novelties than needs, everything here had a purpose. Debby spied a fat calico-fabric tube, with a print of hand drawn multi-coloured beach huts stitched around it. It had elastic at both ends, and a small hanging-loop at one end. She grabbed it quickly.

'Oh, God, Darren, look! I've been after one of these for bloody ages!'

'What is it?'

'It's a bag-bag'

She saw his mouth twitch into an almost-smirk, but he just bit his lip and shrugged.

'Umm… okay, if you say so.'

'Look, noodle-head; you stuff plastic carrier bags, or dusters, or socks, undies or whatever, in through the top and pull them out as needed through the bottom? Mum has one, hanging on a hook inside the pantry. She's had it years! It's brilliant. I didn't think you could even still get them!'

Deciding it was a 'must-have' she cheerfully handed over what felt like an absurdly small amount of money for it, and then decided to splurge on a set of four padded placemats and four napkins, and a generous cotton apron, all in the same fabric. She tucked everything into her hessian carrier bag.

'Bargain!'

Towards the back of the room, she spotted Adrienne Raven. She was deep in conversation with a stunning, very well-dressed woman whose make-up and hair were also impeccable. As they approached, Adrienne looked up and grinned.

'Hi, guys! You made it! Did you have breakfast at Peg's?'

'We did, and it was incredible!' Darren enthused, proffering his hand. 'I'm Darren Davies, and you've met Debby already.'

Adrienne gestured to the woman next to her. 'Debby, Darren, I'd like you to meet my friend Trudie Sangster. She runs the local clothing boutique, GladRagz, here in town, just behind the supermarket. Darren and Debby are staying at Teapot Cottage for a few weeks,' she explained to her friend.

Trudie smiled. 'A few weeks! Gosh, that sounds like heaven! It's a very special little place. I'm sure you'll have a lovely time.'

Debby held out her hand. 'I'm pleased to meet you, Trudie. Tell me, do you have such a thing in your shop as a bathing suit or bikini that would fit me? When my lovely husband sprang this surprise on me, he forgot to mention the small matter of a hot tub that I'm longing to get into!'

Trudie pulled a regretful face. 'Oh no, sorry Debby! I'm still waiting for a lot of the summer stock to come in that was meant to be here weeks ago! The shipment's been held up at customs, largely thanks to all the post-Brexit nonsense that still isn't resolved. Paperwork issues are a mile long, these days. I don't think what I've currently got would appeal to you. It's more the heavy-strapped, tummy-control kind of thing I'd be selling to the octogenarians! Not a single bikini or flattering one-piece in sight quite yet, I'm afraid.'

Adrienne waved a hand. 'Debby don't worry about that. I have a heap of swimsuits I haven't worn for years. You're roughly the same size as me, I think? I'll dig them out, blow the cobwebs off, and drop them down to you later this afternoon. They've seen better days, but they're still good enough for a hot tub, I think, and I won't want them back.'

'That's so kind of you, Adrienne! Thank you. It will save me a trip to Carlisle.'

Trudie looked at her kindly. 'Oh Carlisle's definitely worth a day trip, if you haven't been before. It's the hub of the Lake District. It has a lovely cathedral and grounds, some interesting shops, and some great cafes and restaurants too, if you fancy staying on for dinner. There's a wonderful Italian place on a corner, not far from the pedestrianised area. The name of it escapes me; it starts with S, I think. But the food is just amazing in there! You might also like to visit the John Watt Café on Bank Street. It's been around since the eighteen-nineties, and it has the most *fascinating* history!'

'There's lots of places elsewhere too, that are worthy of a visit,' Adrienne chimed in. 'Most of the Lake District towns and villages are very pretty. Some spots are a bit more touristy and crowded than others, mind you, especially now it's summer. The school holidays don't start for ages yet though, so most places shouldn't be too busy.'

Debby bought a jar of orange and ginger marmalade and some more eggs from Adrienne, along with the last packet of lavender shortbread that was sitting on her table. By the time they left the church hall, laden down with a variety of fruit, vegetables, free range chicken and meat, and a big bunch of lilies for the kitchen table, it was lunch time.

'I couldn't eat a thing,' Darren declared. 'I'm still stuffed from that bloody enormous breakfast!'

'Me too. Let's head home and chill with a book for a bit. I'm keen to try that lavender shortbread later, with a cup of tea. Badger will be pleased to see us, too. I think he'll enjoy this lovely juicy pig's ear from the market.'

'I think he's going to want the steak pie. I might have to wrestle him for that!'

'Yeah, but by the time you've finished wrestling him for it, I might have already eaten it.'

Chapter Three

A few days into their stay at Teapot Cottage, which had passed as peacefully as intended, Darren looked up from his book to see his wife bursting through the front door in a flood of angry tears. She'd been out for an afternoon walk with Badger, and had taken the path that led across the fields and down towards the town. She'd asked Darren if he'd fancied going with her, but all he really wanted to do today was stretch out on the sofa with one of his new 'Grishams.' He'd been enjoying an hour of quiet, until a distraught Debby rushed in, weeping fit to combust. She slammed the front door so hard the crockery in the kitchen rattled. He put his book down, alarmed.

'Debs, what is it, babe? What's got you so upset?'

She sat down heavily, with her head in her hands, sobbing. Her voice was nearly hysterical.

'I just saw a woman coming up the driveway pushing a twin pram. She had two babies, Darren. Two! How can it be fair that someone else has two bloody babies, when I don't even get to have *one*? And why here, outside this bloody holiday house in the middle of fucking nowhere? Does God really hate me *that* much?'

Her rage and anguish were palpable, and Darren was lost for what to say. Was this how it would be for his wife from now on; having hysterics at seeing any other woman pushing a pram? He couldn't bring himself to say, yet again, how unjust life was, or how there was no rhyme or reason for how brutally selective mother nature could be. It had all been said before, many times. It would only add flame to the fire if he repeated it now.

There were no easy answers, for why some people who didn't deserve or even really *want* children somehow seemed to have them without much effort. All too often, those who didn't have the faintest idea how to care for kids properly got to shell them out like peas, while others who were desperately wanting, who would have made the best parents in the world, were cruelly denied that chance.

It wouldn't help, to share his own frustration, at the random, inexplicable harshness of it all. Instead, he put his arms around Debby as she sobbed, and consoled her as best he could, while she got this latest bout of injustice-laden grief out of her system.

'I hate that woman, and her stupid kids. I wish they were all dead.'

Darren's blood ran cold, and he suddenly came close to snapping. He managed to resist the overwhelming urge to shake his wife hard, and scream some sense into her, but he felt completely blinded by a rush of emotion he couldn't even describe. He couldn't let her comment slide.

'Bloody hell, Debs! Can you hear yourself? It's not that poor woman's fault that you can't have a baby of your own! And it certainly isn't her babies' fault that they were born! What's the point of hating people and wishing them dead, over something they can't control? Why should she, or any other woman, not have a baby, just because you can't? For God's sake! You have to get a grip, before all this bitterness drives us *both* bloody mad!'

Being upset, frustrated and unhappy about being unable to conceive was one thing, but actively wishing another woman dead just because she had babies wasn't far short of insane. Debby's comment was terribly unfair, and it gave a glimpse into a scary side of her that he didn't recognise or even want to know. She was getting worse; her randomly unleashed fury towards family and friends who 'didn't understand' was boiling over to include innocent strangers, now!

Darren was sure it was just the anguish talking; that she hadn't really meant what she'd said. When they'd first got together and were happy, before the stress of trying to get pregnant became all-consuming, Debby would never have wished hurt or pain on anyone.

If only she could get pregnant, surely everything would settle down? She couldn't go on like this. Neither of them could. He swallowed his frustration yet again, and hugged her tightly. He felt so inept. What could he say to her? What could he do, to make this freakishly awful situation less horrible?

There was nothing. Today, as every other day, he searched for solutions and came up with nothing. He made them both a coffee and tried to go back to his book, but it didn't work. He'd lost the thread now, and his mind was a scrambled mess again. Debby sat in one of the window seats, sulking, and staring blankly down into Torley valley. She didn't offer any conversation, and he was glad, but the previously companionable silence was uneasy now. He felt a bit mean, for preferring it to a fight or ongoing whining, but it wasn't just his wife who was struggling. He was getting to the end of *his* tether, too.

Half an hour later, a knock at the front door startled them both. Darren opened it to find one of the tiniest and most beautiful women he'd ever seen, looking up at him. She had very long dark hair, the clearest complexion in the world, and the most amazing blue eyes, framed by long, sooty lashes. She was wearing a fern-green velvet cape, and carrying a small basket of strawberries. She smiled warmly and stuck her hand out.

'Hi. I'm Seraphine Raven-Black. Most people around these parts know me as Feen. My dad owns this farm, and this is my step-mum's cottage. She's Adrienne Raven. I think you've met her?'

Darren returned her smile and nodded. 'Yeah, I met her a couple of days ago down at the Farmer's Market.'

'Ah yes, that would be right. Anyway, I thought I'd come and introduce myself to you and your wife. I hope you like strawberries? These are from our farden at the garm.'

Darren looked over his shoulder at Debby, then opened the door wider to invite their guest in. Maybe this nice woman's visit would cheer up his deeply despondent wife a bit. If it didn't, maybe her strawberries would!

'Debs, there's a neighbour here, wanting to say hello. She's come bearing gifts!'

Debby looked up. When she saw the woman standing in the doorway, she blanched.

'You!' she said accusingly.

The woman smiled gently. 'Yes, me.'

Without being invited, Feen came forward. 'I know I'm probably the last person you want to see, and I think I know why, but I do want to talk to you.'

Debby looked away, mumbling. 'Well, I don't want to talk to you.'

'Okay then; you can stay quiet, and I'll talk, and you can throw me out after that if you wish, but please don't do it before you've heard what I've come to say.'

Darren frowned. What was going on, here? Was this little woman well-meaning? As the daughter of the landowner, surely she must be, but it seemed like an odd conversation. He watched Debby closely, preparing to throw their uninvited guest out in short order if she created any further distress. He looked enquiringly over at Debby, and she rewarded him with a glare that could freeze the Sahara. She folded her arms defensively, and stared off into the middle distance. Darren could feel the strength of her hostility. Surely their visitor, Seraphine – Feen? – must have felt it too. But it didn't seem to deter her. In fact, she moved even closer.

She stood directly in front of Debby, took a deep breath, and spoke quietly.

'Despite what you think, I do deserve my children. They were born very prematurely, at twenty-eight weeks, after I was involved in a car crash that nearly cost all three of us our lives. It was out here, on the rain moad, about half a mile down, in fact you can see the sash crite from here.' She gestured at one of the big windows that overlooked the Torley valley.

'I'd dashed out to the supermarket to get some last-minute duff for stinner. It was raining, and dark, and someone on the wrong side of the road smashed into my car and sent me burtling down the hank.

'I'd been married less than a year. I had a very bad concussion, and my babies had to be delivered by C-section while I was unconscious, so I missed their birth, and they fought for their lives, *really hard*, until they were out of the woods. It took months. They had several setbacks, and there were times when we really didn't mink they'd thake it. But they did, and I know how lucky I am. I know how lucky *they* are.'

She paused, then continued, as quietly as before.

'I understand your pain. I can feel it as if it were my own. I know that you want to have children more than anything, and I know how hard it is, seeing other women with kids when you can't have them yourself. I know how hard it was for you, meeing me with sine.

'But please don't hate me. Don't wish me dead, or them. It's not my fault, or theirs, that you haven't got pregnant yet. If I can help you, I will, and I'd be happy to. But you need to be open to it. You can't close your mind and fill it full of hate and resentment. That will poison your ability to do *anything* positive with your life, not just fail to conceive.'

Throughout Feen's quiet narrative, Debby just stared at her, open-mouthed. When the other woman had stopped speaking, Debby erupted.

'You cheeky bitch! Who the fuck do you think you are, barging in here with all that? How *dare* you? What the hell do you think you know about me? About us? I've a good mind to complain to Mrs Raven. You are *so* out of order!'

The other woman sighed heavily, her eyes swimming with tears. 'I know!' she wailed. 'I agree with you entirely! I *am* out of order. I'd normally *never* warge my bay into someone else's life or problems. But out there in the driveway just now, I felt the force of your rage at me and my children, *and* the depths of your despair. And I understood why. And I wanted to reach out to you, because I've felt a similar despair in not knowing whether my children would survive or not. It's an indescribable hell, and I understand it, more than you know.'

Debby shook her head, refusing to be placated. 'What is it you actually want, you weirdo? To gloat? To throw your kids in my face? You want money to go away? *What*?'

Feen shook her head, vehemently. 'No! God, no! I want to *help* you. I'm pretty sure I have the power to help you, and something is driving at my back, telling me I should.'

Feen frowned, and sighed in exasperation. 'It's hard to explain, and most people don't understand, but I have a gift for healing. I got it from my mother. She died, but she left me with the ability to see into souls, and try to heal the tormented ones.'

Debby snorted and looked Feen up and down.

'So that's what you think I am? A tormented soul? Fuck off, you patronising cow!'

Feen's shoulders slumped. She held up her tiny hands in surrender.

'Ok, fair enough. I'll go, and I won't come back uninvited. But if you do want to talk things through and let me see how I might be of help, you only have to ask. I know what it's like to be in that plarkest dace, to be wondering if there will ever be any light at the end of a tunnel you don't know how you ended up in.

'I watched my mother die from bowel cancer. I watched my dad nearly die after an accident in our barn, and I watched my babies' lives banging in the halance for *months*. I've cried more tears and prayed harder than anyone else in this world. So I get it. I know what rage and grief feel like.

'I'll get out of your hair. I promise. I just wanted to reach out to you, that was all. I felt compelled to tell you that you're not alone; that you're not as isolated as you think you are, in all this, that someone else really does understand your pain. I wanted to try and help you, in whatever way I could. I got it wrong. I'm sorry.'

Debby sat, stony-faced, giving nothing.

Feen placed the little basket of strawberries on the coffee table. When she spoke again, her voice was stiff.

'The strawberries are a fift from the garm. I can see I've outstayed my welcome.'

Debby sniped at her, bitchily. 'You think?'

Feen didn't say another word. Instead, she drew her cape around her shoulders and went back to the front door.

'I'm sorry,' she said quietly to Darren, as she opened it. 'If I've done more harm than good, I'm truly sorry.'

Darren didn't have a clue what to say. He was intrigued, confused, and also acutely embarrassed at his wife's attitude, but he understood her outrage at being so deeply intruded upon, in her own private space, by a complete stranger. It was a really odd, uncomfortable situation, and he had no idea how to respond to it.

'Don't worry about it,' was all he could manage. 'And thanks for the berries.'

Feen nodded and left.

Debby was crying hard again, when he closed the door. She was furious. 'How dare she? Who the bloody hell does she think she is? Doesn't she know how rude it is to crash into someone's private space and start spouting off like that? The crazy bitch can't even speak properly! And thanks for standing up to her and defending me, by the way. '*Don't worry about it*'? Clearly you don't give a shit about how I feel.'

Darren was suddenly furious too. 'It's called Spoonerism, Debby. Transposing the consonants on a pair of words. Some say it's a speech disorder; a form of verbal dyslexia. It's not her fault, so don't be so fucking mean. And as for 'standing up to her' and 'defending' you? Well, I agree that she probably shouldn't have come here, but she meant well, Debs! Any idiot could see that!' He was shouting now, and absolutely seething.

'What's the point of attacking someone's best intentions? Why be abusive to them? Why mock their disability behind their back? And why are you taking your stupid, irrational anger out on *me*? You've become such a vicious bloody viper, lately. I hardly know who you are anymore. And I'll tell you something else, Debby. I've had a gutsful of this shit. Pull yourself together, for fuck's sake.'

They both fell into a hostile silence, each occupied with their own angry thoughts. Darren was simmering, but he was also very confused. Feen Raven-Black's visit had been extraordinary. Yes, it *was* out of order. It *was* bordering on outrageous and unacceptable, but something deep inside him believed that she really had come forward with the best of intentions. And how *did* she know what their problems were? Was the cottage bugged? That would be ridiculous, surely? What reason would anyone have, to eavesdrop on a random holiday tenant?

Debby had a few things to think about now, thanks to their strange little visitor. In one way Darren was glad she'd been, and said what she had, if only to try and convince his wife that there was a bigger picture and it was about time she started *trying* at least, to see it. He did believe what Feen had said about anger and resentment poisoning their lives across the board, if they let it. That much was true, even if nothing else was.

Debby's increasing animosity, in almost every direction, was slowly suffocating them both. Today, for the first time, he felt as if he was teetering on the outside edge of a black hole where his marriage used to be. Could he stop himself from falling into it? He swallowed the lump in his throat, as he fought back the tidal wave of sadness that threatened, yet again, to drown him. Once again, his emotions were a jumbled mess.

They had so few options left now, and if Debby wasn't willing to consider them, those options amounted to nothing. Right now, she was still fixated on having a baby herself, biologically. She didn't want to think about surrogacy, fostering or adoption. She wanted to experience pregnancy and childbirth, with everything it entailed, and she wanted it so desperately that nothing else was even a tolerable choice.

It wasn't a stupid thing to want. It was as normal a thing, in fact, as anything could ever be. But the hard truth was that less than half of all pregnancies achieved through IVF in Debby's age group resulted in a live birth. Miscarriages were heartbreakingly common. They'd already suffered the devastation of two. They'd lost one embryo at seven weeks, the other at eight, and both had needed a D & C with recovery time that had shaved more weeks off the dwindling time they had left.

Even if Debby did get pregnant again, there was no guarantee that she would go to full term. The odds were stacked against them, and reducing all the time. Clearly, even with all the supplements, boosters and lifestyle adjustments that were aimed at improving the quality of her eggs, it was going to take a miracle for her to conceive and go the distance. After their last visit to the clinic, when the consultant had gently suggested it might be time to consider options other than pregnancy, Debby had wept for a week.

Feen Raven-Black, that tiny, ethereal woman; could she help them? And, if so – how? The mad thing was, that even though Debby had shut her down completely and more or less thrown her out of the cottage, Darren was still prepared to consider virtually *anything* that might be possible, no matter how bonkers or airy-fairy it sounded. Weirdly, a witch-doctor (or the female equivalent) suddenly seemed like a halfway feasible option.

My God, I'm losing the plot myself, now!

Lots of couples didn't have children, sometimes through circumstance, but equally often through choice. If Darren and

Debby couldn't conceive, no matter what they tried, and if nobody could help, or Debby wasn't prepared to let someone else try, maybe it simply wasn't meant to be. But, although he did believe – rightly or wrongly – that they could still have a full, rich life together, he wasn't sure he'd ever get her to that point. If he could, their life together would certainly be different from the one they'd initially planned, but, at least they'd still *have* a life together. Maybe the real lesson, behind all this brutal conceptional failure, was that nobody could 'have it all.'

Darren was already more thankful than he could ever truly put into words about the random way his own life had changed, off the back of a terrible crime committed by someone who had atoned for it in the hardest way and who, in that process, had offered him a chance to turn his life around. He'd been incalculably blessed, not once but twice now, firstly with a home and career he once thought he'd never have, and then with a wife he adored who – inexplicably – adored him back.

He'd already had enough gifts bestowed up on him to last a lifetime. Who would he be, to want more? As heart-breaking a prospect as it was, that he might never be a father, he didn't *expect* to 'have it all.' He couldn't be greedy over his blessings.

It was different for Debby; he appreciated that. She'd had a fairly average upbringing, and a normal enough education. She came from what most would describe as an average, middle-class family (albeit with a pair of emotionally stunted parents), and she had normal enough expectations of life. She wanted to be a nurse, marry a decent bloke, have a nice house and push out a couple of kids. None of that was too much ask for, was it? Nothing on that list was unrealistic.

Darren would love a family, of course, but while he wouldn't see his life as an abject failure if it didn't happen, Debby absolutely would. The ongoing inability to have a baby of her own was already casting a deep shadow over *everything* for her. Lashing out at complete strangers was a new development, and who knew what else she might do, after that? What was left of their increasingly fragile relationship felt like it was inching slowly but surely towards the edge of that big black hole. How long would it be before he tumbled headlong into it?

An hour later, despite all Darren's attempts to get her past the incident, Debby was still sulking. He was normally very protective of her and would be deeply offended by anyone who upset her. He would also tell someone, in no uncertain terms, to back off. He'd even get physical if he had to. But surprisingly, today, he found himself agreeing with Feen Raven-Black, after she'd waded so weirdly into their space.

Maybe Debs did need that - to be kicked out of her sad little bubble.

She sat, stone-faced, staring out the window down into the valley, merely grunting when he asked her if she wanted another cup of coffee. He took it as a yes, and made one for her, before setting it down on the coffee table with a bang.

'I've fucking had all this, Debs. I feel like I'm suffocating. I'm going for a walk, to get some fresh air. I'll leave you to it. You can sulk on your own, for as long as you like.'

He shrugged into his jacket and whistled quietly to Badger, who needed no second bidding to have a second walk. Debby raised her eyebrows at him but said nothing. She seemed determined to stew in her own sour juice, over the two 'attacks' she'd had, one after the other. But Darren was only half sorry they'd argued. The other half of him was relieved at having let off some steam. Things were boiling away so close to the surface for both of them, it was inevitable that they had to blow at some point, and it was becoming harder to do that without really hurting one another. This holiday wasn't meant to be about continued fighting. He'd hoped for something better, while they were here, but it clearly wasn't going to happen – at least not yet.

He picked up Badger's lead and harness. Some time alone, with his own thoughts, was exactly what he needed. On a visceral level, he missed the beach, with its crashing waves and crying gulls. That was where he always used to go, when he needed to clear his head. Even in the early days, when he was immersed in petty crime and had nothing to look forward to in life, when things got too much he'd scrape up the fare and get on a train to the coast. He'd walk along the beach, sometimes in howling wind and driving rain. But even at those times, when he had to fight with all his strength to stay upright, it still made him feel better.

He missed his flat by the sea. He'd sold it to buy the Exeter house with Debby, but most days he wished they could have found a way to hang onto it. Losing that first and biggest symbol of real independence, and the start of a brand-new life, had been hard. He was mostly pretty happy in his new life, but there would never be a time when he didn't miss that little flat with its view of the ocean, and the time to walk along the beach that sat in front of it, and put the world to rights; in his own head at least.

A hike to the little Tor at the top of Ravensdown Farm would be a good enough substitute today, though. Darren had been keen to go up there, right from when they'd first arrived. Badger always appreciated being out in the open, especially having the chance to run around on a farm. Although he was fully domesticated, the poor dog's face was always a hilarious picture of confusion whenever he saw a mob of sheep. His instincts were telling him that he should be doing *something* with them but, bless him, he just didn't know what it was.

As Darren neared the top of the driveway, he almost collided with Adrienne Raven, who was hurrying towards Teapot Cottage, with her head down. He stepped aside just as she was about to crash into him. She stopped, startled.

'Oh. Hello, Darren! I was just on my way down to see you and your wife. I've just been talking with my step-daughter, Feen. She's in a bit of a state. I believe she's rather gone and put her foot in it? I thought I should come and apologise, sooner rather than later.'

Darren grinned ruefully. 'She did create some sparks, that's for sure. But it's nothing we didn't need to hear. In fact, I've decided to give Debs a bit of space so she can think about what was said.'

He thought for a moment then added, 'I'm going up to the Tor. You can walk with me if you like?'

Adrienne considered the idea, then shrugged. 'Why not? My cake can wait for a bit, and nobody needs me for anything else just now. A walk would probably do me good. I've already got my boots and jacket on. And please call me Adie.'

'A hike like this blows the cobwebs out.'

She nodded, without smiling. 'Indeed it does.'

They set off, up to the gate that separated the farmyard from the public walkway. Darren held it open for Adie, who gave him a tight smile of thanks as she came through. She didn't look at all happy. Darren decided to change the subject for a bit.

'Is it a nuisance for the farm; Joe public tramping past your house and barn to get to it?'

Adie shook her head. 'Not so much now. Most ramblers don't come up this way anymore. We got fed up with people parking right outside the house, so my husband Mark put those big gates up, at the bottom of the drive, and hung some signs along the fence to stop them. The walkway crosses the fields at the other side of Teapot Cottage, on the town side. Most hikers pick up the path from the back of the Bull and Royal pub now, because they can park there, which they can't do here anymore.'

She pointed to the other side of a truly splendid stone farmhouse and explained that the path she was talking about ran along the back.

'Besides, it goes with the territory of farm ownership. It's legal trespass, for want of a better term. We can't change the law, and we're not in a position to complain. We're just lucky that most people are respectful. The gates are all spring-hinged so it's not possible for anyone to leave them open, and we've put a few bins around so people who bring picnics can more easily dispose of their leftovers. Happily, most do.'

Adie went on to say that there had been the occasional time when ramblers had helped the farm. A sheep once had its head jammed into the fence between a post and a tree, and probably would have died if the rambler hadn't managed to free it. Another sheep had given birth in some difficulty, and did die, but a couple of walkers managed to step in and save its twin lambs. 'So not everyone is a nuisance who comes up here,' Adie finished.

'Yeah, I guess you have to take the rough with the smooth.'

They didn't speak again on their way up to the Tor. When they reached the top, Darren was slightly out of breath. For all his fitness, a hill like this was still a bit of a challenge. He looked around, and marvelled at the view.

Adie sat down on a flat rock, and looked at Darren sagely. 'I *am* truly sorry, Darren, about Feen barging in on you both the way she did. For what it's worth, I'm horrified, and acutely embarrassed. She comes across as an odd little thing, and she doesn't have much of a filter at times, especially when she gets a bee in her bonnet like she did today. I first met her when she called on *me* unannounced, when I was staying at Teapot Cottage myself, before I ended up meeting and marrying her dad and everything. I didn't know what to make of her.'

She stared off into the middle distance pulling at her bottom lip with her thumb and forefinger. Darren could sense there was more, so he waited. Adie turned to look at him, smiling just a little.

'But I've grown to love her. She's what a lot of people call a 'white witch.' She is brimming with empathy, and love for nature, and she's incredibly clever in knowing how to help people in crisis. She sometimes just has a funny way of showing it, that's all.'

Adie went on to describe how Feen had a sixth sense, an intuition. She often knew what was going to happen to people before they knew it themselves, and she was a very gifted natural healer. She also had a real affinity for animals and people, especially those who were suffering.

'She means well. She doesn't have a harmful bone, but she's had some pretty big challenges. The accident with her twins is only part of what she's had to face. Her mum died of bowel cancer when she was fourteen. She was an unusual little girl too, and quite detached from the more mainstream kids because she didn't have much in common with them. Some kids had no idea how to take her, so they bullied her, for a long time.

'In my sister-in-law Sheila's words, Feen vibrates to a different frequency. She sees the world very differently to other people.'

Adie pushed her hair back out of her eyes. 'And, because she was quite isolated, growing up, she sometimes just speaks without thinking. She still hasn't fully learned where other people's boundaries are. She just crashes in, determined to help, because that's her focus.'

'She does seem very sweet, if a bit intense,' Darren offered.

Adie thought for a moment, then nodded. 'Yes. Sweet and intense is a very good way of describing her, actually. And you know, it's not my place or desire to intrude, but she did tell me what she sensed the issue is, for you two. I'm very sorry, Darren. It must be hell to want a family so much, and to not be able to make it happen, especially when there's no good reason you can hang your hat on.'

Darren appreciated Adie's apology, and swept aside the notion that it should have been Feen herself who apologised. He understood how embarrassed she might be after barging in and saying her piece with the very best of intentions, with no real clue about how offensive it was, and then realising when the damage had been done. She'd probably appreciate how inappropriate it would be to call again, and try to apologise, especially when she'd promised not to. Debby had been hostile in the extreme, and Darren couldn't blame *anyone* for choosing not to experience that for a second time. Part of him didn't want to go back to the cottage, himself!

He quietly confessed to Adie how he thought that maybe Debby deserved to hear what had been said, and how much he hoped it would make a dent where his own efforts had failed.

'I can't get her past this. It's like she's completely stuck, where she is. I can't move her forward, no matter what I try to do.'

Adie listened without speaking, as Darren poured his heart out, telling her about their long and painful journey through IVF, the disappointment, the tears, the despair, then finally the anger and frustration that he was feeling almost constantly now, in response to his wife's flat-out refusal to do anything but wallow in her own anger and grief.

'I can't call it self-pity, can I? It's not that. It's worse than that, more profound. It's like the very essence of who she is has been dismantled, in this whole fertility process, and she doesn't know how to put it back together. It doesn't help that she's not at all close to her parents, who do I have to say are not very nice people at all. A lot of her friends have abandoned her, too, which hurt her a lot, and a couple of the ones who *have* stuck around have been so insensitive, it's almost cruel. That's made things much harder for her, I think. She feels very alone, abandoned, and unsupported by people she used to think she could lean on.'

He grinned sheepishly. 'I'll bet you're glad you came!'

Adie laughed out loud. 'It's fine, honestly. Sometimes it's good to talk to a virtual stranger. The closer people are, the more judgemental they tend to be. That's what I've found, anyway. Everyone who's even *vaguely* invested thinks they have the best advice to give, and it never seems to occur to them that it's the last thing you really want. They go ahead and throw it at you anyway.' She chuckled, half to herself, and shook her head.

'And as far as friends go, who've turned out not to be friends? Believe me, Darren, I've had my own fair share of *that* lately! I know exactly how Debby must be feeling, over that. It's so hard when the people you've always thought you could rely on disappear when you need them most, when you're at your most vulnerable and afraid. You do end up feeling incredibly alone, and foolish too sometimes, for believing you could depend on them in the first place.'

Adie went on to describe a few of the obstacles she'd had to overcome herself, before she met and married Mark Raven, and Darren concluded that she would be the last person to sit in judgement of anyone else. She certainly wouldn't have offered a sincere apology for her step-daughter if she didn't genuinely believe Feen's intentions.

As apologies went, it was good enough for him. He'd convey the apology to Debby in good time, and she could make what she wanted of it, but right now he just wanted a little headroom; some space away from her. He gently pushed back a small surge of guilt about that, knowing that while she'd discovered that she couldn't rely on people she'd thought of as friends, she probably felt let down by him too. But, just because his wife was a boiling basket-case, it didn't mean he had to end up the same way. No matter how guilty it made him feel, he sometimes had to put his own needs first. A bit of time out, now and then, was critical to his own emotional stability. That much, he *did* understand.

Badger was now spent, from retrieving the stick he'd found halfway up the track that Darren had thrown for him countless times. He lay on the ground, snoring gently. The wind started whipping up, and Adie quickly got to her feet.

'We should get moving again. It's very exposed up here, and the wind can chill you to the bone, even in summer.'

'The view from up here is stupendous! It's a lovely spot.'

She smiled broadly, and bit her bottom lip. 'It is. I have a real fondness for this place. It's where Mark properly proposed to me, over a sausage sandwich and a bottle of pop.'

Darren threw back his head and laughed. 'The very essence of romance! How could you have refused?'

She laughed back, her eyes dancing at the memory. 'Believe me, for him, that *was* romance. He's a darling man, but he's certainly no Romeo! I knew that a sausage sandwich wrapped in tinfoil, and a bottle of pop poured into a plastic cup, was probably as good as it was ever going to get. He did get down on one knee though, which was quite a big achievement for him at the time, because he was still recovering from a very bad accident. So, I didn't even try to hang out for more than that; I just made it simple for him and said yes.

'We also escaped up here after our wedding, just the two of us. But at least, that time, he did make sure we had some real champagne.'

A smile played around her lips, and Darren enjoyed her moment of pure happiness at the memory. It was a far cry from the oppressive, resentful silences and half-hearted attempts at light conversation he'd been having recently with Debby. They'd manage a few hours of normality, but then something would happen. He'd say the wrong thing, or she would make references to babies or children, and the gloom would descend once more. He couldn't remember the last time they'd had a proper belly-laugh.

They'd laughed a lot when they first got together, especially in those first years of marriage, before the seething spectre of childlessness reared its Medusa-like head and parked itself squarely and immovably between them.

It was refreshing to be with a woman who laughed and smiled the way Adie Raven was doing now. This nice lady had certainly had her struggles, but she'd come through them, and seemed to be leading a happy and contented life. She didn't appear to be crippled or overly traumatized by what hadn't worked out in her life. She embraced the new life instead, and was happy and thankful for the joy she had found in it.

Darren hoped fervently that Debby would get to that place, where she could be happy in spite of some of her dreams not coming true, where she could have new ones that would bring her a different kind of joy. And sooner rather than later. How much more strain could their marriage take, before it buckled and broke under the weight of failure and accusation?

As they made their way back down the hill, he asked Adie more about what had happened with Feen's babies. He was surprised when she became slightly emotional, in describing how close the babies had come to dying after such a premature, traumatic birth, and the effect it had had on the family. Darren genuinely felt for Feen's husband, Gavin Black. What must it be like, to be sitting all alone in a hospital with your unconscious wife and unbelievably tiny children, wondering if they would survive or not?

He suddenly wanted to find Feen and reassure her that she hadn't caused the kind of offence that couldn't be forgiven. She'd been through so much, yet she could still reach out to another woman in pain, and try to help. Darren knew that even if it sparked another argument with Debby, he was determined to try and get her to see that.

At the bottom gate, he turned to Adie. Her cheeks were flushed from the wind, but she was beaming.

'Thanks Adie, for the company, and the listening ear. Please tell Feen not to worry. It's fine. Thank her for me, would you? For reaching out? She didn't do it in the best way, I'll grant you, but right now there *isn't* a good way to bring this subject up with Debby. She's hypersensitive, but it does all have to be dragged out into the open, so the outcome may yet be a good one.'

Adie held her hand out. 'I hope so, Darren, and I've enjoyed our walk too. And any time you want to have a chat, you can usually find me pottering around here somewhere.'

A voice rang out, from inside the barn. 'Is that you, love?'

Adie jerked a thumb towards the barn. 'Come and meet Mark. He's the lord of the manor!' Her eyes were dancing merrily again. It was abundantly clear, how much in love she was.

She's a lot of fun, I reckon, Darren thought to himself. *If you really got to know her, she'd be a good laugh, and a good friend.*

As they stepped inside the massive opening to the barn, a stocky, middle-aged man appeared from around the back of a tractor that was clearly in the throes of being fixed. He was swearing softly to himself and wiping his grimy hands on an even filthier cloth.

'Ah, I thought I 'eard voices.'

'Mark, this is Darren Davies, our current tenant at Teapot Cottage. Darren, this is Mark Raven, my husband.'

The man stuck out a grease-stained hand. 'Ow do?' he growled in a deep Lancashire accent. 'Are y'any good wi' machinery, lad? I can't get' bugger to start.'

Darren shook his head apologetically. 'Sorry, Mark. I don't know one end of an engine from the other, I'm ashamed to say.'

Adie piped up again. 'Darren's a vet, Mark. Down near the south coast.'

'Aye, is that a fact? Yer a vet? Ow long 'ave yer bin practisin'?'

'Eight years qualified. Aiming to specialise in farm work, as a matter of fact, but currently working in domestic practice in Exeter.'

Mark pulled an ambivalent face and shook Darren's hand for a moment longer before abruptly letting it go.

'Welcome to Ravensdown. I 'ope y'ave a nice 'olidy at' cottage.'

Darren replied that he was sure they would, and then said goodbye to Adie. As he left, with Badger at his heels, he hoped he'd get chance to go walking with her again.

Chapter Four

Well, thought Adie. *He seems like an interesting character.*

She had the distinct impression that Darren Davies had a big back-story, one that went well beyond the problems he and his wife were having conceiving. He looked to be somewhere in his mid to late thirties, and had only been qualified as a vet for eight years. With the five years of training, that would have put him in his mid-twenties when he started, which was a little late, but perhaps he'd done his degree part time.

Somehow though, Adie sensed there was more to Darren. There was a slight air of tragedy about him, a kind of careworn weariness, or resignation, in his eyes; almost as if he'd survived something traumatic and had been changed in some way because of it. Feen could probably have described it a lot better, and likely would if Adie were to ask, but she wouldn't mind betting there was a lot more to the man than met the eye. He was heavily tattooed, and judging by the deep lines in his face, he looked like a guy who had seen a lot of life, so there likely was a bit of a past.

He was nice enough, and so was his wife, Debby. Adie hoped they'd find some peace together in their marriage, and maybe a stay at Teapot Cottage would help. The lovely little dwelling had a healing quality, something indefinable, that truly touched the people who stayed there. Adie had experienced her own healing there in a way she couldn't have imagined when she'd first arrived, after her own life had spectacularly imploded. She'd been immeasurably hurt, bewildered, and grieving the loss of her marriage. She had also been wildly menopausal with her hormones pinging around in all directions! The cottage had been balm to her battered soul, and she had rebuilt her life within its walls.

Feen's new husband Gavin had experienced an unforeseen healing at the cottage, too. He'd finally made peace with his mother, Carla Walton, after years of bitter estrangement. The pair had eventually reconciled, albeit through a painful process, while Gavin had been staying in the cottage. Even Adie herself, who'd had every reason to dislike Carla because of things that had happened earlier between the two women, had managed to find forgiveness and understanding. None of those steps were small ones.

Perhaps it was Torley itself, she mused, that worked some kind of healing magic on people. A lot of the visitors who came here ended up staying, or at the very least returning for further visits. Many of Adie's tenants at Teapot Cottage were 'repeat offenders,' as Mark liked to call them, with the tongue-in-cheek Lancashire humour he was so well-known for. People kept coming back, craving the peace and tranquillity of Torley.

Tourists were always made to feel welcome, although the town wasn't really much bigger than a village, and it wasn't exactly on the Lake District 'attractions' trail. It was more of a working town, dominated by farming, and with most of its retail and service trade catering to locals. It also worked well for commuters to Carlisle, as a handy and more laid-back alternative to living in the busy city.

It was certainly a friendly place. Most small towns and villages were so, but the 'welcome' some of them offered was all too often superficial, underpinned by a lofty air of superiority or downright nosiness, or an unhealthy, rubbing-the-hands preoccupation with how much money people were likely to spend while they were there. Some places had a reputation for the behavioural oddities of their dwellers, some of whose conduct could be classed as questionable, at best.

Happily, the people in Torley had few such peculiarities. Apart from one or two typical 'prima donnas' and a small handful of gossipy types (who most people simply rolled their eyes at), the business owners, farmers and townspeople were mostly down to earth and practical. They accepted newcomers and visitors as they found them, offering what they had with genuine goodwill, and seldom getting bent out of shape if it wasn't wanted.

Adie couldn't imagine living anywhere else now, and not just because she was married to Mark and had assumed the role of 'Mistress of Ravensdown,' as some of the townsfolk good-humouredly called her. It also wasn't just because the people here had been kind to her at a time when she desperately needed kindness and acceptance without having to explain why. Many had opened their homes and their hearts, and freely supported her, with no questions asked.

Her attachment to Torley wasn't just because of her relationship with the beautiful and enigmatic Feen either, or the fact that the young woman loved her too, and treated her as a vital member of her growing family. It wasn't even the fact that she felt now as if this new family were her very own, with Feen and Gavin to support, and their gorgeous little twins, Alder and Willow, to help nurture. Her own children were all grown up and scattered in different places with lives and kids of their own, but her wonderful salt-of-the-earth new husband had generously embraced them all with open arms, and they were all still a big part of her life. They visited often, and liked Torley too. She also had some truly solid friends here now, who she couldn't imagine being without.

It was probably a combination of *all* those things, she decided now, that had given her such a sense of contentment and belonging here in the lovely little Lake District town.

Having people in her life that she felt she could really trust was critical too, in fact it was one of the things that mattered the most. She fully understood what Darren had said about Debby's turmoil being so much greater for having fewer friends than she'd expected, to support her at such a difficult and traumatic time. When he'd mentioned how upset that had made him feel too, on his wife's behalf, it had brought a huge lump to Adie's throat. She'd become surprisingly emotional, and she'd confessed to him that she'd been there herself, and knew all too well, how painful broken friendships could be.

In the aftermath of her break-up with her first husband Bryan, virtually everyone they knew socially had assumed that the split was all her fault, and even after Bryan's long-standing affair had been exposed, those so-called 'friends' had stayed away. She never knew exactly why that was, but it had decimated her, and left her thinking that if any of them had valued her friendship, they'd have made the effort to move forward *with* her, or at least ring or text, to ask her how she was. But none had, and that had been an incredibly tough lesson.

On deep and painful reflection, she'd come to realise just how much of her old life had been false, and the friendships that had once felt meaningful were all just part of the sham her life had been. So much had been superficial; not just built on lies, but also on false hope, that the people in her circle were genuine and real. But when she finally found the courage to face the truth, it was clear that when the pain of her own grief had stopped her from going to lunch or coffee, to sit around and gossip about other 'friends' who were never there to defend themselves, she no longer seemed to have a valid place in that social scene.

She'd become *persona non grata*, in the end, and the knowledge that *she* was the one they'd all be making mean-spirited comments about, at their pointless long lunches, had stung for quite a while.

Horrible, how the stony silence to my face fronted a bitchiness behind my back that would have deafened me.

It had taken Adie a long time to realise that losing people she'd thought were her friends had been a big part of the grief she was feeling when she'd first arrived here in Torley, with her marriage in tatters, and none of her children really speaking to her. At the time, she hadn't thought much about the betrayal or abandonment of friends. The impact of that hit her later, after the dust had settled on her divorce. She then had to go through the difficult mental process of letting go of those relationships too. But she'd managed to do it, for the most part. She no longer missed a single one of the people she'd once placed so much store by.

She was still very close with Miranda Quirk, who'd been her best friend since primary school. The two women had unfailingly and staunchly stood by one another through thick and thin. Miranda, bless her beautiful heart, had been through some serious fires of her own, but she was still a rock; the true friend she'd always been.

When she thought Adie had gone far enough in her recovery, and the worst of her rawness had healed, Miranda had finally shared what she'd learned about the women they'd *both* once regarded as friends, and how many of them had known about Bryan's affair for a long time.

Some had apparently heard it from their husbands, which begged the question: what sort of women were they, who could come to Adie's dinner parties, month after month, sit at her table, eat her food, drink her wine, and look her in the eye as they pretended everything was great, when they all knew different? Swollen with secrecy and self-satisfaction, they blithely maintained the shallowest of friendships while they quietly waited for her life to blow apart.

Stellar actors, one and all.

But Adie's outage and humiliation had quickly turned to laughter, when the ever-hilarious Miranda had put everything into perspective in a way that *only* Miranda could. When Adie had wondered whether she'd just been blinded by what she wanted to see, and oblivious to any hints that might've been staring her in the face, her funny and ferociously loyal friend had elegantly waved the question away with an impeccably manicured hand.

'Darling, no. The real truth is that some people only want to be friends with you so they can have a ringside seat to watch your anguish, and they'll never tell you that,' she'd declared.

'Then, once you stop being morbid entertainment for them, and become a human being with needs instead, they evaporate like farts out of a bottle! Once they're satisfied that it's *your* life that's hit the skids and not *theirs*, you won't find them anywhere. The only support they understand is the corset kind. You know, the sort that stops their boobs from resting on their bellies, and their spare tyres from falling to the floor?'

Miranda always made Adie laugh, often to the point where she literally couldn't stop. She had an uncanny knack of being able to smell a 'fake' at forty paces, usually before they even said a single thing, and she never held back with her opinions about them. She and Adie had indulged in countless conversations over many decades, about the fickleness of friendship, usually at one of their regular cocktail meet-ups where they'd manage to put the entire world to rights in the time it took to have just two vodka martinis.

Their discussions were often hilarious, and typically peppered with the usual disparaging comments about lying cheating men, the unfathomable challenges of menopause, and how to halt the ageing process at least to *some* degree. But the subject had come up often, of how you could sometimes be completely blindsided by someone's bad behaviour, in spite of how long you'd known them.

Unlike Miranda, Adie had always given people the benefit of the doubt, and sometimes for far longer than she should have. But she'd found it pretty hard to take, when she'd found out how little reward that had brought her, when her own chips were down. A couple of the friendships she'd poured a lot of effort into had imploded without much warning, at the hardest time of her life.

She allowed her mind to drift back, now, to one very significant conversation she'd had with Miranda that had proved to be a real turning point in her grief process.

One of the 'friends' who had let her down was a woman called Penni Pickitt, who Adie had previously thought of as a close and trusted friend. The loss of that friendship had been painful.

It had started unravelling when Penni's dad, Christian, was dying. Adie lived nearby and she used to do his food shopping. She'd grown close to him over the years. She loved him very much and she'd tried, many times, to persuade Penni to visit him more often; before it was 'too late.' But Penni always had endless excuses for not going. When time started running out, the guilt finally kicked in, and she'd tried to offload her feelings to Adie. But Adie was grieving *herself* for the looming loss of her treasured friend, along with everything else that was causing her world to crumble. She'd tried to explain to Penni that she couldn't be her exclusive emotional crutch, because she was struggling herself.

Penni's reaction had been baffling and startling. Instead of acknowledging Adie's own grief, and offering support, she'd disengaged completely. That had been hurtful enough, but the friendship had become officially dead and buried after Adie had gone to the care home, during a pandemic lockdown, to leave a little gift at reception for Christian, and Penni had threatened to call the police. Adie hadn't been trying to break the care-home's code of no entry. She'd just wanted to drop off a present that she thought her dying friend would enjoy. She'd been shocked, and angry, at Penni's threat. She'd struggled and failed, to get her head around the sheer spite and vindictiveness of it.

At one of her and Miranda's infamous cocktail afternoons, Penni's name had popped up in a passing comment, and Miranda hadn't held back at all, in showing her contempt. The conversation had ended up being incredibly funny, and it had completely changed the way Adie was feeling.

'Oh, Adie! Penni Pickitt? For God's *sake*, darling. Don't get me started on *that* piece of work!'

Adie had grinned, and settled back comfortably with her drink, knowing that Miranda had every *intention* of chipping in her penny's worth, with a savage attack on their former friend. And, of course, she'd done exactly that, launching herself full-tilt into one of her uproarious, blistering tirades; that kind that could literally make paint peel. She was a very successful stage actress, and her theatrical, larger-than-life personality didn't have an off-switch. Adie knew they would soon both be shaking with the giggles, as they usually were by the time Miranda finally ran out of steam, fell off whatever high horse she'd jumped on, and started poking fun at her own indignation.

Predictably, before they'd even got halfway through the first martini, Miranda had done what she always did so well, and expertly flipped the tables.

'I know you're still upset about that *utterly* ridiculous woman, but you really must forget about her. The idiot calls herself a 'grief recovery specialist,' which is an absolute *howler*, under the circumstances, don't you think? Her, of all people?

'Adie, a marriage disintegrating, complicated children who won't speak to you, being turfed out of your home and prevented from seeing your lovely dog by a two-faced liar of a cheating, scum-caked husband… these are not small things! Facing an uncertain future at our time of life is pretty frightening too!

'But did that silly bitch care how you might have been feeling about *any* of it, or about how losing her lovely dad was going to hurt you too because you adored him? Of course not! She didn't even *notice* your grief. That woman is so self-absorbed, it's terrifying.'

Miranda had taken a long swig of her martini, and crunched and swallowed an olive, before rolling her eyes dramatically and continuing.

'Don't tell me *you* never noticed Adie, in all the years we knew her, that no matter what any of us had done, Penni nose-Pickitt had done it first, or better? And no matter what anyone else wanted to talk about, she only ever gave it a nano-second's lip service before flipping the conversation back around to herself? She's one of those deplorable people who only listens until they can spot or manipulate a chance to jump back in and talk about *themselves* again!'

Miranda had laughed then, and shaken her head. 'You know, I rang her a few times, in the early days, to talk about something that was quite important to me at the time. My squeeze-of-the-moment had dumped me for a much younger version, and I was a lot more upset about it than I'd been prepared for.

'D'you remember Zane, that luscious, Greek twenty-eight-year-old? Dark curly hair, gorgeous chocolate eyes, but always scruffy, and a bit dusty, like he'd fallen out of an olive tree, or something? Hot enough to melt the Antarctic? Yeah, him.

'Well, I always knew he'd go chasing after someone more his own age eventually, because he wanted kids and he'd never hidden that fact from me. I'd never hidden the fact from him either, that I'd already tottered past the pram-pushing stage by then, but it still hurt like hell when he left. I was a bit of a headcase for a while, if you remember?

'Nobody likes to be abandoned, do they? Or reminded of what a decrepit, ragged old hag they're turning into, trying to stop their foundation from congealing in their facial crags, as time and tumbling oestrogen drag them ever-closer to the scrapheap?'

Adie had laughed with delight, at that. The stunning and glamorous Miranda was a very long way from being ragged *or* bound for the scrapheap, and thanks to her excellent cosmetic surgeon she didn't have anything even vaguely *resembling* a facial crag! But her anecdotes were always entertaining, and her ability to poke fun at herself as well as others, was hilarious. She had no idea how funny she was, either, which made her even more of a treasure.

'Anyway, I was curious to see what Penni nose-Pickitt did with that; as a so-called 'grief recovery specialist,' I mean. But guess what? Every single time without fail, within a minute, we'd be talking about *her* again, and she never once bothered to ask me anything more about why I'd called. We were supposed to be friends but it never occurred to her, to ever initiate contact herself, to ask how I was getting on after my Greek god had chucked me off a cliff and left me in freefall. It was crystal clear to me, that everything I'd said had sailed right over her empty little head!

'You know, I actually timed her, once. It took her precisely fifteen seconds to spin the conversation back around to herself! Fifteen fucking seconds, Adie! Let me tell you, I gave up trying to talk to that dimwit about *anything*, after that.

'Nose-Pickitt hated you, because you had the bare-faced cheek to actually stick up for yourself for once, and call her out! Rude girl, how *dare* you be so bold? And as for her threatening to call the police on you because you'd been kind to her dad? That was more than *slightly* insane, darling. I don't know anyone rational who would do something like that. It really isn't normal behaviour.'

'I know,' Adie had mused. 'I never did get my head around that. It did seem unusually unkind, from someone who tries so hard to convince everyone that she's all sweetness and light, like butter wouldn't melt. I had no idea how two-faced she really was, until that happened.'

'I did care about her grief,' she'd added, as she'd crunched her own olive. 'She said I didn't. She called *me* selfish! I loved her, and of *course* I cared that she was hurting. It was her dad, after all! But I loved him too. I was grieving too, and all I wanted from her, as a friend, was to be validated for that. I know now that she just wasn't capable of offering that. Having no empathy, well, that's one thing. But being so mean? That was something else, wasn't it, Mand?'

Miranda had nodded. 'Yes, it was, Adie. It was vicious, and I'll tell you why. Your relationship with Christian was everything hers wasn't, and she couldn't *stand* it! That's all it came down to. Jealousy, and conscience too probably, because she spent years more or less ignoring the poor man, even when he clearly needed her, and then it became too late. You can't make up for lost time like that.'

'You know, he always used to wish she'd make more time for him. It broke his heart that she didn't, and it always broke mine too, whenever he mentioned it. She never made the effort for him, Mand, and it would have been such a simple thing for her to do. Why wouldn't she do it? I just don't get that. When they're gone, they're gone, you know?'

Miranda had looked at her kindly, with a loving twinkle in her eye. 'You don't know much about narcissists in general, do you, darling? But you need to know how to spot them before another one happens along, wins your trust, and shreds you like a coconut. Penni nose-Pickitt is the purest form of narcissist; spectacularly ruthless, without a care in the world for anyone's needs but her own. Top-drawer manipulator, hell-bent on getting what she wants, no matter who she has to stand on, to do it. And in typical narcissist style, she cast *you* as the miscreant because you dared to contradict her! If there's one thing a narcissist cannot stand, it's being challenged, even when they deserve it.

'She's a fraud too, Adie, pretending to be what she's not! She's not a 'grief recovery specialist' at all, or anything *else* she wants everyone to think she is. As we say in the acting trade, she's just a fur coat and no knickers.'

Adie had shaken her head. 'Sorry, Mand. I dunno whether to laugh or cry about it all, so I guess I'm doing a bit of both!'

Miranda had handed Adie a tissue to wipe her eyes with. 'You loved and trusted someone who turned out to be a hideous human being to you. I've been there too, Adie, and I get it. It hurts. We've all had fake friends that make us appreciate the honesty of our enemies. But, in the end, all you can *ever* do is laugh at them, once you've seen them for what they are, and I think you're finally starting to, thank *God*!

'I remember when you cooked nose-Pickitt a lovely lunch, on her birthday, *and* when you once drove Christian on a hundred and twenty-mile round trip so *they* could have lunch together. I was amazed that you did all that, and more besides. Such selfless things to do; it's just a shame that you ended up doing them for someone so self*ish*.'

'I don't think she remembered any of that stuff, when she did what she did,' Adie had mused. 'My friendship never counted for anything, with her, did it?'

'No it didn't, darling, but that's not your fault. You did the best you could, right up until you literally couldn't. How many hours *did* you spend, by the way, listening to the idiot's endless tales of woe about that man she's been engaged to for a gazillion years who still hasn't married her? She tries to pass that off as him having some mental health condition or other! For God's sake! *That's* a howler too, isn't it? Personally, I think he's the sane one. The man would have to be mentally ill if he *did* let her drag him down the aisle.

'Oh, and let's not forget the fact that her own son doesn't speak to her, and hasn't for donkeys, and won't even let her see her grandsons!'

Adie had laughed again, then. 'That's right! She always had so much to say about the injustice for people who never see their kids or grandkids. I guess it hasn't even occurred to her that there are sometimes very good reasons why certain people don't *deserve* to see them.'

'Yes. And she was horrible to Christian's poor brother too, trying to make sure he didn't find out how sick Christian was, to try and wangle power of attorney before the brother got to do it! Who does something like that, to their own family? She couldn't even *pretend* to have compassion. Fur coat and no knickers, like I said.

'You know, Adie, that lunatic will never hold her hand up to *any* of what she's done to people. She prefers to play the 'poor-me' card instead, dragging sympathy in from every gullible fool who believes her bullshit. And, incidentally, anyone who threatens to call the police on you just for trying to be kind to someone you loved was *never* your friend. *Ever.* Trust me on *that.*'

Adie had nodded quietly at that. While Miranda's indignant rant was pretty funny, the fact that she'd been so crushingly right about everything meant it had still been painful to hear, at the time.

'That silly spineless wonder *always* hated you, on some level at least, to threaten you like that. And she didn't even have the guts to do it directly, did she? She very cleverly engineered another of your so-called 'friends' into doing her dirty work!

'More fool the friend, I have to say, though. Wasn't *she* smart enough to know how cleverly she was being manipulated? Or did she just go along with it, Adie? Because there's only one thing worse than a person who plays one friend off against another, and that's the friend who allows it to happen.'

'Yeah, I suppose. Of course, not long after that happened, that other friend you're talking about showed *her* true colours as well, didn't she; ghosting me for more than a week when I desperately needed help, and was off my head with worry? She was busy travelling, I know, but she knew I was completely distraught and she still ignored me! We were meant to be close friends. I thought she was someone I could confide in. I never thought she'd leave me in the lurch like that. It really hurt.'

'Yes, and when you dared to tell *that* nincompoop how you felt, she dumped you too, didn't she? You weren't allowed to say how upset you were, because – God forbid – that made *her* feel uncomfortable!'

'Yeah, and there I was; the villain again! She told me she was 'done' being friends with me, and that was that. I don't miss her, actually, but I think that's mostly because she tried to bolster her argument by dragging her husband into it. Remember that?'

Miranda had nodded. 'Yes I do. She said he was really angry because you'd 'ranted' at her? I have to say, I thought her using him like that was pretty pathetic.'

Adie had agreed. 'It absolutely was. Using his opinion as ammo to help justify herself was a pretty low blow, even for her!'

'That's classic, textbook manipulative behaviour, Adie. I never knew she was even capable of that.'

'Neither did I, but as soon as she said that, something really odd happened. It was like a switch had been flicked, somewhere inside me. Something just instantly *dissolved*, for want of a better word, and right from that very moment I just didn't want her in my life anymore.'

'She didn't have a good enough argument for abandoning you in your hour of need, Adie. You told her how you felt about it, which you should be able to do within a friendship that's solid. But she chose to see it as an attack, and she used her poor husband to help paint you as the bad guy, to get herself off the hook. That's the most telling part of the entire debacle, darling. Seems to me like she was just looking for an excuse to cut you loose.'

'Well, I did wonder about that. And I guess you could say it worked, because it killed everything stone dead, in an instant. I'd never experienced that before, with anybody. I guess she did what she felt she needed to do, and it's all water under the bridge now of course, but it *has* left me wondering whether she'd ever said a single honest word to me, in all the years we were friends!'

'I don't think you'll ever know the answer to that.'

'Probably not, and it really doesn't matter now. You know what did piss me off though? After all that nonsense, she actually sent me a bloody Christmas card! From her *and* the husband who'd supposedly condemned me too! That was beyond bizarre. Needless to say, it went straight in the bin.'

'That was about *her*, Adie, and whatever need she had, to try and make herself feel better. Just forget her. Leave her to her weird bunch of friends, like nose-Pickitt, and that mad bunch of sex-starved old biddies she introduced you to, who nearly drove you demented. Remember them? The 'Cling and Fling Club,' as we called them? Clinging to that sad, co-dependent clique they've got going online, flinging no end of shit at one another, and hating the rest of the world! Ugh! God, save us *all* from the madness of *that!*'

'You're absolutely right, and I have let it go, mostly. I'm no saint either, of course, and I got things wrong too. A *lot* of things, probably. None of us is perfect, are we? But I did always try, to be as good a friend as I could be, to those two. It just didn't count for much, in the end, did it? My loyalty to them, and my love for them, it meant nothing. All they could see was the worst of me, like you say.'

'You backed the wrong horses, that's all. Instead of picking a pair of decent thoroughbreds that could run with you, you ended up with 'Nincompoop and Pickitt' – a couple of nags that were really only fit for the knackers yard. Fodder for the glue factory, darling.'

Adie laughed. 'Nincompoop and Pickitt! I love that! It sounds like a dodgy law firm in a Monty Python sketch!'

Miranda had smirked. 'And there, I rest my case. They *are* just as ridiculous.'

Miranda's perspective was hilarious, but Adie knew she was right. People who trampled all over you, and then treated *you* like the villain for daring to be upset, weren't 'friends.' The minute you challenged them, they insulted you yet again, then washed their hands of you. Who needed people like *that* in their lives?

'You know what they say, Adie; 'don't wish your enemies dead because you'll end up at the funerals of 'friends.' But I guess you could borrow my red sequined tap-shoes and do an Irish jig on the coffins.'

Adie had giggled at that, but Miranda had turned to her then, and allowed her own grin to fade, as she'd regarded her thoughtfully.

'As the saying goes, Adie, let the trash take *itself* out. But I have to apologise to you, darling. I wish I hadn't been in Lanzarote when you needed help with that crisis you felt forced to ask nincompoop for help with. I'd have been there in a heartbeat.'

'I know, Mand, but I've thought about that too. Maybe what happened *needed* to, so I could get the real measure of a friendship I hadn't known was false. Maybe it was just time, you know, for me to find out the truth and move on.'

Miranda had considered that for a moment. 'Yeah, maybe. Life does show us what we don't expect to see, sometimes. It might feel awful at the time, but it's always in our best interests, isn't it, when we look back? And you've evolved, and become stronger, in the aftermath of your marriage. It makes sense, and it's *good*, that you were able to square that one away without it really bugging you. It shows how far you've come. But there's something else I have to apologise for, Adie.

'I've always had the measure of Penni Pickitt, but I didn't warn you about her, and I should have. In my own defence, which admittedly isn't much good, you seemed to be getting along ok with her. I had no idea how much she'd end up hurting you.

'If I'd seen that coming, I'd certainly have tipped you off about her. I did wash my hands of her, of course, after she threatened you. I have many faults but I'm not disloyal. I couldn't even *pretend* to be friends with someone who caused that much hurt to someone I love. And I do love you, you silly old tart.'

‘Oi, less of the old, thank you very much! I love you too, you crazy cougar-minx! Miss ‘Fifty-five-is-the-new-Forty!’ And thank you for saying all that, and for putting everything into perspective. I’m glad you’re in my corner, Mand.’

‘I always will be, Adie. And for what it’s worth, I’d have punched nose-Pickitt’s lights out for a fiver. Mind you, having said that, she’d probably have put me in jail for it.’

Adie had snorted with laughter. ‘Oh, no! She is *not* worth doing time for!’

‘She seriously isn’t darling, but *you* are!’

‘Well, I’d visit you in jail.’

‘I’d visit *you* in jail, if I wasn't already in there myself. But I’d probably be unable to resist bringing a cake with a file in it, so I’d end up being sprung, and stuffed into the cell next door anyway, wouldn’t I? Then those halfwit women really *would* have something worthwhile to bitch about behind our backs! I do know what they say about me too, of course.’

‘Ah yes, cradle-snatcher, toy-hunter, teen-toter, cougar with claws, mutton dressed as lamb, oh, and that really funny one; *‘lock up your sons!’* That one’s a howler. That *always* has me in stitches.’

Miranda’s eyes had twinkled again. ‘Yes, alright, shut up. But seriously, it really doesn’t matter what those acid-drops think. Half of them are just jealous, not that I blame them for that. I’d be jealous of me too, if I had to wake up every morning looking at a jowly, snoring, shrivel-bollocked old fool like most of *them* do. My boys are always gorgeous! They’re never rich, which doesn’t matter of course, because I have my own money.

‘And I guess the prunes hate that too, as dependent as half of them are on their crusty husbands to bankroll their Botox and browlifts, and foot the bills for all those ludicrous ladies’ lunches, where they all sit around with their bellies on their thighs and their tits on the table. What a waste of money all those tummy-tucks were!’

Adie had been laughing hard by then. She’d known that Miranda had been desperate for her to find some balanced perspective, and it had worked. As another saying went, it’s never the stab in the back that hurts, it’s discovering who held the knife. But, with her cynical sense of humour, and hilariously honest viewpoint, Miranda had enabled her to mend and move on from the odious Penni Pickitt and other quiet assassins.

Adie envied her best friend's carefree take on life. Twice-divorced, Miranda still hadn't found her 'forever' Mr Right, but she still believed he'd show up eventually. She just wasn't going to languish, in the meantime! At almost fifty-five she looked forty, and relished her singledom like a thirty-year-old would. She was having a good time in life, and Adie thought it was fabulous, how 'Mand' could effortlessly 'pull' a man in his twenties, and keep him around for as long as it suited her. She was gorgeous, mysterious, independent and fun. What red-blooded young man *wouldn't* want a slice of that pie? Miranda was milking her assets for all they were worth, and why not? She'd settle down when she was ready. Until she was, life was for living, and she didn't intend to miss a moment of it.

And she was nearly always right, about the human condition. If Adie ever needed a dose of reality, or a different perspective, she only ever had to pick up the phone and talk to her beloved 'Mand.' It was so good to have such a solid supporter in your corner; someone who could see another person very differently from how you saw them yourself, and who wasn't afraid to kick you up the bum by putting things in context for you, when you were so self-deluded that you couldn't see your wood for your trees.

It was also a rare and special thing to be able to say you'd had someone in your life who'd never given you a single wrong or inappropriate word of advice in more than forty-five years, and who'd never threatened to wash their hands of you just because you'd 'screwed up,' by being human and fallible, and you'd somehow managed to offend their precious ego in the process!

Adie giggled to herself again now, as a wave of love washed over her. She really must arrange for Miranda to come and stay again, soon. She breathed life, fresh air and hilarity into every space she entered. Adie adored her.

Another conversation drifted into her mind now; another funny-but-heartbreaking one she'd had with Peg, Trudie, and her sister-in-law Sheila, over one of their regular Friday-morning coffee-and-cake meets down at Peg's cafe. She'd told them ab out her conversation with Miranda, and how valuable it had been, and they'd shared similar stories about being on the sharp end of other women's versions of 'friendship.'

Trudie had talked about a friend she'd had for fifteen years, who she had supported through a long and difficult divorce. The friend was getting remarried, and Trudie was excited for her, but the decade and a half of friendship had disintegrated, virtually overnight, after the friend had asked her to order something special into the boutique for her to wear, and expected to have it at 'cost.' Trudie had been willing to discount the outfit by sixty percent, explaining that she was running a business and had to make a living just like anybody else.

'Next thing I know, there's a mean review left online from her about my shop, accusing me of selling drab, outdated clothes, and trying to rip her off! Two bloody stars, after I offered her a really decent discount on her dream dress! I thought sixty percent was pretty generous, for an outfit like that. It cost hundreds!

'My mark-up isn't what people think it is, you know. It's a living, but I'm only just on the edge of comfortable. That shop will never make me rich. I don't even get much stuff at cost for *myself!* I certainly can't afford to give clothes away, even to friends!'

'Nor should you be expected to, especially to mean ones,' Adie had observed.

'Well, as mean goes, that wasn't the end of it. She rang me, the day after she'd left the review, to say she'd take it down or make it a lot nicer if I'd change my mind and let her have the dress at cost! I couldn't believe that.'

The friends had all been incredulous. Sheila had seemed particularly outraged. 'What? Cheeky cow! Ah well, what's a little bloody blackmail between friends?'

'I know, right? I said no, of course, and I told her to take a hike, and there it was! Fifteen years of friendship flushed down the toilet, because saving a few quid was clearly more important .It wasn't even as if she couldn't afford it! She just wanted to make a point, and everything was lost because of it.'

Peg had chimed in after that. 'That's pretty shortsighted, I'll grant you. Sadly though, I think it's often the case, that friends won't support other friends in business. Like women I've known for years, who I've always had a helping hand for in the past, who would still rather go to a different bloody café than support mine. There's one or two of those, around here!'

Adie had been surprised. 'Really? That's a bit mean. People can be wretched sometimes, can't they? We should all be lifting one another up! Especially as *older* women, who have all been through one kind of mill or another. We'd all do so much better, I think, if we were more of a champion for each other's efforts. As much as I hate to say it, I do believe that some so-called 'friends' are secretly hoping others will fail. That's how I felt, anyway, about some of the people I used to know.'

'Tell me about it!' Trudie had agreed. 'Everyone says they want you to do well, blah, blah, but God help you if you even *look* like you're doing better than they are!'

Peg had chipped in to say that after her first husband died, some her friends disappeared, and she never heard from them again. 'It's like you only see the real measure of someone's commitment to a friendship when there's a crisis, and it never takes long to find out who can't cut the mustard.'

Peg had confessed to how hard it had been, to face everything she had to go through, without the support she thought I could rely on.

'I ended up feeling a bit silly, for thinking that me losing my husband in a car crash should have mattered more to them than their own discomfort. But if they couldn't be there for me in the worst crisis of my life, what did *that* say?

'I cut them loose, but I didn't make a fuss. I just quietly shut the door and moved on. It's easier, sometimes, to just step away. Dignified silence and all that. I'm sure most of them didn't even bloody notice I'd gone.'

Sheila had offered her perspective too, with a cheeky grin, well aware that her Lancashire accent, and the comical way she dropped her 'aitches', always made her stories funnier.

'I've always called a spade a spade, as you know,' she offered. 'And some folks just can't 'andle the truth. I 'ad a friend for a lot of years, right from when we worked together in Preston before we both got wed. She married an Aussie and lives over in 'obart now, in Tasmania, but she were over 'ere one time, visiting relatives. I'd planned to drive an 'undred miles just to spend a couple of hours with ‘er because she said she didn’t ‘ave time to come to my neck of the woods.

‘Well, I couldn’t say I blamed ‘er. We’re a long way north, aren’t we, up ‘ere? So I figured if she’d come ten thousand miles, I could go an ‘undred, right? So we set a date, and I were literally in me car and setting off, and I messaged her, to tell her I were on me way. I got a text straight back, sayin’ sorry but she weren’t going g to be there. It turned out she’d forgotten! She were already ‘alf way to some bloody ‘oliday ‘ouse with ‘er ‘usband for a week. If I ‘adn’t thought to message ‘er, I’d ‘ave driven two ‘undred bloody miles for nothing!’

Sheila had shaken her head, sadly. ‘It weren't the first time I’d made an effort for ‘er, or the first time she’d forgotten me and left me ‘anging, and feeling like I didn’t matter. After that last time, I’d ‘ad enough. I told her I didn’t think there were much point in trying to keep being friends, if she didn’t think I were important enough to make any time for, when I’d always made time for ‘er. She never even bloody replied! That were the end of it. And that were a thirty-year friendship! Clearly she weren’t interested in maintaining it.’

‘That must’ve been horrible, Sheila. So hurtful, after all that time. I'm sorry you’ve all been through so much crap with people too,’ Adie had offered, looking around at her new friends. ‘But I’m glad it's not just me. I did wonder if I was just some kind of too-trusting sad-sack that wandered around with a neon flashing sign on my back, asking people to shit on me.’

Sheila had shaken her head emphatically. ‘Nope. I ‘ate to break it to you, love, but you're nothing special in that. You’re just like the rest of us. No better, no worse, and no less or more unlucky with the freaks we meet in life.’

Adie brought her mind slowly back to the present, now. She shook her head, and sighed gently. She supposed it was probably hearing about poor Debby Davies, and the desertion she was dealing with, that had triggered the return of her own painful memories of the past. But it was clear to her now, in looking back, how much those past conversations had helped her to move on. They’d been immensely valuable, but she knew she wouldn't need to revisit them again. She was in a good place now, having healed and mended as much as she ever would.

She swallowed down the lump in her throat.

It's time to let it all go for good, now; say goodbye to it, for once and for all.

Yes, a lot of 'fly-by-nighters' had come and gone, and doubtless always would, in one form or another, but the keepers had certainly stayed. Miranda, and her new friends; Peg, Trudie and Sheila, had no time for the kind of nonsense her erstwhile crowd had been caught up in; meanness, gossip, and wet-lettuce insincerity.

If she really did want to know how big her bum looked in a pair of jeans, Trudie would be honest. If she ever found herself getting wound up over something silly, Peg would peel her off the ceiling in the blink of an eye and tell her to calm the hell down and have some cake and coffee, and the steadfast, straight-shooting Sheila had no qualms about telling the truth to *anybody's* face. The difference was, these women knew enough about kindness and respect, and any honesty they would offer or be asked for would be given with a good helping of both. They'd been through enough fires of their own to know what mattered in friendship. In a crisis, they'd be there; no question.

Adie also knew that Mark would never lie to her about anything, unlike her ex-husband Bryan. He hadn't said a truthful word about very much at all, in more than half a decade, before they'd broken up.

Honesty was everything. She'd learned that the hard way, after keeping devastating secrets of her own, at enormous emotional cost - and not just to herself.

Sometimes the truth does hurt, she reasoned, *but at least you always know where you are with it.*

Never again would she engage in keeping destructive secrets. Never again would she hide the truth from the people who needed to know it, and never again would she do or say what she didn't mean. Her own naïveté was embarrassing, now that she knew what she'd been up against, with some of the people she used to know and trust. But she'd learned valuable lessons from the cost of her own inattention. She'd also seen a *real* grief counsellor; one who *had* been competent, and understanding (unlike the ludicrous Penni Pickitt), who had helped her, in a few useful sessions. As time went by, and she'd overcome so many of her own life's challenges, she'd emerged with a strength that she once never believed she'd ever have.

But the real turning point for Adie had been meeting and marrying Mark. He had started out as a helpful friend but it hadn't been long before the two of them realised they were in love. They'd been married within a year of meeting, and the time since had been the best of Adie's life.

That's the kind of stuff that's better to dwell on – the kind that reinforces everything I have to be thankful for. But everything feels so much worse, when you're already vulnerable, doesn't it? If I'd been in a better place with my own life, back then, maybe it wouldn't have hurt so much, that the people I loved gave up on me. But despite how painful it was, it's been one of the best lessons I could ever have learned. I guess sometimes you have to go through that kind of fire, to learn how to value yourself enough to raise the bar on who deserves a seat at your table.

Her thoughts turned back to Darren and Debby Davies, and the anguish they were feeling as they struggled to come to terms with their own grief and loss. Darren was worried about his wife, and concerned about her state of mind. Her body had been flooded with hormones while she'd been undergoing her IVF treatment, and Adie understood all too well what an emotional impact haywire hormones could have. It wasn't so long ago that her own hormonal balance was non-existent, thanks to a tough rollercoaster of a menopause that often had her feeling like the most strung-out and deranged human mess on the planet!

For poor Debby, the endless disappointment of unexplained infertility, failed IVF cycles, the frustration of being endlessly poked and prodded by different doctors as they tried to make her conceive, or get to the bottom of the reasons why she couldn't; that would be enough to drive anyone crazy.

But human connections were so important, when it came to dealing with the unbearable, and Debby had lost friendships that had mattered to her too. The pain and disappointment of those abandonments and betrayals must be compounding her anguish. It was pretty hard to face and overcome trauma alone, especially when people you thought you could count on only added to it. Darren had mentioned that Debby's own mother had a crushing lack of sensitivity, and her dad was so disengaged he may as well not be around at all. It was little wonder the poor woman was a seething hodgepodge of conflicting, angry emotions. Who *wouldn't* be a boiling mess, with all that to deal with?

She really felt for poor Debby. Life had been surprisingly cruel to her, and it couldn't have been easy for her to see Feen in the driveway outside the cottage, with not just one but *two* bonny babies. It must've felt like salt being rubbed into the rawest of wounds, after coming here to try and forget for a while, or find a more balanced perspective. Feen had handled things badly too, and was beating herself up for it, but Adie had long since come to believe that everything happened for a reason, even if the reason took a while to appear. Sometimes you had to simply be patient and wait to see what it was.

Maybe Darren had been right. Maybe Feen had acted as a catalyst to fully open a wound, to stop it from festering beneath the surface, and give it time and space to properly heal.

Only time would tell, she supposed.

Chapter Five

Darren still wasn't back with Badger by the time Debby decided to start the difficult job of pulling herself back together. She was still feeling shaky, and slightly wobbly, but she couldn't decide whether it was her own outrage that made her feel that way, or something else. Ever since the woman with the babies had left (Feen Raven-Black, their landlady's step-daughter, if she remembered correctly), and since Darren had waded in and said his own snarky piece before absconding too, Debby had tried very hard to hold onto her outrage, reminding herself over and over, that it was justifiable to be as upset and angry as she felt.

How dare that woman just breeze in here, without an invitation, and openly attack the very core of Debby's anguish? It was like poking a wasp's nest, wasn't it? And that's how Debby felt – like a hot, angry, buzzing mess. Her husband having a rant at her, on the back of a complete stranger doing it, was also pretty hard to take. He didn't often lose his temper with her like that. Clearly, he was a hot buzzing mess too.

Honestly, what had that stupid cow expected? And how does Darren expect me to feel? Where the hell is his loyalty?

But as the time ticked by, Debby realised that she was actively having to try, very hard, to maintain her anger towards Feen or Darren. It was a real effort to stay mad, so it forced her to ask herself – how justified was her anger, really? Her encounter with Feen had certainly been an outrageous experience. It had caught her off guard and rocked her to the core, but had it really been an attack? Had the other woman *really* turned up just to poke the wasp's nest?

The more she thought about it, and the less indignant she allowed herself to feel, the more Debby felt compelled to acknowledge that it hadn't been the case at all. Feen didn't know her, and had no reason to deliberately antagonise her. She had been defensive of herself and her children and her right to have them, yes, but wouldn't *any* mother be that way? Even though Debby hadn't actually uttered the words, that if they were all dead she wouldn't be forced to see them, that apparently hadn't stopped the other woman from feeling the force of her resentment. It must have been a massive manifestation of bad energy.

Maybe that's what's got me so rattled – the fact that she picked up my vibe!

Her mean-spirited, spiteful, jealous thoughts had apparently been so forceful, they hadn't stayed private. And Feen had made an important point. Of *cours*e it wasn't her fault, that Debby couldn't conceive! She'd said it clearly, but gently, with something approaching sensitivity. And she'd backed it up by offering to help, in whatever way she could. And she'd humbly apologised for intruding and making assumptions that it would be ok to come in and talk the way she had.

Debby had instantly rejected her offer of help, dismissing it as nothing more than a simple chance to gloat, thinking; 'how could a complete and utter bloody stranger, with two screaming snots hanging off her hips and clearly without enough common sense to know when to butt the fuck out, possibly 'help' her and Darren?'

She took a deep, shaky breath now, and let the tears come.

Oh my God! What am I becoming? She wanted to help me, and all I did was yell at her, and wish her and her babies dead! What kind of monster is this failure to have a child of my own turning me into? There's so much I can't deal with anymore, and my whole personality is changing. I'm starting to fight with Darren all the time too, and withdraw from him, when he's the one person who loves me the most, above everyone else.

Her own husband was getting sick of her now, and how could she blame him? He said he didn't know who she was anymore, and she couldn't blame him for that either, since she didn't know who she was herself, these days. Their marriage was dying, right in front of them, and it felt like an out-of-control juggernaut that simply couldn't be stopped.

God, I'm so tired! People have been trying to tell me for months, how exhausted I am, but why am I only understanding that now?

She *was* indescribably weary, to her very bones. She was weary of well-meaning family and friends who never seemed to stop asking when she and Darren were going to start a family. She was weary of the people who assumed and implied that she was childless through 'selfish' choice. She was weary of the patronising ones who smirked and patted her hand, and told her it was only a matter of time before she got pregnant. She was weary of the ones who'd given her a nudge and a wink and reminded her that she'd better get on with it, because time was ticking. She was weary of the crushingly rude ones who went a step further with hurtful remarks about being an 'ageing' parent to a young child and creating a burden to it far too young in life. Even her own opinionated mother had waded in, on that one!

'It would be so unfair, wouldn't it, Debby, to leave it much later? If it's really what you want, to have babies with that no-good husband of yours, then you do have to get your skates on. You don't want to look like a granny at the school gates! Imagine how hard your poor children would be teased, or even properly bullied, about *that*! Not to mention having to mop up your dribble later on, because of course they'll feel obliged to take care of you when they should be out having lives of their own, instead!'

But most of all, Debby was weary of the endless, systematic, soul-destroying process of being routinely and humiliatingly fiddled with, by different doctors in different clinics, and always being told the same thing; that nothing was 'wrong' with her.

She and Darren had initially chosen a clinic close to home, but big mistakes had been made there. They'd had a horrendous experience, which had only added to their distress, and they'd felt forced to change to a different clinic. They'd chosen one further afield, but it had an excellent reputation, and they felt welcomed and supported there. They finally started to feel they were in capable hands, but still no baby had arrived.

Debby had been told very firmly, several times now, that her early termination when she was sixteen had in no way whatsoever weakened her chances of having another child. The failure to conceive was, apparently, no-one's fault. It was 'just one of those things' – a cruel, deeply distressing, random hiccup of nature, and there was nobody to blame.

There simply wasn't a medical explanation, and it was impossible to know whether her infertility would have been easier to accept if there *had* been a sound scientific reason for it. Maybe if they'd found something out, right at the start of the process, they wouldn't have put themselves through seven brutal rounds of IVF. They'd tried the back-to-back cycles, as well as the delayed ones that meant waiting until the drugs from the previous rounds had fully left her system. Frustratingly, nothing had 'stuck,' no matter which way they'd tried. Two devastating miscarriages had only deepened their pain, and no more pregnancies had followed.

There were side effects from the treatment too. Constipation had been a major issue for Debby, along with mood swings, bloating, and tenderness all through her body. She also constantly battled to resist comfort-eating, to try and feel better. There were times when she wanted to stuff her face with everything she could find, even though the clinic had told her she needed to keep her weight at an optimal level to optimise the chances of conception. Being enslaved to a calendar was horrible too. That constant reminder, that time was ticking, was unbearable at times.

Only now did Debby realise that throughout the entire three years of trying to conceive through IVF, she'd been in tears for most of that time; anxious, irritable, and hating the world just a little bit more, each time her period turned up. A couple of specialists had told her that her attitude was quite possibly the primary driver for most of her physical symptoms. She needed to relax and stop panicking about the prospect of ongoing failure. That was all well and good, but how the hell was she supposed to stay on top of the hormone-fuelled mood swings that continually sent her into a tailspin of gloom and doom?

As she thought back over it all, her tears welled up again. If only she could just turn off the insistently ticking biological clock that stripped the joy from everything! But, if she was clever enough to do that, if she was *so* superhuman, she'd have conceived without any issues, wouldn't she?

As the problems of the world went, one woman's childlessness was hardly an epic tragedy, for anyone else but herself and the people around her who cared enough to ride the waves of anguish with her. But it still amazed her, how insensitive and downright rude some people felt themselves entitled to be, simply because she couldn't seem to manage to do the one thing she was supposedly designed for; the one thing women were expected to just get on and do.

Well-meaning or not, family or not, the people who persistently ignored her personal boundaries and trivialised her anguish by making crass references to the clock ticking? They just needed to shut the fuck up about it. That would help. The readiness of people like Feen Raven-Black, to wade in on something that was none of their damn business, just made Debby's burden so much harder to bear.

And what about Darren? She knew he longed to be a father. She was grateful for his philosophical approach to it, saying 'if it happens that's great and if it doesn't that's ok too.' But how did he *really* feel about it? Was he grieving? It didn't appear so, but he was usually pretty good at hiding his emotions and she knew the last thing he'd ever want would be to add to her misery by showing his own pain. But what was it like for him, really?

Were men somehow seen as 'less' than what they should be, if they failed to meet society's expectations of reproduction, to continue the family line? Were those who hadn't created children regarded as men to be suspicious of, or feared? Did they feel like failures, in the face of such prejudice? It may be the 21st century, but some of society's old traditions and expectations were still very much in play, especially from grandparents-in-waiting.

Barbara, Darren's mother, had never expressed anything other than compassion and acceptance, after finding out the true situation, but how did she really feel? Was she grieving too? Darren's sister Michelle had two daughters, so Barbara already had a couple of grandchildren, but they lived in Spain, so she didn't see them much. She would probably relish having a grandchild closer, but she was probably more sorry for Debby and Darren for themselves, rather than what her son's childless status might mean for *her*.

Debby's own mother had made her ambivalence crystal clear, about whether or not she became a grandmother. In addition to the fact that she'd never held back with her dislike of Darren, she could come up with a cruel or caustic comment about most other things too, at the drop of a hat. Unfortunately the woman couldn't offer a balance; she didn't appear to be capable of swinging the other way and offering a single scrap of encouragement or support. Debby spent a lot of time trying to pretend that her mother's mean-spirited sniping, or her complete lack of empathy for her torment, didn't matter.

As for her father, Debby had no idea what he thought about *anything*. Don Cameron was present in physical form, but his emotional engagement with Debby and her sister Jayne had always been virtually non-existent. He'd never intervened when he should have, with the power and the authority he had as head of the household, to stop Carole from being such a bitch to her daughters. He mostly stuck his head up his own lardy backside instead, and pretended nothing was wrong. In failing to protect Debby and her sister Jayne from their mother's bitterness, he'd let them down, all their lives, at the most basic level. Debby couldn't rely on him for anything.

She'd once heard him confessing to a visiting friend, over a few too many whiskies late one night, that he should have done more than he did for his daughters. She'd got up to go to the loo, and to get a glass of water, and she'd heard him and his mate in the living room, slurring away to one another. They say; 'get someone drunk and the truth comes out.'

Well, it had come out that night, with Don admitting that he'd been a lousy father for far too long, but while he could admit it to an equally pissed-up friend, he never said it to the people that actually mattered; the ones who fully deserved to hear it. His own bloody daughters. Don was a gutless wonder, if ever there was one. Debby realised now, how little respect she had for either of her emotionally barren parents. It might've been a different story if they'd respected her!

Debby gave herself a mental shake and tried to push away the thoughts about her family that never failed to make her angry and miserable. There was enough going on already to torment her, without dragging all that stuff in too. Better to leave that particular pain parked where it was, in her head, in the place she'd worked so hard to find where she could put it, and keep it from eating her alive.

The back door opened, and Darren cautiously poked his head around it. Clearly, he was testing the atmosphere, and wondering whether it was safe to come in. Badger had no such sensitivity; he simply bounded in and rushed straight up to Debby, as he always did, as if he hadn't seen her for months. The collie was a simple, joyful animal, happy with a walk, a cuddle and a dish of food. She wished she could be so ecstatic with so little.

Darren came in behind him, smiling tentatively at Debby's tear-stained face. She immediately got up and put her arms around him. He returned her hug, and they stood there for a moment or two, wordlessly, just connecting on a physical level, in a way that felt familiar and reassuring.

'I'm sorry', she mumbled into his shoulder. 'I don't know what's happening to me.'

Darren hugged her tighter. 'You're sad. And you're angry, confused, and grieving. I get it. I'm sorry too, by the way. I know it doesn't help, to get pissed off at you. But I'm worried about you. About *us*.'

She nodded, looking at the floor. 'Me too.'

He led her gently to the sofa, where they sat quietly for a while, holding hands.

Debby took a deep breath. 'I know I've had my head up my arse for too long. I know I need to fix that. I don't really know where to start, but I think I need to start with you, because you've been really upset with me today and I need you to be honest with me now. *Really* honest. I want you to tell me everything you feel about me, and about this whole baby situation. All of it, warts and all, whether you think it's going to hurt me or not. I need to know where you're at.'

Darren studied her for a long moment, then took a deep breath of his own.

'Right. Ok, well, since you've asked, I'll tell you; but don't shoot me for saying it, okay? Remember that you asked for it.'

He rubbed his face with his hand and she saw for the first time how tired he looked. It wasn't just a physical tiredness. He was emotionally tapped out too. Why hadn't she seen that before now?

'I feel like I'm living in a pressure cooker, Debby, and the hardest part of it all is seeing you so unhappy, so desperate for a baby. I hate that I can't fix what's tearing us apart, and I hate that I've started worrying now, *really* worrying, that you are losing your grip, and that maybe we aren't strong enough to survive it. I worry about that because of the depth of your anger and your grief, and the way you've started expressing it.

'It all feels like there's a massive intruder into this marriage, and it's so huge, Debs, and I can't control it. I feel like I'm at the mercy of it, living in the shadow of it all the time, and I'm scared to death of what it's going to mean for us. Wishing other mothers dead, and their kids as well? I really *don't* know who you're turning into, and I can't describe how sad and scary it is, to hear you say stuff like that. I'm terrified of losing you; within our relationship, as the woman I've known and loved, or losing you for real, if we don't make it.'

Fresh tears sprang to Debby's eyes again, but she stayed silent, letting him talk.

'The best bit of my life is you, Debs. It's *you*. It has been since the day we met, and I hope it always will be. Yeah, of course I want kids! You're not alone in that, but for me it's not the end of the world if we don't have them, because that's not why I married you. Babies would be the icing on the cake but, to be honest it was a pretty good cake to me already, until all this infertility malarkey started.

'I guess I'm already feeling pretty lucky, after the mess I'd made of my life, to even have *you*. I used to think I didn't deserve a good woman who'd love me. Now I have that, it somehow feels a bit greedy to want anything more, if that makes any sense.'

Debby nodded. 'Yeah, it does. I get that. I really do.'

'And if I had the choice Debs, between being with you and not having kids, or losing you, I'd choose you and no kids. In a heartbeat, babe. Because you are everything to me. *Everything.* And I guess, if we really are being honest here, I wish you felt the same about me. I wish I could be enough for you. It kills me, that I'm not.'

He fell silent then, and Debby squeezed his hand. She dragged a hand through her hair and looked at him, with her eyes still puffy from crying.

'I love you so much, Darren. Meeting you was me getting *my* cake. I just want us to have the icing on it too, and be a proper family, with children! It's all I've *ever* wanted. I just don't know how to want it less, and I can't imagine wanting anything else more. It just feels like such a normal thing to bloody want!'

'But how will we cope if we can't get past it, Debs? If you can't accept it? What will you do; leave me and take your chances with someone else? We're both fine, the doctors have said so, but maybe we're only fine individually. Have you thought about that? Maybe it's the blend of you and me together. Maybe that's what's not working.'

Darren's voice cracked. He sounded so miserable. Debby could hear the anguish in his voice, but he carried on.

'And if you do really wonder about that, if it's something that's weighing on your mind, I'd understand if you went. If you wanted to see if you could have a baby with someone else, it would tear me apart, but I wouldn't blame you, because I know how big this is for you, Debby. I know how important it really is, for you to be a mother, so if that's what you felt you needed to do I wouldn't stand in your way.'

Debby was crying again now, properly crying. Darren, her poor, wonderful husband, with tears streaming down his own face, was prepared let her go and take her pregnancy chances with another man. He really *did* get what a big deal it all was. How could she ever have doubted that? The one thing he didn't get though, was the fact that she didn't want to have a baby with anyone else. She wanted to have one with *him*, her Darren, the love of her life!

She knew she was the love of his life too, and that made it all the more humbling and extraordinary, the fact that he was prepared to sacrifice his love, in order for her to be happy. He was an amazing man. She knew that walking away from him wasn't an option, and she told him so. He reached out and drew her into his arms, holding her close, and burying his face in her hair.

She mumbled into his shoulder. 'So I know I might have to draw some kind of line under this, and try to move on. It's shaping up to be the only choice we have. I'm just not sure how to make that leap though, Darren. How do I get from here to there, before it tears us properly apart?'

'We could still consider adoption, or even fostering, for a while. I know I've a criminal record, but it's all for small stuff, and I've turned things around, so we might still be eligible for one or the other – or maybe even both.' Darren's voice was hopeful.

Debby sighed. She'd heard a lot of people talk about how rewarding fostering was, and she believed every word of it. But the thought of getting attached to a child then having it taken away again? She didn't know if she could face that. A lot of the kids that were taken into foster care had behavioural problems too, or a lot of baggage. Darren would be an amazing foster parent; he could handle almost anything a kid might turn up with. She had no doubts about that, but she seriously doubted her own capacity to deal with it even though there was, apparently, very good training and support given by the authorities to people who entered the fostering system.

Adoption was a long-shot. Darren's criminal record might be more of a problem than he thought, and babies were in pretty short supply. Going abroad was an option, but it could take years, and the amount of bureaucracy was astounding, not to mention the potential problems with cultural differences. That particular path was a battle of its own. Did they have the patience and the stamina, even if Darren was considered eligible? His voice broke into her thoughts.

' .... dogs?'

Debby blinked at him. 'Sorry, what?'

'I said maybe we could just buy a cheap ten-acre block of dirt somewhere in the Outer Hebrides and set up a home for stray dogs?'

Debby laughed, in spite of herself. 'Oh yeah. And how does that pay the bills, exactly?'

Darren shrugged, a smile playing around his lips. 'But think of all that unconditional love! All those waggy tails?'

'Yes, and all that poo, all that bad breath and the endless howling and barking. We'd keep the painkiller industry alive all on our own, with all the headaches we'd have!'

They both laughed, mostly at the relief of the bubble of tension being broken. Debby picked up Darren's hand again. She looked at him anxiously.

'I love you. Totally. You're the other half of me, and my life would be meaningless without you. I know I need help to process this, to really come to terms with the fact that maybe it just isn't going to happen. I don't want it to be that way, so I'm scared to accept that it might, because doing that feels so *final*. It feels like saying goodbye to all my hopes and dreams of ever becoming a mother. If that door does have to close, I don't want to be the one who shuts it.'

She sighed, heavily, and wiped her weeping eyes with the knuckles of her hands.

'Being a mother is what I've always felt I was destined for. But I don't want to be the person I'm turning into either, Darren, wishing other mothers and their babies dead! For fuck's sake, what *is* that? But I genuinely think that the only thing that will stop me from turning into a complete monster, if it isn't a baby, is a change in how I think. I just don't know how to make that happen.' She shook her head in sad frustration.

'You need to talk to someone, babe. A professional. Someone who understands. Someone who won't judge you or make you feel small, who'll show you how to think about it differently. Maybe once you get a different perspective, it might be easier. I dunno, Debs. I'm no shrink, and I'm not you, and only *you* know what you really need. I just know I can't provide it. I'm too close. You need someone objective.'

Debby knew that he was right. He talked a lot of sense, when she chose to listen to him. 'I guess I've always been envious of you being so philosophical about it. I always thought that meant you didn't understand what I've been feeling.'

'Believe me, I do, Debby. I do get it, but only up to a point, I have to admit. I'm just the bloody sperm donor. Mine's the easy bit. I don't have a biological clock kicking me up the arse every other minute. I don't have a deeply ingrained drive to be pregnant. Maybe if I *was* designed to give birth I might be champing at the bit to do it, but I'm not. I'm just a lowly bloke, and most lowly blokes can't really imagine how women feel in *any* situation, especially yours. Because we're blokes, you know? And lowly?'

Debby laughed again. She got what he meant, totally. Only another childless woman could understand the depth of the emptiness that came with being unable to have the baby she longed for.

Darren winked at her, suddenly. 'Hey, just going off on a bit of a tangent, d'you fancy a meal out tonight? We could go down to one of the pubs in town and have supper? Saves cooking. When's the last time we did that, just went out for pub grub, and sat around with a couple of pints, doing the silly nonsense chat thing? It's early, but they probably have a happy hour, or two. We could have a couple of pints before we eat.'

'I'll get my coat.' Debby mentally dragged herself together, determined to show her husband that she was capable of thinking about something other than her childless state, for a couple of hours at least.

They decided to take Badger with them and took the path across the fields down to the nearest pub; the Bull and Royal. They managed to bag an outside table and, over a few pints of ale and a couple of steak-and-chips suppers, they managed to relax and have a laugh. A lot of other patrons made quite a fuss of the incredibly handsome Badger, actually getting up out of their seats and coming over to meet him, throughout the evening. Badger was in his element, solemnly shaking paws with people, and enjoying being lavished with attention.

As the last morsels of lemon tart with blueberry coulis were polished off, the last mouthfuls of ale were swallowed down, and jackets were shrugged back into, the chef came out with a foil-wrapped package, which he handed to Debby.

'Here you go. Some scraps of steak. Quite a bit of fat, but that'll be good for his coat, and there's at least half a sirloin in there that some idiot rejected as being 'too medium,' whatever the hell that means. Your dog may as well have it, rather than it go in the bucket for the pigs. He's lovely. He deserves a treat.'

‘Oh, how kind! Thank you so much.’ Debby was grateful for the offering. ‘He is rather partial to a bit of steak.’

The chef laughed. ‘Yes, I saw, earlier on, when I was taking a break. Looked like you gave him half of yours.’

‘Well, not quite half, but he certainly didn’t miss out. And he won’t with this, either! Thank you again.’

Badger was made a fuss of for a final time and they left the pub, replete with good food and drink, and humbled once again by the kindness of a stranger.

‘I like this place,’ Debby declared as they started their walk back to Teapot Cottage.

Darren took her hand and held it as they walked.

‘I do too. The people around here seem really genuine. There’s no agenda. And all that steak? There’s a fair old bundle there. No pub down south would do what that chef just did. They’d be too hung up on the whole health and safety thing. They’re not supposed to even give leftover food to the homeless. It has to go in the bin. Regulations. It’s so unfair to do that when some of these restaurants and hotels can look out though their front windows, and actually see people living in cardboard boxes at the corner of the fucking street.’

‘Yeah, fair play to the chef at the Bull. The food was good too. We’ll go back, I think, don’t you?’

‘Definitely. And we should try the other pub too, the Feathers, I think it’s called.’

When they got home, the sun was going down across the valley, casting gorgeous warm yellow light through the living room windows. Debby and Darren stood drinking in the view for a while. The warmth of the day still lingered. The cottage didn’t feel cool at all.

Darren filled the kettle and set it on the Aga, going through the motions of making a pot of tea as if he’d been doing it in that kitchen for years. There was a real cosy peacefulness about Teapot Cottage. It felt so homely and gentle. The walls felt wise, somehow, as if they’d borne witness to a great deal in their lifetime. *If only they could talk*, Debby thought to herself as she settled into a window seat to watch the setting sun.

While they’d been gone, Adie Raven had paid them a visit. A carrier bag had been left hanging from the front door handle with an assortment of swimwear in it. Debby sat the bag on her lap, and opened it. A very plain but sculpted black one-piece with a small belt and little gold buckle at the waist appealed to her a lot, as did a pretty halter neck bikini, in pink and white flowers, with an under-wired bra and high-waist briefs. There were a couple of other one-piece swimsuits in the bag, and everything was very nice. It was lovely of Adie to have remembered. A brief note was taped to the bag that said; 'I don't want them back!'

Debby smiled. Kindness was everywhere. But then her smile fell, when she remembered the kindness of Feen Raven-Black, and how mean she had been in the face of it. As Darren approached, holding out a steaming mug of tea, she said;

'I'm going to look out for that little Feen woman tomorrow. If I do see her, I'm going to apologise to her.'

Darren smiled gently. 'That would be a nice thing to do. I'm sure she and her family will appreciate it.'

'It doesn't mean it was okay for her to bang on at me the way she did, though.'

'Of course not. And she probably knows that anyway. I don't imagine you'll have any more problems on that score.'

Now that the swimwear had arrived, Debby decided to try it all on and she was very pleased to find that despite the fact that she'd put on nearly half a stone in weight since the IVF process started, everything fit pretty well. She kept the black swimsuit on, figuring it was as good a time as any to try out the hot tub. Darren didn't need much persuasion, and before long they were both soaking under the stars with their cups of tea nestled into the moulded cup holders at the sides. She grinned at her husband, lying with his head back, eyes closed, a contented smile playing at the corners of his mouth.

'Oh, God, Darren! This is *so* great. I think we need one of these at home. Shall we get one?'

Darren opened one eye, looked at Debby's happy face and burst out laughing.

'Yeah, I s'pose we could. Be great in the winter.' He held out his arms to her, and she drifted into them.

They made love that night, tenderly and with more affection than either of them had felt for a long time. For once, it wasn't about trying to get pregnant, and while that didn't mean everything had been resolved, Debby had come to understand that in some way, whichever way she could, she would have to figure out how to move on. She would have try, at least, to focus on how to build a life without children, and although she knew that the ache of loss would never truly disappear, she hoped it would diminish, at least to the degree where she could still enjoy whatever else life might have in store for her. Letting go of her most heartfelt, cherished dream would be hard. But she had an amazing husband who would support her all the way.

She needed to talk more with Darren about the prospect of being a childless couple, and not just from her own perspective. He'd said, many times before, that he would cope just fine if they didn't have any kids, and she'd always believed him, but with a lot of resentment or frustration. She needed to let go of that, and try to see it more from his side of the fence.

Darren had his own priorities, and the biggest one was Debby herself. Today, they'd had a very deep conversation and both of them had laid themselves and their fears wide open. They knew how much was at stake, but a surprising 'shift' had taken place. She couldn't describe it, because it was so subtle and as yet intangible, but it *was* a definite shift. She wasn't exactly at peace but, for the first time since all the misery started, she was starting to feel that it might be possible to get past it, if she allowed Darren's love to guide and support her. It was mind-blowing, to learn that he loved her enough to let her go, if doing so would enable her to realise her own dreams. That was the most powerful thing of all.

As she snuggled down beside him and felt herself drifting off to sleep, she thanked her lucky stars, for the first time in a long time, for how wonderful her husband was. He had his faults, sure, but he was as strong and solid as a rock. He would never let her down. Strong arms held her, a strong heart loved her, and a growing part of her did believe now, that eventually – whatever came or didn't – they could somehow find a way to make a good life together.

Chapter Six

Darren was roused abruptly by the sound of someone battering relentlessly at the back door of Teapot Cottage. He quickly realised that something must be very wrong, so he jumped straight out of bed and hauled his jeans up over his hips. Why the hell would anyone be banging on the door at this hour of the morning? It was barely half past seven! So much for a lazy lie-in!

The banging was insistent, and didn't stop. Without putting on a shirt or a pair of socks, he ran down the stairs and yanked open the back door. He was amazed to see Adie Raven's husband, Mark, standing on the doorstep. The man didn't waste any time.

'Darren, is it? I'm sorry, lad. I wouldn't normally bother yer so bloody early, but I've a problem I need real 'elp with, an' it can't wait. I need a vet, urgent like. Ours is away fer't weekend, and I can't get 'old o' t'other bugger on call. Can you 'elp us at all? Please, say yer can.'

Debby was behind him now at the door, in her dressing gown.

'Debs, this is Mark Raven, Adrienne's husband. Mark, this is my wife, Debby.'

Mark Raven stepped forward extending a weathered hand. He looked apologetically at them both.

'Ow do, lass? I'm sorry to disrupt yer 'olidy, but we've an emergency at Bracefields, me brother-in-law Bob Shalloe's farm across valley.'

Mark explained that a ram from an adjoining farm had stuck its head through the fence at his brother-in-law's ram, and the two had butted heads pretty hard. Their horns had become entangled to the point where one of the rams had had one ripped out and it was hanging off, and the animal was stumbling around and falling, in shock and pain. Bob Shalloe was reluctant to shoot the poor creature if it could be saved, but it was definitely an emergency that needed to be sorted without delay.

Darren nodded. 'Sure, of course I can help. Let me finish getting dressed, and I'll grab my bag from the truck.'

He looked at Debby. 'Will you be alright, babe, if I go?'

'Yeah, of course. You *must* go. You can't leave an animal in distress.'

Darren looked back at Mark, as he dashed back up the stairs. 'Debs can make you a quick coffee, if you like?'

Mark shook his head. 'No time. We 'ave to get gone. Me sister'll feed us some brekkie when we get there.' He started a little, as if remembering something. 'Oh, an' Adie told me to ask yer if you'd like to go up to't farm and join 'er for breakfast at eight, Debby; save yer bein' on yer own. We might be a while, an' I think she'd appreciate the company, to be honest.'

Darren had amazed himself, at how quickly he'd been able to focus after being so suddenly and unceremoniously bounced out of his bed. He'd managed to go from being sleepy and resentful at being woken from a deep sleep, at what felt like the crack of dawn, to firing on all cylinders and being ready for action in three minutes flat.

As Mark drove, he explained that his brother-in-law Bob ran mostly Herdwick sheep on his land, like Mark did himself, but both Bob and his neighbour were also breeding a small herd each of Improved Haslingden Sheep, otherwise known as 'Lonk', that were native to the Pennines and tended to also do quite well in Cumbria. Unfortunately, the injured ram was a Lonk. Mark pulled a face.

'If bugger needs puttin' down, it'll cost 'im a pretty penny to replace it.'

'I'll do what I can, I promise.' Darren knew that a decent Lonk ram would probably set Bob Shalloe back thousands of pounds. As if to echo his thoughts, Mark spoke again.

'Last year, one went at auction in Clitheroe for seven an' 'alf grand.'

Darren grimaced. 'Presumably insurance will cover a replacement, though?'

Mark nodded. 'Aye, it should, if it comes to that. 'Opefully it won't.'

No pressure then, Darren thought, as he stared out through the windscreen of Mark's Range Rover.

Farm work was an area of veterinary practice that Darren had been itching to get into. Working with livestock offered a unique opportunity to be involved with a huge variety of different species – ranging from rare-breed cows, horses, ponies, pigs and sheep, to high-value alpacas, ostriches and a lot of other birds, including raptors, and occasionally even peacocks! No two days would ever be the same, working for clients with very diverse business and domestic relationships with the creatures and herds they tended and bred, were often intensely proud of, and in many cases truly loved.

A lot of the vets he'd graduated with weren't interested at all, in farm work. The more cynical and less patient predicted it was only ever a matter of time until meat farming ended completely. Others said it was too dirty a job, and yet more thought farmers didn't care about their animals as anything other than bankable assets.

Darren knew all of that to be largely untrue. He hadn't met many farmers, to be fair, but the ones he *had* met seemed to care a great deal about the welfare, comfort and quality of life, of their stock. As for the job being dirty, well, that wasn't a 'thing' for Darren. He didn't mind getting his sleeves rolled up or his hands mucky, and if he had to come home covered in blood, mud, mucus or manure, as far as he was concerned it simply went with the territory. He'd already been throw up on by countless cats, dribbled on by no end of slobbering dogs, and someone's pet parrot had even drawn blood from him once, requiring two stitches, so what was a bit of cow shit, compared to that?

The 'dirty end' of the job is actually most of it. If you don't have the stomach for it, why would you want to be a vet at all? There's a hell of a lot more to it than cute kittens and playful puppies!

He snapped back to the present as Mark turned the Range Rover off the main road and onto a dusty driveway that led up to a tall and imposing house, A signpost at the roadside read 'Bracefields Farm.'

Mark told him that Bob and Sheila had been here for more than twenty years, and it showed. The place was a typical farm; 'bitty' and slightly scruffy, with sheds and other outbuildings of various shapes and sizes dotted around, in different states of repair. Hens, geese and dogs ran loose, cats slept on flagstones in the early-morning sunshine, and farm machinery and implements were scattered everywhere. Some of them looked almost abandoned; as if they'd been exactly where they were for decades, with grass growing up around them, as they rusted gently in the open yard. Bracefields Farm was entirely practical and functional, and made no apology for it.

The house was gorgeous though, and very well-kept. It was Georgian; a square, two-story red-brick 'mini-mansion,' with long, elegant multi-paned sash windows. The top floor had five, in a neat row, and the ground floor had four; two either side of a heavy, panelled wooden door that was flanked by an ornate moulding. The symmetry, so typical of Georgian homes, was stunning.

As Darren and Mark pulled up in the yard, a middle-aged couple came towards them. The woman was wiping her hands on her apron. She looked worried, but she smiled at them both. Bob just nodded, grimly. Mark made the introductions.

'Darren, this is me sister, Sheila Shalloe, and 'er 'usband Bob. Darren Davies is stayin' at Teapot Cottage, and e's a vet. Best I could do, under't circumstances. No offence,' he added with a wink at Darren, who just laughed.

'None taken. Good to meet you Bob, and Sheila. Glad I can help. I love your house by the way. It's a work of art! Do you actually use all those chimneys?'

Sheila nodded. 'Yeah, most of them, at some point or other, over the winter. Case of 'aving to, sometimes, to keep the 'ouse's bones warm. It's a bit exposed around 'ere, and we do feel the wind when it blows in from the Atlantic.'

Bob stepped forward. 'Welcome to Bracefields farm. Sorry to drag you away from your holiday, but we're in a bit of a mess here. The ram's in a bad way, I think. He was half-mad earlier, screaming, butting the railings, foaming at the mouth. Shock and pain, no doubt. But he's gone very quiet in the last half-hour, and I don't think that's a good sign. I could put him down myself, of course, but he's young and rather magnificent, aside from being bloody expensive! I want to see if we can save him first, if you don't mind?'

Darren immediately liked Bob. He sounded well-educated, and he was straight to the point and practical. He seemed like the kind of no-nonsense man who would always say what he needed to in a handful of words, unlike some who would use ten times as many to say the same thing.

'Sure. Let's take a look, and see what we're dealing with.'

As the three men started walking towards the back of the farmhouse, Sheila piped up. 'I've got some scrambled eggs, sausages, and 'ome-made 'ashbrowns on the go. Breakfast will be ready when you are, and remember to ask Dave, too.'

According to Bob, his neighbour Dave Holloway had managed to get his own injured ram into his barn, and he'd asked Bob if Darren wouldn't mind going across and taking a look at it too. Darren nodded. Bob's ram was now lying in the field, close to the fence line, and was bleating quietly. It's eyes were glazed with pain, and the hole in its head was huge. It had lost a lot of blood, from the place where the horn had been torn out, and Darren could see in an instant that the poor animal couldn't be saved. The damage to its head was catastrophic, and its pain was too great. He said as much to Bob.

'I can tranquilise him and try and stitch that, if you want, but his head's torn open. Half his brain's exposed, Bob. He's lost so much blood and he's already susceptible to massive infection. I'm so sorry. I do have to recommend putting him down.'

Bob nodded, curtly. He was visibly upset, and swallowed hard.

'Righto, then. I did suspect as much. It's a devastating injury. I can see that, but I owed it to the poor bugger to try, didn't I?'

'Yeah, you did.' Darren was surprised when Bob handed him a rifle.

'I assume you know your way around one of these?'

Darren sighed heavily, and nodded.

Bob put a hand on the ram's neck and patted him a couple of times.

'I'm sorry, old boy. You'll be missed around here, but I hope you understand. We have to let you go. Can't let you suffer.'

Bob's neighbour, Dave Holloway, came over as Darren completed the unhappy task of putting Bob's ram out of its misery. Mark and Bob wrapped the animal in plastic and put him in one of the outhouses so that Bob could make arrangements for him to be collected by a company who could dispose of him appropriately. He'd been a solid lump of a beast, at least eighty-five kilos, at Darren's estimate.

Dave Holloway took him over to his barn to take a look at his own ram. Luckily, this one had fared a lot better, with only a tear to the base of its horn, that Darren was able to quickly swab and stitch. After an injection of a powerful antibiotic, he pronounced the ram as fit to release back into the field.

It was something, at least. The job hadn't been a double disaster. Dave was upset too, that Bob's ram had had to be euthanised, and offered to share his at tupping time.

'Don't worry, Bob. My ram'll do both herds easily enough, if the insurance doesn't pay out in time.'

Bob gave Dave a hearty slap on the back, and told him that Sheila was expecting him at Bracefields for breakfast.

'This middle-aged whipper-snapper is divorced, and I happen to know that he doesn't take care of himself as well as he jolly-well should,' Bob explained to Darren, with a twinkle in his eye. 'Sheila sometimes takes pity on him, drags him over the fence and fires some food at him. Even a motley dog deserves a bone from time to time.'

Dave rolled his eyes and grinned. 'I may be middle-aged, and I may be divorced, you bloody old git, but that doesn't mean I'm motley, thanks very much. I'm perfectly happy on my own, too, as you're well aware.'

He turned to explain to Darren; 'The ex-wife ran off with one of my sly-bastard mates. Best thing that ever happened, as far as I'm concerned. Losing *two* barefaced liars from my life was the luckiest break I've ever had. I did have to go back to work for a while, mind you, but I've got all my own money again now and I feel ten years younger!'

Bob grinned and clapped him on the back again, and Dave broke into a cheeky, generous grin. It was clear the two men were good friends, as well as neighbours.

Back at the farmhouse, Sheila had put two big platters of eggs and sausages on the kitchen table. She also lifted a big oven-dish of fried chopped potatoes out of her Aga. Darren realised he was famished. He noted that Sheila's beautiful black and brass Aga was three times the size of the one at Teapot Cottage.

She saw him looking at it, and grinned. 'Standard kitchen fayre, up this way. You'd struggle to find an 'ouse in Torley that didn't 'ave an Aga or a Rayburn. You've got that little red one in Teapot Cottage, 'aven't you? 'ow are you getting on with it?'

‘We weren’t prepared for it, but its charming. Gives a lot of character to the kitchen, I’ll say that for it, but I have no idea how to work it. Debby, my wife, plans to have a go at it though. She does have an instruction booklet, and a recipe for something she allegedly can’t get wrong, so I guess that’ll help.’

Sheila laughed. ‘Agas are great. Once you know ‘ow to regulate and use them, which isn't ‘ard, there’s nothing they won’t make a good job of.’

‘Have you got an Aga in your kitchen, Dave?’ Darren enquired.

‘I do, as a matter of fact. It’s only a small one, just two hotplates, but it hasn’t seen any cooking action since Gillian left me. I just use it to dry my socks in, most of the time.’

They all tucked into their plates of breakfast. Mark explained to Bob and Dave that Darren was looking to get more into farm work. Bob seemed impressed.

‘I hear that its getting more difficult to get good newbies. A lot of them are turning their noses up at this kind of work, but the truth is, we need farm vets now more than ever, with the different rare-breed programs going on, up and down the country. Just as we start to need them more, it seems there are less of them.’

‘That may be true, but I haven’t found an opportunity yet. I keep looking, but most of the farm vets in my area are holding onto their jobs.’

‘Well that should tell yer summat,’ Mark observed. ‘It must be a good job, if no bugger wants to leave.’

Darren laughed. He loved the way Mark talked. Sheila, his sister, had a Lancashire accent too, but it wasn't as pronounced. Darren figured that most of the rougher edges of hers had probably been gradually rounded off thanks to twenty-odd years of marriage to Bob, who spoke more like an English gent.

‘I keep hoping for an opportunity to open up in Devon, where I live; somewhere within commuting distance. I’d *love* to be more involved with livestock. Any kind of veterinary work is rewarding of course, but it’s no bed of roses. People think being a vet is a glamorous, feel-good career, and a lot of the time it is, but most people don’t realise that there’s often a fair chunk of heartbreak too.’

He didn't need to point out the obvious; that there were a lot of pets that had to be put to sleep, and how devastating that was, for the owners. It was a tough part of the job, seeing that, even when you knew it was the right thing to do.

He accepted Sheila's offer of a third cup of coffee, and piled two more sausages and another large spoonful of potatoes onto his plate. As he did so, he sent a silent message of thanks into the ether, that Debby wasn't here to witness a carb overload that teetered on the edge of outrageous.

'It's a privilege, to be able to heal the sick, so I'm not complaining, and I know that losses are part of farm practice too. But, if I'm honest, I'd just rather be out in the fresh air, working with a more diverse sector of animal husbandry, helping to keep commerce and industry alive, and being part of the infrastructure that gives some of these rare breeds the best chance to grow and thrive. We've lost so much, over time, haven't we? It's nice to see so much effort being put into bringing some of it back. I want to be part of that, if I ever get the chance.'

Bob winked at him. 'You might get paid too much in mutton chops and not enough in cold cash, though.'

Darren laughed again, and gestured at his plate. 'Well, I don't have a problem being paid in eggs and sausages from time to time, believe me! There are far worse things than this, as a reward for helping out.'

Sheila nodded, and winked. 'Farmers don't mind paying their bills, and they also don't mind slinging a breakfast or a lunch at someone, or putting a couple of organic chickens or a bag of Brussel sprouts into the back of a Land Rover, either. You may end up with a good balance of both. Let's keep our fingers crossed, that you get a chance to follow your dream.'

Soon, it was time to leave. Darren accepted Bob's and Dave's profuse thanks, for getting there so quickly, and getting on with what needed to be done. Each of the two men pressed a couple of big banknotes into his hand, and wouldn't take no for an answer. They believed that his time was as valuable as anyone else's, and it seemed a bit churlish to argue with that, so he humbly accepted their money.

Mark spoke to Sheila, as he got up from the table. 'Adie's asked me to invite yer to ours for Sunday lunch soon. She wants yer to let 'er know what Sunday suits yer best. And you should come too,

Dave, since I'm thinkin' yer could do wi' a decent feed instead of a plateful o' roasted socks.'

On the way home, Mark remarked that Bob would be glad of the matter being resolved so fast, even if it wasn't the outcome he'd wanted. His voice was brusque but kind. 'It were as plain as nose on yer face. Poor bugger were too far gone. I know there were nowt else yer could've done, lad.'

Darren shook his head. 'There really wasn't. It's tragic. He was a magnificent ram, Mark, a beautiful animal. What a terrible waste. It's a lovely breed, the Lonk,' he added. 'They've been around a long time, haven't they? A couple of hundred years?'

Mark nodded. 'Yep. They were bred fer't fells, in Lancashire an' Yorkshire, but they do pretty well up 'ere too. They're officially at risk, on't Rare Breeds Survival Trust list. It's important to keep 'em goin'. Even smaller 'erds, like Bob's an' Dave's, are important. Good meat, good wool, nice and 'ardy. Some o't fancy chefs like 'em.' He rolled his eyes.

'They make good 'otpot, apparently. Interestin' breed, tick a lot o' boxes. People argue about source o't name, an' all. Some say it's summat to do wi't grass they graze on, but others say it's an 'ark back to me own native Lanky dialect, as long an' thin.' He looked sideways at Darren and smirked. 'I like to think the latter.'

'Bob seems like a good bloke,' Darren offered. 'And I like your sister, Sheila. They seem like salt of the earth. I hope they get to grips with the loss quickly.'

'Oh they will, lad. One thing you'll learn fast, if yer do get in to farm vettin' is 'ow practical we all are, about losin' stock. Can't be any other way wi'out it drivin' us barmy. The foot an' mouth outbreak were a worry. It were a while ago now, but I lost me entire bloody flock. Took a bit, to get we're 'eads and finances around that. Me wife Beth cried fer a full week, an' I 'ad plenty o' tears meself.'

'Yeah. I was a teenager then. It was long before I'd even *considered* a career as a vet, but I remember it all playing out on the telly, and all of the entrances to the country walkways around the edge of my town being blocked off to walkers. It was a terrible thing.'

Mark just nodded but said nothing further, and Darren was left to his own thoughts for a while.

This morning's emergency had been a welcome diversion. It had effectively taken his mind off everything else for a while. As much as he knew how important it was to take some time out, to focus on how he and Debby might still be able to make their marriage work despite the cold shadow of infertility affecting their every thought and move, the intensity of having nothing else to think about was crushing. He wondered if they'd made the right decision, to leave home and come somewhere else, just to see if a change of scene and time away from the humdrum of their usual busy schedules could help them find a way forward.

Maybe it was just a fancy excuse for running away, and he wasn't sure if it was even working the way he'd intended. The past few days had been intense, and in spite of what Debby had already said about promising to try and look at the situation a little differently, it would be easier said than done, for her. He felt that they weren't a lot closer to getting onto the same page than they were when they first arrived.

Admittedly, it had only been a day since that important conversation, so he wondered if he was expecting too much. Could a change of environment really somehow miraculously open the floodgates to better understanding on both sides, and a full commitment from Debby to find a new way forward? It was bordering on unrealistic, he knew, to expect some great epiphany or revelation while they were here.

That would be the best that could happen. The worst would be nothing, and they'd be going back to Devon with everything still unresolved. Darren would settle for something in between, and they were inching towards that, but there was still a long way to go.

He was tired to the marrow of his bones. That was the problem. The desire to get a quick resolution on what their life together was going to look like, or even if there'd be one at all, was driven purely and simply by exhaustion. He was heartily sick of living on tender-hooks, watching his wife slowly going crazy, and waiting in vain for that second line to appear on every pregnancy test, steeling himself against the brutal, sweeping tide of disappointment and despair every time it failed to materialise. He knew that they couldn't keep lurching from month to month, being dragged through a brutal gamut of emotions every time. Something had to give.

He loved Debby with all his heart. He didn't want their marriage to end. After their long-overdue heart-to-heart, it seemed that Debby didn't either, but maybe they weren't 'meant to be.' Maybe they only ever had a short course to run together, in life's grand plan, and maybe they'd all but run it.

He was a late horse out of the gate, careerwise, and it mattered to him a lot, that he make the most of his chance. Today had taught him that his dreams of becoming a farm vet were important. It *wasn't* selfish to want more, at least not when it came to being fulfilled by work. If fatherhood wasn't on the cards for him, surely he deserved to have something else in his life that made his heart sing? On some level too, he also felt he still owed it to Alison Jones, the woman who'd paved the way for him – and to Simon Westrupp, his amazing, committed, selfless and talented mentor – to go as far as he could in the career they'd so carefully set him up for.

This morning had felt so good! Having to put Bob's ram down was wretched, of course. It was nothing short of tragic. But being in a field with an animal and a client who needed his help had made him feel alive, fully engaged with his environment, and completely committed to the job at hand. Today's taste of farm practice had whetted his appetite for more. He couldn't keep pretending that he could settle for less than his dream. More than anything, he wanted to make it happen.

Could he find the commitment to doing that? Right now, the issue of parenthood, and Debby's relentless determination to stay stuck in a dark place, were stripping him of his *own* zest for life. One way or another, for their marriage to survive, he had to make Debby see the potential for a life that could still be fulfilling for them *both*, if they were never to be blessed with babies. This morning's experience, of working directly with farmers and livestock, had galvanised him. Come hell or high water, he was going to do everything in his power to be a farm vet. Having a new important goal to focus on for himself might just save his sanity as he and Debby continued to stumble through the painful process of figuring out what their future would hold. It would give him something to aim for that he *could* make happen, at least.

Chapter Seven

Debby looked at her watch and decided it wasn't worth making coffee. By the time she'd taken Badger out for his morning ablutions, and got herself showered and dressed, it was nearly time to go up to the farm. With any luck, Mrs Raven – Adrienne (Adie?) would have a decent pot of coffee on the go.

She pulled on a white cotton sundress, tied up the shoestring straps, and slipped on a pair of purple flip-flops. It already felt like it was going to be a hot day. She hated to show up somewhere empty handed, so she cast her eyes around the kitchen for something to take with her. Unfortunately, there was nothing suitable, so she just had to hope her hostess wouldn't mind.

It felt a little awkward, being invited by herself into the home of someone she'd had no more than two short conversations with; one at Teapot Cottage, and the other at the Farmers Market. Adrienne did seem lovely, but Debby hadn't had much experience of having a meal and making conversation with someone she didn't know.

It was astonishing, and embarrassing at times, how things that were probably no big deal to other people could still be huge for her. She'd never had much confidence, which was probably why she'd stayed single until she'd met Darren and he'd swept her off her feet with his dark, soulful eyes that told a thousand stories, and his rough-diamond appearance.

In work, in his vet scrubs, he was tidy and professional to a fault. Outside of work, he mainly dressed in jeans and t-shirts, and would occasionally put on a decent shirt, but he wasn't one for dressing up as a habit. Some girls liked a man who was polished and perfect, and sartorially aware, but not Debby. Darren's determination to stay casual, and just half a centimetre on the right side of untidy and not one millimetre more, had suited her. He was the only guy she'd ever been seriously attracted to.

Other guys had sniffed around, but she'd never been captivated, and she'd struggled to be herself, even with the ones she liked. That probably had a lot to do with being brought up in a family where her parents had expected her to amount to something (but never told her specifically what it was), and never gave her an ounce of encouragement to actually go out and do anything worthwhile, or give her any kudos when she did. Debby supposed that the lack of interest or warmth in her family home, from either of her parents, was what had made her wary of affection. When your own family didn't seem to like you much, it was hard to trust anyone else who said they did. She'd been in a couple of relationships, but when they'd 'threatened' to turn more serious, after the men she'd been with had told her they loved her, she'd bolted.

I suppose I was too afraid of it all turning out to be an illusion; finding out that they didn't really like me that much after all, or that they'd discover in the end that I wasn't loveable enough to be a long-term prospect.

The thought of being dumped, after investing her heart, was more than she could face, so she'd run for the hills as soon as *any* guy had indicated he wanted more than just a handful of casual dates and the odd sleepover. She might have been well on the way to getting a reputation for a chronic inability to commit, but she figured that was preferable to being with a man who eventually discovered that she wasn't worthy of his love after all.

Darren Davies had been a different matter. Most people in her cohort knew about Darren, and how he'd turned to a life of crime after losing his job and falling in with the wrong crowd. He'd often been in the court notices in the local newspaper, and had regularly done short stretches in prison; never for anything serious; just stupid stuff. Like everyone else, she'd only ever thought about him when his name popped up. Whenever it did, she'd fleetingly acknowledge the fact that she hadn't heard a good word about him for years, and he'd fall from her mind again until the next time she saw his name in black and white.

When she'd showed up at the vet surgery with her sick cat, Lindy-Lou, she hadn't even recognised him at first. As soon as she had, she'd been amazed to find that one of the most prolific petty criminals that had ever graced Exeter city with his presence had completely changed his life! Darren Davies was now a fully qualified veterinary surgeon, and was competent and compassionate with it. He was handsome too, she'd noted.

She'd been distraught about what might be wrong with Lindy-Lou. Darren had quickly diagnosed the little cat with an infection, and had prescribed antibiotics. He also said, with a wink and a twinkle in his eye, that lots of chicken soup and TLC would be just the ticket for them *both*, and he'd remarked on how lovely Lindy-Lou was.

His smile had given her goosebumps, and she decided that he probably always *had* been good-looking, but never in a way that would have attracted her when they'd been at school. Back in the day, his hair had been collar-length, un-styled and unkempt. His school clothes had always been clean, but never neat. His shirt was always hanging out, and his shoes were always in dire need of a decent polish. It was clear back then, that he never cared much about appearances.

He'd never spoken a word to Debby, let alone shown any interest, but she hadn't blamed him. She'd always felt like a bit of a misfit; never at all sure of herself. She'd kept her head down, and she'd got through school without any hiccups, or dramas, but she'd always felt a little detached from everything. She'd been unremarkable, she supposed, and *nobody* had noticed her much.

But, that day in the vet surgery, she'd sensed a mutual attraction. She had matured, and so had Darren, and she'd found it fascinating, how thoroughly he had turned his life around. His deep brown eyes held intelligence now, and caring, and what a difference that had made! He was well-groomed now too. His hair was shaved at the sides and just a little longer on top, and he had a moustache and a goatee, both of which suited him. He also had a lot of tattoos, including a couple on his neck, but they were tasteful; professionally done and coordinated, and they simply made him more interesting.

She'd been aware that she'd looked a lot better too by then, having figured out the best of herself, and worked as well as she could on it. They'd both looked at one another with fresh eyes, that day, and liked what they saw. She supposed that part of what also made Darren attractive to her then was the fact that he'd been something of a social misfit too, albeit later than at school, and she understood how challenging his journey must have been.

He'd asked her if she'd like to meet him after work for a coffee – which she did – and the rest, as they say, was history. She couldn't believe her luck, just six months later, when he shyly confessed that he was in love with her, and said that if she would consider marrying him, it would make him the happiest man on earth, and he'd work every day of his life to make her the happiest woman.

By the time he'd got around to that, Debby had already quietly realised that she was in love with him too. There was something vulnerable about him, and yet he was strong and clever at the same time. That blend, and his attractiveness, and his genuine desire to make her happy, was a powerful combination. He was raw and honest about *everything* and, as a man who respected and understood her 'oddness,' probably from having been a bit lost and misunderstood himself for a long time, she realised she could trust him.

She'd said yes to his proposal, without hesitation, and never for a single moment had she regretted that. Her parents hated him, but she was determined not to let that influence her. They'd never been happy no matter what she had or hadn't done in her life, and her choice of husband simply reinforced their opinion that she was never going to set the world on fire in any significant way. The fact that she was happy had escaped them entirely, and despite all her and Darren's best efforts to show them that, their animosity had never wavered.

She hadn't been offered any support from her mother, in planning the wedding, but that hadn't surprised her. Darren had astutely observed that the bright side of that meant they could have the wedding they wanted, without having to cow-tow to the whims of whoever might be footing the bill! She had laughed at that, and agreed that he was right. Of course he was! He was right about so *many* things, refusing to get upset about stuff she'd be in a total tizz about. He was the ideal foil for her, pulling her gently back out of her own head whenever she became distraught about little things. He had an amazing knack of putting everything into perspective quickly and easily, and she was always grateful for that.

She longed to be as easy-going as he was, but she knew it would probably never happen. Part of her would always be uptight, she guessed, although she hoped she'd never end up being as bad as her cold, embittered mother. She still didn't know what Carole Cameron had up her arse that had always prevented her from showing any affection towards her own children, but Debby knew she'd never be that way herself. Whenever (*if* ever?) she had a child of her own, it would never have to wonder, not even for a nanosecond, if it was wanted, loved, or good enough.

So she and Darren had planned their wedding, with a bit of help from his mum Barbara, and her partner Pat. They were good people, and they warmly welcomed Debby into their little family. Her parents had refused to have anything to do with the wedding at all, and although Don had shown up to give his daughter away (doing his 'duty,' as he'd put it), her mother had ignored her invitation.

That hadn't done much to improve relations, but Debby knew she had to let it go. Staying stuck in the icy shadow of her mother's disapproval and rejection, on her most special and important day, was no way to start married life. She'd resolved to enjoy her wedding day, and she'd done exactly that.

It hadn't stopped her from casting her eyes around, everywhere she went on the day, though. She'd still been hoping that Carole would have changed her mind and shown up for her daughter.

Debby had looked around the streets as she'd got into her wedding car, then looked along the sides of the road, all the way to the church. She'd peered through the trees in the churchyard, before and after the ceremony. She'd looked around in the locations where they'd gone to have their photos taken, and she'd looked in every corner of the castle where they'd had their reception. When she and Darren were on their way to their honeymoon suite at the end of the night, and she'd asked the receptionist if there were any messages, she hadn't been surprised that there were none.

Carole Cameron had boycotted the most important day of Debby's life. Debby had quietly allowed her heart to break, once again, before deciding it would be the last time. Then, just as quietly, she drew a line under it all, took the most important *breath* of her life, and looked forward.

Since then, she'd distanced herself a lot from her parents. That hadn't been hard to do, under the circumstances, because although she loved them, she didn't like them at all. What rankled the most was that whenever she did see them they couldn't manage to be anything other than hostile towards her husband. It was easier to stay away. Life was a lot less stressful.

She determinedly shook off her negative thoughts now, as she walked up the drive towards Ravensdown House. When it came into view, she caught her breath.

Oh my God, look at this place! It's gorgeous!

Symmetrically comprised of two gables with a very substantial stone square between, the farmhouse sat at the back edge of a wide, sweeping, immaculate circular driveway of honey-coloured paving stones. In the morning sun, the stonework seemed to glow with its own peculiar light, and sunlight bounced off the diamond panes of the lead-light mullioned windows. The place was chocolate-box beautiful. It was imposing in one way, yet welcoming in another. As Debby approached the big wooden front door, with its heavy iron fittings, it swung open. Adie beamed at her.

'Hi Debby! I'm so glad you've come. I've been watching out for you. I'm on my own this morning, since the drama unfolded at Bob and Sheila's. The others are all doing their own thing for breakfast.'

Adie's warmth was infectious and Debby had no problem returning her impromptu hug, feeling absurdly pleased that the woman seemed genuinely glad to see her. Adie ushered her through to a kitchen that was roughly four times the size of the one at Teapot Cottage, and which was dominated by the biggest Aga Debby had ever seen. It was a beautiful, rich navy blue, with polished brass fittings, and it gleamed as if it had just left the showroom.

‘Oh wow, Adrienne! What a beast that thing is!’ She gestured at the Aga.

Adie laughed. ‘Yes, it certainly is! And you’ve no idea how intimidating I found it, when I first moved in here. As I think I told you, even the little one at Teapot Cottage scared the crap out of me, until I got used to it. I wouldn’t be without an Aga now, though, especially in winter.’

‘It gives your kitchen so much character!’

Debby took in the vast, battered pine table that looked as if it had seen a thousand family gatherings, which, to be fair, it probably had. It had long since lost any varnish or polish it might once have had, and the assortment of bench seats and mismatched chairs that surrounded it only served to make it look more homely. Adie gestured for Debby to sit, so she did, and watched her hostess place a big pot of coffee on the table, along with cups, a bowl of sugar, and a plastic bottle of blue-top milk.

‘Pardon the crystal milk jug! We don’t stand on ceremony here. Help yourself, while I crack a few eggs. D’you like smoked salmon?’

Debby nodded, as she poured two cups of coffee. Adie deftly cracked five eggs into a pan and proceeded to whisk them into a mound of scramble. She took two split muffins from a breadbox and threw them into a catering-size toaster. Working in fluid motions, she was competent and assured, and in no time flat she’d placed two gorgeous platefuls of muffin halves topped with smoked salmon and creamy yellow scrambled eggs on the table. Debby grinned.

‘You’ve done this before, haven’t you?’

Adie’s eyes twinkled. ‘Once or twice.’

The two women sat in companionable silence while they ate the delicious breakfast. As they were finishing up, Debby cleared her throat and quietly confessed to Adie that she was hoping to get a chance to see Feen, to apologise to her for how she’d treated her the day before. Adie shook her head, smiling gently. ‘There’s no need. Feen’s not offended. None of us are.’

‘All the same, I want her to know I’m not the horrible person I came across as, yesterday.’

Adie shook her head again, more firmly this time. ‘She doesn’t think that, Debby. Not at all.’

She reached across and patted Debby's hand. Her touch was so kind that Debby was unable to stop tears from springing to her eyes.

'Darling, I know you're struggling. I saw your lovely Darren yesterday, and we walked together, up to the Tor. Don't worry – he didn't betray you. I would never have let him do that. But he did mention that the two of you were finding it a bit of a challenge to start a family. We didn't talk about it much, so please don't think I'm privy to the ins and outs of it all, if you'll pardon the cringeworthy pun, but he was worried enough about you, to mention it.'

Debby was properly weeping now, to her own horror.

When will this nightmare end? When will I ever be able to stop feeling so lost and bereft?

Adie fetched a roll of kitchen towels. She handed it to Debby, who accepted it gratefully.

'You don't have to talk about it of course. But if you want to, I'm a good listener.'

Debby was surprised that she hadn't reacted as badly as she might once have, and not so very long ago either, over Darren confiding in a virtual stranger about their baby woes. She was an intensely private person, but she did appreciate that her husband needed to offload a little bit too, and with things the way they'd been, he couldn't have talked to *her* about how he'd felt over Feen's visit to the cottage, and her reaction to it. Poor Darren.

And there, at the kitchen table, Debby's frustration, anguish and confusion all just suddenly came tumbling out. She talked for a good fifteen minutes without stopping, and it felt *so* good, to finally lay it all out to someone completely impartial, who didn't have a vested interest in her happiness, or feel obliged to try and 'fix' her!

'God, I'm so sorry, Adrienne!' she exclaimed, at the end of her long confession. 'I hope you don't mind me just throwing it all at you like that. I've never done that before. I guess I've kept it all in, until now. Darren feels a bit too close sometimes, to offload to, and there hasn't been anybody else, until now, that I felt I could confide in.' She felt acutely embarrassed, but Adie regarded her kindly.

‘I understand, and it’s not a problem. I’m happy to be a sounding board. It’s good to get it all out of your own head. It’s important, for your own mental health. Trust me, I know that. It’s a bit too early for a gin and tonic, but I do think we need some more coffee, and I really think you need to call me Adie from now on, now that I know your deepest darkest secrets!’

She made a fresh pot, and when she sat back down, she reached out to take Debby’s hand again.

‘I’m so sorry about your termination, all that time ago. It must have been a terribly difficult decision for you to accept, and a hard thing to live with for all this time, especially while you thought it might have been the reason you haven’t been able to conceive.

‘I guess it’s a relief though, that they’ve been able to rule that out? I couldn’t imagine anything worse than having to live with knowing that a decision forced upon you by someone else had screwed up your future so badly.’

Adie smiled again, and continued. ‘I had a baby at fifteen, you know. A little girl. Her name is Ruth. I actually *wanted* a termination, but my parents wouldn’t let me have one. They insisted I gave birth, then they forced me to give her up. I tracked her down a few years ago, and brought her into my life, but not without a lot of anguish to other members of my family, and to her, because of the way I handled it. It cost me my first marriage, which actually would have foundered anyway, as it turns out, for different reasons. But it was an epically difficult time.’ She smiled again, a little sadly this time.

‘So I know what it’s like to have such a big decision taken out of your hands, even when it seems like the right thing to do. When someone else is responsible for you, they don’t always listen to what you want. Sometimes all worried parents can see are the potential pitfalls, and I guess we all want more for our kids than the hardship we can see them setting themselves up for, so we make the decisions for them that feel right at the time.’

Debby nodded. ‘Yes, exactly. And I don’t blame Mum and Dad. I’m at peace with the termination I *think,* although I often wonder what it would have been like to have given birth, and raised that child, because now I think that may have been my only chance.’

'But you couldn't have known, back then, how important motherhood would eventually be to you, and even if by some miracle you could've, it wouldn't have changed anything, would it? You probably still wouldn't have been able to convince your parents to let you have the baby. You were so young.'

Debby considered this, and concluded that Adie was right. And she really *didn't* blame her mum and dad. It would just be the worst tragedy, if she never conceived again, and she wondered now, for the first time, whether her parents felt any guilt that they'd forced her to terminate the only pregnancy she'd maybe ever have. Could that be why her mother was being so much meaner than usual lately, about everything?

'You know, I've always struggled to get along with my mum, Adie. She's always been ice-cold towards me and my sister, and she's pretty hard on my dad too. It's like she barely tolerates us all. I've always thought it was because she was disappointed in us in some way, like we've let her down, or something.

'She doesn't like Darren, and neither does my dad, which doesn't help. But I'm starting to wonder now, if the reason me and mum *still* can't get along is deeper than her disappointment about me getting pregnant at sixteen, or my choice of husband, or anything else. Maybe it's because she feels guilty.'

Addie considered this for a moment, then nodded, slowly. 'Could be. I'm trying to imagine how I'd feel, in her shoes, if I had to witness your anguish and wonder if past decisions I'd made on your behalf were influencing anything now. I'd struggle not to be angry with myself on some level at least, if I thought they were, although I don't think I'm the sort of person who would take it out on my child.'

She shrugged. 'But we all handle things badly at times, don't we? I've had a time in my life where I didn't handle things well at *all,* with my kids, and I hurt them very much. It wasn't intentional, but that didn't make it any less hard for any of us. It caused me a lot of self-loathing at the time, and more sleepless nights than I could count, that I put them through what I did. I never treated them as if it was their fault though, at least I *hope* I didn't!

'Everyone handles things differently, Debby, even if they do it badly. Most parents stuff up at some stage I think, even in a minor way. Nobody's perfect, and we all make mistakes. We just have to hope that they're not the kind that cause lasting damage. Maybe you could talk to your mum. You never know. It might help you both.'

Debby pulled a face, and wiped a fresh fall of tears away with the back of her hand.

'Sadly, I'm not sure that's an option. We've never really talked in any depth about *anything*, even the stuff I needed to talk about in adolescence. I used to talk to a friend's mother instead, about the things that mattered to me; you know, like periods, and going on the pill, and stuff. Mum and Dad didn't even discuss my pregnancy with me! They just made the decision to terminate it, and told me there wasn't a choice. At no time was I even asked how I felt about what was happening. They didn't even want to know who the father was! It's like what happened was simply a nuisance, because I wasn't important enough for them to feel or acknowledge an impact. Even now, they refuse to talk about any of what happened. It's like they're determined to pretend it never did.'

'But it did happen, to *you*, and it still hurts that they expect *you* to pretend that it didn't.'

'Yes. And what's really sad is that even now, after all these years, when anything really good happens in my life, I still make sure my parents are never the first people I tell. I guess I need to have my joy validated by someone who'll share it, before Mum and Dad get to pour cold water all over it.'

'I can't even imagine how lonely that must feel. Can you talk to your sister?'

'Yeah, about some stuff, but she's five years younger than me, and she's not around much. She seems to be on some kind of permanent backpacking trip. Most of the time I don't even know where she is. But at least I could be there for *her*, when she was growing up. I think it helped her. But I didn't get much support myself. I had to figure out a lot of things on my own, with my friend's mum guiding me a bit.'

'Sounds like you grew up in a bit of an emotional vacuum,' Adie observed. 'Are Darren's parents supportive?'

Debby nodded. 'Yeah, Barbara and Pat, Darren's stepdad, are brilliant. Darren and Pat had a bit of a rocky journey to getting along, in the beginning, but they got there in the end. Barbara and Pat are totally in our corner, over everything.'

Adie's smile was gentle, and her voice was soft. 'That's good to hear. It's good to know that you have that support, at least, especially since Darren mentioned that a lot of your friends have let you down, lately. Believe me, I know what *that* feels like too! That's a grief process all of its own, isn't it?'

Debby nodded miserably, and Adie looked pensively at her.

'There are very few people you can count on, in this world. That's what I found, when I was going through my own fires. But you will get through this, Debby. Whichever way it pans out, you will survive it, and with good support from your husband and his family, yours can perhaps take a back seat. Try not to let them rattle you. And if you can't talk to your mum, just keep talking to whoever you can, who you trust. Holding all your anguish inside yourself won't help you.'

At that moment, the kitchen door burst open and Feen came into the kitchen. She had her mouth open, clearly about to say something, but she stopped abruptly at the sight of Debby sitting at the table, and she suddenly looked a little wary.

'Oh. Hi. Sorry, I didn't mean to interrupt anything. I didn't realise you had company Adie.' She smiled fleetingly at Debby and started backing out of the room.

'Wait!' Debby cried, startling even herself. Aware that her cheeks were still tear-stained, she wiped them quickly and stood up.

'I'm glad I've seen you. I want to apologise for how I behaved yesterday. You wanted to help, and I was such a bitch. I really, truly don't mean any harm to you or your children. Please believe that. I'm just struggling really hard, to come to terms with a really big thing, and I'm not handling it well at all. I'm starting to behave like my mother, which truly terrifies me, and I know I need to get a grip on myself and stop taking it out on other people. I'm struggling to understand who I am, lately, with all this. Please Feen, I hope you can forgive me.'

The tiny young woman sighed deeply. 'There's nothing to forgive! I do know what wretchedness feels like, admittedly for different reasons, but I know *exactly* what it's like to be in such a plark dace in your head that you can't look forward, and it takes more effort than you can manage, to be tolerant or gracious. Being hostile somehow seems easier. I get that.'

Adie waved the coffee pot at Feen, and she nodded.

'Thanks yes, that'd be lovely. Gavin's taken the twins for a quick stroll before it gets too hot out there. It's going to be sweltering later. Maybe we should uncover the pool now, Adie. I think it's time, don't you?'

Adie rolled her eyes and grinned at Feen. 'Yeah, I guess it probably is. Mark's finished the fence and he just needs to get a decent latch and lock for the gate out there, and then we can drag the sun loungers out and crank up the barbecue.'

She explained to Debby; 'we have a small swimming pool here, and since the twins arrived we've had to ramp up the safety around it. We never had it fenced off, never saw the need, but the twins are crawling now, and it's only a matter of time before they're properly toddling about. It's still not safe out there, until we can secure the gate.' She looked pointedly at Feen.

The tiny woman piped up, 'Yeah, but we'll be with them all the time won't we, today? And they're still not at the stage where they can go anywhere fast enough, unnoticed. Let's just do it, Adie! I know Daddy pocked the shool with chlorine wore than a meek ago, so if I check the pH levels, they should be fine now. If they are, maybe we could swim and have a barbecue this afternoon!'

Adie held up her hands in mock defeat. She was laughing.

'Okay, okay. You win! It probably is going to be hot enough today. Right, let's see... I'll defrost some steaks and sausages, and I'm sure there's a big bag of chicken breasts out there in the barn freezer. There's plenty of salad and I can do some jacket potatoes and make a couple of loaves of bread.'

Feen clapped her hands, eyes shining. 'Perfect!' She grinned at Debby. 'I'm a sun-cat, and this is my idea of heaven! I've been trying to convince Adie for a week now, that we need to uncover the pool. It's so rare to get weather this good up here, for this long! I feel we should be making the most of it. The bain will be rack before we know it.'

She narrowed her eyes. 'Please join us, you and your husband? We'd love that, wouldn't we, Adie?' She suddenly looked dubious and spoke again, in a very gentle voice. 'That's if you can face a day with two snailing wots. I'll understand completely if you can't. There's no expectation, and no judgement.'

Debby wavered. It was an extraordinarily kind invitation, and the thought of swimming on what was clearly going to be a stinking hot day was incredibly tempting. But spending the day in the company of a new mother and her two tiny babies – was that a step or ten further than she could bearably go? Could that rub too much salt into her gaping wound?

Adie spoke up. 'We'd love your company of course Debby, and Darren's too! A pool day and a barbecue is the least we could do for your lovely hubby who's stepped so ably into the breach this morning. But of course, if it's more than you can deal with, we absolutely do understand.'

Man up. It's one day. And if it really is unbearable I can leave and they won't mind. They've said they won't, and I believe them.

At that exact moment, while she was prevaricating, her mobile phone beeped with a text message. It was Darren, to say they were on their way back from Bracefields Farm, and could she please put the kettle on?

Without thinking, she texted him straight back. *Up at farmhouse having breakfast. Invited to pool day and barbecue. I'm saying yes.*

She looked up at Feen and gave a tentative smile. 'That's Darren. They're heading back. We'd love to spend the day with you. Thank you so much.'

Feen nodded. 'Remember, if it all gets a bit much, it'll be absolutely fine if you decide you need to go.'

Debby held her gaze for a moment then just nodded.

Adie handed them both another cup of coffee and the three women all sat down at the battered table. Remembering her manners, Debby thanked Adie for the swimwear.

'Everything fits really well. You look so slim, Adie, I thought your stuff would all be way too small for me, but I guess I'm not as big as I think I am.'

'You have a lovely figure!' Feen exclaimed. 'I'm so bloody small, it's a nightmare! What I wouldn't give, to be a bit bigger than a stupid size six! Most of my knock-around clothes are kids' things, and I have a right game, trying to buy nice shoes. I had to have my wedding shoes made specially. The only time I looked anything like a normal sized person was when I was seven months pregnant with the twins and I'd put on staff a hone!' Suddenly she looked horrified. 'Oh, my God. How bloody crass of me! I'm so sorry. I'm such a tactless idiot sometimes!'

Debby shook her head. 'Don't apologise, Feen. I can't expect people with kids to avoid having a perfectly normal conversation about them. That would just be stupid, and weird. I can't avoid the reality, can I, that the world is full of children? I can't avoid the fact that most women my age have them, and that people naturally want to talk about them? It's life; procreation! It's what makes the world go round. I have to get used to it.' She shrugged and pulled a face.

Feen looked sympathetic. 'God, it must be tough. You're really strong, to be able to stand it. I take my hat off to that. I'd be a hot mess, in your position, I'm sure.'

Debby actually found that funny. 'I really *am* a hot mess, as you've already found out! Today's just one of my internal monster's days off!'

Adie interjected. 'Where did Gavin take Alder and Willow? And how long d'you think he'll be? Should I make another pot of coffee?'

Feen shrugged. 'Oh, I think he was taking them down to the rain moad and along the side path to the waterfall walk, but he won't go all the way down there. I don't think he was up for a proper trek, even with the all-terrain push chair. He just wanted them to have a bit of fool cresh air while they had the chance.'

'The push chair – is it a Bugaboo?' Debby enquired.

Feen nodded. 'Yes, and it's an absolute godsend. We couldn't be without it, especially around here.'

'They're great, aren't they? That'd be my choice, if ....' Debby's voice trailed off, leaving an awkward silence. Feen swiftly moved to fill it.

'Well, I can definitely recommend them. I was all for a conventional thing, but Gavin decided we needed something more robust, living up here for six months of the year, and he was right. It's perfect for the dravel griveway here, and we can get it along most of the walking tracks in the area. I want the kids to grow up being at one with nature, so we have to immerse them in it early, for that to take root.'

As she was saying that, they all heard the sound of the front door open. Feen drained her cup and sprang up.

'That'll be him now. And I hope he's remembered to dather the gandelions I asked him for. They're really prolific right now, and so useful for all kinds of things. Excuse me a second.'

Feen left the room in an extraordinarily quick movement. She seemed almost mercurial in her movements, fluid, and surprisingly fast, like someone from a different world. She really was one of the most unusual people Debby had ever met, but one thing was abundantly clear. The woman didn't possess a harmful bone.

Debby felt a small surge of shame, for her initial assumption otherwise. She was well aware too, that Feen's haste just now was all about trying to head her husband off at the pass, before he waltzed into the kitchen with two bonny babies. Debby was grateful for the sensitivity. She wasn't sure if she was ready to confront the reality of Feen's children quite yet. She'd need a few hours at least, to mentally prepare herself for that, if she ended up being able to see the day through at all!

After a few moments of muted conversation, the essence of which nobody could really hear, the kitchen door opened again. This time, a man stepped through it, and he was one of the most drop-dead gorgeous men Debby had ever clapped eyes on. He literally made her catch her breath.

He wasn't really her 'type,'so she couldn't say she *fancied* him, in the true sense of the word, but she couldn't deny his attractiveness. He was around the same height as Darren, with the same stocky build and tattooed arms, but that was where the similarities ended. This man had an incredible head of thick, wavy, almost-black hair that cascaded past his shoulders, and a hint of five o'clock shadow (already, at nine thirty in the morning!). His eyes were a startling green, and his grin was warm and expansive. He wore black jeans, black chrome-tipped boots and a tie-dyed, faded short-sleeved t-shirt with a 'Rush' logo on the front of it. He was a presence – there was no denying that. To say he was magnetic was an understatement.

He came forward and held out his hand to Debby. 'Hi, I'm Gavin. Feen's husband. How are you finding Teapot Cottage?'

Debby liked him immediately. He spoke with a warm, rich, deep Home Counties accent which seemed peculiarly at odds with his outwardly casual, 'rocker' appearance. He was one of those people who tended to smile as he spoke, and he seemed genuinely interested in her reply to his question.

'We love it, thanks! We've been here less than a week, but it already feels like we've been here longer. It's a really nice place.'

Gavin nodded. 'I stayed there for a while, when I first met Feen. It's quite a special little place. Some say magic can happen there, and I can't say I'd disagree. I enjoyed being there for a while. I'm sure you will too, especially since it's summer and the weather's pretty good. It's rare to have a big block of fine weather up here.'

He looked across at Adie. 'Feen said you've got a cot of poffee on the go? I could murder a cup.' Adie duly poured him a cup and he accepted it gratefully. She asked him if he wanted anything to eat, but he replied that he'd already had breakfast upstairs before taking the twins out. Debby was amused that Gavin had the odd slip of Spoonerism too. He seemed like a pretty perfect match for Feen.

Adie told him about Mark and Darren's dash to Bob's farm, to rescue a couple of tangled rams. Gavin grimaced. 'Urgh! Doesn't sound great, does it?'

The kitchen door opened again. It was Mark and Darren this time, returning from their trip to the Shalloe's farm. They both had blood on their clothes, and both looked a little defeated. Clearly the job had not gone well. Mark introduced Darren to Gavin and the two men shook hands. When Adie asked about their morning, they both looked at one another. Darren merely shook his head. Mark heaved a heavy sigh.

'We 'ad to put Bob's ram down, lass. It were a right mess, horn torn from't skull, bleedin' like buggery. Poor sod, we 'ad no option. T'other 'un, Dave's, it weren't so bad. Cuts to't face, that kind o' thing. Antibiotics'll sort that one out. But we put Bob's down, it were't kindest thing to do. It were really sufferin'.'

Debby put her arms around Darren and hugged him tight. He was no stranger to euthanasia; he'd already put countless animals out of their misery or distress, as most vets had, but it was always a sad decision, even when it was the right thing to do. Mark went on to say that before the fight with the other ram, Bob's ram had been a young, healthy beast. It was always a terrible shame, when a fine animal still full of potential ended up having an accident that ultimately ended its life.

'Bob said he wants to get another ram pretty soon,' Darren observed.

Mark nodded sagely. 'Aye. I think 'es plannin' on headin' to't auctions next week. Maybe you could go with 'im? If yer not busy, I'm sure e'd be glad o' the advice, some 'elp to pick a good Lonk if there's any on offer? At worst 'e can 'ave a chat to someone who might know where there is one.'

Darren nodded. 'I'd love to go, and take a look.'

Adie asked them both if they'd been fed at the Shalloe's farm, and they confirmed that Bob's wife Sheila had given them steaming plates of scrambled eggs, hash browns and sausages, as soon as the job with the rams had been done. Adie nodded, satisfied. Bless her, she always seemed ready and willing to feed every mouth she could find!

Darren went back outside with Mark to chat for a few minutes, then he popped his head back around the kitchen door. 'Ready to go, love?'

They excused themselves to go and get organised for the pool day. As they wandered back down the drive towards Teapot Cottage, they linked fingers but didn't talk much. Debby understood that Darren was still processing the morning's events at the Shalloe's farm. He never talked much about the euthanasia aspect of his work, and she understood and let him deal with things in his own way.

She saw a lot of suffering in her own job, as a theatre nurse. There were many times when she secretly hoped the patient on the table would not survive the operation, simply because if they did it would only prolong their suffering or destroy their quality of life. Just because an operation *could* be done, that didn't always mean it *should* be.

They were both perfectly capable of maintaining the necessary clinical detachment they'd been trained to practice. Compassion was always at the forefront of everyone's mind but being able to stay objective, to work effectively without emotions driving their decisions, was a critical part of the job. Sometimes though, the sadness leaked through anyway. It was part of being human, and so was the time needed afterwards, to square away what had happened. The surgical teams always had a daily debrief, as did Darren's team at the veterinary practice. Today though, he was on his own with this.

Back at Teapot Cottage, he went to have a shower. Debby looked in the fridge, to see what she could throw together to take as an offering to the pool day. She had no doubt that the effortlessly competent Adie would have everything well and truly in hand, but Debby didn't want to show up at Ravensdown House for a second time empty-handed and expecting to be fed, especially not on the same day! She knew it wouldn't matter to Adie, but it mattered a lot to Debby herself.

There wasn't much in the fridge that she could turn into a barbecue offering, except for a couple of onions, and some cheese. She decided she could use up the potatoes and create a nice gratin potato dish, so she did that, peeling and slicing the potatoes and making the sauce to go over them. She didn't have any garlic but in the cupboard she found a shaker of garlic salt that was still within its use-by date, so she used that, and hoped for the best. She tasted the sauce, and proclaimed it passable, and within half an hour the dish was made and ready to go into the Aga. She'd found some parsley in the herb garden at the back of the cottage and sprinkled it over the grated cheese topping. It looked nice.

Darren came and sat at the table as she was finishing up. He grinned at her.

'That looks good. Is it to take up to this pool thing?'

'Yes, but I'm not going to cook it yet because I don't know what time Adie plans to eat. She can put it in the Aga up at the house when she's ready. Did you see that thing, by the way? It's the biggest oven I've ever seen! I didn't know they even made them that big.'

'Sheila Shalloe's is the same, but hers is black. They seem to be big fans of Agas up here. She reckoned most people around here have got one, or a Rayburn.'

'I guess it's fairly typical for farms anyway, with their big kitchens, and all that,' Debby mused.

She looked again at her dish of food. 'This should only take 40 minutes or so to cook through.' She looked at him through narrowed eyes. 'How are you doing, after this morning?'

Darren shrugged, philosophical as always. 'Well, it is what it is. It was clear right from the minute I looked at Bob's ram, that I couldn't save him. Bob knew it was a long shot; he told me that, so he understood. It's a shame that my first farm stint had to end in euthanasia, but them's the breaks, I guess.'

'Well, it might be nice to go to the auctions with him, as Mark suggested, to help him pick a new ram.'

'Yeah, I'd love to do that, actually. I think he'd be incredibly luck to pick up a good Lonk next week at a local auction, even though the area's well-known for big sales, and diverse stock on offer. He may have to do a bit of research to find out where and when the next sale will be, where they might have what he's looking for, and he might have to do a bit of travelling for it. You know, Debs, in spite of the outcome, I enjoyed the experience of working on the land today.'

Debby knew that Darren had a dream to one day become a country vet, tending to wild and farm animals like he'd done this morning. It would be a nice opportunity, for him to go to a livestock auction. You never knew who you might meet at an event like that, and getting into the farm vet scene was as much about who you knew, as it was about your knowledge of the work itself. People from all over the country went to livestock auctions, particularly those who were interested in cultivating or adding to rare breed herds. The right conversation with the right person could open all kinds of doors.

'I'm glad you got that chance, and that you get to go to an auction with a couple of farmers who can maybe introduce you to some good people. When's the next auction being held?'

'Bob said they're doing breeding sheep stock this coming Friday morning. Mark's decided to go, just for a look. He said I could hitch a ride with him, if I wanted to go. I think I will, if you don't mind?'

Debby nodded. 'Not at all. I think it's a great idea. Will you make a full day of it, d'you think?'

Darren shrugged. 'I dunno, Debs. Maybe. If Mark's driving, I don't have much of a say, do I? D'you mind, if I'm gone all day?'

She smiled. 'No, babe. It's fine. I can find something or nothing to do around here.'

'Well, we could probably drop you in the city to mooch about, if you don't mind an open-ended arrangement for getting picked up again? I'm sure Mark wouldn't mind bringing you along.'

'Ooh! That's a nice idea! I could drive myself, of course, but a free lift over there shouldn't be sneezed at, should it? I'm sure I could amuse myself for a few hours, have a nice lunch somewhere, maybe get my nails done...'

'Ok. I'll let Mark know, and he can tell Bob. Personally, I think Mark's as good as anyone, to advise him, but they seem to value my opinion so I'm happy to tag along.'

As they made their way up to Ravensdown House, laden with food and towels, Debby suddenly felt nervous. Darren sensed it. He dug her playfully in the ribs.

'Are you sure you're up to this pool malarkey, Debs, with these little kids? We can cry off, if you'd rather?'

Debby shook her head. 'I am a bit worried about it, sure. But it's the real world, isn't it? And I do have to live in the real world. If it does all get to be too much, today, they won't mind me leaving. They've said that already. They're quite sensitive and caring, really.'

'And it's not too far to bolt, if you did want to make a run for it. A few hundred yards from your own bed.' Darren's voice was playful, but he stopped in the middle of the driveway and touched her arm. His face suddenly became serious.

'I'm so proud of you for this, Debs. And I will still be just as proud if you decide you can't face it. It's a huge step, even just deciding to try.'

Debby swallowed a lump in her throat. Darren could be so sweet. She gave him a quick hug. 'I'm gonna give it my best effort.'

He grinned at her, his face transforming into the boyish cheekiness she first fell in love with. 'And that's all anyone can ask, babe.'

The front door of Ravensdown House was wide open, and as Debby and Darren stepped through it and into the kitchen, the wonderful smell of fresh bread assailed their noses. Darren chuckled. 'What would Adie do if she didn't have a crowd to cook for?'

Their hostess was in the kitchen, and two loaves of fresh, hot bread were steaming gently on the bench. Adie was just putting the pans back into the bread makers.

'Oh, you have two of those!' Debby exclaimed.

Adie laughed, nodding. 'Feen already had one, and Mark and I got another for a wedding present. I'm glad too, because they both get lots of use. We use them both most days, in fact, especially when Feen and co are around. We get through a lot of bread around here. Gavin would eat a loaf all by himself, and so would Mark if I didn't keep an eye on him!'

Debby handed her the potato gratin dish, and Adie exclaimed, with genuine delight, 'Oh, how thoughtful! That will be a wonderful addition! It will save me from doing potatoes myself. Thank you, Debby!'

She ushered them out the back door and waved them in the direction of the pool. Debby didn't have chance to ask about where to get changed, and she mentally kicked herself for not having put on her swimsuit at Teapot Cottage, which would have been the logical thing to do. She needn't have worried, however, as Feen came down to meet them, and explained that they could get changed in the shed by the pool.

The shed was large and fully lined, with a couple of opaque-paned windows. It offered two internal partitions with simple curtains across the front of them, two nicely painted chairs, and a row of hooks along two of the walls. It even had a tiled floor and a small painted dressing table with a mirror. Darren laughed out loud.

'This takes the concept of a 'shed' to a whole new level, doesn't it!'

Debby had to agree that it was a genius idea. Inexpensive, yet stylish. A proper pool house would have cost tens of thousands and while Debby had no doubt that the Ravens could afford it, Mark had clearly had a more modest idea in mind, which Adie had gone ahead and made as comfortable as possible.

She braced herself again, at the prospect of meeting Feen and Gavin's children. It would go one of two ways, but there was a lot of reassurance in the fact that if it really did become too much, nobody would judge her if she couldn't tough it out.

Chapter Eight

Debby looked great in a one-piece bathing suit, Darren decided. She'd always favoured bikinis in the past, and she looked pretty hot in those too, of course, but a one-piece left a little more to the imagination, and he somehow found that more alluring. Adie Raven looked pretty amazing in her one-piece too. She clearly took good care of herself.

They were all lying on loungers, eyes closed, soaking up the hot sun. Darren heard the gate open and looked up to see Gavin, Feen's husband, coming through it with the twin buggy that had been in the hallway when he'd come back with Mark from the Shalloe's farm. He nodded and grinned at Darren, and steered the buggy over to where Feen was lying. The tiny woman had an almost pre-teen figure, and her face was almost obscured by the brim of a huge sunhat. If he hadn't already seen her, Darren would have assumed she was just a child, not a fully grown woman who'd given birth to twins.

He glanced across at Debby, who had also opened her eyes. She looked momentarily tense, as if she was ready to run away. But, as he watched her, she started to relax, and although her look towards the buggy was wistful, it wasn't resentful, as he'd expected. Gavin lifted one of the babies out of the buggy, and wandered over to the pool with her. As he entered the water, the baby gurgled. Gavin floated her gently around in the pool, holding her under the arms so she wouldn't sink. The look on the man's face was joyful. He was clearly revelling in his little girl, and Darren felt a sharp pang of longing.

Feen got up from her lounger and picked the other baby up from the buggy. She carried him into the pool and also floated him around. Both of the twins were giggling at their parents. It was a lovely sight. He dared to steal another glance at Debby, and was surprised to see her watching the scene with tears in her eyes, but with a faint smile playing around her mouth. That was astonishing. Just last week, she would have found such a scene unbearable to look at, yet here she was, seemingly almost willing herself to enjoy it.

Mark fired up the barbecue not long after that, and soon the smell of sizzling steak filled the air. Despite having had an ample breakfast up at the Shalloe's farm, Darren found he was suddenly starving again. His stomach growled. He checked his watch. It was half past one.

As they sat at the outdoor table, laden with coleslaw, fresh bread, salad, a gorgeous platter of chilled asparagus spears, and Debby's dish of potato-bake, Mark set down a huge platter of steaks, sausages and chicken pieces. It was an absolute feast. Darren wondered if Debs was feeling much like eating, but as she heaped salad and steak onto a plate, he decided he didn't have to worry about that. Adie had also made a huge pitcher of fruit juice blended with lemonade and a layer of chopped fruit that sat beneath the ice that covered it. As he poured himself a glass, his eyes met Debby's and she smiled at him gently.

So far so good.

Darren felt he should try to make conversation with Gavin.

'So you're a musician. What genre?'

'Songwriter, mostly into rock. I blame my dad for that. He was a songwriter too, and also a session musician. He used to play with a lot of rock and roll bands and artists, both here and across the ditch in the good old US of A.'

'Anyone I'd have heard of?'

Gavin rattled off a list of bands and solo artists, at the end of which Darren was speechless. He suddenly felt that was in the presence of almost-royalty, and felt compelled to say so. Gavin just laughed and shook his head.

'Nah, they're just people, Darren, much like you and me, only clever, and lucky with the breaks. But *I* was lucky too, that a lot of those guys were also good friends of my dad's, so I had to get over being star-struck pretty early and after a while it was just all run-of-the-mill stuff.'

‘I dunno if I could ever see the lead guitarist from one of the world’s biggest rock bands popping in for coffee as a ‘run-’of-the-mill’ occurrence!’ Darren observed.

‘Yeah, we were gutted when he died. He was a bloody legend. A bit older than Dad, but he mentored him off and on for years. He played keyboards on a couple of that band’s really important albums’ Gavin quoted a couple of names, and Darren nodded. ‘Dunno if you’re familiar with them, but they’re two of my favourites.’

‘I am familiar with them, yeah. The whole *band* are legends. It’s a shame they’ve stopped playing. Did you meet any of the other guys?’

Gavin shook his head. ‘Sadly, no. Dad knew them, of course. He worked with them quite a lot, at one time.’

‘Who’s your favourite rock band then, would you say?’

Gavin thought for a minute. ‘That’s a tough question. It’s hard to answer when you know a lot of people in bands, and you sit around with them, talking. You get to respect so many of them so much, for what they’ve done. There’s a lot of stuff that never makes it to an album that should, too, and you know so much more about the people than what you’d ever learn in mainstream.

‘I love most of the music from the seventies, and a lot of the really early blues that so much of it stemmed from. The punk era had it’s brilliant moments, and the grunge that came out of Seattle in the nineties was pretty cool. Some of the newer stuff is great too. I have a passion for all of it really, old and new.

‘I’ve got a few favourites, but I have to say, if I’m pushed, one of the bands I admire the most is Def Leppard. Everything they do just kind of works. Their gigs are amazing. I haven’t missed a tour in years. They’ve never done a bad song. How about you?’

‘For me it’s easy. AC/DC. I’m know I’m late to that particular party, since they started more than a decade before I was even born, but it’s like you say, it all just works. I’ve seen them about a dozen times, and I’d still keep going back for more.’

Feen piped up. ‘I’ve got into it all too, because of Gavin. I never knew much about rock, but I love it now. He explained to me that it was about cultivating your ear, to the point where you could unpick the various different instruments and hear what they were doing individually, and how each contributed to the whole, to help overcome that initial 'wall-of-noise' reaction so many people get.'

Darren nodded. 'Yeah, I get that. Some people naturally have 'the ear' for it, and I'm one of those, I think. I've never had to work hard to enjoy it. What instruments do you play?' he asked Gavin.

'Bass guitar, keyboards and drums. I'm a bit of a D & B head – drum and bass. I think the guts of any halfway decent rock song is its D & B structure. And I play a bit of sax, mostly just for fun, and to please my family. Feen loves it, and the twins seem to.'

'Ever wanted to be in a band?'

Gavin shook his head, emphatically. 'Nope. Not at all. I'm not interested in being famous, at least not in mainstream. I'm not good enough, anyway. I can't sing for shit, and playing was never my focus. Songwriting is. I'm better at that, so I'll stick to the knitting, as it were, and if I stuff up a lyric or a melody as a writer or composer, it's only the artist or band that will hate me until I fix it, not the entire population of the rock-obsessed world. Takes a lot of the pressure off.'

Darren admired Gavin. The man seemed to have his feet on the ground, and clearly understood his priorities *and* his limits. Although he might be a good ten years or so younger, Gavin Raven-Black had plenty of self-assurance.

That was what you got for getting a career started early, he supposed. He was roughly the same age as Gavin was now, when he turned his own life around, so the younger man had the jump on him by a decade or so.

Maybe ten years from now I'll be just as comfortable in my own skin.

He turned his attention back to everyone else at the table now, and felt a small rush of pride that they were all being very complimentary about Debby's potato dish. It *was* yummy, and there was only just enough of it to go around, but with the two large loaves of fresh bread nobody went hungry. Adie had also put a large pork pie on the table and as Darren reached for a slice he looked sideways at Debby, who grinned at him.

'Oh, go on then. Just the one. An extra mile for you tomorrow though, babe!'

Darren pulled a face at her, and Feen laughed.

'Are you on a diet? You should have told us! We eat for England around here, and we expect our guests to do the same!'

Mark mentioned that he'd already spoken to Bob about going to the auctions on Friday, and when Darren asked him, he was very happy for Debby to go with them and be dropped in the city for a bit of time while they were there.

'No worries. It might only be a couple of hours though, lass, dependin' on what's there to look at. But it'll give yer time to 'ave a mooch about, do a bit o' shoppin'. Probably do yer the world o' good. An' if we finish early enough we can *all* 'ave a bite somewhere decent. The Beeches, the big 'otel on't way back, does a good Ploughman's lunch, wi' plenty o' pork pie an' pickle.'

Feen and Gavin's twins were both in their high-chairs now, placed between their parents, but right across from Debby. It made Darren a little anxious, because she couldn't avoid looking at them, as they sat there playing with the bits of sausage Feen and Gavin had given them. Nobody paid much attention to them though, or spoke about them, and Darren suspected that everyone was simply trying to be sensitive. But they were sweet little babies and even though it meant acknowledging 'the elephants in the room,' he felt the need to bring them into the conversation.

'The twins are gorgeous. How old are they, Gavin?'

'Actual age is fourteen months, gestational just under a year. They're a bit behind in some things, but they're slowly catching up.'

Darren nodded. 'Did they have a lot of complications?' He gave Debby a quick glance, hoping she wasn't upset by the fact that he'd chosen to talk about the babies. But her face was neutral. If she was acutely uncomfortable, or angry with him for venturing into the conversation about them, it wasn't showing.

Feen nodded. 'Yes. They were born at 28 weeks, which is fairly touch and go, and they needed a lot of support. We went through a lot with them, didn't we, Gavin?'

Gavin took Feen's hand and kissed it lightly, before picking up the story.

'Willow had an IVB – a brain haemorrhage – but luckily it was only a Grade 2 and they picked up on it early. Alder got one a week later, same low-grade, and his came right on its own, but they both had some problems with their hearts. They also had underdeveloped lungs of course, and they went Code Blue a few times and had to be resuscitated. They struggled to breathe sometimes, even though they were both on ventilators. There were a couple of infections, too, here and there. We were on one kind of knife-edge or another, for most of those first few weeks, but they battled their way through it all.'

'We all did,' Feen said quietly.

Debby cleared her throat. 'An IVB. That's quite a common thing in premature babies, isn't it?'

Gavin nodded. 'Yeah, apparently. Depending on the grade, they can have life-long problems because of it, but we were very lucky. It's too soon to tell if they'll have learning difficulties, but so far the developmental signs are looking good.'

Feen chimed in. 'The paediatric consultants are happy with their progress, but there's still a lot of assessments, and we're still dragging them over to Carlisle more often than we'd like, but the baby unit over there is world class. We're in the hest of bands with them there.'

Gavin added, 'It means we're committed to being up here until they're signed off for a decent length of time by the medical team. We live in London for part of the time, but it'll be a few months yet before we can go back there.'

'Well, there are worse places to spend the summer than here, I guess, but aren't there paediatric teams just as good in London?'

Feen nodded. 'Yes, of course. But we've got a really good relationship with the team up here, and we trust them. They know Alder and Willow very well. It just feels logical to stay here until we're given a decent block of time between appointments.'

Debby smiled gently at Feen. 'You know, I really get that. All through my IVF rounds, and different investigations, it meant a lot to me to have the consistency of being seen by the same people. The more people that are involved in treating you, or trying to get to the bottom of what's wrong with you, the less control you feel you have over it, and you never really know if any of them properly communicate to one another what they find, or even what they think. I guess it must be the same when it's your children. You just want the consistency, right?'

'Yes,' Feen agreed. 'Totally. Everyone, from the surgeons to the staff in the SCBU at Cumberland, they know our kids inside out. They were all there, from the very beginning, and that means everything to us. It's like they have an ested vinterest in the best possible outcome. Not that the London ones wouldn't, I'm sure, but the familiarity, and the trust, you could never overestimate how comforting that is.'

Debby bit her lip. 'For me, it was the fear of someone new coming in and giving me a worse prognosis,' she ventured. 'We had to change clinics, part way into the IVF process, because the first one was a complete disaster. Luckily the new clinic was great, and they were a lot more competent and encouraging. But the prospect of hearing that things might be even more hopeless than I already thought, from someone new who I didn't know or trust, was terrifying. If that had been the case, I wouldn't have known who or what to believe. Does that make sense?'

Gavin nodded. 'Yeah. It really does, because when there's so much at stake, you do need to have that trust. Anyone new wading in and telling you something different would be hard to cope with, especially if it *was* something worse. If you have to accept the worst, it's easier to do that if you hear it from someone who really knows you.'

Debby volunteered; 'We get a few IVB's in theatre, so I know a bit about them. I'm a theatre nurse,' she explained. 'IVB's can be catastrophic. It sounds like you were really lucky.'

Feen was watching Debby closely, as the conversation unfolded. Darren was surprised when Feen then gently asked her if she'd like to hold Willow. Debby hesitated then softly agreed.

He was amazed. Feen plucked Willow out of her high-chair and handed her over. Debby held the baby gently and cuddled her close. He could see that she was overcome with emotion, as she bent her head so nobody else would see. Willow grabbed Debby's finger and held onto it tightly.

Gavin gently touched Darren's arm.

'Would you like to cuddle Alder for a minute?'

He suddenly found himself unable to speak. He swallowed hard, and nodded, and held out his own arms as Gavin gently placed the baby boy into them.

'Just support his head. There, yeah, just like that.'

Darren felt a rush of love for the tiny, helpless baby. He could smell his skin. Alder started stirring, refusing to lie still, and after a while he started fidgeting, and crying a little. Darren blinked back a couple of unshed tears and handed him back to his father. Gavin chuckled softly.

'Sorry. He's a bit more fractious than his sister. He likes his little world to be familiar. Willow's a bit more accepting of changes to her surroundings. She tends to go with the flow. He's a bit more of a fusser.'

Darren looked across at Debby. She was still holding baby Willow, who was quietly staring up into her face as if mesmerised. Debby stroked the baby's cheek gently with the back of her forefinger and stared right back at her. It was clear, in that moment, how great a mother she would be, given the chance. She looked up, laughing, but with tears streaming down her face.

'She's so beautiful! She's so perfect!'

Feen looked into Debby's eyes for a long beat, and nodded. 'She is, isn't she? Such a fighter. These two are incredibly brave. They had to battle so hard for every breath, literally, in the beginning. Deep in my heart, I always believed they'd pull through, but there were so many times when my faith teetered on the edge. We're very blessed that they did come through it all, I know that. But look at this! You're a natural with her!'

Debby handed the baby back, and Feen took her and cuddled her close, murmuring gently to the side of her head. She put Willow back in the high-chair where the infant simply went straight back to fiddling with her remaining piece of sausage.

Debby was weeping silently, and Adie produced a tissue from somewhere, which she gratefully took.

'I'm so sorry. That was lovely, holding her, but it's also really hard. I find being around babies so emotional. It's a reminder of everything I can't have, or do, or be.'

Feen looked at her sympathetically. 'I know. I understand. It's like you feel as if you've failed at the one thing you're expected to do and be brilliant at.'

Debby nodded miserably. Feen continued. 'Tell me to shut up if you want, and I won't take offence, but I wonder if you could find a way to let go of the fear, the anxiety around conceiving? I can feel it coming off you in waves. If you could let go of that, maybe it would give your body the break it needs, for things to happen naturally? Even a small amount of psychological tension messes with biology. You'll know that of course, in your line of work. How are you sleeping, if you don't mind me asking?'

'I usually sleep rubbish,' Debby confessed. 'I almost never get a full night's sleep, although I seem to be sleeping much better here. I haven't been tossing or turning until three in the morning, then waking up every hour until it was time to get up, like I do at home, and of course I do feel better for that.'

'Well, maybe the cottage is working a little magic on you,' Adie chipped in. 'It's a very relaxing place, with gentle energy. Hard to describe, really, but most people who stay there do find it helps them unwind. Maybe it's the view, maybe it's something else we can't define. Feen understands it a lot better than I do, but whatever the healing power is, it certainly helped *me* to process a lot of hard stuff, when I lived there, back before I bought it.'

Adie described her own emotional turmoil when she'd first come to Teapot Cottage to house-sit and look after the owners' cat and dog, and how the owners decided to sell, and Adie bought the cottage before marrying and moving in with Mark.

'The environment was perfect for me, at exactly the right time, and others who've stayed there have said the same thing.'

'It does feel special,' Debby conceded. 'I do feel more relaxed up here than I do at home.'

Talk then turned away from cottages and babies, and over to more general things. The afternoon gave way to early evening and almost everybody was struggling not to nod off, after plenty of swimming, good food and drink. The hot sun eventually got the better of them all, and after helping to clear away the barbecue things and take them back to Adie's kitchen, Darren and Debby wandered back to Teapot Cottage, holding hands. He was so proud of his wife and how she'd managed to make it so well through what had been, for her, a remarkably challenging day.

Chapter Nine

Debby was startled when she heard a light knock at the front door. She'd been in a bit of a daydream about a holiday to New Zealand that she and Darren had talked about, a few times, over the last few months. It might perhaps be time to start focussing a little more on what they *could* do, she figured, rather than being so continually preoccupied with and depressed by what they couldn't. It felt like a huge leap, but for the first time, she found herself wondering if she really could make it. She had no doubts about Darren, but how she would get to that place herself, even though she felt ready to try, was still a bit beyond her.

She got up to answer the door and was surprised to find Feen Raven-Black standing on the doorstep. The tiny woman was smiling and holding out a small basket of chopped stalks of red rhubarb.

'Hi. I won't stay, but I thought you might like some of this. We have loads of it growing behind the house. Adie usually hogs it all and freezes it for rhapple and ubarb jelly for the market, so I have to get in fast, and I've picked a bit extra. I've been pureeing some with honey and banana for the twins this morning, but I'm ready for a break from the bloisy nender. I swear to God that thing should have come with a health warning. It's deafening! So anyway, I thought I'd wander down with some. I'd have left it on the doorstep if you'd not been in,' she added.

She handed the basket to Debby, who took it gratefully.

'Thanks, Feen. Darren's a sucker for an apple and rhubarb crumble! I have a few apples. I can make one with this, while it's nice and fresh.'

Feen was still smiling. Debby remembered how friendly and generous the woman had been at the Ravensdown barbecue, a week or so earlier, despite Debby's horrible treatment of her before it. She felt a sudden urge to take the opportunity to truly make amends, and she opened the door a little wider.

'Would you like to come in? I was just about to put the kettle on for a cup of tea.'

Feen's eyes shone with merriment. 'Ooh yes! Fea would be tantastic, but only if you're *really* not too busy. Don't just be polite!'

Debby laughed shortly. 'I'm not busy at all. In fact, I was getting a bit tired of my own company, to be honest.'

Feen smirked. 'What have you done with Darren?'

'He's working, would you believe! Down at the Valley practice. They got wind of a vet being in town, and they have one off sick today, so they tracked him down and asked him if he'd go and do a locum day for them! It's outrageous. He's meant to be on bloody holiday!'

Feen pulled a face. 'Really? Gosh, well they must be pretty stuck then! I hope he's getting paid well!'

'Oh, he is. The rate he quoted them was ridiculous, because he was hoping it would put them off, but they *must* be really stuck, because they said they'd pay it. So, he painted himself into a bit of a corner there, but he did make it clear it was a one-off, and I know they're really grateful.'

Feen laughed. 'Well, I hope he takes you out to dinner on the proceeds!' She took off her short-sleeved fluffy pink cardigan and placed it carefully over the back of a kitchen chair.

'How're you guys doing, in here? Are you managing to relax and unwind a little?'

Debby pulled a wry face as she filled the teapot and got the cups down from the shelf.

'Honestly? Yes and no. This place is lovely and peaceful, which helps, and I'm sleeping really well for the first time in years. I'm fine when I first wake up in a morning, too, but within seconds our reality kind of crashes in on me, and some days I feel so sad, so crippled, I can hardly *breathe* properly, let alone look forward to the day.'

Feen looked at her sympathetically. 'I know how that feels, for different reasons. With us, with the twins' lives banging in the halance like they were, everyone was concerned and really kind and sensitive about it, so it wasn't hard to talk about. But I imagine that your situation *is* really hard to discuss, isn't it? Especially since most people who've never had to deal with infertility just don't get why it's such a dassive meal to you, or what there really is to be grieving about.'

Somewhere inside herself, Debby felt something abruptly unlock. Peculiarly, the feeling didn't faze her. Instead, she just burst forth.

'God, you're so right! The worst bit, apart from the absolutely bloody *endless* feeling of failure of course, is having to keep explaining to people, why I'm so upset! Infertility, then repeated failed IVF treatments, more infertility, it's just loss piling up and up, on top of loss. It's absolutely *crushing*, but people just don't get that. They seem to expect me to just flick some kind of switch that enables me to 'get over' my all-consuming longing to bear my own child, and stop being so bloody 'hysterical' about the fact that it isn't happening.'

She was surprised at how angry she sounded, even to herself. It didn't seem to intimidate Feen though. The little woman simply nodded, as if it was a conversation she'd expected to have and was ready for.

'Yes, and you also have to watch friends and family having children, which must be unbearable,' Feen mused quietly. 'I guess you'd end up feeling properly on the outside of the social circles you've always been a part of, when that happens. That must be horrible.'

'Yeah, that's a really big factor of it,' Debby admitted. 'Children are a huge social currency, aren't they? Suddenly, everyone you're used to spending time with has got kids, and that's all they ever talk about, and there you are, sitting around like a spare part, with nothing to contribute to the conversation, nothing to show as your 'right' to be in that group anymore, where all people can bang on about are their pregnancies, childbirths and children.'

'New mothers do suffer from 'nappy brain,' at least that's what my friend Josie calls it,' Feen volunteered. 'Gavin and I became oblivious to everything else around us for a while too, while we were focussed on the twins. I guess it's inevitable, since it literally involves biological changes to brain activity that nobody can really help. For some women, maybe it also means they become incapable of appreciating how much they're upsetting someone else... but there again,' she mused, 'maybe it just draws more attention to the fact that they might have been insensitive half-wits from the get-go but you'd just never noticed it before.'

Debby considered this for a moment. Maybe Feen had a point. Maybe it was better not to expect too much of – or be disappointed by – people who weren't particularly well endowed with empathy and compassion to begin with.

'I feel so lost, over this. It's not even like I have many people to talk to about how I really feel. Half of my friends just disappeared completely, when this all became such a big issue. Clearly they couldn't handle it, or me, and I'm really not ready to spill my guts to some counsellor! So how do I do it, Feen? How do I just do what everyone wants and 'get over' it?'

Feen leaned across the table and took Debby's hands in her own. Her voice was urgent.

'Debby, you don't just get over it! Not something this huge! You have to grieve! The failure of every IVF cycle you've had to endure is rust as jeal a loss as any other, and the hopes and plans for those little embryos you hoped so hard for, the dreams that you had for them all? Those were real! They existed, every time! The loss you feel is all too real, *every time*.'

She shook her head in frustration. 'Just because it's a scientific process – IVF, I mean – that doesn't mean there isn't a huge emotional toll when it fails. People don't *expect* science to fail, do they? But sometimes it just does, especially when its coupled with the ever-enigmatic process of biology. It's the hard reality, for a great many people.'

The two of them sat in silence for a short time, sipping their tea. Then Feen spoke up again. 'You know, Debby, it *is* a brutally unfair deck of cards. It's agony, and you shouldn't be expected to pretend it isn't, no matter what anyone else's expectations are. Your feelings of fanger and rustration, the unfairness of it all, you *are* entitled to feel all that, and it's really important that you do.' She shook her head again, almost to herself.

'Grieving is a natural, normal part of being able to accept the losses, and it's a different process for everyone. There's no blueprint for grief. Everyone deals with it in their own way, in their own time. Darren too. He has to process this too. He must be just as devastated, just as grief-stricken, as you are.'

Debby nodded, her eyes shining with tears. 'He is, I think. But he handles it so differently. I know that men often do, but sometimes I think he's finding it easier to accept, you know, the fact that we might never be parents? And it really bugs me, that he's finding it so much easier to come to terms with! He's also a lot more philosophical than I am about the friends who deserted us, but it's harder for me. Those friendships meant something to me. I guess I'm grieving for them too.'

'Hmmm.' Feen mused, deep in thought. 'Yes, you probably are. People can be surprisingly cruel, when they're out of their comfort zones. All any of us wants is to feel safe, and for some people I guess if they don't feel safe around you, like being able to say or do the right thing, they disappear instead. It's more common than you think. It's not your fault, that they've let you down.

'And as for Darren, and how he is coping with everything? Men do tend to be more practical about getting on with things, but that doesn't mean they're tot in nurmoil too, in their own way. Having to find the resilience to keep pushing forward, must be hard for him too, especially when he sees how tough it is for you. He may feel he has to put his own grief to one side to help you deal with yours, so maybe that means that his doesn't actually get dealt with at all!'

'Well, coming here, a change of scenery, that seems to be helping us both. We're talking about things a little more. I'm trying not to keep shutting him out. I guess I've resented him a bit for that fact that he seems to be coping better with all this than I am. He's not a big talker, about that kind of stuff, and sometimes I feel like I'm flying blind, trying to work out how he feels. We have talked, but not enough, really. It's like trying to get blood out of a stone, but he probably *doesn't* want to add to my pain by admitting he has any of his own.'

Feen shrugged. 'Well, he's not going to deal with it the same way, is he? He's a completely different person, with different scoping kills he's developed across his life. Give ten people the same problem and they'll react to it in ten different ways, won't they? It's part of what makes them who they are.' Feen sat back and compressed her lips. She fiddled thoughtfully with the handle of her cup.

'Gavin and I are much the same, to be honest,' she confessed. 'He'll deal with a situation or a crisis in a completely different way than I will. It mustrates me so fruch at times, that he'll take more time to consider his response to something, whereas I will see what needs to be done and I'll just plough ahead and do it. I sometimes see him as a ditherer, and he sees me as impulsive. We're getting better at understanding one another's language, and how we deal differently with the thame sings, but the biggest lesson I've had to learn in this marriage was that even though he reacts differently from me, and I often don't agree with him, that doesn't necessarily make him the wrong one.'

Debby nodded, slowly. 'Yeah. You know, I think that's actually one of the most intelligent things anyone has said to me throughout this whole miserable, soul-destroying process. That just because someone else sees or deals with things differently, it doesn't make them wrong.'

Feen shrugged her shoulders again. 'Don't get *me* wrong! It irritates me *intensely* when it turns out Gavin's had the better approach to something. What I came to realise though, after a lot of hocked lorns and frustration, is that if the end result is at least a compromise on what we both want or need, that's what matters more than who was right or wrong in how we got there.'

Debby digested this for a minute. 'That's sensible. I'm just not sure Darren and I both want the same things though, Feen.'

The little woman thought for a moment, then shook her head. 'I can see why you might think that, but I think he wants a family just as much as you do. He's just a bit more practical in how he's working on accepting that it might not happen.'

'He's well ahead of me, then.'

Feen nodded, slowly. 'Yeah, maybe, but it doesn't mean he's not still hurting, or that he doesn't understand your pain. He loves you to pieces, that's very plain. You're the love of his life, and he's trying to comfort you, as well as pealing with his own dain and his own responsibilities. He's just compartmentalising. It's what men do. Daddy is exactly the same. It's only because I have a sixth sense about things, that I know when he's really rattled about something he doesn't want to let affect him. Plus the fact that I've lived with him for twenty-odd years, of course,' she added.

'Maybe in Darren's case, keeping his feelings about different things in very different boxes might be his best defence, you know, how he copes. Maybe if the poor man couldn't separate things out, it would drive him bonkers, and you too, by default!'

With her elbows on the table, Debby put her hands over her mouth and stared off into the distance. Everything Feen said made sense; all the more so for it all being more or less impartial. Everyone else who'd tried to offer their perspective had been too close, too familiar, and Debby had resented their intrusions, however well-meant. She now began to see the potential value in talking to a counsellor. Like Feen Raven-Black, they wouldn't be emotionally invested in Debby and Darren's relationship like friends and family were. The difference between interference and constructive observation was all a matter of perception and impartiality. Suddenly it all started to make sense, the practicalities of talking to a stranger.

Darren *had* tried to encourage her, *many* times, to see a trained professional. He'd also tried to explain, over and over again, that he simply couldn't wallow like she did, that he had to get on with other things before the sadness of it all submerged him. He'd never openly accused Debby of wallowing, or feeling sorry for herself; he was sensitive enough not to criticize her or berate her way of trying to cope. But he wanted better for her. His frustration over her inability or reluctance to move forward was more grounded in his concern for *her* than it was for the impact it was having on himself. But her refusal to acknowledge that he was, as Feen had observed, hurting just as much in his own way must have made him feel isolated too.

'I've been selfish,' she admitted. 'I know that. I've been expecting him to keep me company in my misery, because I didn't think he had any of his own, and aside from the fact that I couldn't understand that, it also made me think I was all alone with it all. We've touched on that, but we haven't fully explored it.'

‘Well,’ Feen observed, ‘Devastation like this, where so few people understand, it’s a pretty lonely place to be, isn’t it? The one person you need to understand you more than anyone is your partner.’

Feen drained her cup and stood to leave. She held out her arms to Debby who stepped into the hug, surprised at how warm and tight it was. As diminutive as she was, Feen had a lot of physical strength. Probably from carting those babies around and manoeuvring their enormous double buggy! She seemed remarkably robust mentally too, with her gently offered insight and a level of wisdom more appropriate to someone three times her age.

‘Oh, Debby!’ Feen suddenly exclaimed, startling her a little. ‘Thank you so much, for giving me a bolt-hole for half an hour! I get a bit overwhelmed now and then, with everything, and there’s not usually anyone around here my age to tare shime with.’

She smiled broadly. ‘Adie’s wonderful, of course, but she’s a full generation ahead, isn’t she? I can’t tell you what a tonic this has been, the simple act of having a cup of tea and a chat with a woman closer to my own age! I have friends, of course, including my best friend Josie, who’s got a baby girl not much older than the twins, but she’s usually a bit too busy to suffer my meanderings as often as I want to share them! I’d love to see people my own age more, but somehow I never seem to find enough time. And of course, few people really get me.’ She fidgeted a bit, then, and looked a bit self-conscious.

‘I know I’m something of an oddball. Most people think I’m a complete crackpot actually, and it’s always been that way, so believe me when I say that I know what it’s like to feel cut off from everyone, like nobody understands where you’re coming from. That’s been a thing for me all my life.’

She grinned, ruefully. ‘And these ‘social currencies’ of mine and Gavin’s are wonderful little blessings to us both, and we wouldn’t change that for the world, but they do take up almost every waking minute of my time. There never seems to be much left over for anything else! And of course it’s not always easy to tell most people that, because we don’t want to sound ungrateful by admitting that it’s not all runshine and soses. But gosh, what lovely company you’ve been!’

Debby was gobsmacked. 'I'm so surprised you'd say that. And I've been on the outside of most things all *my* life too, in one way or another. I can't even get along with my own family! My sister is lovely but continually AWOL, travelling somewhere in the world with intermittent contact, and my parents are a work of art, and I don't mean that in a good way! I haven't got much in common with anyone either, so I understand what you mean. It's hard being different, or feeling like you don't fit in anywhere. I only started to feel like a normal person when I met Darren! I'd gone for nearly thirty years feeling like a fish out of water. And now this infertility malarkey is keeping me there.'

She hugged Feen spontaneously. 'Thank you for saying such a kind thing. It makes me feel less of a freak. I'm something of a misery-guts most of the time these days, I'm afraid, and I've had no real idea how to turn things around. But that's all about to change. Talking to you has made me realise that I do need to talk to a professional; someone who can help me come to terms with having to create a different life from the one Darren and I had planned.'

'I don't find you miserable, Debby! Not at all. Yes, you have a lot on your plate to accept and overcome, but it doesn't define you, and it doesn't mean you're not interesting! I'd love to talk more with you sometime about your work as a neatre thurse, for example. I'd find that fascinating. I'd love to hear more about what you do, and of course how you met Darren! I'm a sucker for a romantic story, and I have a pretty good one of my own! Maybe we could do coffee in the town sometime, away from the guys and the kids? A good family friend has a nice local café.'

'Yes, we've been there already, and met her. Peg, isn't it? She's nice. And yeah, I'd like to meet for coffee.' Debby admitted.

She suddenly felt humbled and almost embarrassed by Feen's words. This incredibly generous little woman sounded genuinely sincere with her compliments, and it was so nice to be seen as a whole lot more than just a defunct baby-machine with a 'failed' sticker plastered across the front of it. Or a deranged, ranting mad woman, who wished serious harm on complete strangers. Debby found herself smiling, in spite of everything, and looking forward to the prospect of a girly coffee.

'Great!' Feen clapped her hands. Then her face became a little more serious.

'Debby, I know that the stress of infertility is a terrible, crushing thing. I totally get that you can become so focussed on getting pregnant that you can literally forget what you used to do for fun. And even though I've never actually had many friends to lose, I also appreciate how hard must be, to be deserted by people you thought cared enough to stick around. I've seen Adie go through absolute hell, over that. Let's touch base again in a few days and plake a man. Maybe do lunch. The Feathers is nice for a lub punch. Let's have some fun together!'

The two women swapped mobile numbers so they could message one another. Feen then left, after insisting that Debby make a promise to text her whenever she wanted to talk.

Once she had gone, the cottage seemed strangely quiet. Debby felt a little shivery, and was almost tempted to light the fire, even though it was a warm day. It seemed a bit silly, but she instinctively realised that what she still really wanted was a little more company. She didn't feel quite ready to be completely on her own again, so she compromised and lit a candle instead. A living, moving flame – even from something as small as a candle – often made her feel like there was someone else in the room. It was a small thing, but an immensely comforting one.

Darren wasn't due back for another few hours, so she busied herself with making an apple and rhubarb crumble for their supper. She put the rhubarb on to boil in sugared water, and mixed her crumble topping at the kitchen bench while her thoughts bounced around a bit. For once, she deliberately decided against trying to stifle or deny them.

Feen was right about so many things. Debby was starting to realise that she had become so focussed on trying to conceive, and trying to deal with the devastation of every failed attempt, she'd forgotten what she used to enjoy, or what used to made her laugh. Life was still going on, outside the door, out in the world. It all rolled relentlessly forward, in its own indomitable way, with few people ever knowing, and even fewer really caring, about the challenges others faced behind closed doors.

There wasn't much point in beating yourself up forever about a fact of life you couldn't change. Wouldn't it be better if she could find a way to accept it, instead? To find a way to step back into the world and be a part of it all, instead of disengaging and staying in the shadows of her own sadness, risking her marriage and a lifetime of potential happiness that could still be possible in a different way?

Darren was carrying on. He was out there today, answering a frantic call to help people and animals in need. He didn't let his or Debby's grief stand in the way of doing what he loved. Her parents hadn't put off their trip to the Amalfi Coast this summer, had they, because of Debby's grief? They'd *never* do that, so it probably wasn't an appropriate comparison, but her sister Jayne cared about her a lot, and she'd still gone off travelling yet again, in spite of Debby's grief. Anita, her closest friend, hadn't put off starting her little business selling children's clothes from home on the internet, had she, because of Debby's grief?

People were getting on with life. Even the people who really, truly cared about how Debby and Darren were coping, were all getting on with their lives. Until today, Debby had resented that. But her thinking had somehow shifted, and she wasn't sure how much of that was down to talking with Feen Raven-Black, or the change of environment, or simply her own evolution. Perhaps it was some peculiar combination of all three. But *something* had changed.

Somehow, without her realising it was happening, the burden of resentment or anger or confusion towards her family and friends had started to lift. She could feel it lightening around her, and she actually felt slightly ashamed, now, that she'd begrudged everyone else their right to live like normal people and enjoy their lives; that she'd somehow expected them to be paralysed by her grief in the same way she was herself. That was completely unreasonable, of course and on some rational level she'd always known that. Now, though, she actually felt and understood it.

What had Feen said? It made perfect sense, in Debby's own context. *Even though they react differently than me, and I might not agree with them, that doesn't make them wrong.*

Another important thing Feen had mentioned, which was only just becoming clear to Debby now, was the fact that she had to forgive herself for being human in her misery.

Debby knew that the people who loved her wouldn't be resentful of her unfair expectations of them. They'd know that her behaviour was driven by anger, loss and bereavement, and they'd understand. They would forgive her, and of course they'd want her to forgive herself. She decided in that moment that she would do exactly that.

There *was* no right or wrong way to react to the agony of infertility. It *was* okay to hurt, to be bereft, to be desperately afraid of what on earth might be next, what on earth else could fill that aching void that was meant to be filled by a child of her own. She *was* entitled to feel those things.

What she was *not* entitled to do, though, was blame anyone else for it all; not her family, not friends, not women she saw in the streets with their babies, not Darren, and certainly not herself.

According to the experts, Debby's inability to conceive was not related in any way to her early abortion. So, she had two choices, didn't she? She could either acknowledge that as fact, or continue to beat herself over the head with it, tormented by her own arrogance in assuming she knew more than they did.

It was all about the 'why,' wasn't it? That deeply ingrained human need to understand the reasons for everything? But what if there really was no 'why,' here? A lot of things in life just didn't have an explanation, it was as simple as that, and you could drive yourself mad trying to find one, including clinging to a belief about something every expert in their field had already told you wasn't a factor.

I have to acknowledge that this failure to get pregnant isn't my fault. I did not cause this. Nothing I did, or failed to do, makes me responsible for this. And I have to stop allowing people, however well-meaning, to disrespect my boundaries and feelings by criticising my failure as if it is my fault!

As revelations went, this was huge. It represented the kind of forward mental movement Debby had been in desperate need of. Oddly though, it was not a cataclysmic, or even a mildly dramatic revelation. It was more of a previously-unseen door being quietly pulled open, waiting for her to stand up straight and look through it, to the view beyond. Suddenly, she realised that a life without children did seem like it might one day be possible.

A Spell To Increase Fertility and Promote Pregnancy

You will need ~
A new moon
**Four crystals: moonstone, carnelian, fluorite and aventurine (to represent the four seasons and the four elements in the astrological calendar)*
**A small crystal bowl full of distilled water.*
**Four raspberry leaves*
**The unopened buds of four white roses.*
&Sixteen white votive candles
**A long Silver ribbon.*
**A small purple velvet pouch.*
**A photograph of the intended mother to be*
~

Beneath your Spell Tree, on the night of a New Moon, give thanks to your tree for its shelter and hosting. Give thanks to the New Moon and acknowledge its unseen presence.

Place your bowl on the ground and surround it with each of your crystals in four corners. Frame four candles as corners around each crystal. Place the photograph of the mother-to-be beneath the bowl, facing upwards. Place the rosebuds in the bowl, and lay a raspberry leaf on top of each one. Create a circle around the entire arrangement with the silver ribbon, and light the candles. Draw down the energy from the moon with your hands sixteen times.

The Incantation (once):
'Bless-ed Mother of Earth and Sea, Mother of the Fertile, hear my plea.
Moon Mother, Sun Mother, Sacred be.
Grant my wish to the Mother to be.
Make her womb open and ready to be
the home for the longed-for child.
Keep her heart open and ready to receive
the gift of the longed-for child.'

Give your thanks to the Sacred Mothers, gather your things, place the rosebuds, the raspberry leaves, the silver ribbon and the photograph of the mother to be in the velvet pouch then bury it underground in a place where the next full moon will cast its light.
Make a gift of the four crystals to the mother-to-be so she can keep them by her bed, so their power will work while she is sleeping.

Chapter Ten

Working wasn't much fun when you were meant to be on holiday. Darren's conscience pricked him hard, as he bandaged the leg of a seriously hostile tomcat after he'd finished draining and cleaning the awful abscess from its latest fight. It had hissed at Darren and bitten him hard – enough to draw blood – forcing him to sluice his own wound, and disinfect and bandage it before he could even get started on dealing with the battle-torn cat itself. The bad-tempered old feline was well known to the practice, apparently. Nobody found it pleasant to treat, especially since its owner was allegedly no less belligerent and difficult to deal with –and astonishingly ungrateful, to boot.

The whole point of getting away for a month was to do just that – get away. Take time out. But here he was, stepping into the breach for the fourth time in a fortnight, up here in Torley where there seemed to be a chronic shortage of good vets. It wasn't the pick of places for most people, he had to admit. Not a lot going on up here, on the face of it at least, and possibly a bit too quiet for anyone who wanted to have a good social life as well as a decent job.

Valley Veterinary Practice was the only surgery in Torley. There were three vets, but Stan Biggar, the oldest one, had dropped to part time to protect what was left of his failing health, and was making plans for retirement. One of the other vets was currently away on holiday. Evidently, the practice usually coped well with local demands, but the past two weeks had been busier than usual, which had put the service under some strain, and a promised locum had let them down at the last minute. When they'd caught wind of a vet being here on holiday they'd approached Darren, humbly and with much respect, to ask if he could possibly do a day of small surgeries to help them out.

As much as he'd wanted to say no, Darren found himself compelled to help. His work was a vocation, after all, and – if he was honest with himself – he figured could use a day away from Debby. Her bumpy encounter with Feen Raven-Black had been difficult to smooth over, and although she'd settled down afterwards, even to the extraordinary extent of being able to have a pool day with the other woman and her family, and then a couple of coffee dates with Feen, he still found that being around his wife could be horribly intense. She was weepy, quiet, and not very communicative. He knew she was going through a massive process, of letting go of her cherished, heartfelt dreams of motherhood. She was trying to come to terms with the prospect of being childless, and trying to imagine what kind of life they could have without the much longed-for babies.

It was a very big journey, for which there was no road map. She just had to navigate it as best she could, and he wasn't sure if he should be hovering or making himself scarce while she went through the process. Although she'd said she had no intention of leaving him, he was well aware that it was a choice she still could take. While she took the necessary time to work through her options and reach the most important decisions of her life, all Darren could do was wait, support her as best he could without smothering her, and hope that everything would somehow settle in a way that would let them move forward. Debby was finally talking to her sister a bit too, and he knew she'd also talked to Adie and Feen a handful of times since the pool day. He hoped it had helped.

Talking to others never really worked for him. A problem shared being a problem halved wasn't something he could relate to very well. He needed time and space to get to grips with big decisions. He didn't get there by talking to others. He retreated into himself, to think things through on his own, and he generally found the input of others to be more distracting than helpful.

The criminal lifestyle had evolved over time, after he'd lost his first job and fallen in with the wrong crowd. It was no excuse, but Darren knew exactly how and why it had happened. He'd hated himself for it, so when the opportunity came to change the direction his life was taking, it hadn't been hard for him to accept it. Thanks to the actions of a now-dead woman who'd been both cursed and blessed with stupidity and wisdom in equal measure, he'd been able to turn away from the life of crime he'd been embroiled in, and make something of himself. It was still really hard to believe sometimes, how dramatically his life had changed, or the incident itself that had been responsible.

In the course of committing what he'd describe as a 'routine burg' in a house in an affluent neighbourhood, Darren and his young accomplice, Tom Findlay, had been sprung by the owner of the house, Alison Jones, who'd come home without warning. Everything had gone horribly wrong from that point. Tom Findlay had lost his life that day, at Alisons' hands, and the days and weeks that followed had been indescribably wretched for all concerned.

The shock and heartbreak of what had happened to his young friend had forced Darren to realise how warped his life had become and that something really big had to change if he ever hoped to escape the revolving door of prison, and being miserably defined and eternally condemned, by the events of those few weeks.

Alison Jones had recognised Darren's intelligence. She'd understood how much more there was to the petty thief who'd stood before her back then, in abject shame for his part in what had turned out to be the most tragic set of consequences imaginable, and she'd gone on to set the wheels in motion for him to become the person she knew he was capable of being.

Alison hadn't meant to kill Tom, and she had recognised the devastating impact of her actions. She acted in the best way she could to right the wrongs, to help repair the lives she'd shattered. When a hole gets torn out of your life, it's not always possible to fix it and not leave a scar, and Alison knew that. After she found out that she was terminally ill, and before she took her own life, she did the best she could, to heal the scars she'd inflicted, and make life meaningful again to the people left behind who'd known and loved Tom Findlay.

Vet training hadn't been difficult either, really, for Darren. Long, yes, and demanding of massive commitment, but he'd been prepared to make it, and with the help of Alison Jones' vet friend Simon Westrupp, who'd overseen his practical training, he'd come to fully embrace and truly love it. Compared with the challenge of squaring away the dichotomy of hating Alison Jones for half of what she'd done, and loving her for the other half, the long years of study, training and work to qualify had been easier than he'd anticipated.

Darren had made up his mind to make Alison and Simon proud of him, and he'd worked his arse off, to do just that. He figured that wherever Alison was now (and he wasn't entirely sure whether she was – or even *should* be – in heaven or in hell), she'd be looking at him and nodding, with a half-smile on her face, and saying; 'See, I knew you could do it, and look at you now!' He also knew how happy she'd be to see her dog, Badger – Darren's dog now – so cherished and happy in his new life.

The Darren Davies of the time, reformed criminal and recently qualitied veterinary surgeon, had never made any bones about his past. He hadn't spared Debby any of the details of exactly what his life had been like before they'd met. But asking her to be his wife? Well, that had been a whole different kettle of fish. That decision had been the biggest and most terrifying of Darren's life.

He remembered back to the time when he was deciding whether or not to propose. People might have thought that some of the decisions he'd already made in life, like turning to crime, or taking a golden opportunity to turn his life around again, would have been massive, and they certainly were. But compared with the conundrum of whether he should ask Debby Cameron to marry him, those other choices had been easy.

He'd walked for miles along the beach with Badger on a cold, grey Sunday morning, with the icy sea wind snatching at his face and stinging his eyes. A lot of things had gone through his mind that day, as he worked his way through all the potential scenarios, of Debby saying yes, or saying no, and what either choice would mean for him and his future. Back then, he was still very much in a place where he was pinching himself for his good fortune, and still repairing his shattered self-esteem. A large part of him seriously doubted whether he had any right to expect any more from life than what he'd already been given.

He'd also wondered, as he'd battled the howling wind on that beach, how he would deal with the rejection if Debby's response to his proposal was to say that he'd been a fun distraction for a while, but he wasn't 'marriage material' for an intelligent woman with a career of her own, who didn't need a partner with a shady past pulling her down. If she turned him down, he'd be gutted, but he'd reasoned it would be fair enough. He had a decent job and a seaside flat, but what else did he have to offer her, really?

They'd only had a handful of dates, when he realised he was falling for her, so he knew he had to tell her the full story (and not just what the papers and the six o'clock news had said), before he ended up losing his heart completely. That way, if she did walk away in disgust, he'd be better able to survive it.

She hadn't walked away. Not that night, and not since. He'd made sure she knew everything about him, warts and all, and she'd still accepted his shy proposal, offered almost casually as his buffer against rejection. In doing so she'd made him the happiest man alive.

As he'd already acknowledged, many times over, he'd been given an extraordinary amount of good fortune already, with a career handed to him on a plate, a dog he cherished and a wife he adored. They lived in a decent house, they didn't go hungry, they had a social life, family who cared (on his side at least) and careers they both enjoyed that gave them the ability to have a few little luxuries, like nice cars and holidays abroad. He'd decided that for him, that could be enough. After a lot of hard soul-searching, he had managed to find a peace within himself, but it hadn't come easily, and it had come largely unnoticed by his wife, who was tied up in knots with her own grief and pain.

One of the hardest parts of coming to terms with everything by himself was when bad news came in when he was working. Debby always did her best not to bother him at work, but there were times in the IVF process when her period would come, or when she'd get the news that no embryos had attached, and she'd let him know while he was at work. He didn't mind; he needed and wanted to be there for her, and of course he was always waiting too, for good news. But bad news derailed him just as much as it derailed her, and it was always so tough, hearing her crying on the end of the phone. It meant he occasionally lost his focus, and that wasn't good.

He'd decided to come clean and confess to his boss and his team, why there were some days when he wasn't capable of speaking, when all he wanted to do was lock himself in the loo and cry, or rush home to comfort his wife. It was laying himself bare in a way he didn't really want, but he needed to be honest, and it really did help, that others understood and cared what they were going through. His colleagues had immediately stepped up, and held him together, and he was convinced that the support he got at work was pretty much the only thing that had prevented him from losing the plot completely.

So far, he and Debby had managed to hang on, riding the choppy waves of infertility together. But what if she wanted to walk away *now*, and chance her arm with someone else? He could hardly stand in her way, could he? It would be the most devastating thing imaginable, to lose her now, after everything they'd been through, but as heart-wrenching as it had been to tell her that he wouldn't stop her if that was what it took for her to be happy, he did mean it. Somehow, he would find a way to pick up the pieces if she left him for pastures new. He loved her enough to want her to be happy, even if it wasn't with him.

Work, however unexpected and random, was providing a little here-and-there respite that he sorely needed. The chance to get out of his own head for a while was helping to keep him sane.

This month in the Lake District was 'make or break' for their marriage. They both knew it. So far, if you didn't count the faux-pas with the bag of baby clothes mysteriously appearing in their holiday luggage, and Debby's encounter with Feen Raven, and her attitude to both, things hadn't gone too badly. She hadn't mentioned the bag since Darren had put it back in the truck, and she'd mended the fence with Feen.

They'd even made love a couple of times since they'd been up here, without prior scheduling, for the first time in probably two years. It had felt wonderful, and right, and real to him, to be spontaneous; to feel less like a performing seal who only seemed to be wanted when the time was right for conception.

They'd fallen asleep together in the lovely big bed, beneath the crocheted patchwork throw, and cuddled up like they always used to. But it was a small boat they were attempting to sail, on very rough seas, and he was a long way from being sure they wouldn't end up capsizing completely and drowning in a storm they seemed powerless to escape.

Chapter Eleven

Adie and Mark were jolted awake by the sound of someone battering insistently at the front door of Ravensdown House. Mark jumped out of bed straight away, and pulled on a pair of pyjama pants, but Adie was a few beats behind him, mentally. With blurry eyes, she looked at the bedside clock, as Mark flicked the light on. It showed twenty to four in the morning.

Who the hell? she thought groggily to herself, as she roused herself fully and hurriedly threw on a dressing gown and followed Mark downstairs, praying that whoever was trying to batter their door down hadn't woken the twins.

The hammering at the front door continued and Mark got to it first. Adie could hear a woman's strident voice; 'Somebody! Anybody! Please! Please help me!'

As Mark opened the door Adie looked beyond his broad shoulders and was startled to see a wild-eyed Debby Davies staring at them. Mark opened his mouth to speak, but Debby jumped in first.

'Help me! There's something seriously wrong with my husband!' Her voice was shrill, and panicked, and she abruptly turned and fled back down the drive towards Teapot Cottage. Without a word, Mark stuffed his bare feet into his wellington boots and grabbed his Barbour jacket from the peg by the door, and tugged it on over his bare chest as he raced after Debby. Adie felt she had little choice but to follow, and tore down the drive, and in through the back door of the cottage behind Mark.

'He's upstairs, on the bed! I've called an ambulance, but I don't know what else to do! Help me! Please!' She was in tears now, and frightened out of her wits. Mark ran up the stairs, with Adie following close behind. The bedroom stank of vomit and sweat. As soon as Mark looked at Darren, he swore. 'Jesus Christ! What the 'ell's 'appenin? Darren? Darren, what's up, mate? Talk to me if yer can.'

Adie knew something was very badly wrong. Darren was sweating profusely, breathing shallowly, and a dark blotchy rash had started to creep across his arms, chest and neck. He looked at Adie and Mark through eyes that were half glazed over, and he tried to speak, but couldn't.

Debby was behind them now. 'I was woken up by the most almighty bang, really loud, like a ten-ton concrete block had landed on the roof. It shook the whole house! I realised the bed was soaking, and he's been sick all over it. He's been shaking, constantly. I've tried to get him to look at me, but he can't focus. I don't think he can move his head.'

Adie looked at Darren again, and a cold finger of fear scored her spine. Whatever this was, it wasn't good. Mark kept talking to Darren, but he remained unresponsive, with his whole body shaking uncontrollably. Debby was desperate, shaking too, and crying hard.

'I think I know what it might be, but I hope to God I'm wrong. Please, God, please, let me be wrong.' She was almost babbling now, distraught and fearful, saying the same thing over and over again. 'I think I know what I'm looking at, but please, God, *let me be wrong.*'

Blue lights flashed in the bedroom window as the ambulance drew up at the front of the cottage. While Mark continued to try and get a response from Darren, Adie went downstairs to let the paramedics in. She showed them upstairs then followed, hovering in the hallway as the bedroom became crowded. They assessed Darren, with grim faces. One of them shone a light into his eyes, and even from back in the hall, Adie could see him flinch. They were talking to him, trying to get a response in much the same way Mark had been trying. Clearly, they were deeply concerned. One of them left the room and pushed past Adie, saying he was going to get a stretcher.

Suddenly it was quiet in the bedroom. Adie was suddenly terrified. What did that awful silence mean? The next words she heard frightened her to the core. It was Debby's voice, suddenly flat, devoid of all hysteria.

It's sepsis, isn't it? I did the glass test on him, and the rash didn't fade. It's Pasteurella multocida, something all vets worry about. He was bitten by a cat a couple of days ago,' she explained.

The paramedic still in the room responded with a grim nod. 'It does look like sepsis, I'm afraid. What you're suggesting is incredibly rare, but it's possible. We'll know more when we get him over to Cumberland.'

Mark cleared his throat. 'You go with 'im lass, in't ambulance. I'll follow in me truck, and meet you at th'ospital. Adie'll take yer dog back to't farm, to sleep in't kitchen. She'll keep 'im safe up there.'

Adie could see that Debby was deeply afraid. As the paramedics expertly loaded Darren safely onto the stretcher and moved him downstairs, she spoke to them quickly, saying she believed, as had Darren himself, that he'd cleaned the cat bite wound as soon as it had happened, and been sure he'd done it properly. 'He's a vet, and I'm a nurse, so we do know what to do, to prevent infection.'

She grabbed a handful of clothes and headed for the bathroom to get dressed. Mark put an arm around Adie. 'Can you sort this lot out, love? I need to get dressed and follow 'em. I can let yer know any news when I hear any.'

Adie nodded, suddenly remembering that she too was in her night clothes and slippers. 'Yes, of course. I'll get this bedding in the wash, and everything cleaned up, and I'll take the dog back to the house and try to get him settled.'

Debby came out of the bathroom and gave Adie and Mark a weak and wobbly smile. 'I have to go. Thanks for your help.' She rushed down the stairs and Adie heard the doors of the ambulance slam shut. Mark quickly kissed her and left to get dressed so he could follow the ambulance to the Cumberland Infirmary in Carlisle.

They're not mucking about. There's no time to lose.

Sepsis. Adie knew very little about it, other than the fact that it was an incredibly serious, life-threatening bacterial infection. She knew that if it did develop, you had to act fast. *Really* fast. She prayed they'd get to it quickly at the hospital, and that Daren would be ok. She also sent a silent prayer of thanks to the angels for her husband Mark, who hardly knew these people, but had offered to stay by Debby's side at the hospital, while they worked on Darren. He knew she'd need the support, in case the worst happened. She'd also need a way to get back to Teapot Cottage, at some point.

She set about cleaning up the cottage, getting the sodden sheets in the wash, and rolling the remaining bedding into a ball to take up to the farm to wash in the bigger machine in the barn. She bent to give Badger a reassuring cuddle. He'd been whimpering softly throughout the events of the night.

'Come on, gorgeous boy. Let's get your bed and your bowls, and maybe a toy too, hey? I have a nice cosy place for you to sleep, by the Aga in the kitchen, up at the farm. I've got a very special bone for you to chew, and your mum and Dad will be back before you know it.'

The dog followed her, reluctantly at first, then with a little more confidence. After ensuring the cottage was securely locked up for what was left of the night, Adie made her way back up the drive to Ravensdown House. Mark's truck was gone, but the house was ablaze with light. Feen was in the kitchen, in her dressing gown, and she was making a pot of tea.

'God, Feen, I'm sorry! I guess you couldn't avoid being woken by the bedlam.'

Feen sighed and shook her head. 'I think we might've heard the door go, but at our end of the house it's all quite muffled so we didn't think anything of it. Probably thought it was you or Daddy moving around. But then when that siren started up, we came tearing down the stairs to find the front door wide open, and you two nowhere to be seen! We wondered what the hell had happened!'

Adie smiled grimly. 'I'm so sorry. That must've been really scary.'

Feen nodded. 'It was. But Daddy rushed back and filled us in, as he was getting dressed to follow the ambulance. It's just terrible. I hope Darren will be ok.'

Adie cocked her head on one side and looked at Feen shrewdly. 'Any insights?'

Sometimes, in certain situations, Feen would already know what to expect. This time, however, she simply shook her head. 'Not really. I beel a fattle. A fight for life, but I can't sense anything beyond that. The outcome isn't showing itself to me. Hopefully, it will, but for now I'm not much clearer than you are.' She looked anxious. 'Daddy said they think it's sepsis.'

Adie nodded, grimly. 'It looks like it. They have to examine him properly, to know for sure. I guess we'll know later this morning. I've been cleaning up sick and stuff, so I'm going to get this dog settled and go for a shower.'

Feen handed her a mug of hot tea. 'Take this with you. By the time you're ready to go back to bed, it should be cool enough to drink.'

Adie smiled at her gratefully. 'Did the twins get woken in the fracas?'

Feen grinned. 'Yeah, for a nanosecond. They had a little whine and then dropped off again. Gavin's back in bed.'

'You should head that way too.'

'I just wanted to make sure you were ok. I will go up now, though, with my cup of tea. See you later.'

She stepped forward and the two women exchanged a warm hug. Adie mumbled, half to herself. 'That poor couple. As if they haven't been through enough!'

'I know,' Feen agreed. 'But for tonight we can't do anything more. I guess you'll be at least half awake until Daddy comes home, or tones or phexts with news at least, but do try to get some rest at least, Adie. You've done all you can, for now.'

Two hours later, at just after six-thirty, Adie heard Mark's truck in the driveway. *I must've dozed off,* she thought to herself. She had tried to remain alert, but it hadn't worked. She hurriedly checked her phone to see if she'd missed any texts or calls from Mark, but there were none. Either the news was too bad to not say face to face, or he wanted to just let her sleep. She prayed it would be the latter. She got up and made her way down to the kitchen. The poor man would be in desperate need of a decent cup of coffee.

She met him in the hallway. He was taking off his jacket and boots, and he looked bone weary. He looked at her bleakly and she held her breath, steeling herself for the worst news.

''E's still alive, lass. It's sepsis, and' it is that thing Debby said it were, from 'is cat bite. They've pumped 'im full of antibiotics, an' put 'im in intensive care. 'E's on a ventilator. They can't predict nowt else yet. It's a waitin' game. But 'e's in't right place, love. If they can, they'll pull 'im through.'

As Adie prepared a pot of strong coffee, Mark went on to explain that he'd left Debby at the hospital with Darren but had instructed her to call him or Adie when she wanted picking up to bring back. Adie figured Debby wouldn't want to leave Darren's side under any circumstances, to go anywhere.

She decided that she would go over to the hospital herself with a few things from the cottage. She reasoned Debby would probably forgive her for going through the couple's belongings at least to the point of being able to collect a few of their toiletries, something of Darren's own for him to sleep in, and maybe some fresh clothes for Debby. And food. As much as the poor woman probably wouldn't feel like eating anything, she'd need to keep her strength up. Cumberland Infirmary were excellent at supporting loved ones and allowing them to be near to the sick and injured, especially in times of real crisis, and would sometimes even offer cups of tea if they happened to be there when the patients were getting theirs as scheduled, but they didn't run to providing meals. Adie wasn't sure if Debby had even taken any money or a bank card with her, to buy anything from the hospital restaurant.

She had some hearty chicken soup in the freezer, precisely for a time when someone in her family might be under the weather and in need of a pick-me-up. She'd reheat that and take it, in a flask. She said as much to Mark, and he nodded. 'Aye, love. Mebbe she'd appreciate that. I'll take dog for a run in't field now, before I start fer't day. I want to check't roof at Teapot Cottage too. Debby said she 'eard an ear-splittin' bang on't roof, like a concrete block landin' on it, or summat. That's what woke 'er up, apparently. Sounds bloody weird. I'll take a look.'

'The dog's name is Badger,' Adie offered. 'And after the run you'll be going nowhere until you've had a shower and a decent breakfast, and a half-hour nap.' She raised her hand as Mark started to complain. 'And I'm having none of your protests, thank you very much. You've been up since half past three. I promise to wake you after half an hour, but you can't go out there and put in a full day's work on an empty stomach and too little sleep.'

Her voice was firm, and it was a rare occasion when she steered her husband. He knew his own mind and didn't take kindly to being told what to do, but she made sure her tone of voice conveyed how firm she intended to be, today. He slumped back in his chair, in defeat.

Adie knew he had to deal with the farm's growing lambs today. They needed tagging, and they were eating more and more, and had to regularly be shifted to new pasture. It was a job for the quad bike and the sheepdogs, and Mark was keen to get going, mindful that heavy rain was forecast for later in the day. He had a lot to do, before the fine weather broke, and she understood his determination.

Farm work was simple enough, but it could be demanding, and most of it simply wouldn't wait. She'd learned that well, a couple of years ago after Mark's accident, when she'd stepped into the breach to help Feen run things while he was laid up for several months. As Mark rose to go and have a shower Adie added, gently, 'and yes, thank you, it would be good to find out what might be wrong with the cottage roof.'

Two hours later, after collecting a few essentials from Teapot Cottage, Adie was on the road to Cumberland Infirmary. She had Feen with her, as the two women had decided to have lunch and do a bit of shopping in the city. Adie didn't go to Carlisle very often, so she always tried to make the most of it when she did. There were one or two household items she needed, one of which was a new mattress protector for the bed at Teapot Cottage. Feen could do with a bit of time away from the twins, and Gavin was working but happy to watch Alder and Willow at the same time, while his wife went out for lunch. He was an absolute diamond.

She remembered now, how seriously alarmed she and Mark had been, when Feen had first introduced them to the long-haired musician as her future husband, within just a day of meeting him. But one look at his daughter's dreamy face had been enough for Mark Raven to know that she had lost her whole heart to the handsome rocker in an instant, just like he'd done himself with her mother Beth, back in the day. He hadn't been excited about the prospect of his only child having already decided to marry someone she didn't really know, and a leather-clad 'headbanger' to boot, but he accepted it with as much grace as he could muster, and kept his panic largely to himself. After all, the pot couldn't fairly call the kettle black, could it? And, as Adie had pointed out, for Feen to have been lucky enough – as lucky as Mark himself had been with Beth – for the feeling to have been mutual, well, it was the best they could ever hope for, wasn't it?

Feen had been a similar age to Mark when he'd fallen for her mother, but he was more than a little worried about the fact that his daughter was in many ways quite naïve and vulnerable. He'd raised Feen singlehandedly, after Beth had died, and he was still very protective of her. Complications with Gavin's family on the back of past events hadn't helped matters, in the beginning, and it had taken a while for the dust to settle, and for both families to adjust to being related by marriage.

Once everything did settle though, Mark and Adie realised how perfect Feen and Gavin were for one another. The horrendous accident last year, where Feen's car had been forced over the bank on the road into Torley town on a night of filthy weather, had forced the premature arrival of the impossibly tiny twins. It had been a desperately anxious time, with the twins' lives hanging in the balance. But little Alder and Willow had proved to the world just how tough they were, and they'd pulled through with no discernible complications. Adie would never forget how devastated Gavin had been, at the prospect of losing his new little family. They were the rock of his life, and he adored them. Mark and Adie knew Feen couldn't have found a better partner to go through life with, and they both loved Gavin very much.

'You're deep in thought,' Feen observed, cutting into Adie's musings. 'Anything you want to share?'

'Oh no, not really, darling. I was just remembering the last time we were at Cumberland. It was after you'd had your accident, and Gavin was distraught about you and the twins, just like I imagine poor Debby is right now, about Darren. I'm sure she's probably seen this kind of thing a lot, in her work as a nurse but it's a lot different, isn't it, when it's this close to home? I just hope the worst doesn't happen.'

Feen bit her bottom lip, thoughtfully. 'It's a rare thing, for my intuition to fail me. But in this case, I'm afraid it has. I have no idea what will happen. My window appears to be closed, Adie.'

'What, just for this? Or for everything?'

Feen shook her head. 'No, just for this. I'm still sensing most things around me as usual, but somehow there's a real block in front of this thing with Darren and Debby. I don't understand it, but I'm going with it. It may change. For now, I'm as much in the dark as everyone else, and I can't offer anything. I'm sorry.'

'D'you think it might be because she shut you down so hard that first time you tried to talk to her?' Adie was curious now.

Again, Feen shook her head. 'No. Because I've picked up on things about her since then. The pool day, I saw her heavily pregnant. That's not to say it was Darren's though, because I didn't see him in her picture. Only her. I dunno what to think about that, Adie. I saw her pregnant and happy, contented, but she was by herself in the vision. I'm trying not to dwell on that.'

Adie pulled a wry face, as they pulled into the hospital car park. 'Sorry, I won't keep asking. The last thing we need is for something to be manifested that isn't even there!'

The ICU was very quiet. Adie rang the bell and waited for a couple of minutes, until a nurse opened the door and agreed to go and get Debby. She came to the door and stepped out into the corridor. Her face was tense, and blotchy. She looked like she'd been crying for a week. She gave Adie and Feen a tight smile and took the bag Adie offered.

'He's really ill,' she said flatly. 'He might not make it.' Her bottom lip wobbled a little, but she managed not to cry.

Adie placed a hand on Debby's shoulder. 'You look exhausted. Shall we get a cup of coffee, downstairs? Can you leave him for a short while, d'you think?'

Debby nodded, shortly, and let out a heavy sigh. She rolled her shoulders and moved her neck from side to side.

'Yeah, I guess I could. Nothing's going to change in the next half hour or so. Even just to see the sky for half an hour, that would be something.'

It seemed as if Darren had, as suspected, developed sepsis after treating a cat, on one of his help-out days at the Lakeview Veterinary Practice in Torley. It had bitten him on the hand, and he'd immediately flushed out, cleaned and dressed the wound. 'We both know to do that, you know, attend to potential infection immediately, in the course of the job?' She closed her eyes.

‘I know cats can be bad, but he knows that too. I just know he would have done all the right things, in response to being bitten. I don’t doubt it for a minute. But he clearly didn’t get rid of all the infection. He did mention, more or less just in passing, that a feisty old cat had bitten him, but he didn’t say anything else about it, and I thought nothing of it, because it’s such a common hazard.’

Darren had gone to bed early, claiming he was feeling a bit rough and had a headache, but he’d played it down so she hadn’t been too concerned.

His blood pressure had been dangerously low, on admittance to the hospital, so they’d applied vasoactive drugs to help bring it back up. He was on a ventilator, and was being given corticosteroids to reduce his inflammation, and antibiotics through an IV drip. A catheter had been inserted so they could monitor his urine output, which was another potential indicator of organ damage.

He hadn’t woken up yet. There was a marginal improvement in his overall condition, with reducing inflammatory markers, but he was a long way from being out of the woods.

‘They got him just as he was going into severe septic shock. If I hadn’t woken up when I did, he would have died. There’s no doubt about it.’

She added, half to herself, ‘If it hadn’t been for that big bang on the roof that scared me fully awake, I wouldn’t have woken up at all. He’d have died right there in the bed beside me.’

Tears suddenly sprang to her eyes again. Adie leaned forward and patted her hand. ‘But he didn’t die, darling. They’ve got him, and you know better than anyone else, that he’s in the best place. This is a very good hospital, remember, and I do say that with some authority, after seeing what they pulled Mark through in here, a couple of years ago, not to mention how well they took care of Feen, Alder and Willow after their big accident last year.’

Debby nodded. ‘Yes, Cumberland’s gone through a rough patch in recent years, like a lot of hospitals have, but it’s one of the best in the country now, especially for critical care, and if anyone can save him these amazing people will. I know they’re doing their best. Anyway, thank you for bringing stuff in for us. And for taking care of Badger. I’ll see if I can get him into a local kennels for a while, at least until we know what's happening. Can you recommend a good one?'

Adie and Feen both shook their heads. 'No. Forget kennels, Debby. Badger will be just fine with us,' Adie reassured her. 'His food is all there, at the cottage, so we'll bring that up to the farm, and he can stay with us. His bed is already in the kitchen. He's just lovely, but he will be missing you both, and will probably be a bit confused, so do try to get back when you can, even just for a little while. Just call us when you want to come back for a bit, and one of us can come and get you.'

'You're all so kind. Thank you, and I'm so sorry for waking you in the middle of the night. You must've got an awful shock. I hope the cottage is ok too. The roof, I mean. Whatever that bang was, it sounded horrific.' Debby rose from her chair. 'I'm going to head back up now. I don't want him to wake up and wonder where I am. Not that they expect him to wake up just yet, but you never know…'

Adie's heart went out to her. 'That's right. You never know.' She gave Debby a quick hug.

As Debby left, Adie turned to Feen. 'Mark was going to take a look at the cottage roof. He hasn't messaged to say he found anything. Debby said she heard a massive bang, like something enormous and heavy had landed on it. Whatever it was, thank God it woke her up.'

Feen looked speculatively at her for a moment, then spoke quietly. 'There's nothing wrong with the roof at Teapot Cottage, Adie. Debby was in a very deep sleep when Darren went into shock. The cottage created its own warning to her. That's all it was.'

Adie stared at her stepdaughter. She had heard a lot of strange things come out of Feen's mouth over the past few years, but never anything as bizarre as this. 'Are you saying what I think you are? That the cottage *itself* somehow knew Darren was ill and created a loud bang to warn Debby?'

'Yes,' Feen said simply.

'Do you know how crazy that sounds?'

'Yes.'

Rattled, Adie immediately texted Mark, to ask him what he had found at the cottage. She didn't expect an immediate answer, and was astonished when her phone rang straight away.

'Allo, love. Good timin'. I were just stoppin' fer a wee. I've 'ad a good look at cottage, and there's nowt to be concerned over. It's a funny thing. Roof's perfect. I even went up into't loft space an' all, to 'ave a look around. There were nothin'. All a bit of a mystery if y'ask me, but reassurin' I suppose. Maybe she were dreamin'?'

'Yeah, maybe she was. That was probably it.' Adie rang off and looked back at Feen, who had an enigmatic smile playing about the corners of her mouth.

'Let me guess. No sign of anything untoward?'

Adie gave just one brief nod. 'Correct. No sign of anything untoward. Mark wondered if Debby had been dreaming.'

'No. She wasn't. The almighty crack across the roof was real. Without that, she wouldn't have woken up, and Darren would almost certainly have died. And he's not meant to, and it's clear to me now since Daddy's call, that he won't. He is going to survive because she needs him. She's already pregnant.'

Adie blinked, and shook her head, lost for words. As the two women left the hospital and looked for a nice lunch spot in Carlisle town, she wondered – and not for the first time – just what it was about her slightly off-the-wall daughter-in-law, that made her so matter-of-fact about things that most didn't make the blindest bit of sense to most rational people. She also wondered – as she had a hundred times in the past – what latent power lay within the walls of Teapot Cottage and why it felt, to everyone who went there, like the most enigmatic place on earth.

Chapter Twelve

A nurse was adjusting Darren's drip when Debby arrived back in the ICU. She gave Debby a small smile, but quietly informed her there was no discernible change. Not yet.

Well, at least things haven't got any worse. That's something at least.

She sat down heavily in the chair next to Darren's bed. She picked up his hand and kissed it. She whispered quietly, hoping he could hear her, but not wanting anyone else to.

'Come on, babe. Wake up. I really need you. Badger needs you too. You're our world, Darren Davies, and our lives would be utterly meaningless without you. Come back to us, okay? Please?'

How would I live without him? How would I even breathe, without him? He really is my world.

What if Darren didn't recover? Well, that was a thought her mind refused to consider now. Back in the bedroom at Teapot Cottage, where he lay, mumbling quietly, and fitful and feverish, when she'd pressed the glass over his rash and it hadn't faded, she'd been terrified.

The sepsis was an extreme response to the infection Darren had picked up from the cat bite that he'd taken care of, but clearly not well enough. The remaining, probably miniscule, droplet of infection that had evidently entered his bloodstream very quickly had triggered a chain reaction throughout his body. Neither of them had realised how sick he was, when he went to bed a little earlier than usual. He'd complained of a headache, that was all. Debby remembered telling herself at the time that he didn't normally suffer with headaches, but he hadn't thought it was a big deal himself, so she'd put it out of her mind.

Without urgent treatment, sepsis can kill. The infection rages, and can cause irreparable tissue and organ damage, and all-too-often death. Debby prayed she'd got him to hospital in time. For the first time in her entire life as a theatre nurse, she'd felt the desperation of knowing someone was critically ill but being unable to do *anything* to try and fix it herself. Never in her life before had she felt so powerless. Never in her life had she borne witness to the person she loved the most in the world being in very real danger of dying, right in front of her eyes, with nothing she could do to help stop it.

The ambulance had arrived within a few short minutes. Torley had an emergency response hub, in the centre of the town, and Teapot Cottage was just a short stretch away. She'd never been more grateful for anything in her entire life, as she was for seeing those blue lights flashing. But she had never felt so wretched, so desperate, when it left again with them both in the back of it, taking the man she loved more than anything else in the entire world to a place where he might be saved.

In all the drama that had unfolded at the cottage, she'd all but forgotten about poor Badger, but she knew the Ravens would take care of him. They were good people, and it had been so wonderful that they'd come all the way to Carlisle to reassure her Badger would be just fine, and to bring some personal effects; boxer shorts and a clean t-shirt for Darren, a change of clothes (including underwear!) for her, and deodorant, wet wipes, shower gels, body lotion and hand cream. Feen had known Debby would likely want a shower, but she advised that the soap in the hospital bathroom wasn't the best quality. 'The lotions will help counteract the dryness,' she'd said.

One of them had been thoughtful enough to bring Debby's cleanser, toner and moisturiser too. The two women were incredibly kind and thoughtful, and for once Debby swallowed down her indignation at the thought of someone going through her drawers and seeing what she had. As a very private person, she would normally be absolutely horrified at the thought of anyone going through her things, but these were not normal times, and Adie Raven was the kindest person on the planet. She wouldn't have a care or a comment to make, about the colour or condition of Debby's knickers or what perfume she used. The woman just wanted to help, and Debby appreciated it.

She noticed now, for the first time, that Adie and Feen had brought everything in the little holdall that had somehow made its way into their luggage for the holiday – the one that had the baby clothes in it. *I thought Darren had put that back in the truck! I saw him do, that. I'm sure I did! How the hell did it get back into the house?*

It made sense, of course, to find the smallest available bag for what were, essentially just a handful of helpful items. But Adie or Feen must have emptied it, to put everything in.

Adie said she'd cleaned up the bedroom, done the laundry, and would there would be clean sheets and a duvet cover back on the bed again by the end of the day. Feen was going to go down and sort that out. But the baby things were probably somewhere in the bedroom, in plain sight. Debby knew she would have to deal with them when she went back to the cottage, and she wasn't looking forward to that. Maybe there was a local charity shop she could drop them off at, so they could be appreciated by someone who *would* have a use for them.

Oddly enough, though, Debby wasn't as upset as she normally would have been at the prospect of walking into a room to a pile of knitted baby clothes. Her stomach wasn't churning at the thought. Also, interestingly, she wasn't feeling the usual dread that governed her every waking moment, about her inability to get pregnant. Only a quick, here-and-gone flash of sadness washed over her, when she thought about all the beautiful little garments she'd so painstakingly knitted and crocheted, and what a waste it all had been.

She looked in despair at her husband, lying motionless in the bed, with drips and monitors all around him. Only the sound of the ventilator, and the quiet beep of the monitors could be heard in here. That, and the sound of Debby's own breathing as she continually fought to steady herself to prevent the fear from engulfing her.

He is more important. He is all that matters now. He needs to survive. I can face a life without babies, but I can't face a life without him. If that's the trade-off, so be it.

In the instant she had the thought, she knew it to be true. With Darren's life hanging in the balance, his survival really *was* the only thing that mattered. And perhaps, if he recovered fully, they could consider adoption, or fostering. Did the maternal instinct fail somehow, if you were given a child to care for that wasn't your own? For the first time, Debby was willing to consider that maybe it didn't. She'd felt a swell of love when she'd held baby Willow, at the pool day with the Ravens. That was a good enough sign, wasn't it, that she could still cherish a child she hadn't given birth to?

Maybe she could talk to people who fostered, or who had adopted children, and find out from them what it was like to raise a child they hadn't borne themselves. And maybe she could have some of her questions answered, about the kind of support offered to 'parents' of fostered children, to help them cope with the loss when the time came for those kids to be moved on. She already knew that a lot of kids stayed in contact with their foster parents, long after they'd left and become independent adults. A lot of those bonds, forged in many cases through adversity and challenge, remained strong and permanent.

Maybe certain alternatives were possible. But oh, how she still longed to be pregnant! To feel new life growing inside her, created by the unique and special blend of cells from herself and her gorgeous husband. To feel and see the swell of her belly and breasts, and truly know the miracle of conception and birth. To bring a child into the world and prepare that child for life in that world. For so many years, that deep, desperate longing had driven every decision Debby had made, and Darren too, by default. She knew it wasn't so black and white for him. He thought someone else's child could be a viable option for them, but she hadn't been able to understand why.

She realised now, in the dim quiet of the hospital room, that her refusal to accept other possibilities was underpinned by fear. Agreeing to consider other motherhood options always felt like an admission of defeat, and how would she live with the ongoing longing that might never go away even if she wanted it to? What if she was left with a crippling guilt, that she'd given up too soon? When would be the 'right' time to throw in the towel? And, if she did, would it still drive her mad, but just in a different way?

But since last night, everything had tilted, in her world. Faced with the very real possibility that she could lose the only man she'd ever truly loved, her perspective had totally changed. Nothing mattered more, now – nothing at all – than Darren pulling through.

She kissed his inert hand, as her tears fell. Inside herself, something quietly shattered. She felt her hope fly away now, and she allowed it to take her breath away with it. Then she made the decision, equally quietly, to start pulling back together the pieces of herself that were left, that would hopefully be enough for her to make a path she could walk down, towards a different kind of future. She whispered to Darren, quietly.

'I've been such a fool. Forgive me. I've wanted your child so much. But I've got to come to terms with the inevitable, don't I? I know it isn't going to happen for us. I guess I've suspected it for a long time now, but I've put so much energy into denying it, and lashing out, and refusing to accept the reality.' Debby's voice cracked.

'I have to stop. I know that, and I will. I *will.* And I'll see a good counsellor, someone who can help me accept everything, and find a way to move forward. You were right about that, and Feen has already helped me to see the value of it. But the thing is, babe, I can't do any of this without *you.* I can't draw a line under it all and move on to a different kind of life from the one I always imagined and dreamed of for us, if you're not there to help me do it. I need you, so much. I love you, *so* much. You're the other half of me. Nothing means anything without you. Please come back to us, me and Badger. Please come back, Darren.'

* * * * *

Debby took a short walk around the hospital grounds, and then grabbed a quick sandwich and a cup of tea in the restaurant. She decided to have a long, hot shower, and change into the clothes Feen and Adie had brought for her. She unpacked the little holdall and resolved that after she'd freshened up herself, she would give Darren a cooling sponge bath with his own shower gel. She reasoned that even if he was still asleep, he might still smell the familiar fragrance, and maybe it would help.

Unpacking the bag was easy, until she reached the bottom and pulled out a small, lemon-coloured baby hat. A lump formed in her throat again, and fresh tears started falling.

Could her world be any more turbulent right now? Barely big enough to cover her fist, this tiny little hat represented something so much bigger than its woolly little self. It somehow reinforced to her now, quietly and brutally, the fact that there would never be a baby.

She needed to find a reason not to see the little lemon token of love and hope as a symbol of her unbearable plight. Maybe she could donate it to the neonatal ward here in this hospital, where love and hope were so important, and so powerful. Maybe she could donate *all* of what she'd made, in gratitude for all the staff who battled so hard, every day and night of every week, to save the lives of so many people who needed their help.

She felt a lot better after her shower, putting on some clean clothes, and indulging in a spray of perfume, which Adie or Feen had thoughtfully included in the bag. One of the nurses handed her a bowl, and she ran some lukewarm water into it, and a couple of squirts of Darren's shower gel. After drawing the curtains around him, she slowly and gently began to wash him. The love she felt in that moment, the tenderness she had for him, made her cry all over again. He was so vulnerable here, lying in this bed, with an uncertain road to recovery ahead of him.

'If you're going to fiddle with it, at least do it properly.'

Debby couldn't believe what she'd heard. While sponging Darren below the waist, in complete silence, she was more than a little startled to hear his voice!

'Oh, my God! You're awake!' She stared at him. His eyes were still closed but he nodded stiffly.

'It would seem so, although I really wish I wasn't, because I feel like shit.'

Debby pressed the call button for the nurse and took Darren's hand in both of hers. 'Keep your eyes closed for a bit, babe, and don't talk anymore. You're in the hospital. You've got sepsis, from that cat bite you got. Remember it? The bite? You've been really ill for the last twelve hours. You're in intensive care.'

Darren's eyes flew open, and Debby caught the panic in them before the light forced him to close them again. He sighed, heavily. 'God, can you kill the lights please, Debs? It feels like razorblades in my head. I remember the cat bite, yeah. Are you sure it was that? I thought I'd sorted it.'

His voice was barely audible. 'Mangy old bastard,' he mumbled, half to himself. 'Should've put the fucking thing down.'

'Don't talk. Just rest,' Debby pleaded gently. She looked up as the nurse came in, with a doctor right behind her. They then ran a few quick tests, asked a few questions, and arranged for Darren to be given some solid food, which he said he could manage. After saying how thrilled they were that he didn't have any discernible cognitive damage at least, they left again, to arrange a few more tests.

Debby was overjoyed, and suddenly resolute. Left alone again with Darren, she sat beside him and took his hand. She couldn't stop the tears from falling yet again, but this time they were tears of relief.

'You've given me the worst fright.'

Darren squeezed her hand, pulled it up to his lips, and lightly kissed it. His voice was low, and a little gravelly. 'I'm sorry, babe. I did clean the wound thoroughly, when it happened, but I guess it just goes to show how vulnerable we can be. And how riddled with bacteria some of those beat-up, bastard bloody toms can be. It's good lesson for next time.'

'You were delirious, mumbling away to yourself, and I do have to say the language was astonishingly bad.'

Darren grinned. 'Probably a throw-back to my past life. I used to swear all the time. I was terrible.' He fell silent. Clearly, he was still very weak. Even his voice had no strength in it. Debby took a deep breath.

'There's stuff I need to say. It's nothing to worry about, but I need you to listen, and let me take my time saying it all. And don't interrupt me, okay?' He nodded, and she carried on, with her hand still held tightly by his.

'I've been sitting here for so many hours, willing you to wake up. My head went to the worst place, Darren. The place where I lost you. Because I know what sepsis is, and what it does, and I knew there was a very real chance that you might not wake up at all, and even if you did, you might not be the man I know anymore.'

She closed her eyes momentarily, as more tears threatened. 'As you can see, I'm a bit weepy and over-emotional, and it's not just because of that, or because of the fright you gave me when I first realised you were so sick, in the middle of the night. It's also because I made a few decisions while I was willing you to come back to me and Badger.'

She suddenly felt shaky, but she knew he would understand, and she knew she couldn't stop now. He lay there, propped up in bed, looking at her with such gentle kindness, she could hardly stand it.

What did I ever do to deserve this amazing guy?

'I've decided to see a counsellor, who can help me draw a line under the whole baby thing. Adie has recommended someone she went to, a while back; a woman called Dawn Mott. She's pretty good, apparently. And once I'm in a better place with it all, maybe we can think about fostering.'

Darren stared at her. Still, he respected her request to listen, without chipping in. He gave her an encouraging smile, to continue, so she did.

'I know making our own family is not going to happen for us, and I know I have to accept it. I couldn't, before. I wasn't willing to give up trying, and not just because I was so desperate to have a baby. I didn't want to give up because they said they couldn't figure out a good medical reason, why we've never managed to conceive. Part of me always kept hoping that it still might happen.'

Debby gave up and let the tears come. There was no use trying to fight the huge, engulfing tsunami of grief. Through her sobs, she soldiered on. 'But when you were lying there, so helpless, when I thought about what my life would be like without you, I realised that you getting better was the only thing that mattered. And that's when it hit me. If I have you, that *can* be enough for me, because nothing in my world would ever make sense again without you.' She sniffed, loudly and snottily, and reached over for a tissue to blow her nose.

'Nobody gets me like *you* do, Darren, and I'll need you more than ever, to help me. It will be a different kind of grief, a kind of letting go, I suppose, but I think I already started letting go of it all, when nobody could tell me whether or not you were going to be okay. In those first few hours, when everyone thought the worst, I think that was the beginning of the change in how I felt, about the importance of a baby to our happiness. I know I've talked about moving on, but I was still so unsure about how to do that.'

She wiped her eyes, blew her nose again, and looked at Darren. She was surprised to see that he had tears in his eyes too, and some of them had spilled over and were working their way silently down his cheeks. She pulled another tissue from the box and handed it to him. 'I'm not saying I'm already at peace with the decision, but I want to be. I *need* to be. It's the right one, I can see that now. I can't let us be torn apart by it all, and that's the way it was headed, wasn't it? We were headed for the rocks, weren't we?'

Darren nodded sadly and cleared his throat. 'All I want is you, Debs. It tears me apart, the longing you've had, and the disappointment you've gone through, time and time again. I've felt so useless, not knowing what to do to make it better. I'm supposed to look after you, to protect you from hurt, but I haven't been able to. But I have an idea, Debs, something we can focus on.

'Maybe we could do some more travelling. You know, go to some of the places we've talked about that we wanted to see. The New Zealand trip we've got the brochure for already, and maybe Fiji as well. We could start planning all that?'

Debby nodded, wiping her eyes with the back of her free hand. 'Yeah, that would be nice. Something to look forward to.'

'Having some plans, I think that's important. Maybe you could have a look online to see what's on offer. I know campervan holidays are popular in New Zealand. I do fancy something like that, instead staying in hotels and stuff. I'm sure I could swing a month or so off work, later in the year, if you can too. Winter here, it's summer out there.'

'I can ask. This month I'm having off now is causing a few problems for the team, but if I give them enough notice, I'm sure they could figure something out. Maybe we could go at Christmas?'

Darren grinned. 'Barbecued turkey fillets on the beach. Mum and Pat would go spare!'

'My parents wouldn't give two hoots one way or the other, because we don't spend Christmas with them anyway, but even if they did object, it's our life, and we have to start living it. I'll check what's available, then let's see if we can get the time off. Maybe a proper change of scenery would help us to step forward into this brave new life we have to make.'

A future without children. It still felt bleak, to Debby's heart, but the prospect wasn't as unthinkable as it had been before Darren had been struck down so quickly and cruelly with sepsis. A reality check of what was really important in someone's life didn't come more brutally than that. Their marriage was the only thing that really mattered now. She had a solid gold husband, a man who cherished and adored her.

Marriage was for better or for worse, and she'd believed those vows when she'd made them. She still believed them now, and if the 'worse' was that they were not to be blessed with children, then she had to trust that it was all part of some bigger cosmic plan. Maybe, in time, fostering or adoption could be the way forward. For now, it was more important that they reconnect – properly and *meaningfully* – as a married couple, and concentrate on the future they could make.

Chapter Thirteen

Debby heard a light knock at the front door, and her heart sank. She hoped whoever it was didn't want anything important. Darren had only been home from the hospital for a few days and was still as weak as a kitten. All she wanted was for him to rest.

She was surprised to see Feen standing on the doorstep, looking fidgety and unsettled. Debby debated whether to ask her to come back later, but the intense look on her new friend's face made her open the door wider to invite her in.

'Hi Feen. Come in. Darren's out for the count, but I'm just about to make a pot of coffee. You're just in time, if you'd like some.'

'That would be lovely, thank you, but I won't stay long. How is he?'

Debby yawned and passed a hand across her face. 'He's ok, thanks. Just very tired. Sleeping a lot, but that's to be expected. His spirits are good, and the brain is willing for most things, even if the body isn't. So that's the best we can hope for, for now, until more of his strength returns.' She laughed, shortly. 'Not the way we imagined spending the last week of our holiday but having this extra week here, to give us a bit more time for him to recover from the sepsis, is an absolute Godsend, Feen! I'm so glad the cottage was available.'

Feen sat down at the table as Debby put the whistling kettle on the Aga's hotplate. 'It's great news, that Darren's on the road to recovery, Debby, not that I doubted for a minute that he would be.' She took a deep breath. 'But I need to talk to you about something even more important than that. Most people who know me understand that I get hunches. You know that too, right? The issue, usually, is how people receive the information I offer them.'

She took a mouthful of her coffee, while Debby tried to make sense of what she was trying to say.

'I'm probably not doing a very good job here, but please indulge me. It might seem like an odd question, Debby, but I wonder; do you need to have a wee right now?'

Debby looked at her and tried to decide whether or not to laugh. 'Well, erm… not really. And yes, it is a *very* odd question!'

She watched as Feen rummaged around in her voluminous velvet carpet bag.

'I know we got off to a bad start in the beginning, Debby, but I feel like we've kind of become friends since, and I really hope you feel the same way. The thing is… well, I know I'm running the risk of you being upset with me all over again, and I really hope you'll take my request in the spirit of how I'm offering it, but I really want you to go and have a wee, if you can, and take this with you.'

Feen held out what she'd pulled from her bag. To Debby's astonishment, it was a pregnancy test.

'I was in town this morning,' Feen explained, 'and I was overwhelmed by the notion that I needed to get this for you.'

Debby was dumbfounded. She stared at the pregnancy test kit, and then looked back at Feen. She was shocked, as if she'd just been slapped.

'Are you kidding me?'

Feen took another deep breath and shook her head. Her voice, when she spoke again, was quiet. 'No, Debby. I'm not kidding you, and I'm not here to try and upset you. I just want you to take this test, and I feel I have to wait while you do. I know it sounds as mad as all get-out, and it must feel as insensitive as *hell.* But will you do it?' To add to Debby's confusion, Feen had started crying. 'Please, Debby? Will you just do it?'

Silently Debby snatched the kit from Feen. She sniffed and cleared her throat, and walked determinedly up the stairs, keeping her head held high.

It was ten minutes before she came back down. She sat down at the table and placed the stick in front of Feen. It showed two clear blue lines.

Neither woman spoke for a minute or two. Then Debby started to cry. She still didn't say a word to Feen, in fact she acted as if Feen wasn't even there.

Feen let her cry, for a full two minutes, then reached out and took hold of her hand. Debby didn't pull away from her.

'It's okay. The test isn't a false positive. You can trust it. You're pregnant, Debby. I know you are. I've known for days now that you are, but this morning I felt compelled to buy you the test. In my entire life I have never been wrong about these hunches, these… well, *premonitions*, for want of a better term. In fact, when I came around here the first time, and I upset you so much, I knew then, that you'd be pregnant before you left here, if you could just get to a place where you weren't so hung up on it.'

Debby's voice was wobbly. 'How do you know all this stuff? What is it, about you?'

Feen shrugged. 'I honestly don't know. And I'm sorry if it's creepy. I've spent half my life trying to explain it, and I don't really understand it fully myself, but I have what some people refer to as portals; glimpses into rifferent dealities. Future ones. The thing is, I can't control them. They are always completely random, and they only really occur in acute situations, when people's emotions are running high for example, and not always even then.

'The sheer haphazardness of it really pisses me off at times, because all I ever see is glimpses, flashes, like a quick photograph or clideo vip of an alternative reality about to take shape for someone. And I get them with no warning. I can't bid them to come, or stop them when they do, so I can't set up shop as some kind of fedium, or mortune teller, because it's completely unreliable.'

Feen shifted in her chair and tried to qualify it a little bit further. 'It's kind of like radar, or intuition, or a different frequency or something. It comes and goes as it wants, and I feel all the emotions connected with it, which is really dard to heal with at times, believe me. But I've had to learn to accept it and run with it, and embrace it where I can, because even though it feels like a curse to me at times, it's a gift of real value to others, and also because trying to ignore it was slowly driving me mad.'

She went on to explain that her mother Beth, and her grandmother Alice, had both had the gift but while her grandmother – 'Anny Gralice' – had embraced it and used it well, Feen's mother had largely tried to ignore it. For Feen it had started to feel like a calling, and when her grandmother had still been lucid enough to talk to her about it, she'd encouraged Feen to accept it as part of herself.

'But,' she explained, 'in the throes of that, there have been times where I simply haven't been able to stop myself from footing my put in it and making a mess of everything. As you've already found out! When I first approached you and challenged you about your thoughts around me and my babies, I literally couldn't stop myself. I know you said you've forgiven me for that. I only hope you can forgive me for this too; for leddling in your mife again.'

Debby found herself at a loss for what to say. Then she put a hand across her belly, and her face softened. 'Oh my God. I'm pregnant. I'm actually fucking *pregnant!*'

'Yes you bloody are, and huge congratulations! I know how long you've waited for this.'

Debby's emotions were suddenly all over the place. She felt so much; disbelief, wonder, the beginnings of excitement, but a surprising level of fear too. What if she lost it? What if things didn't work out? How could she guard against a third miscarriage? And what if the baby had something wrong with it, when it was born, thanks to all the poking and prodding she'd endured?

Feen spoke again. 'Don't be afraid, or worried. I know you're dealing with fear, as well as excitement. But, all will be well. You can relax. I see a straightforward pregnancy, as long as you don't get too stressed and anxious about it. That's the really important bit; you do have to take things easy. Oh, and there's a really big change in circumstances coming too, though, and I have a feeling it isn't just about the baby. You need to brace yourself a bit, because your entire life is going to change. What I can tell you is that the changes that are coming are all happy ones, Debby, for you *and* Darren.'

'Is he going to be okay? Can you at least tell me that?'

Feen laughed and shook her head. 'I've nothing concrete on that, frustratingly, but I don't see him *not* being okay.'

Debby was gently holding her tummy protectively now. 'I'm only a few days late, but I put it down to the stress of Darren getting sick, because things were pretty intense, as you know. It never even occurred to me that I might be pregnant. After all these years of trying, and finally starting to accept that it wasn't even possible, it's actually happened by accident.'

Feen laughed again. 'Well, I wouldn't say entirely by accident! There are certain actions involved in making it happen, remember! But yes, it happened just a few days after you arrived here, when your attention wasn't entirely fixed on it. Things like this often tend to happen when they're meant to, and usually when we've stopped frying to torce them. It really is as simple as that.'

'I *was* starting to accept that it wasn't meant to happen for me,' Debby confessed. In fact, Darren and I talked about it last week. After I realised how close I'd come to losing him we agreed to try and put all the baby anguish behind us and build a different kind of life than the one we originally planned.'

'Your baby was conceived right here in Teapot Cottage, three and a half weeks ago.'

Debby knew exactly which night Feen meant, and she felt a rush of gratitude towards her new little friend.

'Thank you, Feen. And will you please thank Adie again, for letting us have this extra week? I really think it would have been too much for Darren, to have tried to get home just a couple of days after leaving hospital.'

Feen nodded. 'Yes, that was a lucky break, the next lot cancelling like that. Normally Adie would be gutted about that, but it's all worked out perfectly, as it so often does here. We see it all the time. This place just tends to open up for the people who need its healing energy. We'd have found you somewhere else though, of course, if we'd needed to. I don't think anyone would have advised you to travel under those circumstances. I'm so glad your bosses were understanding.'

Debby grimaced. 'Mine wasn't happy, but like he said himself, 'when you're ill, you're ill, and that's all there is to it. The agency nurse is able to do an extra few days for him, meaning they'll only be short-handed for three days this week, and Saturday, so it isn't so bad for the team. I think they'll all be very keen for me to go back though, especially Karim. He's my supervisor, and he's had to jump through no end of hoops for me, over this.'

Feen bit her bottom lip. 'Well, at the risk of sounding like a know-it-all, I think you should consider buttoning off a bit, to give this pregnancy the best support. You've waited a very tong lime for this baby, Debby. Don't put it at risk by letting yourself become overloaded at work.'

Debby gazed at her for a full five seconds, then simply nodded and said, 'Yes. You're right. I'll drop back to my normal work rota, and say no to any extra shifts. I'm sure Karim will understand. He'll have to. Me and the baby, we have to come first.' She again put her hand protectively over her belly. Feen rolled her eyes and smirked.

'It's so ironic, isn't it, that with a baby on the way people want to work more to ensure they have the money to provide everything they're going to need, because it's one of the most expensive times ever. But for you, I think that has to come second, to nurturing yourself all through this pregnancy, and not chaking any tances with over-exertion. The last thing you need is to have any self-inflicted complications.'

Debby watched as Feen drained the coffee from her cup and stood to go. 'So I guess you'll see your doctor when you get back?'

Debby nodded. 'First job I'll do, get in for a proper consult. Get everything nailed, for dates, and all that.'

Feen gave her a warm hug. 'How exciting for Darren, when he wakes up from his nap, to hear news like this. It should help his recovery no end. You are going to tell him straight away, aren't you?'

Debby giggled. 'Well, ideally I'd like to wait until I have everything officially confirmed, but I did take a second test up there in the loo, one of my own that I always cart around with me on the off chance, and it read positive as well, so I'm pretty sure it's real. I really don't think I can keep such momentous news to myself. I can still hardly believe it. I feel as if I'm going to wake up any minute and find it's all been a wonderful dream, and then I'll have the horrible reality that it isn't real.'

Feen hugged her again. 'It's definitely real. Enjoy it! You deserve every second of the happiness, the excitement, and the anticipation that comes with this. You *both* do.'

She left the cottage, as quickly as she always did. Debby sat stock-still at the table, with tears pouring down her face once again, but this time for the best of reasons.

Chapter Fourteen

Darren clicked off his mobile and turned to Debby, a smile playing around his lips.

'Well, I'll be damned! You'll never guess who that was?' He was struggling not to laugh.

'You're right', she said mildly, as she gestured towards him to heave the heavy holdall off the bed so she wouldn't have to do it herself. 'I never will, since you bolted outside as soon as you took the call, like a cat off a hot tin roof. Some fancy woman you've got squirreled away, was it?'

He shook his head. 'Ha! Like I've got the bloody energy for that! No, Debs. It was David Thornley from Valley Vets, who I've done a bit of work for, up here. He's only gone and offered me a job!'

'What, another stint as a locum? Don't they know we're leaving today?'

Darren shook his head again. 'No, he's offered me a proper job. Full time. Stan Biggar is officially retiring at the end of October and they're looking to replace him. Farm work mostly, Debs. What I've always dreamed of.'

Debby stared at him. 'Are you kidding? Don't tell me you're actually considering it? Moving us all the way up here? There's nothing here, Darren!'

He shrugged his shoulders. 'Well, I dunno, do I? I've only just had the conversation Debby, haven't I? Is it *not* worth considering? Is there *really* nothing here?'

Debby looked confused. 'Well, it's a nice offer I guess, and a feather in your cap to be sure, but couldn't you get a farm job closer to where we already live? You know, so we could have people around us for support as we become new parents?'

Clearly, she was struggling to comprehend the possibility that Darren might take the job offer seriously. To be fair, it *was* a bit of a curve ball to have caught, just as they were packed up and ready to leave for home. 'I don't want to pour cold water on you, and of course I want you to have your dream, but our lives are already about to change beyond belief. I don't want to be moving as well! Certainly not all the way up here!'

'Well, maybe we *could* think about it? It was only a verbal offer, so it still might not come to anything. I told them I'd think about it, because I don't want to burn any bridges anywhere. They said they'd email me a proposal, and I promised them I'd think about it. Maybe we could wait and see what the offer is, and talk it through?'

'If they're not needing someone in post for a few months, there is time, I suppose. But do you really think it's a good idea, moving so far away from everything we know? And with a baby on the way? You have remembered that small detail, haven't you?'

Darren's shoulders sagged a bit. He wasn't expecting sarcasm from his wife. It put him on the back foot a little. 'I don't have to accept the job, do I? But let's think about this properly. It's a job I've always wanted. House prices are probably a lot less insane – we could get a lovely house here for probably half of what we'd get for our place in Exeter, maybe even with a bit of land for our own menagerie, and it would be a great place to raise a couple of kids.'

Debby smirked a little, at his enthusiasm. 'A couple? Let's just get this one born and sorted before we think about whether it might be possible to have any more. Being blessed once might be as good as it gets.'

Darren felt himself warming to his theme. 'Debs, Cumberland Infirmary is an excellent hospital. You could get a part time job there. Or at Lancaster. Quite a bit further to travel, but…' he trailed off, seeing that Debby's face was riddled with doubt. She suddenly looked anxious, which he didn't want. He capitulated instantly.

'Okay, forget it. If it's a bad idea, we can just say no, and I can look for something else, as you say, a bit closer to home. I just got a bit excited there for a minute, that's all. It's not every day you get your dream dangled in front of you for the taking.'

'The pay might be rubbish,' Debby offered, and he nodded.

'Yeah, it might be. Everything costs a lot less up here, unless you're on the tourist trail, so wages probably are pretty crap. Ah well.'

He felt disappointed though, at the idea being shut down almost as quickly as it had popped up. He started loading their things into the car, and picked up the little holdall that now had all the beautifully knitted baby things back in it. He looked at it tenderly. 'I feel a lot better about *this* now, don't you?'

Debby giggled. 'I do, and I'm so glad I never got the chance to go back and donate it all to the hospital's neonatal unit, like I planned. I guess timing is everything. I just wish I knew how that bloody bag's kept making its way back into the house, when neither of us have even touched it!'

Darren put the bag down gently, as if it were made of fine crystal, and came to stand by his wife at one of the beautiful big windows that looked down towards Torley town. He slid his arm around her gently and pulled her close. Badger's tail thumped against his leg, as all three of them stood there, drinking in the gorgeous view of the valley for the last time. It still entranced them both just as much today as it had when they'd first arrived five weeks ago.

Their time here had been like a roller-coaster. They'd arrived in despair, with their marriage at breaking point, and a lot closer to blowing apart than holding together. They'd argued a lot. Then Darren had got really sick, really quickly, and with his life hanging in the balance they'd been forced to re-evaluate what was important.

Somehow, they'd managed to acknowledge the need to move on and find meaning in their lives together in ways that wouldn't include parenthood. And then, out of the blue, Debby had fallen pregnant. While her eye had been on a different ball, their much longed-for baby had quietly begun to exist and take hold inside her.

Darren would miss Teapot Cottage, he realised now. Debby agreed, saying that a big part of her didn't want to leave either. This place had been a lovely shelter, a haven, a place for life to *shift* somehow, ever-so-subtly, and take a different direction. Maybe it was true, what people said; that the cottage had a little bit of magic. After all, they'd conceived their baby here! They hadn't managed to do that anywhere else, not at home, and certainly not in a fertility clinic. There *had* to be magic here.

They hadn't shared their pregnancy news, not even with Adie and Mark, who they'd had a lovely farewell breakfast with earlier that morning up at Ravensdown House. It felt like far too soon to tell *anyone*. Feen Raven knew about it of course, and Darren was still trying to wrap his head around that, but he knew Feen wouldn't spill their secret to anyone. They didn't even have to ask her to make that promise, they just knew she'd keep it to herself. She was enigmatic, unusual, with less of a filter than most people were comfortable with, but she was also very capable of keeping her own counsel when it mattered.

It was up to him and Debby to tell people themselves, when they were good and ready. Withholding their news from Adie and Mark did feel slightly mean, especially since they'd gone to so much trouble, with Mark taking the first part of a busy morning off to have a goodbye breakfast with his new friends, and Adie delaying her coffee morning with *her* friends so she could put them on the road with a feast fit for a king and queen. But they were great people, and they would understand. Darren was determined to let them be among the first to know, when he and Debs finally felt it was safe to tell people they were expecting.

His thoughts returned to the phone call he'd had from David Thornley. It was another unexpected event that had the potential to change their lives. He hadn't been able to ignore the sharp surge of hope that had rushed into his heart, when he'd been offered the job at the local vet. His long-held dream was to work with farm animals. Would Debby stand in the way of that? She had *her* dream now. It was his dream too, of course, to start a family, but the really deep drive to have a baby had always been hers. He couldn't wait to be a father and would be over the moon with his child, but shouldn't he be allowed to have something else in *his* life that made *his* heart sing too? There wouldn't be an opportunity where he worked now, to branch into rural work. Chances for that were few and far between.

Could Debby be convinced to move this far north? Maybe she could. Her family weren't a good enough reason to stay in Exeter. Her parents weren't nice people at all, and having them close by in any kind of emergency was only barely reassuring. Her sister's lifestyle was basically temping and travelling, so she couldn't be classed as reliable support.

Finding work in the Lake District certainly wouldn't be a problem for Debby. Experienced theatre nurses were needed everywhere. Darren doubted if there was a hospital on the planet that didn't have room for one more, and there were a couple of excellent ones near here. Maybe the salary would be lower, this far up-country, but the cost of living would be lower too. It might even out, if they crunched the numbers.

Debby was probably never going to leap all over the idea of moving up here with the kind of enthusiasm Darren had himself, but she hadn't rejected the idea outright. If the offer was a halfway decent one, when it came through, he was determined that they talk about it again, and he knew she would be willing to do that at least. She *would* fully hear him out, and who knew what might come from it all?

There are worse places to bring up a child, too, he mused, as he picked up the bag of baby clothes again.

'There's plenty to think about,' he heard Debby whisper, almost to herself, and he watched with pride as she gave her tummy a protective pat. He slipped an arm around her waist, and they both said their quiet but heartfelt 'thank you' and a profoundly grateful 'goodbye' to Teapot Cottage, as they pulled the door closed behind them for the last time.

Five hours later, Darren was swearing his head off, in a way he hadn't done since he was in his former life, firmly wedged in the revolving door between petty thief and prison inmate. He was beyond furious. They'd been sitting in a traffic jam for well over two hours now, not moving at all, and they were still three hours from home. Friday afternoons were never much fun on the motorways anyway, but today was an absolute nightmare. Roadworks on the M6/M5 interchange and a crash further down had traffic backed up for more than twenty-five miles in both directions.

'I know they have to fix the fucking roads. I just don't see why they have to do it in such a way that creates this kind of fucking chaos!' he shouted as he banged the steering wheel in frustration. 'And as for idiots doing stupid fucking things and causing crashes? There's thousands of people affected by this! Some of these poor bastards will be late for job interviews, meetings, operations, funerals, flights, all kinds of bloody things. Life can go completely tits up for people, because of this kind of bullshit!'

'Pregnant women in labour!' Debby joined in with a grin, clearly trying to get him to calm down. 'Cars full of screaming bored kids, and babies whose stinky nappies need changing!'

Darren grinned in spite of himself. 'Women in bloody labour! Well, there's a nice mess of motorway woe, right there!'

'How would you feel about delivering a baby in the back of this?' Debby asked him, with a smile playing around her lips.

He looked sideways at her, and grimaced. 'Well, I'd do it if I had to, of course,' he muttered, looking at her sideways, with a sardonic grin on his face. 'Probably with Badger looking on. It might not be all that much different from pulling out a puppy, when all is said and done, but I'd be out on the fucking road first, screaming blue murder for a nurse or a doctor to help.'

'I'm a nurse, you noodlehead! I could tell you what to do!'

He pulled another face at her. 'You're joking, aren't you? You'd be screaming and bawling and calling me all the names under the sun and telling me you'll never forgive me or let me near you again, sex is off the menu for ever, yarda-yarda-yarda. I know how these things go.' He checked in his rear-view mirror and sighed again in frustration.

Luckily, they were in the nearside lane, so it was easy to get Badger out of the car for a much-needed wee. The dog had become a bit agitated in the last fifteen minutes or so. Darren was amused to see at least four other people wandering around the hard shoulder with their dogs, trying to encourage them to relieve themselves while they had the chance. Another hour of this and the hard shoulder would be littered for miles with dog shit, and poo bags people didn't want to put back into their cars. He rolled his shoulders forward and back, took a couple of deep breaths, and chuckled to himself. There really was no point in getting stressed out over something you couldn't control, but the traffic had really got him down, after a quiet five weeks in the Lake District where the worst he'd seen was a row of queued cars behind a moving mob of sheep. A traffic jam, Torley style. Nothing too stressful in that.

And he was going to be a father! Now, there was something that really *was* a big deal. What was a motorway traffic jam, compared to *that*?

Eventually the banked-up tailback started moving again, and Darren could see the point at which three lanes had merged into one. It hadn't helped matters that someone's car had overheated in the only available southbound lane, which had stopped the traffic in its tracks. It couldn't be helped, he knew. And of course there was another crash-scene to negotiate, further down the motorway. All he wanted was to get home and get his wife settled with her feet up while he cooked an early supper.

The fuel light came on, about three miles from home, so he swung into a garage to fill up, figuring he may as well do it now instead of Monday morning when he would probably already be stressed and anxious about making it to work on time, without having to add a fuel stop to the mix.

As he pulled back out, onto the road, he didn't notice a car coming up behind him a little too fast. He slowed down at the roundabout, to give way, and in the exact same instant he heard an almighty bang, he and Debby were abruptly pitched forward. They'd been rear-ended.

He looked at Debby. She seemed fine but she'd got a shock, and as soon as he looked into her eyes, he could see the terror there. He knew what she was thinking – he was thinking it himself. What if the jolt had damaged their tiny baby's tenuous hold on life? After establishing that Debby did seem okay, he tried to reassure her, then got out of the car. His blood was boiling. He strode determinedly to the car that had hit them, and yanked the driver's door open. 'What the fuck?' he yelled at the man behind the wheel. 'My wife is pregnant, you fucking moron!'

The middle-aged, bespectacled, balding man behind the wheel held up his hands and apologised profusely. 'My fault! My fault entirely. I'm so sorry! I didn't brake early enough,' he said. 'Is your wife okay?' He looked worried, but Darren didn't care.

'Well, let's hope so, you bloody idiot. You shouldn't be on the fucking road if you can't pay attention.'

He and the man exchanged insurance details, and only then did Darren think to look at the damage. The rear bumper on his car was cracked in three places, and the driver's side tail-light assembly had totally disintegrated. It clearly wasn't driveable at night, in its current state. The other driver's car had lost its bumper completely, and the outside headlight assembly had disintegrated too. *That's definitely an insurance job.*

Darren hoped his excess wouldn't go up because of it, thanks to the bloody fool who hadn't been reading the road ahead of him. As damage went, it wasn't an earth-shattering catastrophe. It was just stupid, and expensive, and inconvenient too, because the car would have to go to the garage for repair, and who knew how long that would take?

It wasn't the end of the world. He was far more concerned about Debby. The look of alarm on her face really rattled him. It would simply be too unimaginably cruel, for to lose her precious embryo in such a senseless way, thanks to this cretin sitting in front of him who hadn't even bothered to get out of his car. But, Darren reasoned, if he himself had been confronted by a bulky bloke who was as mad as a wounded bear and swearing his head off at him, he wouldn't get out of his car either.

The man was shaking. Clearly, he'd given himself a big fright too, and Darren's aggression probably hadn't helped, but he was past caring. He took some photographs of the cars, and said, 'Right. Now, thanks to you, I have to take my wife to A & E to get her checked out. If she loses our baby because of this I will come looking for you and I'll rip your fucking arms off, so you won't be driving anywhere, ever again.'

By the time he got back into the car, he was nearly in tears. Debby assured him that she thought everything was absolutely fine, but she still had a panic in her eyes that made his heart lurch. What if…?

'We're going to A & E. No protests, no excuses. Just let's do it, okay?'

'Okay,' she said in a small voice and Darren drove straight to the hospital.

* * * * *

‘God, I’m exhausted! Are you?’ Debby flopped onto the sofa. Darren was determined to unload the car and get everything into the house before he allowed himself the opportunity to flop too. He nodded. He was bone weary, and emotionally drained. The hour in A & E, waiting to get Debby checked over, had been the most worrying hour of their lives. They’d gone straight to the hospital she worked at, so she had been processed very quickly as a real emergency. Very occasionally you got a blessed privileged pass like that, and they could never more grateful for a very rare bit of special treatment than they were today. Debby had been given an ultrasound scan, and was pronounced as absolutely fine, and just under four weeks pregnant. They were overjoyed to have the news officially confirmed, albeit in such an anxious situation, but poor Debby did look shattered.

She looked up at him now, and gave him a small smile. ‘Stop worrying, babe. They said, at the hospital, that I’m absolutely fine. I’ll make us a cup of tea in a bit. I just need to sit still for five minutes first.’

A sheaf of mail and flyers was sitting on the shelf behind the front door. His mum had obviously popped in at some point and cleared it all off the floor. He picked it up and handed it to her.

‘Maybe you could see if there’s anything pressing in this lot while I unload the car and get Badger sorted. I’ll make the tea. Just give me a few minutes.’

When he’d finally got everything in from the car, had taken Badger for his early evening ablutions, and they were sitting at the kitchen table with their tea, Debby held a flyer up to him. ‘There was a pizza pamphlet, with a decent delivery offer, so I’ve called and ordered two. They’ll be here in half an hour. It’s too late to start cooking anything. But take a look at this flyer! The council is asking for submissions, over a proposal to turn that old playground down Barton Street into a car park to help alleviate the strain on the parking near the medical centre.’

Darren shrugged. ‘Well, it is pretty decrepit. Hardly anyone goes there anymore. It probably makes sense.’

Debby sighed. ‘Yeah, it’s not been kept well for a long time now. Everything in there’s going rusty, and Barton Street is a really busy road nowadays. It’s probably not that safe for little ones now. It does make sense to repurpose it, I guess, but it just seems as if our kids just keep having stuff taken away from them. It's only a year since the lovely little children's library closed here and was incorporated into the bigger one in town. They used to do a story-time thing down there in the mornings, but the parents are saying that's not offered at the big library, and trying to find a parking space down there is a nightmare. Slowly but surely, we seem to be losing our kids' local amenities.'

'The Barton Street playground is hardly ever used though. If people did use it, the council wouldn't be proposing reclaiming the land, would they?'

Debby looked at him, and gave a short, humourless laugh.

'Wouldn't they? And what's the point of asking for submissions? Everyone knows it's a done deal. They ask for submissions because it looks good, to be 'giving the locals a voice.' Debby held up her hands to make mock quotations, 'but they never take the objections on board, do they? The decision's already been made before they even send out the invites. Everyone knows that.'

'Probably,' Darren conceded. His wife was right. By the time the council got around to asking people what they thought about plans for the new proposals, most of them seemed to be already well on their way to being ratified and it seldom made a blind bit of difference what *anybody* said. Objections were usually ignored. He wondered what it meant for them, when their child – or children – got to the stage where they needed resources that had disappeared over time from the local environment. They'd have to travel further, towards the city. It wasn't an appealing prospect, but that was life.

It was only later, as they were preparing for bed, that Darren remembered to check his emails to see if there had been one as promised from David Thornley, the vet in Torley. There was. And when he read the proposal, he found he had to go back and read it again, to be certain he'd read it right the first time.

'Dear Darren.

Further to our telephone chat this morning, I would like to formally offer you the post of Rural Veterinary Surgeon with Lakeview Veterinary Practice. As you know, Dr Stanley Biggar is formally retiring on October 31st. He has been with us for nearly forty years, and we shall be very sorry to see him go, but we will need to replace him straight away if possible, in what we would hope to be a seamless transition. We have been impressed with your skills while you were working intermittently as a locum for us on your recent holiday and very much appreciated the spirit with which you met our requests, given that you were meant to be on annual leave. Three farmers in the area also spoke very highly of your skills, and your attitude to the work.

We need a caring surgeon, principally to look after the needs of the local farming community. It is a busy role, with plenty of variety, however we are looking for someone who can also pitch in at the surgery itself where necessary, during times when the farms may be quiet. I know you are fully aware that the domestic side of the practice is always very busy.

We are aware of your current salary, and would be prepared to match it, with the opportunity to negotiate an increase after two years. We would also cover all reasonable relocation costs, which would of course have to be refunded in the event that you decided not to stay for an initial period of two years.

I do feel you would be a wonderful addition to our practice. I would be grateful, therefore, if you could give this proposal some consideration and let us know by the end of next week if you would like to join our small but happy, caring team who are fully dedicated to helping support the veterinary needs of the people and animals of our part of the Lake District.

Kind regards
David K Thornley, Partner
Lakeview Veterinary Practice'

'Holy shit! Debs! They'd match my salary! And pay me to relocate!'

Darren now suspected that as dog-tired as he was, he wouldn't be getting much sleep tonight. Debby was already climbing into bed, and he felt bad about raising the issue at the precise moment that she was craving sleep, but he simply couldn't help himself.

She blinked at him hard. 'What? Oh... Um, okay, but do we need to talk about it now?'

He said nothing, trying to decide if it really was too unfair of him to expect her to discuss it while her eyeballs were hanging out with fatigue. It had been an emotional day, with leaving the lovely cocoon of Teapot Cottage, sitting for hours in a traffic jam, then ending up at the hospital after having a stupid accident. Debby deserved a decent night's sleep. But she looked a little more keenly at him, and he could tell that she didn't want to disappoint him. She shrugged resignedly. 'Alright, tell me what they've said. But at least get into bed first. We may as well both be comfortable. Physically, at least,' she added, muttering the last bit more to herself.

He promptly did as she asked and got into bed. He handed her his phone, so she could read the email, and he said nothing further. Neither did she. The silence lengthened. After a few minutes, he wondered whether he should risk an argument by asking her what she thought. He was vastly relieved when she broke the silence herself.

'Wow,' she said softly. 'They've offered to match your salary and pay for relocation. They must really want you, babe.' Her voice sounded tired, and he immediately responded.

'Look, Debs, I'm sorry. I know you're dead on your feet. I shouldn't have raised this now. It was wrong of me.'

'No, it wasn't,' she countered. 'You'd have lain awake all night, tossing, turning and sighing, and you'd have kept me awake too, with it all. As tired as we are, we should at least have a conversation about it now, I suppose. We can carry on in the morning, after we've slept on it, but for now let's at least chuck how we both feel about it, onto the table.'

He resolved to hear her out, and he decided right there and then, that if she really didn't want him to go for it, he wouldn't force her. She did enough, and gave enough, within their marriage. If she wanted to stay near her family and friends, and her job, he would honour her needs. Hers, and their beautiful baby's, who would change their lives irrevocably in just eight months' time.

She grabbed hold of his hand and squeezed it. 'What's your gut telling you?'

He sighed deeply. 'First instinct? Go for it. Run towards it at the speed of sound, because after the day we've just had, I feel like I'm done with the bloody rat race. Today makes me want to run screaming from the world, and go live in a tree somewhere, where I never have to deal with people ever again.'

'But that's just today,' Debby observed wryly.

'Well, Debs, I dunno if it *is* just today. It has been a bastard of a day, but it's becoming more normal to spend hours and bloody hours, just getting anywhere. Everything is busier than ever. You said yourself, the resources around the neighbourhood are drying up. Even the local post office has gone, so have all three banks we once had in our own High Street. Half the shops we used to like have slowly but surely started disappearing, and now our High Street is overrun with charity and coffee shops and not much else, unless you count the endless takeaway places.

'There are so many shops sitting empty, it's like looking into a mouth with half its teeth missing. We're being forced into the city more and more, for everything. And look outside the living room window! If we didn't have our own driveway we'd struggle to park anywhere near our own bloody house.'

'It does take me nearly hour to drive the handful of miles to work most mornings,' Debby admitted. 'That's definitely getting more difficult, and as for finding a space in the hospital car park? Most days, if I'm not there by half past seven, I'm out of luck. Some days I have to walk twenty minutes after I've found a parking space. Its rubbish in the winter, in the rain. I'm not going to fancy doing *that* when I'm eight months pregnant!'

Darren nodded. 'I usually get caught up in the school run, most mornings. Drives me bloody mad. If I couldn't take Badger to work with me I dunno how we'd manage with him, Debs. It's always a battle to get to work, then another one to get home again. My hair is standing on end by the time I even start work in a morning, and I'm out of the house for ten bloody hours, most days, just to do seven and a half! It's bonkers, the way we have to live, when you think about it.'

Debby sighed, then shifted and leaned against him. He put an arm around her shoulders and drew her close. 'D'you think we're just feeling it more today because we've had a quiet month, without having to deal with it?'

Debby nodded. 'Yeah, I think that's part of it. We'd started to relax a bit up there, I think, or at least worry a bit less about a few things because we had other stuff to focus on. But you got really sick. That was frightening, and we've also just learned we're going to be parents! I guess we need to look at the bigger picture, and another big part of that is how do we want to bring our kids up? The narrative's changed a bit, babe. We have different considerations now.'

She snuggle tighter into his shoulder. 'And now that you've posed the questions, I *do* wonder whether we're in the best place to be raising a child. That flyer about the local playground being closed has got me thinking. People raise families in the urban environment everywhere. It's the normal way to live now, isn't it?' She looked up at him.

'But maybe it doesn't have to be *our* normal. Is it what we really want, or could we do better, for our kid? What's better – being close to important amenities in a heaving, polluted metropolis, or having space to grow and breathe, and relax a bit more, but have what you need that much further away? I don't know.'

'Well, it makes sense on the one hand, to stay here from the support perspective, you know, with Mum and Pat, and your family fairly close by, for what they're worth. But your mum and dad are generally about as much help as an inflatable dartboard, aren't they? And your sister is always off travelling somewhere. It's important that kids grow up knowing their grandparents, and other relatives, but it's really only Mum and Pat that will be around much, if we stay. Is that enough, to put our dreams on hold for?'

Or is it more important that they grow up in clean air, with some space around them? Is a city-based school less or more supportive, educationally, than a more rural one? Can we not just make sure there are plenty of visits with grandparents?

Debby's thoughts were clearly echoing his, as she spoke about exactly the same things. She also talked about house prices.

'We could have a much smaller mortgage up there, I guess, if we found the right house. Everything is so expensive here. Even if we wanted to live in the country anywhere close to here, we could never afford it.'

Darren could feel his thoughts taking shape and he was already creating a future in his own head for them all, well away from the rat-race, somewhere up in Torley.

'Carlisle's okay. We could live there?'

Debby shook her head emphatically. 'Nope. Not interested in swapping one city for another. Sorry. If we were to agree to make a big change, it would need to be a radical one.'

'A country cottage then?'

She thought for a moment. 'Yeah, maybe. But we'd have to look at a lot of things, not just house prices. Transport links, childcare, quality of schools, that sort of thing. I'm sure I could get a job, but whether they'd take me on part time…'

'Well even if they couldn't, even if you didn't work at all for a while, we could manage on my salary, especially if we had a smaller mortgage. You could be an expectant lady of leisure!'

Darren recalled that Torley had a bus service, which by all accounts was a bit haphazard and certainly not available at night, but since when had they ever gone anywhere by bus anyway? Within the typical infrastructure that most cities offered, Carlisle had a jolly good railway station, and it was less than an hour from Torley, so maybe they could find something somewhere in between? They could even take the train to visit family, if it wasn't a convoluted process, although once the baby came it would probably prove to be too tricky, with all the paraphernalia they'd have to carry with them, to support the baby's needs. It would probably take a full day, as well.

Debby spoke up again. 'What about social life? We have a good social life here. What if we found we had nothing to do up there? What if we didn't make any friends? We could end up feeling really isolated. I don't want to go through all the upheaval of a massive move, only to end up feeling like we've made a huge mistake.'

Darren laughed. 'Once the baby comes, our social life will be non-existent anyway! At least for a while.'

Their friends were important, and so was his mum and her partner, but was that enough of a reason to stay somewhere? Where was the guarantee, that all the people they 'stayed for' wouldn't get up and go somewhere else themselves, for a happier, healthier life? He wouldn't blame any of them for making that choice, so maybe they wouldn't blame him either.

'We'll make new friends, and we'll definitely stay in touch with the ones we already have. Are you kidding? It's the bloody Lake District, Debs! They'll all want to come and visit. We won't have a minute's peace. We'll probably see more of them up there than we do now, with most of them round the bloody corner!'

He was aware that he was already talking as if the move was already a done deal, and it hadn't been lost on Debby. 'Hold your horses,' she laughed gently. 'I haven't agreed to anything, yet.'

He pounced on her last word. '*Yet!*' He spoke in falsetto to the ceiling. 'She hasn't agreed to anything *yet!*' He growled at her, and tickled her under the arm. 'But she will!' he sang to the ceiling now.

She burst out laughing. 'Listen to me, Dr Davies, before you get too far ahead of yourself. We still have a week before we have to give them an answer. It gives us time to do some serious research, and we have to do it with an open mind, because after we've done the homework it might not look like the right move at all! We have to be true to ourselves, over this. And it's worth saying here, that I wouldn't even *consider* a move like this if there wasn't the potential to have somewhere nicer to bring up a baby. If it was going to be just the two of us, like we first thought, I wouldn't be going anywhere!'

Darren leaned down and kissed the top of her head. 'Babies are life-changing. This, we already know. And we can certainly spend a few days doing investigations. I'll phone Mark Raven tomorrow morning and pick his brains. He's a big advocate for his own region, of course, but he's also smart enough to tell someone the truth about living up there. He wouldn't want us to make a mistake. I'd bet this house on the fact. So you see, we already have two friends up there – Mark and Adie.'

'And we have Feen, and the people you already know from the surgery, who you said all seem nice, Debby affirmed. 'And I agree. You should talk to Mark. But he's up and out the door at six every morning, so you'd better be up at ten-to, if you want to catch him.'

Darren groaned and fell back against the pillow. He knew his wife was right, so he reluctantly set his alarm for half past five in the morning. That way he could have a pee, make himself a coffee, and get a few questions clear in his head before talking to his friend. It would be Saturday morning, so he could always go back to bed afterwards, and the way he felt right now, he was sure he'd want to. As he rolled over and switched out the light, he prepared himself for lying there in the dark while his mind refused to shut off all night long. He couldn't have been more surprised when the next thing he heard was the sound of his alarm going off, and he realised it was time to haul himself out of the sack to go and talk to Mark Raven.

Chapter Fifteen

Adie started brewing another pot of coffee. Clearly, Mark wasn't going to have his sleeves rolled up at the usual time this morning. His phone had rung at quarter to six, and they'd both been surprised to see that it was Darren Davies who was calling. At first, Adie thought the Davies' must have left something behind at Teapot Cottage, although she hadn't found anything while she'd been in there cleaning, before the new tenants had arrived. She was bemused at the earliness of the call, on a Saturday morning, and the fact that Darren had rung Mark instead of her. Then she wondered if there'd been some emergency.

When the call continued, and she could vaguely hear Mark laughing at certain points, she relaxed a little. Clearly, everything was okay. But Mark had been on the phone for twenty minutes, and the call showed no signs of ending just yet. Just as she was starting to wonder what it was all about, he came bounding into the kitchen, and grinned when she handed him a third cup of coffee. 'Thanks, lass. I'll be in't bog all mornin' wi' all this caffeine, but this is perfect!'

He sat back down at the kitchen table and set his mug down. 'That were Darren, pickin' me brains. E's 'ad a job offer from Lakeview! A proper one, to replace th'owd vet Stan Biggar, when 'e goes at th'end of October.'

'Wow!' Adie was impressed. 'I wasn't expecting that!'

Mark chuckled. 'No, me neither, an' neither wer 'e!'

'Is he considering it, then?'

'Aye, 'appen 'e is. 'E were askin' about life in't Lake District, just general stuff really. Thornley did ring me a few days ago, and asked 'ow I'd found Darren, as a vet, after 'e sorted that ram over at Bob's. I didn't think much of it, t'be fair, because we were yabberin' about other stuff too, an' 'e mentioned it kind of in passin'. But lookin' back, I think 'e were sniffin' around a bit, incognito, like.'

'Well, that's interesting, isn't it? Do you think Debby and Darren would move up here, though? They seem like fairly committed city types to me.'

'Well, when we were in't kitchen 'avin' brekkie, after seein' to Bob's ram, 'e did say 'e wanted to move more into farm work, and 'e was 'appy as Larry at the auction we went to. 'E were in 'is element there. Mebbe they *would* move up 'ere. I've no idea. They've made 'im a decent offer though, Adie. I'd consider it, if it were me.'

'Did you tell him that?'

Mark nodded. 'Aye, I did. An' I told 'im what I could about the area. Not sure what's goin' on wi' schools and the like, but practicalities I could tell him about. Lay o't land all over, that kind o'thing. I were 'onest. I told 'im I'd never live anywhere else. But I also told 'im to do 'is own research, to make sure they knew what they were comin' to. I didn't dress it up, but I didn't dress it down, lass. 'Appen 'e'll make 'is own mind up.'

How exciting! Adie knew Darren Davies wanted to do more farm work. He'd said as much in the conversations they'd had. It was clearly an important dream for him. Torley wasn't everyone's cup of tea, though, it had to be said. City people often found the quaintness of small-town life a bit too intense, along with the fact that most people knew a little more than they probably should about their friends and neighbours, and the gossip could get a little out of hand if you weren't careful about what you told people.

Still, the townsfolk of Torley had readily taken Adie to their hearts, and she felt sure they would do the same for Darren and Debby if they chose to move to the area. Debby could definitely be a bit prickly at times, and she was also quite private, especially about her struggles with trying to have a baby. Adie wasn't entirely sure whether she would feel comfortable with the locals trying to find out more about her, in the interests of making her welcome. Darren would breeze it. He was a likeable sort who didn't seem to have much to hide.

She said as much to Mark, who pulled a face at her. He gestured for her to sit at the table with him, so she did, and she found herself growing more and more fascinated by what he went on to tell her about Darren Davies.

'So, let me get this straight. He was a small-time crook, in and out of prison, and his friend was murdered, and the person who did it put him through vet school?'

Mark nodded. 'Aye. In a nutshell, that's it. It were a few year ago now, and it were a mess, Adie, and it were in all't papers at the time, I believe. The woman killed Darren's friend after they broke into 'er 'ouse, then she panicked an' buried 'is body so nobody'd find out what she'd done. But it all came out in't wash, and it turns out she 'ad a brain tumour. It's a long story, Adie, by't sound of it, an' I don't know all't details, but Darren were wantin' to know if people'd judge 'im on what 'appened.'

'Well, he'll have to let the practice know, if he does take the job, won't he?'

'They already know. 'E told 'em when 'e went in, on't first day. They're not under any illusions about what they're gettin'.'

Adie shrugged. 'Well, I guess if its good enough for his employers, it should be good enough for everyone else. I knew he had a back story. You can tell, just by looking at him, that he has an interesting past. There's just something about him. But he's a nice man, I think, and I hope he does take the job and they do move up here.'

Adie meant it. If everyone were judged on their past mistakes nobody would get very far in life, would they? At some point, you had to acknowledge that everyone deserved a second chance, and it certainly seemed as if Darren Davies had made the most of the rather peculiar opportunity he'd been offered, to reinvent himself. Good for him! It seemed like an incredibly interesting story, and she was looking forward to one day hearing it in his own words, if he was ever up for telling her.

* * * * *

The following afternoon, as Adie was setting seven places at the table for Sunday lunch, she wondered how Debby and Darren were getting on, after going home on Friday. Darren was still quite weak after the sepsis episode, and there was still much to be resolved about their infertility issues. They also had a big decision to make now, about whether or not to move to Torley!

She was struggling to keep the couple out of her head, and she wasn't really sure why. It was probably because there was a chance they'd be coming back, but it was also because Debby Davies was so desperately unhappy. It was horrible seeing *anyone* in such a distraught and bereft state, and feeling so powerless to change it.

Adie had been impressed with Debby's courage, in fronting up for the Raven's pool day and barbecue, when so much of her was probably breaking apart, inside. She'd put on a gutsy, determined face, held her own in conversation, and had even given baby Willow a cuddle, which must have thrown up all kinds of emotions for her.

She is one incredibly brave woman, and far stronger than she believes herself to be. But if Feen's right, and she is finally pregnant, they must be asking themselves all kinds of questions, around this job. I know she doesn't get along with her parents, but Darren's are down there too, and it's a big wrench to leave your family and make a new life at the other end of the country. Nobody knows that more than me!

Then Adie shrugged to herself and decided that it was probably inappropriate to allow herself to get too close to any of her tenants, particularly the ones that had big problems to resolve. It wasn't normally difficult to keep the right amount of distance from the people who came into her orbit and left again, but this couple had struck a chord.

Was it because she'd had a baby herself, as a young, naïve teenager? That was probably part of it, she supposed. It was something few women could fail to have lasting feelings about, and of course they would empathise with another woman who'd found herself in a similar situation. But Adie also understood that dwelling too much on someone else's issues would lead her into uncomfortable territory, if she wasn't careful.

Lending an ear and a bit of distanced perspective to a stranger was one thing (and only if they asked for it, even then!), but Adie was really only just emerging from a fair amount of drama of her own. In the past couple of years, she'd managed to square away a painful divorce, re-establish her relationships with her kids, sell a house and buy another one, relocate and remarry, and help to steer her new stepdaughter through marriage and a catastrophic start to parenthood after an accident that had prompted the premature birth of her twins. Getting involved with the troubles of a couple of virtual strangers wouldn't help the exhaustion she was already feeling after all that!

Adie cast an eye over her table, and proclaimed it ready. Feen and Gavin still were here, with the twins, and she quickly set their highchairs off to one side, by where they normally sat. Bob and

Sheila were finally coming over for lunch too, after weeks of being busy at the weekends with other things. And their neighbour, Dave Holloway, was coming too.

It would be nice to see Dave again. It was a bit of a surprise, that Mark had invited him, but Adie didn't mind. She'd met him a couple of times at the last two Ravensdown Christmas-night parties, and she'd also bumped into him in town once or twice. He seemed nice enough, and she remembered that his wife had left him, a few years ago, so he was on his own. Feen had mentioned that he had two sons, that she'd been at school with, and they were working in different jobs elsewhere in the country now. Neither seemed to want to take over the farm, which was a small one, and probably didn't offer much of a steady income, especially to a young man looking to provide for a family. But, from what Mark had said, Dave Holloway was really only farming as a hobby anyway, purely for the enjoyment. He'd made his money as a broker, importing and selling high-end American classic cars.

It's always nice to have a guest at the table. The more the merrier.

Within half an hour, everyone had arrived, and the kitchen was a riot of different conversations. Adie gave up trying to tune into any of them. She concentrated instead on getting all the food onto the table, with Sheila's help, and finally everyone could sit down and start helping themselves.

As things quietened down, she saw that Gavin had started chatting with Dave.

'So you're Bob's neighbour – the one with the rare breed sheep herd, is that right? I was sorry to hear about your ram being involved in that awful set-to with Bob's. It sounded horrendous. He's alright, isn't he though, yours?'

Dave nodded. 'Yes, he's doing okay, thanks. Better than Bob's poor little sod.'

Gavin pulled a face. 'On a brighter note, I understand you used to import classic cars from the USA? That must've been interesting. I love some of those old beasts! Especially the stuff from the fifties and sixties. I have a collection of vintage motorcycles, and a couple of veterans. It's mostly all British stuff, that belonged to my dad. I'm a bit of a retro-head, for that sort of thing. Do you have any cars yourself, still?'

‘I do, yes. I have a ‘65 Chev Impala, a 1963 Dodge Dart 270 convertible, and a 1958 Studebaker Silver Hawk. I’m often asked why I kept those three, because there were a lot of motors that came in that most people thought were far nicer. I dunno, though. I just really like these ones, I guess, especially the Dart. It’s nice to have a classic rag-top, although the weather up here means I only get to take the poor old wench out for a spin half a dozen times a year, on average! But they’re probably going to end up as part of my retirement fund, eventually.’

‘Sounds great. I’d love to see them sometime. I know that’s cheeky, like fishing for an invitation, but I shamelessly admit to that being the case. Sorry.’

‘We had a couple of ‘57 chevvies as our wedding cars,’ Feen offered. ‘They were beautiful!’

Dave laughed. ‘Yes, those are such icons, aren’t they? I moved a lot of Chevs, back in the day. They were very popular. You can come over any time, and take a look at my cars, and I can show you some pictures if you’re keen? I kept good photo records of every car I brought in, and where it went. I had a good connection to a few hot-rod clubs, on both sides of the ditch, and I used to get a lot of stuff in on request.’

Feen giggled. ‘It must’ve been such fun, shopping vicariously for something so amazing!’

Dave grinned, and nodded. ‘It’s always more fun when its someone else’s money, that’s for sure.’

The doorbell rang, and Feen smiled gently, as if she’d been expecting it. Adie made to get up, but Feen motioned for her to stay sitting.

I’ll get it,’ she sang, as she left the room.

Mark shot an enquiring look at Adie, and she simply shrugged. ‘No idea; we’re not expecting anyone, that I know of.’

Feen came back into the kitchen, followed closely by Carla Walton, Gavin’s mother. Carla looked at everyone sitting around the table, and immediately became embarrassed.

‘Oh, shit. Sorry. I didn’t mean to intrude! I didn’t even think about what time it was! We usually have Sunday dinner much later, at home.

‘I’m working on a retro table in my workshop today,’ she explained, ‘but I’ve run out of the bolts I need for the legs. Dad doesn't have any, and I can get them from the local supplier, of course, but I'd have to buy a bag of a hundred, which is crazy when I only need four, and I also don't want to have to go all the way to Carlisle on a Sunday afternoon just for that! I wondered if you might have any, Mark? I can replace them for you, later in the week.'

She them mumbled something about not really understanding why she hadn't thought to phone first. 'I just had a brainwave and acted on it.'

Adie pulled out the one spare chair at the table and motioned her over. 'It's fine, Carla. It's nice to see you, actually! And yes, please, do have some lunch with us. There's plenty.'

Carla still looked uncomfortable. 'No, I really don't want to barge in on your lunch. I'm sorry. As I said, I wasn't thinking about what time it was. I just get a bee in my bra when I can't crack on with what I'm doing. Need to get sorted quickly, to keep going. Patience being one of my strongest virtues, and all that.'

Mark pointed at the spare chair. 'Sit, woman,' he growled. 'Yer family. Get some scoff down yer bloody neck. No excuses. I'll look for't bolts for yer, when I've 'ad me afters. Apple pie and ice-cream. You'll 'ave to wait until then, so yer might as well eat summat.'

Carla shrugged. 'Okay, if you insist,' she muttered, and after stroking the cheeks of the twins, Alder and Willow, and cooing at them for a minute or so, she sat down in the empty chair opposite Dave.

'Hi Mum,' Gavin piped up. 'This is Dave Holloway, Bob and Sheila's neighbour. Dave, meet Carla Walton; my mother, and the town's most prolific stripper. As in furniture, by the way, not clothing.'

Dave burst out laughing, as Carla rolled her eyes, and Adie noted that she suddenly looked a bit shy, as Dave stuck his hand out at her.

'Good to meet you, Carla.'

'Pleased to meet you too, Dave. As my son says, with his most excellent brand-new and hilarious joke that he's never told before, I restore old furniture.'

'Is it you who's got the shop in the town; 'Carla's'?'

Carla nodded. 'Yes. Best shop in the Lake District, and run by the most charming woman in Torley town. Everyone loves me.'

'You get some nice stuff in, don't you?'

Carla inclined her head. 'Yeah, it's nice by the time it goes in the window. Some of it's in a pretty sad state before it gets to that, and I've been known to turn the air around me a sweet shade of blue when I can't get something to look the way I want it to. But it's nice to see the fruits of the labours of frustration, and even nicer when someone else falls in love with a piece too.'

The twins were throwing their broccoli around, so Adie's attention was diverted for a while but she quickly handed Carla a plate, and told her to help herself. When she looked back, a few minutes later, she could see that Carla had 'clicked' rather well with Dave, and the pair were already deep in conversation about their shared love of all things retro; mostly cars, motorbikes and furniture.

'I tend to gravitate towards things that remind me of myself; you know, a bit weathered, with a few creaks and dents, here and there,' Dave offered.

'I feel the same. Furniture should have character, so I'm always at great pains to ensure that what I sell looks a bit like me. You know, past its best, but not *quite* dead. Still has a bit of life left in it, on a good day.' Carla talked in her usual classic, deadpan tone of voice. Dave got it, and his eyes twinkled.

'So we're talking about a pair of pretty feet at the end of elegant legs then, are we, for starters?'

Carla grinned, and gestured to her bosom. 'Well, I'm not *quite* as flat as an occasional table, am I? No, I was thinking more along the lines of something being freshly pulled out of the skip at the end of the road and tarted up, with all the cosmetic help it can get, to look halfway decent.'

Dave winked at her, as he passed her the platter of roast potatoes, and told her she looked a lot more than halfway decent to him. Adie was surprised to see her blush!

Sheila was asking Feen about her latest work remit, designing jewellery for the famous dress designer Gina Giordano, and Feen was describing the latest colour schemes she was working on for the upcoming autumn fashion line. Bob and Mark were having a riveting conversation about fertilizer. Everyone seemed perfectly happy, chattering away and enjoying the food, which was just how Adie liked it.

Carla left, soon after Mark had found the bolts she needed, and Dave Holloway offered to walk her to her car. He wasn't gone long, but when he came back into the kitchen he winked at Gavin. 'Interesting lady, your mum. Seemed pretty keen to get home and get that table finished! Either that, or my rugged good looks and charming demeanour were just too overwhelming for her.'

Later, after everyone had gone, Feen came in to help Adie with what was left of the washing up. The dishwasher was well and truly full.

'Today was fun,' she remarked, as she picked up a tea towel. 'It was nice to have a new tace at the fable. Dave Holloway made me laugh when he said how much happier he was without his 'cheating little scutter of a wife.' I'm glad he finally feels that way, because I picked up that he's had to do a spair bit of fadework to get there. But he's a nice man. I like him.'

'I do too,' Adie agreed. 'And I'm glad Carla dropped by, today. That was unexpected, but it's good that she's finally started to feel she can come here without being dragged, kicking and screaming, which is sometimes how it feels of course, inviting her to anything. She still has a bit of a chip on her shoulder, I think. But those two seemed to click, actually; her and Dave, unless I've lost my touch for reading signs?'

'No, you haven't,' Feen smirked. Her face was full of mischief, and she didn't even try to hide it. Adie took one look at her and rolled her eyes.

'Alright. What's happening, there? Come on, out with it!'

'Well, all I can say, or at least all *should* say right now, is that those two are set in stone.'

Adie gaped at her. 'What, you can see that? They met barely two hours ago! They're an item *already?*' She was incredulous.

Feen inclined her head. 'Yes; not that they know it yet. But he's going to call in for a coffee this week, down at her shop, and he's going to prise her away from her hammer and nails next weekend and take her out to lunch. A month from now, those two will be joined at the hip, and that's the way they will stay.'

'Well, gosh! Who the hell saw that coming?' Adie then pulled a face. 'Well, I guess *you* did.'

'Adie, I saw it months ago. They've met before, very briefly, at that very first Christmas party that you came to here, when you were housesitting at Teapot Cottage, before you bought it. Carla still had her heart set on snaring Daddy, at the time, and Dave was still grieving over his marriage heading south. Neither of them paid any attention to the other. But trust me; that has all changed today.' She beamed, and held up her hands in mock surrender.

'Serendipity, Adie. Why else has her dad just happened to run out of long bolts today, of all days? And Carla has somehow finally managed to find enough confidence to turn up here without warning? And just when a certain huggedly randsome and eligible 'farmer' who is in fact her destiny, just happens to be titting at the kitchen sable, having never been invited to lunch before?

'Don't worry,' she added, half to herself. 'I plan to give Gavin the heads' up tonight, about all this. He has another stint as best man, coming up.'

Adie sat back down at the table, suddenly overcome with laughter. 'Oh my God, 'titting at the sable'? You really do make me howl sometimes, Feen, and you don't even have to try!' She wiped her eyes with the back of her hand, and shook her head.

'Well, I'll take your word for the fate part. It's not completely far-fetched I guess, when you consider the magic that constantly hovers around in here. It never ceases to amaze me. It's that old 'fairy-dust' thing again, isn't it? But I do hope she'll be nice to him, Feen. If he's been through the mill, he won't need anyone else treating him badly or taking him for granted.'

Feen shook her head emphatically. 'She won't treat him badly, and she will never take him for granted. And vice versa. Those two are both straight shooters, who will always know where they stand with one another. They're going to discover, very quickly, what soul mates are. They will value one another so much, you wouldn't believe. Oh, and they'll be Darla and Cave, won't they!'

Feen smirked, then asked if Adie knew when Debby and Darren would be coming back. 'I see him accepting the job he's been offered. It will be nice to have them around too, once they've resolved all their issues.'

'*Will* they resolve them, d'you think?' Adie was keen for any nuggets Feen could offer about the Davies' future plans.

Feen nodded. 'Yeah, I think they will. They're going to be happy.'

She put her elbows on the table and briefly put her head in her hands. 'I see a lot of work, physical and emotional, and I see a fair few problems with her mother. But I get a sense that none of it is insurmountable.'

'I haven't been able to stop thinking about those two,' Adie confessed.

'Me neither. There's just something about them, isn't there? Debby could be a nice friend for us both, you know, Adie. She's like, half a generation between us, isn't she? Relatable for both of us? Anyway, we'll see what happens. But I think those two will be just fine, in the end.'

Feen then left, to go for a walk with Gavin and the twins. Adie knew Mark would already be asleep in his armchair, but she fancied a fresh cuppa, so she decided to brew a pot of tea. She was glad he'd managed to find the bolts Carla needed, so she could carry on with her project this afternoon.

Feen's take on the new relationship that her mother-in-law was evidently about to start with Dave Holloway was fascinating, and kind of amusing, since Carla was about as prickly as a fistful of hedgehogs, and Dave was still getting to grips with his wife leaving him for his best friend. But they shared the same sense of humour, and they both loved all things vintage and retro. They seemed to bounce off one another pretty well, at lunch. How lovely it would be for them both, if a romance did blossom as Feen was predicting!

Feen's intuition was no less baffling this time than it ever was, but Adie had no cause to doubt her stepdaughter. Feen was surprisingly insightful and accurate with her glimpses of the future, for so many people, but Adie still found herself amazed beyond belief, at how many extraordinary evolutions and outcomes she'd born witness to, since she'd first come to Torley herself, as a half-deranged, seething hotbed of hormones and hysteria, with her world in tatters, convinced that her life was over. She'd long-since sailed past the point of being surprised for very long by *anything* that happened around Ravensdown and Teapot Cottage!

There's magic in them thar hills, she thought to herself. It was the kind of magic that healed hurt souls and brought hope to the grieving, where epiphanies abounded, and where lives could and very often did begin afresh, with a joy that had once seemed so far out of reach.

Chapter Sixteen

'Honestly!' Debby fumed. 'You'd think we were moving to the bloody Outer Hebrides, or something! Why can't my bloody parents just be happy for us? More to the point, why do they even *care* what we do? They never did before! Why pick *now* to have an opinion?'

'Because you've just told them, in two sentences, that they're going to be grandparents, and that you're moving miles away so they can't enjoy the fact. Of *course* they're unhappy. What did you expect?' Darren's tone was mild, but his observation was true enough, as much as Debby hated to admit it.

'I must say, your mum and Pat took the news about the move a lot better than expected. I could see how disappointed they were, but they took it on the chin. Why can't my mum and dad be the same?'

'They're very different people. Just give them time, Debs. It's a lot for them to get used to all at once. They'll come around.'

'Will they? They didn't even want to see the details of the houses we're going to look at. They're not interested in us, or this baby, or where we want to live, Darren. I don't even know why it's important to them that we stay around the corner! They've never visited us, and they certainly don't care about what *we* want. Mum actually told me I was selfish, can you believe that?'

'I can. But you know, becoming a grandparent probably puts a few things in perspective. Maybe your own mortality suddenly starts rushing towards you much faster, and maybe the need to put things right before you shuffle of the mortal coil starts to rear its head. Who knows? She's a funny old bag, your mum. She's impossible to read. But she loves you really.' Darren's eyes danced as he smirked at her.

'*Really?* Well, she's got a bloody strange way of showing it,' Debby grumbled. 'No matter what I've done in my life, she's never been supportive. Even when I told her I'd decided to go to nursing college, all she did was shrug, and tell me it was 'fine, if it was what I wanted.' There's never been a scrap of enthusiasm for anything I've ever done. It's as if she just can't bring herself to be happy for me. She's never been proud of a single thing Jayne or I have *ever* achieved. She didn't even come to my graduation! She didn't go to Jayne's either, but Jayne seems to deal with it better. And as for refusing to come to our wedding? Well, that's a hard one to forgive *any* mother for, isn't it?'

Darren nodded, sagely. 'Yeah, that was mean of her. On the one day of your life you really need to come first, she couldn't even give you that, could she? But at least your Dad showed up, to give you away.'

'Yeah, at least there was that, although I did have to pressure him, and even after he caved I know he had a row with Mum that went on for weeks, before and after. I dunno what her problem is, Darren. I've *never* known. But sometimes it's just too much to take, and I have to step back. I think living in the Lake District will give me some much-needed space. Not that she bothers with me much, it's just that whenever she does, it's never for anything nice, and whenever she pops her head above the parapet for something, she can never resist having a dig at you, which really pisses me off.'

Darren pulled a face. 'I'll never understand her either, or your dad. He's such a wet lettuce, Debs. A man should be a bloody man. Why does he never stand up to her? No relationship should be so imbalanced that she gets to wear the trousers all the time! It's like he doesn't have a mind of his own. It's really hard to have respect for someone like that. I *have* tried, with him, but I can't get there. I've given up.'

'I know how hard you've tried, babe. But it's okay to give up. You have my blessing on that. The truth is, they don't deserve your respect. They treat you like shit, and it's okay for us *both* to decide we've had enough of that. I've decided that the increased distance between us will be just fine!'

'What about when the baby comes? Will they want to be involved, d'you think?'

Debby shrugged and pulled a face. 'I'd be surprised. They don't even seem interested in the pregnancy, so I doubt they'll have much interest in the baby. It'll just be seen as yet another thing that shackles me to you, in their words. Me being with you makes them hostile, so they probably won't want anything to do with our little new arrival.'

She ignored the small wave of sadness, at the thought of her parents wanting no contact with their grandchild. Still, she mused to herself, it's better to have no grandparents at all than hostile ones. What would be the point of that? No child deserved to be ignored, or looked down on and sneered at, just because of who its father was. She shook her head and shoved the thoughts aside. There were more important things to be thinking about now than her wretched, ridiculous parents.

After researching house prices and talking to estate agents in Exeter and Carlisle, Debby had also found some helpful information about the quality of schooling. Ofsted reports were a mixed bag, but there were a number of nurseries and schools with good ratings. She had also emailed the HR department of Cumberland Infirmary, detailing her experience and enquiring about vacancies. She'd had a swift response to indicate that yes, the hospital did have a handful of vacancies that might suit her skills.

Darren's telephone chat with Mark Raven had been helpful too, and he'd also had a conversation with Bob Shalloe, who he also respected very much. Both men had affirmed their own love of the area, as farmers and family men, and both thought the opportunity Darren had been offered was a good one. That was helpful, because they both seemed trustworthy. They called a spade a spade, and they knew that with a baby on the way, the decision Darren needed to make was life-changing. They knew it wouldn't be right to give him anything less than the best advice they could offer.

The local estate agencies in Exeter thought they would sell their house within a couple of weeks, if they were realistic about their price. There was a waiting list, apparently, for properties in and around their area. There didn't seem to be much on offer around Torley though, which did unnerve them a bit, but a handful of places did seem like they might be worth a look.

They arranged to go back in a week and do some viewings. It meant even more time off work, but with rostered days off and a couple of shift-swaps, it only amounted to two days. Their bosses weren't happy but they didn't quibble much. Before Darren had taken the time off to go up to Teapot Cottage in the first place, he hadn't taken any leave for almost a full year. They'd been reminding him to start using up his holidays, and he still had a few days owing, so they didn't have much choice but to let him take them.

He'd asked Lakeview to give him a few more days to reach a decision, while he sussed out property in the area, and he felt that was reasonable under the circumstances. They readily agreed, and he appreciated that. Their willingness to be flexible boded well, for working in the practice full time.

Teapot Cottage wasn't available, as Adie only let it for a minimum of seven days at a time, and someone was already booked to stay there on the same weekend, so Debby had booked a room at The Beeches, the big hotel between Torley and Carlisle. It looked a bit posh, and it was a bit pricey, but it did include a buffet breakfast that was rated by guests as excellent, and it wouldn't hurt to spend a little time in Carlisle on one or two evenings, finding supper places, and generally checking out the city's social scene. Adie and Mark had already invited them to Ravensdown House for Sunday lunch.

They had six houses to look at, after viewing the details and photos online. One place was more or less an apartment, with steep stairs in a poky hallway, near the centre of Torley town. It didn't even have room at the bottom of the stairs to park a pushchair, and Debby wasn't sure how practical it would be with a new-born. The next place was a tall townhouse, fairly new, and built on three levels. It didn't have a garage, and there was only one parking space. They didn't have a garage where they were now, but making a life-changing move meant they were looking for something similar to what they currently had, if not more, but they didn't want to settle for less.

Another of the houses was a semi-detached cottage. It was on a main road, but set back quite a bit, with a good front garden. It looked like it had potential. It didn't have a garage either, but it did have space to build one, and it would be possible to do that, subject to the necessary planning permission, which the agent hadn't thought would be too much of a problem. It had a lovely walled garden at the back too, which would be great for Badger, and perfect of course for children. That was the house they were most interested in.

There was a very spacious flat above a shop, which they initially rejected, but were persuaded by the agent to take a look at anyway, since it had four big bedrooms and was all on the same level once you'd made it up the stairs. The town centre was quiet at night, the agent reasoned, and the property came with the option of buying the shop below, which could provide them with a subsidiary income if they wanted to rent it out.

A three-bedroom semi-detached house, similar to the one they were selling in Exeter, was more towards Carlisle than Torley. It looked okay, but it didn't have much of a garden, and it was very close to a blind bend on a busy road. It didn't look particularly inspiring, but in keeping with the comment on the listing that said, 'must be seen,' Debby wasn't about to rule it out before she saw it.

The last house on the list was the one she was the least convinced about. Scruffy wasn't the word for the place; the blurred photo showed a detached cottage on an acre and a half of land. It was empty, and had been for years. It looked almost derelict, and the rooms looked poky and dark. Darren seemed keen to see it, as it had the kind of outside space he was dreaming of, and it also had a couple of out-buildings he thought might be useful. He'd cajoled her into agreeing to view it and she agreed, but only because they had nothing to lose, since they were up there anyway. She felt a bit despondent about the houses they were going to see. The pickings seemed slim, compared to what she'd hoped for.

The Beeches Hotel didn't allow dogs to stay, so Badger was spending the weekend with Barbara and Pat, Darren's mum and step-dad. Debby had made them promise not to feed him fish and chips. Pat ran a chippy in the town, and everyone knew the dog was very partial to a piece of battered fish.

'You can let him have a sausage or two, but no more, and definitely no battered fish!' Pat had given her a salute, but he'd done it with a wink and a worrying twinkle in his eye. Debby knew that Badger would be spoiled rotten with him and Barbara, and as she and Darren pulled away after leaving Badger in their care, she wasn't going to put any money on Pat obeying her request not to give the poor dog at least one plateful of cod in beer batter and a pile of chips and gravy!

They met the agent in Torley town centre on Friday morning. He introduced himself as Lance Martin, and he seemed very friendly and enthusiastic. The first house he showed them was the one above the shop. The space was huge, and to some extent it was a blank canvass with plenty of potential. They could bring internal walls down, or put them up, more or less where they wanted. It certainly had possibilities, but Debby simply couldn't see them living there, as a family. The stairway leading up from alongside the shop itself was narrow and dark, and the windows upstairs were all very old-fashioned – and not in a good way. They would all need to be replaced, and the cost would be enormous. The central heating system was antiquated and would also need replacing. The place didn't have a scrap of insulation either. Debby could see it draining away any and all reserves they might have, after selling the Exeter house.

This place is a money-pit. The asking price is only the start. She tried to get enthusiastic about it but she just couldn't warm to it. Neither could Darren, so they quickly ruled it out.

The next one on the list was the townhouse, which was disappointing. The rooms were tiny. So was the garden, which didn't get any sun, thanks to the other townhouses that overshadowed it. It wasn't what they wanted at all. As predicted the apartment, with its impossibly cramped stairway and no garden at all, was really only fit for one person; probably one who never wanted to spend much time there.

Sadly, the semi-detached cottage with the lovely walled rear garden had sold that very morning. As they were literally on their way to see it, Lance Martin's phone had rung, and someone at his office reported that the owner had accepted an offer higher than the asking price, half an hour earlier. Debby felt gutted. That had looked like the place with the most potential. She'd been looking forward to seeing that one the most. Darren's shoulders sagged a little. He'd been interested too, in seeing it.

Everyone thinks house hunting is fun, she said to herself, *until they have to do actually do it, and realise that what they want is harder to find than they thought.*

The other semi-detached house, towards Carlisle, was still on their viewing list but the only other place in Torley itself was Appletree Cottage, the derelict house she'd been dreading being dragged to see. She would happily have told Lance Martin to forget it, but Darren was surprisingly curious to take a look at it.

After coming off the main road and driving down a narrow lane, they pulled up alongside Lance's car. Debby couldn't muster much enthusiasm. So far, the homes on offer had been a crushing disappointment, and she didn't expect this one to be any better. She sighed as she got out of the truck.

It wasn't very far to walk, but she was glad she'd worn flat shoes, because what used to be a driveway down to the house was littered with lumps, rocks and potholes, and overgrown with weeds. Stumbling was a real risk, and that was the last thing she wanted to do, newly pregnant and scared to death that she might not go to full term. Gingerly, she picked her way down, and waded through the bushes behind Darren and Lance. More focussed on where she was putting her feet, than on what was in front of her, she virtually crashed into her husband who had stopped to take a look at the house from the gate at the bottom of the 'drive.'

'Oops! Sorry. Oh, what? Oh, my God, will you take a look at that?' She could see why Darren had stopped in his tracks. The old place, even in its poor neglected state, was stunning. She had not expected *this*!

The cottage was kind of like a scaled-down version of Ravensdown House, with two symmetrical gables flanking a central square block. This cottage had mullioned bay windows too, but some of the diamond-shaped leadlight panes windows were missing. The front door, which was set off to one side, looked a bit rotten in places. The walls had been rendered a very long time ago, and the rendering was falling off in a few patches, offering a glimpse of what looked like stone underneath. But, as tatty and forlorn as the poor place was, it had a real air of old-world charm about it. Debby couldn't tear her eyes away from it.

Looking around, she could see that at one time it had had a substantial sunken front garden, probably about fifty-feet square. Off to one side and all across the back were high walls, made of the distinctive stone of the region. Moss and weeds were growing out of the stonework in different places, but she figured a decent water-blasting would clear a lot of that away. In front of the two walls were lower ones, showing that there had been raised beds, at one time, but everything was so overgrown, it was impossible to tell what might have been planted there. Brambles grew in every direction, some of them with thick, heavily barbed stems. She saw and felt the sadness and neglect, but she also felt something else that she could never have gleaned from the agents' photos of the place. Hope. Possibility. Potential. She tried not to get too excited as they approached the front door.

Inside might be a very different matter.

Darren, thus far, had said nothing. His face was a study in neutrality, and since Debby had complained from the outset that the place looked too far gone and depressing to even warrant a visit, she knew he would be reluctant to say anything positive, even if he felt it. After expressing her initial reaction to the place, she wasn't ready to say anything either, not until they'd seen the inside.

The rooms were quite small, and they walked straight into the first one from the front door. There was no hallway or foyer, and a stone staircase sat directly opposite the front door. The view from the little bay windows would certainly be lovely though, if the garden were sorted out. *You could plant a proper old English garden out there,* she mused.

Debby moved towards the bay window in the first room and peered out. It would be quite something, to look out and see a beautifully restored garden, full of flowers of all different kinds and colours. Turning on her heel, she took a good look around the other downstairs front room, which also had a pretty bay window, but was only accessible through a narrow door from the first room. A very poky kitchen sat at the back, with two separate small rooms of indeterminate use behind it. One looked like it had been a laundry, the other possibly a pantry. The configuration was weird, to say the least, but it wasn't the end of the world.

She started up the stone stairs at the side of the room which ran directly up from inside the front door. She picked her way up slowly, testing the handrail for stability. It was surprisingly sturdy, and the stairs seemed strong and stable. Up on the first floor, she found two double, front-facing bedrooms, and a smaller third. A fair-sized bathroom offered an ancient claw-foot tub and a filthy toilet, with a dented metal cistern that was bolted close to the ceiling. A rusty cheap chain, with no bottom handle, hung forlornly from it. An outsized sink, cracked right down the middle, completed the dismal picture. The floor was tiled, but most of the tiles were chipped and broken. What she could see underneath were floorboards. They seemed a bit stained and ugly, but she had a feeling that with a good strip, sand and polish, they might come up quite well.

On closer inspection, it seemed that all of the upstairs floors were wooden boards, with the same kind of potential. The two double bedrooms looked out onto the garden Debby could already imagine. The third bedroom, tucked alongside the bathroom and facing the rear, overlooked what appeared to be fields, but it was difficult to see for sure because a couple of really big trees that were too close to the window were blocking most of the light and view.

Something in Debby's heart quietly went 'click.' She went downstairs to look for Darren, and was surprised that he'd already gone outside to look at the outbuildings, before he'd even taken a peek upstairs. She found him at the back of the house, fighting his way through a tangle of bushes that had grown over the door of what looked to be a small stone barn of some kind. It wasn't a big building, but there was certainly enough space for one car, and a workshop could easily be built at the end with the door. There was a window, too, but the glass had long since gone, and the wooden frame was rotting. The earthen floor gave off a dank smell, but it wasn't repulsive.

Further along the back of the house was another stone dwelling that had clearly served as a chicken house in the past. Laying boxes were still in evidence, and the empty feed troughs still had a few feathers and random bits of straw in them. Again, the smell wasn't horrible, but the air of neglect was heartbreaking.

Someone loved this poor old place once. What happened?

Debby turned to look at Darren, and was astonished to find that he was shaking. His eyes were dark, with pupils almost fully dilated, and they glistened with unshed tears. She grabbed hold of his hand, in alarm. Was he having some kind of fit? Was this a delayed consequence of the sepsis?

'Babe, what is it? Are you sick?'

Darren squeezed her hand and laughed shakily. 'No. I'm not sick – unless you want to call it lovesick. Debs, I think this is it. I think we're looking at our new home.'

She realised, in that instant that her husband was simply excited, to a state he couldn't contain; to a level she'd never seen before. She had *never* seen him shake with excitement.

'You haven't even seen inside yet! Upstairs, I mean.' She dragged him back around the front of the house and in through the front door. At the top of the stairs, and out of earshot of the agent, she finally admitted that she felt the same way.

'This is a gorgeous little house. At least, it *could* be gorgeous, but it would need a lot of work. This could be our bedroom, this lovely big one. It would get the most sun. The other could be a guest room. Little room at the back could be a nursery, then used as a single bedroom when the baby gets bigger. Bathroom needs replacing, and all the floors need reclaiming, walls need a bit of replastering in places, and then a decent lick of paint, but that's all that's needed up here. Oh, and probably some roof insulation.' She frowned at Darren.

'Downstairs is a nightmare, though. We'd have to knock out walls, make it as open plan as possible, at least take out the wall between those two front rooms, but one of the little rooms could be turned into a cloakroom with a loo and basin, since it backs onto the kitchen where there's already some plumbing. The kitchen's a disaster too, by the way. We'd need to rip out what there and start again, and don't even get me started on what that poor garden needs, out there! It's beautiful here babe, I'll grant you, but think of the cost! We'll be skint for bloody years!'

'Debs, I don't care. I really want to do it; fix this old place up, if we can. I don't want to look at anything else. I don't even want to see the last place on the list. This is it, for me.'

At that moment, Lance came up the stairs, and asked them what they both thought. Debby stepped in front of Darren and began to speak before he had chance to. She was terrified that he was about to throw them both into a fire they wouldn't be able to get out of!

'What's the situation with this place?'

Lance pulled a face. 'The owner left the country twenty years ago. Until five years ago he was renting out, through an agency, but since the last tenant bought her own place and left, it's just sat empty. It no longer met the new criteria that had come in, for rental through an agency, and because he was overseas he wasn't easily able to manage it himself. I think it all got a bit 'too-hard-basket' for him, to be honest. When it fell into disrepair, the nearby neighbours contacted him to do something about it. He lost interest in it a long time ago, and didn't want to invest anything in it. He finally rang me last week and instructed me to list it. It went on the market the day before yesterday.'

'Is there much interest yet? From other viewers, I mean?'

Lance nodded. 'Yeah, quite a bit. We've done two viewings already, and we've another seven scheduled for tomorrow. Saturdays are always busy. Look, I know it's a mess, but places like this don't come up very often, so if you want to make a move on it, I'd suggest you don't wait.'

He smiled deprecatingly. 'I know that probably sounds like standard estate agent patter, but I'm not trying to strongarm you into making an offer. Really, I'm not, because the place will probably sell tomorrow anyway, with all the viewings we've scheduled, and I'd bet my own house on the fact. So, to all intents and purposes, it doesn't matter who buys it. I'd just like to see it go to someone who's going to love it, that's all, instead of some greedy investor who'll do the minimum work on it then charge some poor sod a fortune in rent. Or some developer who'll tear it down and build a dozen poky townhouses on the land.' His face softened.

'I'd like to see this old place restored and loved. And just between you and me, I think the entire house is slate-stone, underneath that horrible rendering. I'd bet my house on that, too. If you took it all off, it'd be stunning.'

Debby liked Lance, and she felt he was being honest. The place needed a lot of work, and it wasn't somewhere they could comfortably move straight into. But, she reasoned, they could probably get a good-sized caravan down that driveway if they cleared it. As long as they could get the power connected, they could live in that, even with a baby if they had to, until the house was liveable.

She turned back to him. 'Can you give us five minutes please? Oh, and could you remind me again what the asking price is?'

Lance told her, and added, 'but he might take an offer of a few thousand less maybe, if it helps. Now he's made his mind up to sell, I know he's quite keen to get shut of the place. Righto then! I'll leave you two to have a chat. Give me a shout when you're ready.'

After he left the house to wander around the overgrown garden, and give them a chance to talk privately, Debby turned to Darren. 'It does have real potential. Do you want it?'

He simply nodded, unable to speak. Debby rushed on. 'Okay, well, my terms are a comfy caravan that we can live in here while we work on the place until we can live inside it, and I want the power connected straight away so that we can get set up. I want the entire downstairs gutting, walls down – even if it means RSJ's. I want everything open plan, a new wood burner in the middle of the room, with dual doors on both sides, and I want an Aga. If you can give me all that, Dr Davies, we have a deal.'

She felt extremely wobbly. Never in her life before had she taken such a massive decision so quickly. Buying a house was a really big deal, and buying one that was all but ruined was even more so. But she had to admit that she felt the same way Darren did, about this place. They'd come here out of open curiosity on his part, and out of unwilling dread on hers. She hadn't expected at *all*, to be so overwhelmed by how this old, neglected house had spoken to her. Nobody had loved the poor place for a very long time. It begged her, silently, to love it, and she was astonished to find that she did. She already did! She could see herself and Darren here, with the house nicely renovated and upgraded, with a beautiful garden to enjoy. She already knew how special this place would also be for the child they were soon to have.

I must be going soft in the head, she thought to herself. *Is it the hormones, the whole pregnancy thing, that's got me so overwhelmed and wobbling like a jelly in the breeze? Or is it my husband who is so in love with this old wreck of a place, he can't even string a sentence together?*

On the most rational level, buying this sad little house seemed like utter madness. But, on a visceral, primal level it felt like buying it and breathing new life and love into it was the only thing they could do.

Their parents were all going to proclaim them as stark raving mad, of course. Debby's would just walk away, shaking their heads, and wanting nothing to do with it. But here, just a mile and a half from Torley town, in the middle of tranquil fields where all she could hear was birdsong, she felt like this was a sanctuary; somewhere she could sit and literally unplug from the world. It really didn't matter if nobody else understood. She did, and so did Darren, and that was enough.

Her lovestruck husband finally found his voice, but it came out as a whisper. 'Debs, we could afford this. We really could. And what's more, we could afford to fix it.'

He was right. The valuation on their Exeter house meant that equity they would have after the sale, even with the exorbitant agency and legal fees, would pay for this old place outright, and go a good way towards the renovations it needed. They could at least put in a decent kitchen and a modern bathroom, as a good enough start to make the place liveable.

'Yeah, we could. A decent caravan might make a dent in the funds, but we could always sell it on again, I guess.'

'Or keep it, as an extra guest room,' Darren's voice was more normal now, but Debby could hear the excitement in it.

'So, what do you think?' She squeezed his hand, knowing he would say yes. The idea of walking away from here and never seeing this house again, even in its current sad state, was unthinkable to her now.

Darren cleared his throat and took a deep breath. 'I say we do it. And I say we offer the asking price, because if we don't, someone else will.'

'I agree. Maybe the owner *would* take a few thousand less, but this place is a rare and wonderful opportunity. We won't be the only people who can see the potential in this place, and the last thing we need is to end up being gazumped. Alright, let's find Lance.'

They found him outside, sitting on the edge of a stone step leading down to the once-lovely sunken garden, and after establishing that yes, the roof was sound, and yes, the plumbing and electrics would all need to be redone but it would be straightforward enough, they told him they wanted the house. Debby was anxious to impress upon him her fear of being gazumped. He waved her fears away with the back of his hand.

'We don't play those sorts of games. If an owner accepts an offer, we halt all subsequent viewings. In the case of this place, even if someone did come in and want to see it or offer more, I'd tell them we'd have to wait and see if the first offer fell through before we would talk to the owner about theirs.'

'Really?' Debby couldn't contain her surprise. 'I thought most owners and agents were out for all they could get. I know I wouldn't be best pleased if I trusted an agent and found out later that they could have got more for my house!'

Lance sighed. He glanced at the overgrown garden, with a hint of sadness on his face, and gave a short laugh. 'We would only talk to the owner if a new offer was significantly more. It's all in the sales contract they agree to, with us. And I'm going to be completely honest with you now.'

He looked around the garden and up at the house again. 'I wouldn't have said anything if you hadn't wanted it, but the owner, Chris Marsh, is a very good friend of mine. I used to play here, when I was a kid, with my best mate Steven. Chris and June were his parents. We had a lot of happy times here. Unfortunately, Steven died of an undetected heart defect when we were sixteen. Just dropped dead on the footie field at college, with no warning, and it was devastating for Chris and June. She never really got over her grief, and her health nosedived. She died a few years later, and Chris moved to France and rented this place out.

'We've always kept in touch, me and him. We have Steven in common, of course, and we still talk about the old days. Chris was almost like a second dad to me, for a while, even after Steven died. It all changed after he moved away, of course, but he's entrusted me with Appletree Cottage and he's asked me to try and find a buyer who wants to love it back to life. I'm fairly sure you do, and since you're also more or less cash buyers, I'm a hundred percent confident in saying that it's yours if you want it.'

Darren was looking at Lance intently. 'That must've been awful, losing your mate like that. I'm so sorry for your loss. I know too well, how tragic the death of a lad so young really is. I lost a friend too, at that age.'

Debby knew that Darren was thinking about Tom Findlay, the young boy who was killed back when he and Darren were living a different life, as a pair of low-rate thieves. Tom had been sixteen too.

Lance nodded. 'It was. It hit the whole community hard, here. Everyone loved Steven, and some say he'd have made Carlisle United, eventually. Life goes on though, doesn't it? We have to pick up and carry on.' He looked up at the cottage again.

'But please don't see this house as tinged with sadness. It's not. They were a happy family and, as I say, we had a lot of fun in this garden. I think I laughed here more than I did anywhere else.'

'Well, we're hoping that children's laughter will fill this garden again one day soon,' Debby said, unwittingly rubbing her belly as she said it. Lance's face lit up.

'Are you expecting?' He was beaming. In spite of herself, Debby grinned back at him. 'Oops! Yes, but it's still a secret. That little nugget popped out by accident. We haven't told anyone yet.'

He laughed and gave a knowing nod. 'Waiting for the twelve-week scan? We did the same. We've got three, me and my wife Maggie, and we kept it to ourselves every time, until we were sure. It's a happy secret to have, isn't it? A very special time to cherish, just as a couple. Things change a lot, once everybody knows. Is that why you're moving up here from Devon?'

Darren explained his job, and the offer he was about to accept. 'We don't want to bring our kids up in the city. We appreciate what cities have to offer, but we want to do things a little differently.'

'Ah, well, you're less than ten minutes from Torley town here, and that's got most of what you need. Carlisle isn't far to go, if you fancy a bit of decent shopping or culture. And you're only half an hour away from a main motorway. So, you're not as much in the wop-wops as you think. You can have the best of both worlds here.'

Debby explained that they'd done a little research into childcare facilities and schools, and Lance nodded. 'Ofstead ratings are okay here, right across the educational spectrum. You've got the University of Cumbria, with its main campus here, but there's one in Ambleside as well. They also have one in Lancaster and of course

Lancaster Uni itself is rated one of the best in the country. They're commutable from here, at a push.'

'What does your wife do, if you don't mind me asking?' Debby enquired. She was keen to find out a little more about Lance Martin and his family.

'She's a nurse.' He responded, and she laughed out loud. He giggled a bit, but clearly it was only because he thought he should. Debby quickly cleared up his confusion.

'Me too! Theatre nurse. I'll be looking to go back to work after the baby comes, part time if I can.'

Lance's laugh was genuine this time. 'Mags is part time, because our youngest is only six. She's on the gastro ward at the infirmary.'

Debby told him she would love to meet Maggie some time and pick her brains about what it was like, to work at the local hospital. Lance agreed. 'I'm sure you'll get to meet her very soon. We only live another half a mile long this lane. We'll be neighbours, more or less.'

They all walked back towards the road. Darren had stayed quiet since Lance had mentioned losing his best friend at such a young age, but Debby knew his mind was working overtime. They hung back while Lance contacted the owner. He seemed to be on the phone for a long time, but it was probably only about five minutes. To Debby, it was the longest wait of her life, to be told that yes, the owner was happy to accept their offer, and the house would be theirs if they wanted it.

After Lance had promised to get the ball rolling, and they'd organised a structural survey, he shook their hands and told them they were free to stay on and look around the outside of the property. After indicating where the boundaries were, he returned to his car, saying he needed to get back to the office quick-smart, to start cancelling the viewings scheduled for the following day. They waved him off, and both said in unison. 'He's a really nice guy!'

Debby was looking forward to meeting Maggie Martin. To have someone nearby, more or less her own age, who was in the same line of work, was an incredibly lucky thing. Maybe she'd make a new friend fairly quickly!

She and Darren decided to take a walk around the boundary, which proved fruitful. In one corner of the land there appeared to be a very small ruin; another outbuilding that had literally fallen down where it had stood. It was overgrown with ivy and thistles, but the stone was still visible.

Darren was excited. 'Debs, look! All that stone – we could use that in the house somehow, I'm sure. And that old chook house? I could finally set up my wood lathe, in there.'

Debby was pleased to see that the entire property was dry-stone walled. Some of the walls had partially collapsed, and definitely needed some attention, but they would work in the short term, in keeping Badger safe. At the back of the house, the two big trees that were encroaching and blocking out the light from the third bedroom were apple trees. With a serious prune, Debby figured they could probably keep them. They were, after all, the cottage's namesake! There was just enough space between them to string a hammock, and it looked as if the afternoon sun would be lovely in that space, filtering through the leaves. They could build a patio outside the back door. It would probably have more shade than sunshine, but they could still make it a nice outdoor living area, with their barbecue and their outdoor furniture.

Eventually they starting walking back to the car. Neither wanted to talk much. The enormity of what they'd just committed to was slowly sinking in. They were both happy, Debby could clearly see that, but they were a little daunted too.

There's a lot to do here, she repeated to herself as she stopped, turned back, and took one final look at the house, now mostly hidden from the road by the trees at the edge of the garden in front of it. *But I think we can make this place every bit as spectacular as it once was, and deserves to be again.*

Before they drove back to The Beeches, Darren called into the vet surgery. 'Since we're up here, I think it would be a nice thing to do to go and see David Thornley, and accept the job offer in person, shake hands, that sort of thing.'

'That's a great idea! And then, we can grab some late lunch at Peg's tea shop, and then head to the hotel. I dunno about you, but I intend to make the most of the spa, for what's left of this afternoon.'

Darren was anxious about showing up at the vet practice unannounced, but he needn't have worried. As soon as they walked through the door, the receptionists beamed at them, and one immediately picked up the phone. Less than half a minute later, David Thornley was striding through from the back, and extending his hand to Darren. 'Hi! It's good to see you, Darren, and this must be your wife, Debby?' He turned to Debby and she was delighted to see such a twinkle in his light grey eyes.

'Hi. Dr Thornley. Nice to meet you.'

He turned back to Darren. 'I don't suppose you've got an hour spare, to do a hernia op on an old spaniel?' He bellowed with laughter at the look on Darren's face. 'Kidding! Well, kind of. Stan's not in today, and we're as busy as usual.'

Darren laughed too. 'Not a chance, mate. But I do have some news that might cheer you up, if you've time to hear it. Can we step into your office for a minute?'

Debby waited in reception, chatting to the two receptionists between the comings and goings of various clients and their different critters. Everyone seemed nice. When Darren finally emerged, both he and David Thornley were laughing and clapping one another on the back. David turned to the receptionists. 'Meet the new vet! Starting first week of November, and I think you already know how he likes his coffee.'

Cheers erupted from behind the desk. Everyone was grinning, and one of the receptionists came around and gave Darren a quick hug. 'Welcome to the team,' she told him, and then glanced over and smiled broadly at Debby. 'And welcome to Torley, Mrs Davies! I hope you'll be happy here in our funny little town.'

Arrangements were quickly made for everyone to meet Debby and Darren for a celebratory drink in The Feathers as soon as the surgery closed at six. Debby suggested to Darren that perhaps he could ask Mark and Adie Raven, and Bob and Sheila Shalloe as well, if they weren't busy.

Ravenous, they both headed to Peg Tripper's tea shop, and she was so surprised to see them, she almost dropped the tray of quiches she was carrying. 'What are you two doing back here? You only just left!'

The sat down and told her the news about the house. Peg was immediately excited. 'You mean to tell me you've bought Chris and June Marsh's old place, Appletree Cottage, on Turnbull Lane? I didn't even know it was on the market!' She seemed astonished.

Debby laughed at her surprise. 'It only went on a few days ago, and we were only the third people to view it. I don't think they even had time to get signs up.'

Pet shook her head. 'Well, I never! I think a lot of people are going to be disappointed about missing out on that! It's a bit of a wreck, but it's got real potential, and *tons* of history.'

'So, you're familiar with it, then?' Debby enquired.

'Oh yes! I live next door to it! Mine's the house just behind it, a few hundred yards back towards the town. You'll have driven past my place to get there.'

'Is yours the bungalow, with the big, long porch across the front? With the red telephone box in the garden?' Debby had noticed it as they'd driven past.

Peg nodded. 'Yep. That's me. BT were ripping out the phone box outside the shop here, about three years ago, and I asked them if I could buy it. It's a great landmark,' she giggled. 'It's how people manage to find me. Most folks don't even know where Turnbull Lane actually is, and there are only a dozen or so houses on the entire two-mile stretch. The Marsh's place can't even be seen from the road, the way it is at the moment, all overgrown and everything.'

Peg seemed to be genuinely delighted for them, especially when Darren told her he'd been offered a job with the local vet surgery and had just accepted it, and that Debby was hoping to eventually find work at Cumberland Infirmary. She clapped her hands with genuine pleasure. 'My God! What a lot of big changes for you, all at once! How exciting is all this? It will be nice to have you in town! I'm thrilled.'

Debby invited her to six o'clock drinks at The Feathers, and she happily accepted, saying she'd try to get her husband Eric there too. He was co-managing a farm on the other side of Carlisle, but she hoped he could finish a little early. 'He won't have had a shower or anything, but hopefully he won't be too smelly!'

After a delicious lunch of quiche and salad, with crusty bread and two pots of coffee, they made their way to The Beeches to spend a couple of hours in the hotel's gorgeous spa.

Debby had never seen Darren so happy and excited. She couldn't remember ever being this happy or excited either. A new life was drawing them to this lovely little town and its friendly, welcoming people. That, and finally having their much longed-for baby on the way, all just felt like manna from heaven.

Chapter Seventeen

Thank God for Mum and Pat, Darren thought to himself as they loaded the last of their things into the caravan. *I dunno where we'd be without them.*

The time between selling their house in Exeter and completing on the Torley house had gone by in a blur, between pregnancy scans and classes, midwife appointments, and shopping for prams and other paraphernalia. They'd also had to organise transport, find storage for everything in Carlisle, try (with no success) to smooth the ruffled family feathers on the Cameron side, find a team of cleaners, buy a decent caravan, arrange for the power to be switched on at Appletree Cottage, and get final readings. By the time they'd done all that, and tied up all kinds of other loose ends in Exeter, they were both beyond exhausted.

Darren had been determined that Debby have minimal stress throughout the entire moving process, so he had organised the packers, movers and cleaners to get the Exeter house sorted for handover, and his mother and her partner Pat had gone beyond the call of duty in helping them get everything finalised. Pat was even taking a load of other essential stuff that they were going to need, all the way to Torley for them in his work van, shutting his chip shop for two days in order to do it.

Debby's parents had been no help at all. They were staging a silent protest by refusing to lend a hand in any direction. Darren couldn't bring himself to say much to Debby about it, because the last thing he wanted to do was upset her, but he was really annoyed at their ongoing lack of support. They'd never offered help with anything before, but their daughter was pregnant now, for God's sake! What were they thinking, in refusing to give her their blessing to go and start a new life with her husband and child? Were they really that mean-spirited that they couldn't make things easier for her, in even the smallest way? Couldn't her mother have wrapped some bloody crockery, or cooked them a basic meal when they were doing thirty things in one day and were too busy or exhausted to make time to cook and eat?

Clearly not. Debby had expressed her frustration at the outset, even before they'd bought Appletree Cottage, that her mum and dad were behaving like she was moving to the other side of the world, instead of just five hours up the bloody motorway. Their selfish behaviour took his breath away. They weren't even nice to her, most of the time, so why should they even care if she moved away? None of it made any sense at all. It wasn't even about the baby. As predicted, and as with everything else that was going on in their daughter's life (especially the fact that she actually wanted to *have* one), the Camerons expressed no interest in being grandparents.

Darren continually bit his tongue. His mum Barbara had noticed too, that Debby's parents were conspicuously absent from the general melee. He'd told her how he felt about it, but she'd just shaken her head.

'There's no fathoming some people, love. It's best not to try. They're hurt, and they're reacting. It's not what you or I would do, but we judge by our own standards, don't we? Try not to condemn, Darren. They don't know how to behave any better, or maybe they do and they just don't want to, but that's all there is to it. You just have to accept it, let it go, and get on with things.'

Barbara had gone on to say that maybe once the baby came the Camerons might thaw a little, but she also said she hoped their treatment of their daughter wouldn't end up backfiring on them. Darren knew what she meant. Debby was very hurt about her parents' disinterest in her new life. If she still felt that way when the baby arrived, maybe she wouldn't want them involved. He couldn't imagine they'd want to be, but nobody could predict how the new arrival might make them feel. Praying for a wake-up call felt like a step too far, but who knew? He'd been surprised by enough in life already, to know that he could never rule out the potential for a miracle, especially when it came to a new baby arriving. That tended to bring out the best in a lot of people.

He shrugged to himself now. It would be up to the three of them to work things out. He kept out of things as much as he could, and he didn't let their insults drag him down. According to them, he was abducting Debby against her will, and intending to hold her hostage in the sticks, away from civilisation. It would actually be pretty funny, if it wasn't so insulting to his wife, that they truly believed she wasn't capable of making any decisions for herself.

The truth was, if she'd said no to moving, it wouldn't have happened. No matter what Darren's own dreams were, he was always going to put Debby's and the baby's needs first. Whatever Debby needed, she would get. The fact that she loved Appletree Cottage as much as he did was just lucky. They were on the same page about it, with equal enthusiasm and vision. Their commitment to their new home, and their new life in the Lake District, was equal too. Surely, most parents who wanted their kids to be happy would see that as a good thing?

Carole and Don Cameron had never warmed to Darren, and he fully understood why. His past was what it was, and there was no escaping it, but if their daughter was happy, wasn't that more important than what they thought of the man who made it so?

Debby *was* happy about the decision to move and start a new life in a gentler place. He knew it – and he knew *her* – as well as he knew the back of his own hand. She didn't pretend about anything; she simply wasn't built that way. She always said what she meant, and she always meant what she said. You always knew where you stood with her. It was one of the things he loved the most about her. If she'd even so much as wavered slightly, in her enthusiasm for Appletree Cottage and their proposed new life in Torley, he would have challenged her until he got the truth out of her, and it wouldn't have taken very long. If she hadn't wanted this as much as he did, he would know it by now, and they'd be staying put.

Debby had another reason to be happy too. She'd contacted Cumberland Infirmary again and had been warmly offered some part time work. After a hastily-arranged online interview, she'd accepted a temporary contract, to start as soon as she wanted, on 15 hours a week. She could do three days at five hours, or five days at three hours; it was her choice. The shift rotation would include weekends, but they could live with that for a while. After the baby came, the hospital would either have her back on the same basis, or talk about a more permanent post, when she was ready to return. It was a loose arrangement, nowhere near as secure as what she'd had in Exeter as a permanent full-time post, but it did get her foot in the door there.

She was thrilled about it, especially after her supervisor at Exeter had spoken to Cumbria in support of her application. Karim, her supervisor, had said he would happily recommend her to *anyone*, because she was highly qualified and experienced, she'd been a dream to work with, and the loss of her would be keenly felt by everyone in her team. It wouldn't be possible to get a better commendation than that. Karim had always staunchly supported Debby, and she was going to miss him too.

Darren had also been thrilled to learn that the references David Thornley had taken up, at Lakeview, had revealed something similar. His current boss (his mentor Simon Westrupp, who had provided his initial training and guided him unfailingly through the entire process of qualifying as a vet), had stepped up as a staunch referee and come up trumps for him. The future was looking as secure as it could, at this point. Debby and Darren had sold one house, bought another, found new jobs, made a few new friends, established a good antenatal care system in Cumbria, and were moving to the other end of the country.

And all without a single positive word of encouragement, and without a single solitary scrap of support or constructive help, from the Camerons.

C'est la fucking vie. I hope the bastards choke on their indignation.

But thinking about his in-laws, and the appalling way they were punishing their daughter for daring to have a life of her own, was taking Darren nowhere. It was a sheer waste of energy that was needed elsewhere, so he deliberately threw them into his mental dustbin, and jammed the lid firmly on top of them.

He checked his watch again now. They were only about half an hour behind schedule, which meant they'd arrive in Torley about four in the afternoon, if the traffic wasn't too bad along the way. School traffic was inevitable, but it would certainly help if they could at least get off the M6 before commuter time kicked in!

Debby and Badger were already in the car waiting, with a flask of hot tea and a cool-bag full of sandwiches, fruit, cake and cold drinks that Barbara had thoughtfully provided. They wouldn't have to stop for anything other than a wee along the way. Darren raised a hand and gave a short whistle to Pat, who had already hooked up the caravan and was ready to pull away. Pat flashed his lights briefly, and Barbara gave them the thumbs up.

Three hours in, after getting past the snarl of road works that were still continuing at the M5/M6 interchange, they stopped at the services to let Badger stretch his legs. Everyone seemed happy, and chatty. Darren watched his wife with so much pride, as she came back from the loo, with her hand across her baby bump. The gentle swell was obvious now, and after a horrendous month and a half of being plagued with morning sickness, her body had adjusted to the changes. She was doing just fine now.

They arrived in Torley, as predicted, at ten to four. The sun was already low in the sky though, as the autumn was well underway. He was glad they'd made it without a hitch. He was due to start work the following week, and wanted to get a handle on cleaning up Appletree Cottage first so they could at least store the contents of Pat's van in there. He was beyond grateful that Pat would be there to help him with the dreaded task of guiding the caravan down the overgrown, weed-infested, pothole-pitted driveway, and into the garden to sit alongside the cottage.

When they arrived, however, Darren was gobsmacked at what he found. The driveway from the road down to the house, which had previously resembled the crater-ridden surface of the moon, had all been expertly levelled off. Someone – he had no idea who – had also cleared the overgrowth from both sides and taken all the debris away. A well-settled, tightly-packed layer of gravel was now sitting neatly over the long swathe of packed-down earth. The driveway was as solid as a rock. He turned to Debby. 'Did you know about this? Did you arrange someone to come and do this?'

She stared at the driveway in disbelief too, and then looked at him, blankly. 'No. I don't know anything about it. But how wonderful!' She started laughing. 'Maybe there are faeries here!'

Darren got out of his car to take a closer look. Whoever had cleared the driveway ready for their long 5-berth caravan had done an expert job. Darren knew it would be fine for at least a year before it would need to be done again. It was an extraordinary thing to have happened. *Someone is looking out for us*, he told himself. If anyone had asked him what he would appreciate the most, at this point, it was having the driveway made suitable for reversing a caravan onto the property. Someone knew that, and they'd come along and done it. Who he had to thank, for such an extraordinary act of kindness, he really didn't know.

But I'll make it my business to find out.

He could have got the caravan down the driveway himself, as it turned out, but he was still glad that Pat and Barbara were there. He wanted them to see the cottage, and he hoped they'd have the imagination to see it in the same way he and Debby did.

Even with the driveway cleared and newly smoothed, it still took longer than expected to get the caravan backed down it, and into a stable position alongside the house. Pat was a marvel with the reversing, as Darren and Barbara guided him down. At the bottom, they had to turn it around so that its door opened towards the drive, rather than into the wall of the house. It also meant that the back window, in the caravan's separate bedroom, looked out onto what would eventually be their beautiful front garden. The turning space they needed was still overgrown, so in the end they unhooked it and manually wrestled it into position. It was heavy, but between the three of them they managed to do it without losing control of it or hitting it against the wall of the house. When it was properly positioned, Pat set about stabilizing it. Only when everything was sorted, with the caravan being deemed fit to set up temporary home in, did he even raise his head to look at the house itself.

'Good Lord! It needs some bloody work, chum!'

Darren laughed, and so did Debby. 'Take a look inside.' He tossed Pat the front door keys, which they'd just picked up from the agent, on their way here, and Pat caught them deftly.

'I have to anyway, to hook up the electrics. Where's that cable?'

Mercifully, thanks to Lance Martin, the power in the cottage had been connected, and it wasn't long before they were all sitting around the caravan's little table, holding steaming mugs of tea. It was a bit cramped, for four adults and a very exuberant dog, but nobody seemed to mind. Pat and Barbara both thought the house was reeking of potential.

'I can see exactly why you've fallen in love with it,' Barbara enthused. 'It will be gorgeous when you've done it all! A lot of work, as Pat's already said, but goodness me! What a crown jewel you'll have, at the end of it. And maybe I can help with a bit of advice on interior decorating, if you like? You know, since I did that course and everything, a few years ago?'

'Thanks, Mum,' Darren grinned. 'That means a lot, that you see it the same way we do. And I'm sure Debby would love to pick your brains about what to do on the inside, wouldn't you, Debs?'

Debby nodded. 'I really would, Barbara, thanks! If I can get this place looking as lovely and cosy as you've made yours, I'll be thrilled. I do have some ideas, but I'm open to new suggestions.'

Pat chuckled. 'Is there a plan to be in before the baby arrives? Or is that a bit much to think about yet?'

Debby shrugged, and grinned at him. 'I dunno. We can't get the rewiring done until the end of November, and the plumbing's not being done until then, either. The delay is because all the local contractors are really busy. They were the earliest dates we could get, believe it or not. We have to go shopping for a bathroom suite, and a kitchen in the meantime!'

Darren studiously avoided meeting her eyes. She didn't know yet that he'd already ordered her dream kitchen, the one she'd picked out of a brochure and shown to him in a fit of near-hysteria because she loved it so much. It was a traditional kitchen with a modern twist; all green glass wall tiles, polished wood surfaces and doors, and brass fittings. It came complete with a stand-alone island. He'd also ordered a dark green Aga, just like the red one she'd become so enamoured of at Teapot Cottage.

The kitchen had been an eye-wateringly expensive purchase, and he was glad she hadn't seen the state of their bank account yet, with such an enormous luxury-kitchen-sized hole in it. He hoped he wouldn't have to explain it for another day or two. If he could keep her distracted that long, it would all come together nicely. He planned for her to get the phone call on Monday morning from the kitchen company, just after he'd left for his first day at work, asking her to let them have a time to come and measure up for everything. The plan was to have the kitchen installed in time for Christmas, after all the plumbing and electrical infrastructure was completed.

Feen Raven-Black had recommended her friend's husband to come and do the re-wiring, a guy called Tony Valley, who ran his own local domestic electrical business. He was good at his work, and fair with his prices, and Feen was sure he'd give them the best deal possible. The plumbing would also be a big job, but Tony knew someone he regularly worked with, and so they'd managed to schedule both guys to come at the same time. With those two things out of the way, the kitchen could go in without too many problems. Darren bit his lip and grinned at his step-dad.

'Pat, I can't thank you enough for all your help. It's made all the difference. But, at the risk of pushing my luck a bit further, could I ask one more favour? Before you and Mum go back in the morning, d'you think we could go over to the DIY superstore, over in Carlisle, and pick up the bathroom suite we've decided we want? If we could get it in your van, it would help me a lot. I still have to buy a trailer, and I'd rather not right now, if I can avoid it. All our money's needed elsewhere.'

Pat nodded. 'I understand that, of course. And sure, we can do that. It'll be fun. Maybe we could get the wall and floor tiles for your bathroom too, if they have something you'd like.'

Debby shook her head. 'Wall tiles, yes, maybe. Floor tiles, no. The floors are wooden planks, Pat. We think they might be something lovely, like beech or pine. We want to get a proper look at them, to see if they'd clean up alright, before we decide if they need to be covered instead.'

'Well, you can't put your suite in until the floor's done,' Pat observed.

Debby laughed. 'I guess that's true. But at least if it can sit in one of the other rooms, *ready* to go in, its one less thing to worry about. The guy who's coming with the electrician, Tony Valley, can fit it all. We could get it delivered I suppose, but while you're here…' She trailed off, not wanting to labour a point that Darren had already made.

Pat winked at her. 'Well, if you like, we can go and have a quick look at the floors upstairs now, while there's still enough light left. You need a few lightbulbs in the place, don't you? Put those on your shopping list.'

He drained his cup and stood up. Darren resisted the urge to stop him. Pat was the type who sometimes got a bone between his teeth and he wouldn't let go of it until he was good and ready. If he wanted to chip away at the horrible floor tiles in that manky bathroom, Darren wasn't going to hold him back!

Sure enough, on closer inspection, the entire upstairs flooring was wooden planks. Pat had a chisel, but he didn't have a sander, so they couldn't determine much about the quality of the floorboards in the bathroom, other than the fact that they seemed solid, with no water damage or rot. Once he'd jemmied all the tiles off, which hadn't taken long, he stood up and stretched his back.

'That was a lot easier than I thought but I don't think they were laid that well to begin with, to be fair. Your claw-foot tub is worth a bob or two,' he observed. 'It's cast iron. Get that recoated, put some nice new taps on it, and it'd be lovely.'

Darren had to agree with him. The bath would look lovely, restored, although it wouldn't be in keeping with the modern bathroom they'd decided on. 'Maybe we could set it up in a corner of our bedroom, if the plumbing would allow for it,' he suggested, and Debby nodded slowly.

'Hmmm. Not the worst idea you've had. There's a chimney breast at one end of the bedroom, and I'm wondering if there's a bricked-up fireplace in there. It's a big room, so it wouldn't surprise me at all if there was.'

'Well, if that was the case, it certainly would be lovely to have a bath set up near it, wouldn't it, in the wintertime?' Barbara enthused.

Darren was thrilled at how positive his mum and Pat were being. They were a far cry from Debby's surly parents, who weren't even prepared to look at photographs.

It was nearly dark now. Darren had booked Pat and Barbara a room at the Bull and Royal in Torley town for the night. He'd also booked a table for the four of them to have supper together, and he planned to take Badger, who he assumed was still as welcome there as he'd been when they'd stayed at Teapot Cottage over the summer. A nice pub meal would be just the ticket tonight. Pat hung back as they were leaving the house.

'I just want to check one thing before we head off. I was looking at the pitch of the roof, outside. Did anyone say anything about a loft, or an attic?'

Darren shook his head. 'No. We haven't even thought about that. We saw the inspection that said the roof was in good order, but nothing was said about space up there.'

Pat stroked his chin thoughtfully. 'Hmmm. I'm going to take a quick look, if you don't mind?'

'How are you going to get up there?'

'Give me a leg up, chum!'

Fifteen minutes later, Pat confirmed that Appletree Cottage did indeed have an attic, and he thought it was big enough to provide them with one reasonable sized extra room. 'It wouldn't be a show-stopper, but it's an option if you want to expand at any stage. A loft conversion wouldn't hurt the resale value either. You'd just have to think about access. You'd need to put a staircase in, somewhere.'

Darren was pleased at Pat's news, although he didn't think they'd be devoting any time or attention to a loft conversion just yet! It was definitely food for thought for later, though. He was grateful to Pat for having the insight to check out the potential. All it meant though, was that there would be even more work to do.

The following morning, before heading to the DIY store in Carlisle, they popped into Ye Olde Torley Tea Shoppe for a slap-up breakfast. Darren introduced Pat and Barbara to Peg Tripper, who made them every bit as welcome as expected, and told them she hoped to see them again. Darren reassured her that she probably would, and she beamed at them all. He liked Peg a lot. He was pleased they were going to be neighbours, and thrilled when she invited him and Debby to dinner at her house that night. 'You can't be on your own for your first night here! Come next door and have tea with me and Eric. I've three cats, but they'll make themselves scarce I'm sure, so you can bring your lovely dog. We'll only be having steak pie and veg, but there'll be lashings of gravy, and I think I can rustle up a jam roly-poly and custard for pudding, if you need extra tempting.'

It was only after they'd unloaded their new bathroom suite from Pat's van, and waved him and Barbara and on their journey home to Exeter, that the enormity of exactly what he had Debby had achieved finally sank in. They'd pulled it off! They'd made the break, picked up the keys to their new house, and they were about to embark on the biggest set of adventures so far, of their lives together. Darren wasn't sure whether the fluttery feeling he suddenly felt in the pit of his stomach was fear or excitement. When he described it to Debby, she admitted to having it too, and they both decided that it was probably perfectly normal – and therefore perfectly okay – for it to be a little bit of both.

Chapter Eighteen

They were in the middle of repaving the front patio area that ran the length of the house, when Debby started having cramps, and pains in her back. She stood up and blanched. As soon as the colour drained from her face, Darren knew something was badly wrong. Fearing the worst, he rushed her to Cumberland Infirmary and he knew, in that moment, that even if he lived to be two hundred years old, he would never be able to forget the fear in her eyes, or the terror in his own heart.

Fortunately, the antenatal unit at the hospital quickly established that her cramps were nothing serious. It was, the doctor said, quite simply a 'perfect storm' of bodily complications. As Debby's uterus was growing, the ligaments were being stretched, and she also had a bad bout of trapped wind. The pain she experienced was severe, and that alone had been enough to scare her witless, but after waiting for such a long time to have a child, the thought of anything happening to rob her of that was more than she could bear. She'd become hysterical, which hadn't helped. At one point, while she was waiting in A & E to be assessed, her cramps were so bad, and she felt so wretched and terrified, she just dissolved into racking sobs and cried that she just wanted her mum, of all people!

It was the most out of character thing Darren had ever heard her say, and it seemed a bit churlish to ask her if she was sure, or expect her to wait until they knew what the assessment would show. So he immediately texted his mother-in-law and told her that Debby was at the hospital being assessed with intense stomach pains, and 'asking for her mother.' He wasn't sure if it would hinder or help Debby to have Carole there, if the news was as bad as they feared. But she said it was what she wanted, so he complied. He held off telling Barbara and Pat, deciding that he wouldn't worry them unless there was a real need.

Don and Carole Cameron arrived first thing the following morning, as grim-faced as usual. Neither of them gave Darren more than an initial, abrupt greeting, and Don didn't even talk much to his wife. Carole wore the trousers in the family, and Darren figured that Don had probably long-since decided there wasn't much point in saying anything of note, because she wouldn't listen to him anyway. Darren actually felt a bit sorry for him, but he'd gone past the point of being interested in how the man really felt about anything, since he'd never extended any overture of friendship; probably because Carole would never have let him hear the end of it if he'd tried. He was nothing but a wimp, as far as Darren was concerned, and the usual lack of conversation suited him just fine.

The hospital had already confirmed that neither Debby nor the baby were in any danger, although the recommendation was that Debby should stop trying to lay heavy concrete paving slabs immediately, thank you very much. Darren decided that they wouldn't get any argument from him. If she tried to insist again, about helping with heavy manual work, he wouldn't cave into her demands.

After the Camerons were informed of the situation, they looked him up and down with their usual disdain, before barging straight past him, into their daughter's room. Darren didn't even have to open his mouth, to be sneered at or belittled, and he figured Debby could do without feeling like she had to defend him yet again, so he decided to leave them to it for a while. He was hungry, so he followed his nose to the hospital restaurant and ordered a cheeseburger and chips, and a double-shot cappuccino.

It was a relief that nothing was wrong with Debby. With any luck, he'd get to take her home in the next few hours, but he certainly wouldn't be inviting her parents to come and see their new house.

After finishing his lunch, he made his way back to the ward, and was surprised to hear Debby's strident voice. She sounded angry and upset and he was immediately alarmed.

‘And another thing. I’m sick to the bloody back teeth of the way you behave towards my husband. You’ve always treated him like a second-class citizen, which he is not. You’ve always looked down on him like he’s something on the bottom of your shoe, which he is not. And I would like it to stop now, please, for once and for all. You ‘tolerated’ him, as you so generously put it, while we were living in Exeter, but since we left, your treatment of him has been horrible, and downright mean. If you can’t be respectful to the man who actually makes me happier than I once ever dreamed I could possibly be, then you can both fuck off, and I don’t want to see either of you again. Enough is enough.’

Debby had never sounded so angry. She would no doubt be furious with Darren, for calling her parents in the first place (even though she’d kind of asked him to), for what had amounted to a false alarm. She’d howled that she just wanted her mum, when she was in pain, and he’d complied by getting her parents to come up here. But instead of being a comfort, they were making her blood boil, and that wasn't good. He needed to put a stop to that, *right* now.

When he walked into the room, the Camerons predictably ignored him, and they pointedly rolled their eyes when he tried to explain to them that after getting excruciating pains in her back and belly, and being rushed to A & E, in tears with fear and pain, Debby didn’t need anyone winding her up.

Her mother tutted and continued to ignore him. ‘Mind your language please, young lady! If you’re angry at us being here, that’s one thing, although you did *request* us to come, as I understand it. We came, and we are doing our best, and it is not acceptable for you to swear at us. We’re your parents. Show some respect, please.’

That was it. That last remark tipped Debby totally over the edge, and she lost it completely. As Darren watched, in horrified fascination, the last of her control flew away from her. Even to his ears, her voice sounded shrill, hard and uncompromising. ‘Respect?’ She roared the word at them so hard they both flinched.

‘You want to talk to me about respect? Where’s yours? You’re a pair of intolerant, prejudiced, patronising *bastards!*’

She was bellowing for real now, and never in her life before had she lost her temper with *anyone*, to such a degree. Her parents were incredulous, and absolutely horrified, but she didn't stop. 'Why have you always thought it was acceptable to treat Darren like dirt? He's my *husband!'*

Her fury was something to behold. Again, her mother tutted, bristling with offence and indignation. 'You are clearly upset about this little scare you've had with the baby, so I'll overlook what you just called us.'

Debby was not to be placated. She continued to yell at her mother. 'Little scare with the baby? *Little scare*? I thought I was going to fucking lose this child! I was in pain, Mum, and I was *terrified.* So don't you dare try and minimise that! And, while we're on the subject, it's not the main reason I'm angry. Being terrified and patronised is bad enough, but I've had a guts-full of you trying to make me feel bad for marrying a man you don't happen to like, and blaming him for *my choice*, in wanting to get as far away from you as I can! It was my choice! You're monsters! You're not even prepared to try and *pretend* to be happy for me.'

She drew a big breath. She wasn't finished yet. She was on a roll, and for the first time in her life she was telling her uptight, snobby parents exactly what she thought of them. Darren was mesmerized. As agitated as she was, and as unwise as it was to let her stay that way, he didn't want to stop her at all. He knew she had to get this out. She'd tolerated their terrible attitude for long enough, and now she was blazing. He thought it was long overdue, and fair enough. Something inside him glowed with pride, as Debby unleashed her pent-up fury, over so very many things, directly at her mum and dad.

'If you can't see how happy Darren makes me, and for the life we've chosen together, get lost. You won't be missed. I'd rather not see either of you, *ever again*, than have to stomach another God-knows how many years listening to you relentlessly belittling and whining about the man I love. If you think I want the kind of role models for my child that can only focus on the worst of people and ignore the best, you can think again. I won't let you anywhere near her! NOW GET OUT!'

Her last words were delivered with such force they made her hoarse. She literally had no voice left. She fell back against the pillows, spent, just as a nurse came running into the room, demanding to know what all the swearing, shouting and bawling was about. Debby was puce, and crying, and shaking with rage. Her mother was also in tears now, and her father just stood beside her bed, saying nothing, and staring at the floor with his jaw working hard and his mouth set in a grim line. He was furious and embarrassed, but he didn't look up. Darren sprang forward and gathered Debby into his arms. He looked over his shoulder at Carloe and Don, and shook his head angrily at all of them.

'Get out, both of you. Right now, before I knock you both spark out. I'm not fucking kidding.'

'What on *earth* is going on in here?' the nurse demanded. 'You mustn't upset yourself like this, Mrs Davies! Please! You can't be this agitated! We've only just got you stabilized!' She looked at Darren, frowning. 'What is all this about? You can't be letting this happen, or threatening people in here! This is a hospital, young man, and we will not tolerate violence or abuse. I will have to call the police if this carries on!'

She then looked at Don and Carole, with her hands on her hips, as they continued to stare off in different directions, and neither was prepared to meet her gaze. 'Have I to throw somebody out?' she demanded.

'Yes!' Debby tuned to look at her. 'Get rid of these *bastards*!' She found enough voice to shout the last word, and the nurse told Don and Carole quietly, but firmly, that they needed to leave straight away before she had to call security. They instantly complied and left without another word.

Debs was angrier than Darren had ever seen her. He knew that part of it was the displaced fear she'd felt when they thought she might be losing the baby, and the rest was all the bottled-up rage she'd been trying not to show for far too long now. But the mood she was in was not going to help keep her stable. He needed to calm her down.

'I'll take it from here,' he said to the nurse, who shook her head at him. She wasn't happy at all.

'This simply will not do, Dr Davies. If people are going to upset her this much, they need to be kept away. She absolutely cannot be allowed to get into a state like this again.' Her tone held no compromise, and Darren nodded.

'Don't worry. I won't let them come back in.'

She sighed and met his gaze. 'If this does happen again, we'll have to ban those people from visiting. And no matter what happens, you really mustn't threaten them again like that. Not in here, anyway. Please, kindly tell them not to come back. In fact, scratch that. They're outside, hovering in the hallway. I'll tell them myself.'

'Okay, thanks, and I'm sorry.'

The nurse nodded curtly and left the room. Darren pulled a face at her, behind her back, hoping it would make Debby laugh. It didn't, but when she spoke again her voice was mercifully normal.

'I'm sorry you had to witness that, but it's been a long time coming. They're a piece of work, coming in here behaving like they have. I'm sick to bloody death of it. They haven't even asked if we need anything! I dunno why they're even here. Why did they come – to gloat?'

Darren shrugged. 'I dunno, sweetheart, but I'm sure it wasn't to gloat. They're your mum and dad! They wouldn't want to see you suffering.'

'You're always so generous about them. Why? They've always treated you so badly! You've never been good enough for them, and they've never been shy about reminding you, or me, of the fact. They never miss a chance, do they? They don't deserve your generosity, or to be excused by you, of all people! It's unforgiveable, the way they treat you. I'm not tolerating it anymore.'

'So I heard,' Darren said wryly.

'I meant every bloody word, and I'm glad the nurse threw them out, because they weren't listening to me, or you. They just stalked straight past you without even acknowledging you, didn't they?'

He chuckled. 'Yep. More or less. No change there, though. I'm an ex-con, Debs. They'll probably *always* hate me. It's worse now because we've moved away, and I've got you up the duff, so you're completely under my evil control now. They can't control you *themselves* anymore, or keep a close eye on how thoroughly and completely I'm destroying you.'

He shrugged lightly, and pulled a face. 'It's okay Debs, I've learned to live with it. It's really no skin off my nose. I didn't marry them. I married *you.*' He picked up her hand and kissed it. 'And oh, my God, how spectacular were you, just now? Terrifying in your fury, and completely beautiful with it. You're my hero. Good on you, for finally standing up to them.'

'They're assholes. And it's perfectly alright if you want to agree with me. I know you've always held your tongue, and there've been times when I've had no idea how you managed to do that, but you can say what you want about them now. You don't have to worry about what I might think. I know what they are.'

'A pair of self-serving wankers?' Darren spoke in a deadpan tone, making his expression into that of an ape, which he knew usually made her laugh. He had to calm her down, no matter what it took.

Finally, she laughed. 'Yes. Wankers. That's perfect.'

It was good to hear her laugh. He'd been distraught, and desperately afraid, that they were going to lose their baby. All he cared about now was keeping Debby's God-awful parents away from her.

If they come back here and she doesn't want to see them, I won't be letting them in. Then they'll find out just what kind of stuff I'm still capable of saying to people, if the mood takes me. Then, if they need a <u>*genuine*</u> *reason to dislike me, they'll have one.*

There was no way he was going to stand for his wife becoming hysterical again because of them. He turned to ask her an important question.

'By the way, just now, when you were ranting at Carole and Don, I heard you refer to the baby as 'she.' You told them you wouldn't let them anywhere near 'her.' D'you know something I don't?'

She shook her head at him. 'Scout's honour, I don't, babe. It was a heat of the moment thing, when I was screaming at them. We said we'd wait, didn't we? We said we didn't want to know the sex, and I still feel that way, but I really am starting to feel like I'm having a girl. I dunno why, and I wasn't going to say anything to you, but I guess that's been blown out of the water.'

Darren couldn't help the grin that was spreading across his face.

'What?' Debby demanded.

He shook his head. 'You're going to think I'm mad, but I think you're having a girl, too. I dunno why I feel that either, but I keep thinking about little dresses, and dolls, more than I'm thinking about toy trucks and water pistols.'

'Will you be disappointed if it's a girl?'

'What? Are you *kidding*? I'll be over the bloody *moon*!' Darren bit his bottom lip. 'Daughters can be a bit more difficult to manage though, can't they? I wouldn't let her date until she was eighteen. Well, probably more like twenty-one. Or maybe twenty-seven.'

Debby laughed again. 'Whatever we end up having, you're going to be a great Dad!'

'I hope so. But I'm bloody terrified, I have to be honest. I'm excited, but I'm scared shitless. It's all so real, Debs! The scare we've just had, it's brought home to me just how important this really is, this parenting malarkey. I hope I don't make a complete mess of it all.'

Debby bit her bottom lip. 'It's okay to be scared. A big part of me is too, because there's no blueprint for how we handle this. No roadmap, and no manual. We'll be flying by the seat of our pants with *all* of it, with only our own childhood experiences to guide us on what not to do, and maybe a bit of advice from family and friends who've done it. And let's face it, my childhood experiences are no kind of role model, are they? But it's the same for everyone, isn't it? And not ever parent messes up, do they? Most end up doing a brilliant job. Their kids turn out great, and I bet we'll be in that basket.'

She sounded convinced, and convincing, so he let it go. But he *was* scared to death. At least he'd been able to admit it.

The nurse came back in, with a very stern face. 'Your parents are still here. They're refusing to go until they've seen you again.' She looked decidedly unimpressed.

Debby shook her head emphatically. 'No. Absolutely not. I don't want to see them. I wish they'd listen to me for once, but they just won't, will they? Not even over this.' Darren could see she was at her wits' end about it, and about to get riled up again. The nurse said she would go and tell them, but Darren stopped her.

'No, let me. I'll talk to them.'

'Darren…' Debby began, and then stopped. He turned to face her.

'No, babe. You leave this with me, please.'

She bit her lip and nodded. 'Alright, but don't be too hard on them. Please?'

He shook his head. 'Sorry Debs, I can't promise that. I'll do my best, but I think the time for playing nice is over.'

She stated at him for a moment, then closed her eyes and quietly nodded. 'Okay.'

Darren was seething. It was about time Carole and Don heard a few home truths, and if the end result was even more frostiness, well, they'd all just have to find a way to live with it, wouldn't they? It was one thing to treat him and Debby like dirt. Actively winding their daughter up after the scare she'd just had? That was a different thing altogether, and he wasn't going to let it slide.

Carole and Don were standing near to the reception desk, looking anxious and upset. Carole saw him coming and folded her arms across her chest. Don just stared at the wall, in typical Don-like fashion. Darren decided to get straight to the point with them, without giving them a chance to speak first, because he doubted it would be any kind of apology, which was the only thing he would have wanted to hear.

'Don, Carole. I thought you'd left. Debs did make it plain, didn't she, that she'd asked you to leave? Did you not understand her?'

Neither parent knew how to respond. Darren had never challenged them before, not in all the years he'd been married to their daughter. They were surprised that he was confrontational with them, albeit politely, and they weren't quite sure how to respond.

'Umm, well she did say that, yes. But I'm not convinced she doesn't need us,' Carole stammered, clearly not wishing to talk to Darren at *all*, let alone have to defend herself to him in any way. Her eyes were darting in all directions; she clearly didn't want to look at him. But he wasn't letting her off the hook.

'Well, I'd say she's made it pretty plain that yours is the kind of help she can do without. I texted you last night and asked you to come because I thought it was the right thing to do for her, for all of you, actually. But she's told me I was wrong to do it, and that's good enough for me. So you probably do need to leave now, please, before that nurse over there decides to make good on her threat to call security, and you need to know that if she doesn't, I will.'

Carole shook her head adamantly. 'Oh, don't be ridiculous! Nobody is going to call security! Debby doesn't know what she's talking about. This anger, it's just her fear coming out, about maybe losing the baby. She needs her own mother. You have to let me back in there. Stand aside, please.'

Darren stepped forward, not enough to be menacing, but far enough to communicate to Carole that she couldn't push him around. 'Carole, I don't 'have' to do anything, least of all that. And I'm not standing aside for you anymore. I've done enough of that, over the years. I've had enough of you sweeping me aside like my concern for my wife doesn't match yours.'

He ran a hand through his hair, suddenly feeling desperately weary of all the discord he'd endured for so many years with his wife's parents.

'And let's face it, none of us really knows, do we, what you're actually concerned *about.* I think we can safely say that it isn't Debby's welfare. Like most things in your fucked-up little world, this is all about you, and whatever weird needs you have. Oh, and while I can't even begin to understand what it is that's put the red-hot poker so far up your arse that you can't even walk straight, Carole, what I do know is that this is where you need to lose the attitude; right here, and right now.'

Darren took a deep breath and ploughed on, deliberately ignoring the look of high dudgeon that suddenly swept across his mother-in-law's haughty face. 'I can live with the fact that you don't like me. I can also ignore the fact that you're a small-minded bigot who can't see past her own prejudice. That doesn't matter either. You don't mean a *thing*, to me. The fact that you can't acknowledge how happy Debs is with me is annoying and frustrating to us both, but you know what makes me sick to my stomach, every time I look at you? It's the way you somehow think it's okay to keep treating your own daughter like shit.

'You've done nothing but punish Debs for having a mind of her own, for making choices you don't like. Well, I've got some news for you, Carole. She's not some kind of 'failed clone' of you. She's her own woman, and she's amazing. For the love of God, why can't you see the best of what you created, rather than bitching and whining about how disappointed you are with her? If you can't see how happy she is, and how beautiful, talented and special she is, I'd venture to say there's a lot more wrong with *you* than there is with *her.*'

He turned to his father-in-law who was, as usual, staring off into the middle distance and refusing to engage in conversation. What a bloody featherweight! Darren felt the last vestiges of respect he once had for Don Cameron flying away, since it appeared he couldn't even defend his own wife against disrespect. What kind of man would stand there and tolerate that? Darren would punch out *any* man who spoke to *his* wife that way.

He was as mad as hell, so he decided he may as well finish what he'd started, and say his piece to Don too.

May as well be hung for a sheep, as a lamb. There wasn't much left to lose now, was there?

'And as for you, Don, why do you always stand there and let this ridiculous, sour-minded wretch of a woman fight for the last word? Even when she gets it, she's still as miserable as sin! Why do you always act like you have no opinion one way or the other, about *anything*? If you really do agree with her on every pathetic thing that comes out of her mouth, then you're just as bad as she is. But if you actually *don't* agree with her, why can't you find the fucking balls to stand up and say so?'

At one time, out of deference to Debby, he wouldn't have ruffled their feathers in such a way, but they'd all gone beyond the usual icy politeness now. Circumspection really was officially in the toilet. The wisdom of so deeply disrespecting his in-laws no longer mattered.

Don compressed his lips into a thin line and looked directly at Darren with open hostility now, but still he said nothing. Carole was bristling with indignation but also refusing to speak.

Darren could see that both of them were livid, but he'd gone well past the point of wanting to cut them any slack.

'The funny thing in all this – at least it *would* be funny if it wasn't so heart-breaking for Debby – is that for all your big education, and your critical social standing in your local community, you find it so easy to look down at me for who I used to be. You just cling like a pathetic pair of limpets to your rock of disappointment that your daughter didn't marry someone 'brighter and more intelligent.' You haven't the faintest fucking clue what it takes for a person to turn their life around like I have, or become as spectacular as your own daughter has managed to do with no encouragement from either of you! So, who's wearing the 'stupid' hat here *really*?'

He shook his head at them both. 'Debby is a brilliant, bright, brave and beautiful woman. She is extraordinary. And yes, there isn't a day goes by when I don't thank my lucky stars for the fact that she chose me, in spite of who I used to be. But she did that. She. Chose. Me. Not the other way round. And why did she? Because she saw past all that. She saw how hard I've fought, and for how long, to make my life better. If you can't see or understand it, that's fine, just keep filling your boots with your prejudice and narrow-minded bullshit. But don't keep crucifying Debs just because she somehow turned out to be a better person than either of you!'

Neither Don nor Carole said a single word throughout his rant at them. 'I'll ask Debs again if she's prepared to see you, but even if she does, it won't be today, so you really do need to leave. And, if she is interested in seeing you again, maybe tomorrow or the day after, my advice would be to choose your words wisely, because it might end up being the last conversation you'll ever get to have with her.

'You know, In spite of who you are, I want our baby to know all its grandparents, on both sides. But, if Debby decides she doesn't want you involved in our lives anymore, I'll back her all the way. She comes first, for me. She always has, and she always will. You? You're nowhere.'

He didn't give them a chance to say anything. He simply turned away from them and walked back into Debby's room.

She was asleep, now. He wasn't sure if she'd heard him talking to her parents or not. None of what he'd said was untrue, but he still didn't feel too comfortable about saying horrible home truths to them, no matter how much they might need to hear them. It felt like setting a bridge on fire, albeit one he wasn't interested in crossing.

Debby's anger had shown him that she'd had enough of the bickering too, but he didn't want to burn any bridges for *her*. They'd both reached the crunch-point they'd always known they'd get to, at some stage, but he wanted her to be able to cross the bridge back towards her family if she decided she wanted to, at some point in the future. But, for now, it just wasn't possible for either of them to keep walking on eggshells around people who had no respect for how they chose to live their own lives, and no inkling of what they were going through. The way Debby's parents had behaved today had just become one insult too many, and it had sent Debby over the edge.

She *was* beautiful. She *was* brave, and smart, and funny, and amazing. She was his wife, and she'd been through enough heartbreak. After the rockiest journey imaginable, they'd finally got to a place where they could start looking forward to the bright future ahead of them. Darren wasn't going to let anyone upset the applecart, least of all her miserable mother and father, who seemed completely incapable of anything but sourness and spite.

A few minutes later, the nurse peered around the door, saw that Debby was asleep, and gave him the thumbs up. She whispered to him, 'Well done, you! And I bloody *would've* called security!'

He grinned at her, and she gave him a wink and a smirk, and left again. He'd noticed her hovering around in the background when he'd been talking to (or was that *at*?) Debby's mum and dad. She'd remained close by, and she probably would have called someone to get rid of the Camerons if they'd tried to muscle in again, but they must have sensed that everyone was at the end of their tolerance, because they hadn't pushed any further. They left, without further complaint. He wondered if they were still lurking around outside somewhere, but he wasn't going to go and look. He wouldn't give them the satisfaction.

They didn't matter one iota to him, and he wasn't about to let them think they did.

After a time, he gently kissed Debby's hand, and quietly left the room. He needed another good strong cup of coffee. As he was leaving he mentioned to the nurse that her parents couldn't be allowed in to see Debby unless he was there, or unless she specifically asked to see them. The nurse nodded, and smiled.

'Your wife should be able to go home in a couple of hours actually, Dr Davies, as long as she remains calm until then. She really has been alarmingly distraught. We won't be at all happy about her leaving until we're sure she's not going to get herself so worked up again.' She added that while everything seemed absolutely fine with the baby, they very much wanted it to stay that way. He confirmed that they wouldn't get any dispute from him about that.

Down in the restaurant, he was surprised to see Don Cameron sitting by himself, in one corner. Carole was nowhere to be seen. Darren didn't want to get into another difficult conversation, one-sided or otherwise. He chose to ignore Don, and went to sit at the other side of the room.

He was dismayed when the other man got up from his own chair, and approached him. He opened his mouth to warn Don off, but the other man simply held up a hand, and quickly said, 'I'm not here to pick a fight. I just want a chance to speak, if you'll let me.'

Darren figured the least he could do was give the man five minutes, although he certainly wasn't expecting to hear anything positive. He inclined his head towards the spare chair, and steeled himself for what was coming. 'Make it snappy, Don, because I haven't got long. Debs is asleep, but it's been a difficult twenty-four hours for her, and as soon as she wakes up I'm taking her home.'

Don sat, but he didn't speak for a moment.

'Get on with it, man. As I've said already, I haven't got all day.'

Don cleared his throat. 'Yes, of course. Sorry. I just want to say that Carole can be a difficult woman, and I know that, well enough. She's especially difficult when it comes to the girls, Debby and Jayne. She had all kinds of grand plans for them when they were little. She didn't get the life she wanted when she married me, and she's always said it never mattered, but I think it always has, really. Three years after we got married, I went into the family firm. I took the easy option. Played the safe card. Carole didn't want that. She saw it as a dead end. She always said I could do more, be more, go further. She was ambitious for us all. Always was.'

He took a short sip of his coffee, and continued. 'I think she felt trapped, after I chose security over ambition, but I just wanted to provide for her and the kids, you know? I knew I was never going to set the world ablaze, working for my father, in a mid-stream law firm, but I knew I'd always have a job. My family would always have a roof over their heads, food on the table, a nice holiday every year. I managed to get Debby through nursing school, and Jayne through university, so neither of them had to start their working lives saddled with any debt. But Carole's always had that air of disappointment about her, like I let her down, and I suppose I have, in a way.'

Darren set his cup down, folded his arms, and cocked his head on one side, and picked up the conversation.

'And Carole always thought Debby had sold herself short, picking up with an ex-con with a rap sheet? I get it, Don, I really do. I punched above my weight, and Carole couldn't stand it. She wanted more for her daughter than what she'd settled for, herself. And that's it, isn't it? Carole thinks Debby's settled, like she feels she did herself, instead of hanging out for more.'

Don nodded, sadly. 'We already had the girls by the time Carole realised we were never going to live the life of Riley in Dubai, or Los Angeles. We were stuck in Devon, and always would be. I told her she could leave if she wanted to. But she didn't.'

'She just stuck around and made your life miserable instead,' Darren observed.

Don shrugged. 'Well, to be fair, it hasn't always been miserable. We got on with it all, you know, like you do in life. Earning a living and raising kids, paying off the mortgage as quickly as we could. It hasn't been a massively exciting life, I know that, but you grow accustomed, I suppose. We have had our fair share of good times, over the years. There were true moments of loveliness actually, along the way. And I guess I could have listened to her a bit more, and gone for something a little more exciting. I just thought I knew best. I'm as much to blame as she is herself, really, for how she is now. Don set his cup down and meet Darren's eyes.

'We do love one another, you know. Always have, but Carole's a bit of a snob, or at least she tries to be, and most of the time I just find it easier to let her have her own way. It's not that I have no balls, as you put it, but sometimes a quiet life is worth more than arguing over silly little things, because she'd ultimately get her own way anyway, on most stuff. If I roll over early, it saves a lot of unnecessary drama. But I do know how that looks, from the outside,' he added, pulling a face.

'I wouldn't call your daughter's happiness a 'silly little thing,' Don.' Darren said quietly, and his father-in-law had the grace to look uncomfortable.

'No,' he admitted. 'And you touched a nerve back there, upstairs, when you accused me of having no balls, because I know that's exactly how it must seem. And because I've always let Carole have her own way, it's turned her a bit. She can be really nasty sometimes, I know that, and I don't suppose she has as much respect for me as she would if I'd put my foot down occasionally, over the years.'

Don gave Darren a tight smile. 'But when it comes to balls, I certainly think *you* have them, for what it's worth. It does take a lot of guts to do what you've done, turn from a life of crime to becoming a veterinary surgeon. It's an extraordinary journey, really.'

'You've no idea what it took, or the hell I had to go through, to make me realise I needed to change my life. I *wanted* to change it, Don. It was an active, conscious choice, but it still wasn't easy. Nothing born of heartbreak ever is.'

And it deserves a bit of fucking respect, from you and your shrivelled up, bitter old wife.

'Where is Carole, anyway?'

Don chuckled humourlessly. 'God knows. Probably back at the Beeches, where we're staying. I gave her a bit of 'what-for' actually, because I realised you were right. We need to support *both* of our daughters more, whether Carole likes it or not. And I told her so. I told her to piss off, actually.'

Darren let his eyebrows shoot for his hairline. So, the old fart could actually find his backbone, could he, when it suited him? Don couldn't stop his face from breaking into a grin and, to his own astonishment, Darren had to laugh a bit, himself.

'I guess she loved that, huh? Stormed off and left you to it?'

Don nodded, pensively, chewing his bottom lip. 'Yes, she did. She took the bloody car and left me stranded, to make her point, I suppose. And since my wallet's in the glove box, I'll have a bit of a palaver in paying for a taxi. But I'll figure that out, and I guess we've both given her something to think about, haven't we? You *were* right, you know. Us old 'codgers,' sometimes can't see what's under our own noses. Too comfortable, and too set in our ways. I told Carole she had to start thinking about being a bit kinder to people, if she wasn't going to end up alone, and even more bitter and twisted.'

He stuck out his hand to Darren, who was struggling to know how best to respond to his father-in-law's surprising revelations. 'She and I will probably keep bumbling on as we've already done for decades, but I think it would be helpful if you and I could at least agree that Debby's happiness is the most important thing to us all. Truce?'

Darren accepted and shook his hand.

'Truce.'

It was a breakthrough of sorts, but he felt he had to make another point. 'Look, Don, I hope you don't mind me saying so, but as one man to another, if you two can't or won't change the way you feel about your daughter's choices, it might end up costing you more than you think.'

He didn't have to state the obvious; that Debby was on the verge of denying her parents any access to their baby's life. Darren didn't want it to be that way but, as he'd already said, he would stand by her if that was what she felt she had to do to keep them from creating more trouble.

His father-in-law agreed. 'You're probably right. In fact, I know you are. And I do like the way you're protecting my girl. It's what any father would want.'

He shook Darren's hand and stood up. 'I'd better go and find this blasted woman. She's probably wearing a track in the carpet, pacing up and down on it. Give Debby my love, won't you? And tell her that Carole is only trying to do what she thinks best, even if she's rubbish at it.'

He gave another tight smile. 'There I go again, making poor excuses for my wife's bad behaviour. I know I have to stop that. But you don't change a lifetime's habits in the course of one conversation, do you? I'll have to work on it.'

Darren wisely made no comment, but also rose from the table. He resisted the urge to offer Don a lift back to the Beeches Hotel, even though he and Debs would have to drive right past it. Confessions were one thing, but he still felt a long way from being able to extend that kind of olive branch just yet. Don should sort himself out, over this and everything else. He checked his watch. It was time to get back to Debby. As Don turned away from him, he thanked his father-in-law for his time. 'I appreciate you talking to me, Don. Maybe one day you might like to hear my full story, actually from *me*.'

Don closed his eyes briefly, then smiled. 'You know, I think I might like that. Thank you too, Darren. You've torn the top off a can of worms today, but it's probably about time.' He left without saying anything else, and Darren took a deep breath.

Wow! What a breakthrough! Completely unexpected, and much appreciated, but if anyone had told him, before today, that he'd have thrown a verbal bomb at his in-laws and his father-in-law would turn around and thank him for it, he'd have thought they were stark raving mad.

Don Cameron had always taken the line of least resistance with his wife, and it had served him well enough, for long enough. But Darren could feel that something had shifted for Don today, as a result of Debby's baby scare and hearing a few home truths. Sometimes it was only at the bleakest of times, that you saw what people were really made of. After the hurt, the resentment, the frustration and the fear came tumbling out; that's when what was important (and what wasn't) often became a lot clearer. Don seemed clearer, about a few things at least.

Darren still didn't care much if his in-laws liked him, as long as they kept a respectful distance when asked to, and didn't interfere and meddle where it wasn't wanted. But now, he thought, he could perhaps find some respect for Don Cameron if he had the chance to talk to him more. He wasn't sure he'd ever warm to the glacial, haughty Carole, but Don seemed like a reasonable character underneath the carefully constructed detachment he'd maintained from the moment Darren had been introduced to him.

Darren knew Debby had told her parents about his past, about the fact that he used to break into houses, and that he'd been in prison a few times. She'd told them about the deaths of Tom Findlay and Alison Jones, and everything else that came after. But there had never been a discussion about it as a family, with Darren included, and that hadn't helped. Fair judgement could only come from clarity, and clarity hadn't happened because Darren's side of the story had never been acknowledged or heard.

Carole Cameron had drawn her own conclusions about her daughter's new boyfriend and had simply slammed the door on the possibility that he actually could have learned from his mistakes and become a better person in the process. He longed for a chance to fully demonstrate that. Debby always said it was enough, that he was who he was, and did what he did, and made her happy, and that they should judge him on that. But a chance to fully explain himself would make all the difference to how *he* felt about *them*, as well as how they felt about him. That way, if they still hated him, it really would be all about their own attitude, rather than what they assumed, or thought they already knew. If they still chose to despise him and berate their daughter, they could at least do it as an *informed* choice.

Carole was a narrow-minded, intolerant bigot, but maybe her husband really could become the kind of father his daughter needed. Only time would tell.

Debby was astonished, when he told her about everything that had happened, especially her father's confession about putting his own need for a quiet life ahead of addressing the family fighting that constantly raged around his head.

'I knew he did that. I heard him confess it once, to a friend. Mum can be such a bitch, sometimes. She's been that way for such a long time now and I don't remember as well as I probably should, if she was ever different before, because I've been so frustrated with her for so long.' Debby's eyes filled with tears, and Darren picked up her hand, and gently stroked the mound of her thumb with his own. He stayed quiet while she continued.

'She's always acted pissed off, and I've never known why. As kids, it was really hard for me and Jayne to know how to respond to that. We had no idea how to make things better. Everything we did and said was wrong. All it ever did was make her even more disappointed in me.'

'Debs, if you've disappointed her, that's on her, not you. You're amazing, and you've nothing to prove.'

'She said, several times, that she thought it was probably your fault that I couldn't get pregnant. Even after I told her we'd managed to prove that it wasn't. I don't suppose she ever wondered if maybe it was because she'd forced me to have a termination when I was younger. I don't know if that ever crossed her mind. If it did, she never said it. God forbid she would take responsibility herself for anything. And do you have any idea how horrible it is, to find your own mother despicable?'

Darren blew air out from his mouth. 'No. I love my mum to bits, and I'm amazed that she never found *me* too despicable to love. But, you know, we've managed to prove that the termination wasn't responsible, so if Carole ever did wonder, she's off the hook for ever having to admit to that. But, on a much brighter note, Mrs Davies, I'm allowed to take you home, so I suggest we go and rescue poor old Badger, who's probably cross-legged behind the caravan door, and bursting for a pee.'

As they came out of the hospital, Darren put an arm around Debby and pulled her close to him. She turned her face up and kissed him long and hard. He hugged her tightly and then affectionately flicked her nose with his finger, before they set of again towards their car. They didn't see Don Cameron, sitting on the wall at the side of the hospital while he waited for his taxi, watching them as they left.

Chapter Nineteen

Adie struggled mightily with her own annoyance, and fumed quietly to herself as she left Teapot Cottage. She'd made the usual 'welcome' visit this afternoon, to check that the new tenants were settling in alright. Most people were happy, and were usually keen to say so, but Carole Cameron hadn't been particularly forthcoming, in fact she'd been teetering at the very edge of being downright rude and dismissive.

I know the woman probably has things on her mind, but all I'm trying to do is help her settle in here. Does she really have to be so unpleasant?

Feen was making lunch when Adie came back into the kitchen at Ravensdown House. She immediately looked concerned when her step-mother didn't smile straight back as she usually did. 'Everything okay down at Teapot?'

Adie pulled a face and shrugged. 'I guess so. Mrs Cameron didn't complain about anything, but she wasn't even vaguely friendly. She was quite ungracious actually. It's no wonder they're not staying with Darren and Debby, if she's like that with them too. I can't see Darren putting up with that, under his own roof. But, ours is not to wonder why, is it? As long as they're comfortable enough, I'll leave them to it. I'm sure they'll holler loud and long, if anything's not to their liking. I'm sure *she* will, at any rate.'

Feen smiled sympathetically at her. 'I think that family has some big issues to work through, Adie. They're not far short of completely estranged, and there's a lot of work to be done before they can fend their mences. I think you *should* stay away, for your own sake. I have a feeling Mrs Cameron will see the error of her ways and correct her appalling behaviour in all the different directions she's cast it, but that will come in her and the cottage's own time, and nobody else's.'

Adie nodded, in resignation, then turned her attention to her baking for the following morning's Farmers Market. She was running behind, and didn't want any further distractions. The Cameron's could do what they liked, but she wouldn't be going out of her way to be friendly to them again.

After lunch, she put the lavender shortbread in the oven. When it was ready to bring out and leave to cool, she decided to head down to Peg's café for a late afternoon brew. Hopefully a decent conversation would restore her equilibrium, after Carole Cameron had treated her friendly visit with open condescension. She, Trudie, and Sheila usually had coffee at Peg's café on a Friday morning, but they hadn't managed it today, for different reasons. Trudie's assistant was off sick, and Sheila was over in Lancaster, catching up with an old friend who was only going to be there for a couple of days. Postponing the coffee morning had left Adie feeling a bit deprived. She treasured her Friday mornings with her friends. She resolved to try and pop into Gladragz too, to say a quick hello to Trudie before she closed her shop for the day.

Peg was overjoyed to see her, which just in itself made her feel better. 'Hi, love! I'm glad you're here. I missed you a bit, this morning! I'm closing early, because it's been really quiet today. There's a craft market on, over at the Beeches hotel, and I heard they're doing cream teas, so I think most folk have gone over there for the afternoon.

'But the urn's still on, and I think I've a couple of slices of carrot cake left, if you fancy one. I might even join you. All on the house, at this time of day, since they'd only be going in the bin.' Peg cocked her head on one side. 'You seem a bit out of sorts. Is everything alright?'

Adie shrugged and mustered a small smile. 'Yeah, it is. I've just got a pair of very unhappy tenants who don't seem to know how to be anything but rude, and it's pissed me off a bit.'

Peg grimaced slightly. 'Well, I know how that can be. Some of the people I get in here make me want to crack a cake plate over their bloody ignorant heads. But I think a pot of tea and slice of cake might set you straight. If you'd rather be on your own, that's okay, love.'

'Oh no! Do, please, join me. That's why I came. Everyone else is too busy, distracted or unpleasant to have any time for me today. I'd be grateful for a decent conversation.'

Peg gave her a wink, then brought over a tray with a pot of tea on it, and two plates with a generous slice of carrot cake on each one, with a fan of delicious, whipped cream sprinkled with chocolate at the side. 'Here we go. I can't do a cream tea, but I can pipe a bit of cream onto a slice of cake, for wickedness. I think your waistline can stand it. Sometimes I take the left-over cake home for Eric, but I've noticed him getting a bit thicker around the middle lately, so I think I'll have to start cutting back on the carb-laden treats I'm feeding him.'

'Well, it's pretty hard to resist your cake, Peg. How *is* Eric, by the way?'

Adie was quite fond of 'Peric' Tripper. He'd stepped in at Ravensdown Farm as temporary manager a couple of years ago after Mark had suffered a bad accident that had left him unable to work for a while. He'd broken his neck and torn his liver. Peg had been supporting Feen and Adie with food and a bit of cleaning while they'd been running the farm between them, before Eric Tripper had shown up to help. Eric had taken a shine to Peg, and they'd got married last year, in a simple ceremony at the registry office in Carlisle. It was sweet, that they'd found one another after many years alone, and were now no longer facing the prospect of ending their lives as singletons.

'He's fine, thanks. Putting on a bit of weight, as I say, but otherwise keeping fairly fit. He's been co-managing a place over the other side of Carlisle. It's over in Northumberland, halfway between here and Hexham, so there's a fair bit of travel, but he likes the job, and he's managing it okay so far.' She looked keenly at Adie. 'You do seem really down, love. Is there anything I can do to help?'

Adie considered for a minute. 'You know Peg, most of the time having people in Teapot Cottage doesn't give me any headaches, and some of the guests that stay there are absolutely wonderful. But occasionally I wonder why I bother to rent it out, when I get miserable people like this lot waltzing in and being all snotty. They're Debby Davies' parents, and they don't seem at all happy to be here. I get the feeling there's lots of 'shyte,' as Mark would say, going on with that family. It's none of my business, of course, and I do want to keep it that way, but Debby's mother is a piece of work. She really got under my skin today, and I do sometimes wonder what the hell I'm doing, running a business. Do you ever regret doing it?'

Peg shook her head. 'Not really. Like you, I have my moments, but they're few and far between. I'm lucky though, I suppose. Obnoxious people that come in here are never around for longer than it takes for them to chuck a slice of cake and a cup of tea down their throats. I might feel differently if I had horrible people under my nose for a week or more, I'll grant you, but most of your tenants are pretty good, aren't they? Don't let a few bad apples taint your barrel, love.'

Peg sipped her tea and continued. 'At one time, I never imagined I'd *ever* be running my own business, and certainly not in a backwater like this! I used to teach Latin, at a school in Manchester, but after my first husband Andy was killed in a car crash I had to make a new life for myself, and I wanted it to be completely different.

'His life insurance paid off the house and gave me a lump sum so, after the dust eventually settled – which took a while, as you can imagine – I cashed everything in and moved up here. I'd been up here with him, a few years before, and it came back into my mind after he'd passed. It somehow seemed like a place where I could reinvent myself, if you know what I mean. Quiet, not too touristy, but rugged and easy on the eye. I liked the slower pace of life here. Torley kind of 'called' to me. So I came back up here, and took a look around. I bought Stable Cottage, and this little café, and I've never looked back.' Peg drained her cup, and carried on.

'We didn't have any kids to disrupt, so it was an easy decision for me. It's harder when you've got roots in a place, but Andy was my home, when we were together. It never mattered where we were, but that all changed when I found myself on my own. I wanted to put roots down *somewhere*, and this is where I felt I needed to do it. I'll end my days here, and that suits me just fine.'

'You've made a real success of this little café, Peg. And I never knew you used to teach Latin! Feen would be interested to know that, I think. She loves it, as a language.'

'Well, she would of course, as a witch. It is a lovely language. Most people don't bother with it anymore, of course, which is a real shame, in my book. I always found it fascinating.'

Adie chewed her bottom lip for a few seconds, before she spoke again. 'You know what, Peg? I think Mark and I need a decent holiday. I know we did that safari trip last year with Bob and Sheila, but that wasn't really a holiday, in the true sense of the word. It was full-on, every day, from sunrise till sunset. By the time we got on the plane to come home, I was knackered!'

'Well, it's certainly been a full-on few of years for you, hasn't it, when you think about it? Your marriage ending, Mark's accident, then you relocating and getting remarried, then another grandchild, then Feen's wedding, then all that business with her accident last year and the babies being born so early, then racing around on safari! Managing the weekly Farmers' Market, as well. You've had a lot going on, in such a short space of time, love. And now you've got stroppy tenants to manage too.

'You *are* exhausted! The fact that you've let these current idiots get under your skin is proof of that. Normally you'd just shrug it off as the nonsense it really is, wouldn't you? I think a holiday would be the perfect antidote. Maybe it's easier to plan, now that Mark's got a farmhand.'

Adie agreed. 'He's still always busy, though. I know what he'll say when I ask him if we can take a break. He needs one too, but he won't button off.'

Peg chuckled. 'We might have to stage an intervention, then! Kidnap him while he's distracted, and bundle him onto a plane to somewhere that will force him to relax.'

Adie clapped her hands, laughing. 'That's an excellent idea. You know what? I'm going to do exactly that. To hell with his excuses. The farm won't fall apart if he takes a couple of weeks off – especially now he has help – but *I* might, if he doesn't. I *am* exhausted, and I never really noticed how much, until you just said it. There really has been a lot going on, and you're absolutely right. I probably wouldn't be so rattled about that horrible Cameron woman if I wasn't so tired, and that's not going to fix itself, is it?'

Peg laughed gently. 'No, love, it isn't. So you need to run away and kick your shoes off, and lie on a beach, get some heat into your bones and sand through your toes, and get some of your energy back.'

'Got it in one. We went to Bali for our honeymoon, and we loved it. Maybe we could go somewhere tropical again.'

'The photos were amazing,' Peg affirmed. 'It even made *me* want to go, and I'm usually quite content in my own back yard! There's nothing like a tropical landscape to make you feel a bit restless.'

'Yes, I'm restless, as well as tired.'

‘I’m sure Mark will understand. Just talk to him, love. He adores you. He wouldn’t want you feeling like this, if there was something he could do about it. You don’t need an intervention, just a good heart-to-heart. Tell him how you feel. I don’t know who *wouldn’t* feel overwhelmed, with everything you’ve had to deal with.’

‘Yes, I’ll talk to him, and I’ll manage to persuade him somehow, one way or another.’

They chatted for a bit longer about life in Torley, and who was doing what, and going where. Adie felt her frustration finally start to lift. She scooped the last forkful of Peg’s delicious carrot cake into her mouth and washed it all down with her last mouthful of tea. Peg’s remaining waitress had already lowered the café’s blinds to the halfway point and was now quietly cashing up at the counter. Adie was aware that it was four o’clock on a Friday afternoon, and that her friend would want to finish cleaning up and go home.

‘Darling Peg! You’ve cheered me up a lot. Thank you!’

She gave Peg a warm hug, then quickly trotted along to Gladragz, just as Trudie was thinking about cashing up too, and getting ready to close for the day. The two couples had made a loose arrangement, earlier in the week, to meet at the Bull and Royal for dinner the following night.

‘I just wanted to firm up tomorrow night with you and Kevin, Trude, and since I was already in town, I thought I may as well do it face to face. I get so fed up with everything being done by emails and texts. What’s wrong with an actual conversation, from time to time?’

Trudie smirked at her. ‘I agree, and while you’re here, take a quick look at the sale rale. I restocked it today. I’m sorry about missing this morning’s coffee meet, by the way. Staff sickness, it’s never helpful, is it?’

‘That’s okay. Actually, I’m looking for holiday clothes, and I know it’s the wrong time of year, but I’ve decided to put my foot down and drag Mark away on holiday. I think I’m experiencing what some might call ‘burnout.’ It’s been a tough couple of years for us all, and last year’s safari holiday with Bob and Sheila was fabulous, but it certainly wasn’t restful. I need a week or two just blobbing by a pool somewhere.’

‘I’m not at all surprised, sweetie. You’ve been on quite a rollercoaster for a long time now. I’ve been asking myself how long it would be before you and your family could slow down a bit. It's been one thing after another, hasn't it? I think it's well past time for you to take a decent break.'

Adie laughed. 'That's exactly what I need to hear! I threw myself on Egg's mercy for tea and cake just now, after letting an ignorant tenant get the better of me. She recommends staging an intervention and kidnapping Mark, so I'm going to drag him off to Barbados. I've always fancied going there, and sun frocks are what I'll need.'

'Ooh, Barbados! What an excellent idea! I wish we could do that.'

'Well, why don't you come with us? You and Kevin have been working your butts off too, and when did *you* last go on holiday? I know Kevin's the same as Mark; work, work, and more bloody work, but maybe he needs a break too?'

Trudie looked pensive. 'Yes, he really does, Adie. He hasn't had any proper time out of the business since everything came right again after that God-awful Covid pandemic. He even kept working when he had the flu last year, which I nagged him about for weeks. I thought it was stupid, what he did, but he insisted. He's terrible for taking time off.'

Both women laughed. 'I have a savings account,' Trudie mused, half to herself.

'Of course, you have!' Adie giggled. 'You probably have a dozen different savings accounts! Your husband is a financial advisor!'

'Well, I think there might be enough in my personal one for a decent holiday. Let's talk it through tomorrow night, over dinner. In the meantime, why don't you have a rootle through the two biggest boxes in the stockroom, marked as 'summer stock'? They're just inside the door, on the right. You might find something in there. That delayed summer shipment came in so late that a few things never even made it to the rails. I'm still deciding whether to return what's left to the supplier or save it for next spring, now, but you're welcome to take a look.

'It all needs washing and ironing, of course, so bear that in mind. There's also some swimwear on a rack at the back in there. Most of that did go, but there might still be something there that takes your fancy.'

Adie held up her hand for a high-five. 'Great, thanks! I'll check out some holiday places and prices tonight too, and we can talk about it over dinner tomorrow. What time do want me to book for?'

After organising to meet Trudie and Kevin at the Bull at seven the following night, Adie snuck out to the stockroom of Trudie's gorgeous shop, after her friend assured her she wasn't in a rush to get home. She found the boxes and indulged in a bit of a rummage. She pulled out a gorgeous shirred-busted cotton sundress with spaghetti straps. It was in a beautiful shade of turquoise, printed with darker blue and green peacock feathers, and it had pockets, which Adie always adored. 'Pockets are so handy on holiday! I can go out for dinner with just my phone and my room key.'

Trudie nodded. 'Keep digging! I know there's another dress in the same style in there somewhere, in a different colour. Orange, I think?'

Adie rummaged again and found an identical dress, this time in burnt orange, with lime green printed leaves. She yelped with delight.

'Ooh, yes! These are just perfect, and I know I don't even need to try them on. I can tell they'll fit just fine. Shirred busts and billowy bottoms hid a multitude of sins. I will take a look at the swimsuits too, since I've given all mine away to Debby Davies.'

Adie flicked through the rack.

'Some of these two-pieces are gorgeous, but sadly I think my bikini days are well behind me. I don't want to traumatize small children by putting my wobbly bits on show, so I think I'll take this nice floral one-piece, and I do love that black and white one, so I'll have that too.'

'Monochrome never dates, and that one has a sculpted waist so it will give you some shape.'

Adie laughed. Well, that takes some doing, these days! Even with the yoga and scooting around the farm, usually on the hunt for my missing husband, my post-menopausal lump of a body still needs all the help it can get!'

Trudie just shook her head, laughing. She rang up Adie's purchases and knocked a generous twenty percent off the total. Adie knew there was no point in protesting. It was just what Trudie did, so she accepted with good grace. 'Are you able to order in any summer stock items at the moment? I'll probably want a few more things, like a decent lightweight pair each of black and white crease-proof trousers and decent pair of denims. I already have a ton of tops but my jeans and pants all need replacing.'

Trudie assured her that she'd find something appropriate, fairly quickly.

'See you tomorrow night! And thanks for the discount, my darling!'

As she headed back towards her car, Adie already felt a lot less gloomy. Peg Tripper was always good company and full of sage advice, and Trudie was always positive, and fun to be around. Clothes shopping was *always* exciting, and Adie was thrilled at the thought of her and Mark's lovely friends joining them for a fortnight of tropical relaxation. They never seemed to spend enough time together. Phone calls and texts, the occasional catch-up dinner, and the dash to find a decent dress at short notice, were all well and good but it wasn't the same as relaxing by a pool or a beach together. They were well overdue for getting a bit tipsy and putting the world to rights with a few too many gin and tonics.

The Camerons popped into Adie's head again, briefly, as she drove past Teapot Cottage on her way back to the farmhouse, but she pushed them from her mind. Whatever was going on with that weird family, it wasn't up to her to sort out, or even get involved with. All she could hope for was that they'd all find a bit of peace in the coming days.

Feen was still in the kitchen when she walked back in.

'Did you have a good catch-up with Egg?'

Adie nodded. 'Yeah. I called in at Trudie's too and did a bit of retail therapy.' She lifted her bags to show Feen. 'I'm sorry about before. I don't usually let people get me so rattled.'

She was suddenly horrified to find tears springing to her eyes. Feen was horrified too. 'Adie! Oh, my goodness! What on earth's the matter? Come and sit down!'

Adie just shook her head. 'Oh, I'm just tired, Feen. I'm exhausted, actually. I feel like I'm at some kind of tipping point, or something. I need a break, and I'm worried about what might happen if I don't take it.'

'Then you must take it,' Feen said decisively. 'Get Daddy to take you away somewhere. It's funny that we're having this conversation now, you know, because I was only saying to Gavin last week, that you've been humping through joops for more than two years now. You've faced challenge after challenge, and you've dealt with everything brilliantly, but I do think you need a break. Even good things happening can be exhausting! And let's face it, that safari you guys went on, with Aunt Sheila and Uncle Bob? That wasn't a break, was it? You never had a down-day, in the whole time you were in Africa. Lovely holiday, but completely exhausting, with the flong lights at either end.'

Adie explained that she'd been having a coffee with Peg, and the subject of a holiday had already come up. 'Maybe I could drag your dad away somewhere hot and relaxing for a couple of weeks. I'm thinking Barbados. I've always wanted to go there. I saw Trudie too this afternoon, and she said she and Kevin may be up for coming with us.'

Feen agreed. 'I think it would be wonderful for you all to get away together for a little while. What a lovely idea! Why *not* go to Barbados, if you're looking for a place to soak up the sun and do nothing? You'd love it, I think. Gavin and I spent a douple of cays there, on our honeymoon cruise around the Caribbean. It was beautiful, Adie. Find a good resort that has a great spa, and have a few massages. In fact, I think you should book one for every day, so you can come home all floppy and fully relaxed.'

'Yeah, that's what I'm thinking. A quiet place that's right on the edge of the sea, with a good restaurant, and hopefully an infinity pool to lounge around.'

'That sounds perfect! You need to talk to Daddy, and I'm sure he'll try to put you off, but I think you should fut your put down. You have to do this, to save your sanity.'

The sound of crashing cymbals came from upstairs. Feen looked at the ceiling and grinned, stuck a finger to her lips to indicate 'shh,' and motioned to Adie to follow her upstairs. They snuck up the stairs and peeked through the gap in the living room door.

Gavin was messing about on one of his keyboards. He had given Willow a child's tambourine and Alder a triangle, and the twins were bashing them both pretty hard. They were in deep concentration, and they looked adorable.

Adie's heart swelled. They were great little kids; bright and inquisitive, with eyes like saucers, always fascinated by what was going on around them. They laughed a lot at Gavin when he was working, especially when he started pulling faces at them and mimicking the sound the keyboard made on certain notes, or fired up different musical sounds to make them sit up and pay attention.

When he was in charge of them, he never got as much work done as he would've liked, but he never complained. He adored his kids, and Adie knew he was a truly committed dad. She and Feen watched the trio from just outside the door for a few minutes, then Gavin felt them watching, and he looked up and beamed at them both.

'Salutations, ladies! Have you come to be thoroughly entertained by this incredibly talented young duo? They're showing real promise; I should get them signed up. They'll have their first recording deal in no time at all.' He blew a kiss at Feen. She caught it with her hand and threw it back to him.

'Perfect timing, if you have,' he continued, 'because I've cracked this riff. Listen to this.'

He splayed his fingers over the keyboard and a lovely melody came forward. He began to sing, and while his voice would never make millions for him (he always said he was far better with a pen than with a microphone, and most other people agreed), it wasn't the worst voice Adie had ever heard. Her own was far worse.

So, you've made up your mind there's no reason to stay.
But before you turn an' walk away,
Tell me, baby, what you're gonna to do,
'cause I'll always care what happens to you.

Feen clapped her hands. 'You got there in the end! Well done! I know how tricky that one was. It's nice. Simple, and perfect for being so. I like it.'

'Me too!' Adie piped up, pleased that Gavin had made a breakthrough. She knew that the song he was working on was for a band that had been around a while, who had done the pub circuit in London before being offered a record deal. They had a lot of music, and had already been noticed with a rock ballad they'd written themselves, but the record company wanted better lyrics than they'd come up with for four of the songs they wanted to put on their first album. Gavin had come up with beautiful lyrics, but the last half of the chorus had been a real thorn in his side, because part of the melody on it had changed as well. Adie was pleased that he'd finally nailed that sticking point. The song was ready.

'I'm glad you've got that sorted, Gavin. Congratulations! Excuse me, guys, but I'm going to go and find Mark, because I need to talk to him about this holiday. Join us for dinner tonight, though? Just a lasagne and garlic bread, but there'll be plenty.'

Mark was getting out of the shower when she found him. She asked him to meet her downstairs, and when he came into the kitchen she handed him a beer and sat down with one of her own. He looked at her, warily.

'What's this, then lass? Summat on yer mind? Can't be owt bad, if yer givin' me a bottle and not crackin' it over me 'ead.' Adie smiled gently and took a deep breath.

'We need a real holiday, Mark. I'm worried about myself. I've started to feel overwhelmed, almost all of the time. I spend a large part of each day trying to motivate myself to do anything, and I've been trying to get to the bottom of why that is.'

Adie found herself fighting back tears now, and she turned to Mark and let him see them. She saw his eyes narrow with concern, but she ploughed on. 'I've come to the conclusion that I'm completely exhausted. Ever since we met, well, I should say since before I even met you in fact, everything has felt so up in the air. I feel like my feet have hardly touched the ground. I've been keeping on top of everything, but I can feel myself crashing, and for the first time in my whole life, I'm really worried about myself.'

Mark got up and came around the table. He gathered her in a big bearhug. 'Oh, lass! I had no idea you were feeling like this! Why didn't you say summat before now?'

'I thought I was on top of it,' she mumbled miserably, into his chest. 'But I really don't think I am. Something really upset me today that normally wouldn't. I need a break. I want us to have a real holiday.' And I don't want you to tell me we can't do it. We *have* to.'

To her surprise, Mark agreed. 'No, it's all good. Of course we can go, lass. It's just a question o' when, really.'

'The sooner the better,' Adie told him firmly. 'You've got help, things are very manageable around the farm, and I can get someone to run the market for a couple of Saturdays.' She held up her hand as Mark started to protest. 'No. No arguments. I'm booking us a holiday for two weeks, and we're going as soon as I can get it organised. You've said we can go, and I don't want you to fob me off with vague promises of 'whenever'. This has to happen soon, for me. I need this.'

Mark held her away from him and regarded her intently. Then he gave a simple shrug. 'Okay. Book summat. Tell me what to pack, an' what day to be ready, and we'll do it. I do know 'ow much you need a break. I prob'ly do too, if I'm 'onest.'

'You do,' Adie agreed. 'I really think it's not just me who needs to unplug for a couple of weeks. Oh, and Trudie and Kevin might be coming too. I hope that's alright?'

Mark nodded in agreement. 'Yeah. That'd be nice. Kev an' I can chuck a few rounds o' golf in somewhere, mebbe, and you lasses can get sozzled by't pool. But it can't be any longer than two weeks Adie. I can't bugger off an' leave things any longer than that.'

She explained to him about her thoughts for going to Barbados, and he nodded.

'I said we could talk about it all tomorrow night at dinner. You did remember we were going to the Bull for a meal?'

'Yep. All good.' He picked up her hand and kissed it, and winked at her. 'And I don't suppose, since I've been so kind an' accommodatin' about it all, I could interest you in an early night?'

Adie laughed at the cheeky merriment in his eyes. She leaned forward and gave him a kiss. 'Play your cards right, and you never know what you might get. What's more, I might be interested in a few steamy nights in the tropics, too. Something rather interesting on the beach, and I don't mean the cocktail.' She giggled softly, as Mark pretended to look scandalised.

'Sand in me nether bits? By 'eck! I'll have to give *that* some thought!' He slapped her playfully on the backside as she moved away from him.

She decided that the Camerons, and anyone else with attitude, could go and hang themselves. She was looking forward to a happy holiday now, lying on the beach or by a pool, with a good book, and her handsome (and hopefully undistracted) husband. If their lovely friends could come too, it wouldn't be far short of perfect.

Chapter Twenty

It hadn't been the worst idea to house her parents up at Teapot Cottage, Debby decided. Darren had booked them in with Adie Raven, after Don Cameron had called to ask if it would be okay for him and Carole to stick around for a bit.

They'd been surprised at Don's request, but encouraged by the fact that he'd been respectful enough to ask, rather than simply assuming. Darren and Debby had talked it through, and they'd reluctantly agreed that it might not hurt to see if some improvement could be made in their relationships, after the potential breakthrough Darren had felt with Don.

'Adie said she could make it available for five days, until the next people come in next Friday, so I just bagged it. They might be better off there than in some soulless hotel, Debs. The Beeches is lovely, I know, but it's a bit of a trek from here and Carole likes to keep things simple, doesn't she?'

Darren had gone on to observe that her parents seemed to be constantly at loggerheads now. 'Have you noticed that, by the way? I hope they can stay in a two-bedroom cottage for a week without killing one another!'

'I don't suppose it's much different from how they are at home,' Debby had responded. 'I'm sure they'll manage at Teapot. Mum might hate it, like she seems to hate everything else. Some people are never happy, no matter what you do for them. Even if she loves the place, I'm sure she won't be grateful, so don't expect that.'

Darren had rolled his eyes and grinned at her. 'Wouldn't dream of it!'

She hoped Don and Carole would appreciate Darren's gesture, but she doubted it. No matter what her poor husband did, it would never be good enough for the endlessly picky, critical Carole.

As insistent as her parents been, about wanting to stick around for a while, it was certainly out of the question for them to stay at Appletree Cottage. The house was still something of a building site. Debby couldn't expect her mother to tolerate the day-to-day disruption, like everything being covered in dust and the drains blocking up intermittently. Carole wouldn't be able to hold her tongue, and Debby would probably have committed murder within two days. It was far better to have her parents at a manageable distance, thanks very much, so she didn't have to spend every waking minute trying to figure out how to avoid cheerfully throttling her mother, leaving the body on the floor, and skipping away with nothing on her conscience.

Darren's accidental meeting with Don Cameron in the hospital canteen had turned out to be a revelation, though. After Darren had set him straight about a few things, Don had finally stepped up and said how he really felt about the state of his family's relationships, and what he intended to do about it all. He and Carole had decided to stay for a few more days, in case anything else went wrong for Debby after her scare over the health of her baby. Apparently, they wanted to support her!

Debby was astonished. Privately, she thought the best thing they could possibly do, to achieve *that* goal, was get back in their bloody car and go home. But it wouldn't have helped, to have said so. Fighting with her mother, or with Darren about them being here in Torley, wouldn't help her keep her stress levels down. She had no choice but to go with the flow.

Don's next overture was to take her out for a 'slap-up' lunch in Torley. They went to the Feathers and spent two hours eating, drinking, and talking about their lives as a family. He explained his apparent indifference to Carole taking her frustration out on her daughters.

'I know you and Jayne have never bonded with her, Debby, in spite of how much you both tried. I know you did, because I could see it, and I could see the pain it caused you when she just kept turning you away. I tried, more times than you'll ever know, to stick up for you girls, and believe me there were times when I went hammer and tongs at her over it; always out of earshot, because I never wanted you to hear us rowing, over you. I never knew what she might say that would hurt you even more.

'But, whenever I challenged her about the way she treated you both, she made my life a living hell.' Don ran a hand across his face, and carried on. He was talking quickly. His words were coming out in a rush, like it was important that he get everything out before he lost his nerve and clammed up again like he'd always done before.

'I know it's no excuse. I allowed her to bully us *all*, and I threw you both to the wolves in the process. I live with a lot of shame about how selfish I've always been, in trying to put a quiet life for myself ahead of all that. I should have been a lot firmer with her, and I wasn't. I was a lousy parent, and I let you down. I'm sorry.'

Debby was gobsmacked. It took her a moment to square away everything he'd just said, and when she looked at him, she was shocked to see the tears in his eyes. 'Oh God, Dad! You haven't been a lousy parent! Please don't think that! Yes, I've needed a lot more than you gave me, emotionally, but even though I didn't get it, I've always adored you.' She felt like crying herself, now.

Don reached out and covered her hand with his own. 'Thanks for saying that. But I know I could have done more. I *should* have. I did let you down over that, at least. Your mother loves you more than you could ever imagine, but I don't have to tell you what a difficult and complicated woman she is, and as much as I've always loved and understood her, and seen what everyone else didn't, I also do see what everyone else *does*, Debby. I know what she's like, and I know how impossible it must feel, for you and Jayne, and while I'm being honest, I think that's why your sister stays away so much. It's easier for her, I think, than coming home and making choices that your mother probably won't be happy with.'

Debby nodded. 'Yeah. You might be right. At least while she's not around, she doesn't have to make excuses, or keep having to stick up for herself, does she?'

Her father looked sad, and Debby gently flipped her hand so she could grab hold of his thumb and squeeze it. She wanted to throw her arms around him and hug him, but he wasn't big on public displays of affection. Frustratingly, the barrier that had always been there still stood between them. He sniffed a little, and she handed him a napkin, in case he might need it.

‘Debby, I have to tell you something, about your mum. She’ll hate me for doing it, and she might never let me hear the end of the betrayal, but I’ll have to take that on the chin, because I can’t keep putting my own comfort first. I feel like I have to betray her, because I think it’s more important now, that you understand something very big, about her.’

Debby went still as Don took a deep breath.

‘Your mum had a very difficult upbringing herself. We told you and Jayne that your maternal grandfather Paul died of cancer when you were little. Well, he didn’t, Debby. He was murdered one night, in a pub, after a really bad fight that he’d started himself. He used to get pissed and pick on anyone for a scrap. But one night he chose the wrong bloke, stepped him out, and the guy broke a bottle and stabbed him in the neck. He died in the street, bleeding out from a severed carotid.’

Debby started at him in horror. ‘What? Are you serious? Is that what really happened to him? My God! Why didn’t you or *someone* tell us the truth?’

Her father sniffed again, but this time it sounded a little more decisive and controlled. ‘Because he was a nasty bastard, Debby. An abusive, belligerent drunk, and he regularly battered his own wife, and he didn’t spare the children either; your mother, your Aunt Denise and your uncle Graham. He used to hit them and scream at them. He never abused them sexually, but he was a savage to them mentally and physically. He always told them they were useless, that none of them would never amount to anything, and he was never shy of giving a hard back-hander to any of them.

‘He never hugged or kissed your nan, and he used to ridicule her and tell her she was soft if she tried to cuddle the children, even when they were upset and needing comfort. Standard text-book power and control, really, I suppose. Anyway, your mother always said that she could never bring herself to have that conversation with you and Jayne, which would have been inevitable if we’d told you the truth about what happened to Paul.’

‘So, let me get this straight. We grew up thinking my grandad died of an illness, and we never knew what he’d done to mum. To Nan. To any of them.’

‘The family never spoke of it, Debby. Your nan made all of them swear never to speak of what had happened, not to anyone.’

'But Dad! That's really unfair! Surely they *all* needed to talk to *someone*? A counsellor, or therapist, or something? They must have been so traumatized!'

Don nodded, sadly. 'They were, love, they all were. But it was a different time. Back then, people didn't talk about how they felt. They were see as soft in the head, if they tried! There was a lot of misplaced pride in that family too, Debby. Louise, your nan, never wanted anyone to know that her husband had beaten her and her children, and ruled them by fear, because of the *shame* she felt. And she certainly didn't want anyone to know how relieved she was that her husband was dead, because that would have been unseemly. No matter what had happened, she believed she'd have been harshly judged for that and, sadly, she was probably right.'

Don's voice was quiet. 'Nobody knew what Paul had done to his family, so she had to play the grieving widow. She went to her own grave, keeping up appearances. It was tragic.'

Debby thought of her poor abused grandmother, and her traumatized mother, and her aunty Denise, and her uncle Graham. What a terrible way for them to grow up. She could see now, why her mother had always seemed so stunted in her maternal abilities. Her own role models had been paternal violence, and maternal timidity and secrecy. It would never have been safe to be anything but guarded, living with a man who viciously beat and belittled you. Poor Carole had grown up with very little self-esteem as, no doubt, had her siblings, whom Debby had seldom seen since she'd grown up herself. She didn't know them well enough to be able to say for sure, but she was willing to bet that their lives had probably been adversely impacted too.

Don was speaking again, and Debby turned her attention back to him.

'I know that some people go the other way, like you have, after a difficult upbringing. You're going to be the most wonderful mother imaginable, in spite of what you were deprived of. You won't be a restricted one because of it. I know that your mother *wanted* to be that person; the one who turned things around, but I think she was too damaged. She didn't know how to be soft, Debby. She was too afraid to even try, and then that just became something else that she could hate herself for.'

A lot of things were beginning to fall into place now, in Debby's mind. But one thing still confused her.

'Why are you and Mum here, Dad? Why are you hanging around?'

'Because we genuinely want to help you. I want to, and believe it or not, your mother does too. We want to help you, with the house. We've not done anything to help you in any way at all, and I'm well aware of that. But this baby-scare you've just had, well, it frightened me and your mother; the thought that we might lose our first grandchild. I never realised how important it was, to be a part of this baby's life, until we thought we were going to lose the chance.' Don shrugged, apologetically. 'And the thought of having to watch you being destroyed by losing this baby too, after losing two already, well, that made us want to be here for *you,* to help you get through that, if it happened.

'And I know we've made a right mess of our chance to be involved. We've stuffed things up bigtime. But you know me, Debby. I'm a practical sort, so I thought if maybe I could help get the house ready for the baby, it would get you out of the caravan and in there a bit sooner. Your mum's got a real bee in her bonnet about you still being in that caravan with a new baby. I can imagine its comfortable enough, but she can't.'

He looked at her, and his eyes were still moist. 'I guess by now you've probably cracked on well with the house itself, but maybe I could start doing some work on the front garden for you? I'd like to do that, if you'd let me?'

Debby swallowed the lump in her throat. 'That would be lovely, Dad. I know you've a green thumb. We'd love you to be involved, in whatever way you'd like to.'

Don patted her hand. 'Then consider it done.'

She laughed at him. 'Well, I dunno about done, Dad. There's a hell of a lot of work to do out there!'

He winked at her. 'You leave that with me.'

As they left the pub, Debby gave in to her impulse to hug him tight. 'Thank you, Dad. You know, we've never done it before, had a daddy-daughter lunch. This has been such a wonderful thing, even if the news you've given me isn't.'

Don cocked his head on one side. 'But don't you see? It *is* wonderful. Not about poor old pisshead Paul, who never took any of a thousand chances to be a better man, but it explains something important about your mother. Surely that's valuable?'

She realised he was right. 'Yes, of course, looking at it that way, of course it is.' Debby was suddenly pensive. 'Dad, d'you think I could go and see Mum? D'you think she'd want me to?'

Don closed his eyes, briefly, and smiled. 'I think she would. I think she'd appreciate it more than you know, not that she'd ever tell you, of course. Anyway, I'm off to do a few errands. I'll see you later.'

Debby blew him a kiss as he started his car and left the pub car park, waving and tooting his horn.

She sat for a few minutes in her own car. The familiar frustration she always felt whenever she thought about her mother was curiously absent now. Instead, she just felt sad, and sorry that she hadn't known all these things about her, years ago. It may have helped Carole enormously, and her daughters too, if she could have been honest about her own life. *It's hard to be supportive or helpful if you don't understand what's going on,* she muttered to herself as she started the car and drove towards Teapot Cottage.

It was funny to be back here, she thought to herself as she knocked on the front door. Thanks to their stay here, and the people they'd met, she and Darren's lives had changed completely. It felt strange to be knocking on this particular door, knowing that someone else would be opening it, and it was even more strange that it would be her own mother!

Carole was surprised to see her, that much was clear. 'Oh…' she said, and just stood there, staring at Debby, clearly at a loss for what else to say.

'Hi Mum. Aren't you going to ask me in?'

Carole looked flustered. 'Well, do you *want* to come in? I thought I was the last person you'd be wanting to see.'

She held the door open wider, nonetheless, and Debby stepped past her, into the lovely cosy living room with its beautiful big windows affording the spectacular view of the Torley Valley, with its little town nestled near the bottom. It was nice to be back here.

'I love this view! It's really something, isn't it? I used to sit here for hours, in that window seat, just gazing out at the landscape. I have a real soft spot for this place.' She turned to her mother.

'I was in turmoil when we came here, but this cottage soothed me. It worked some kind of magic on us, I really do believe that. We conceived out baby in here, and life looks very different for us now. I do think it's all thanks to this place, really. It has such an amazing vibe about it. How are you settling in?'

Carole shrugged. 'Alright, I suppose, considering we're only here for five days. It's a nice cottage. Feels cosy. It's a certainly a lot more peaceful without your father stomping and harrumphing around. How was your lunch with him?'

'Good, thanks. It was good. I really hope we can do it again sometime. He said to tell you he had some errands to run and that he'd be back later, in time for supper I think.'

Her mother nodded curtly. 'He's picking up some food for tonight. God knows what. Do you want a cup of tea?'

'Yes please!' Debby sat down at the kitchen table while her mother set the whistling kettle on the Aga and started preparing a pot of tea. 'How are you finding the little red beast? I was scared stiff of it when we first arrived here, but I fell in love with it, hence the one we've got on order for Appletree Cottage. Darren bought me my dream kitchen, including an Aga just like this one, only dark green, and then he just let the installers call me to ask when to bring it. I've never been so surprised in my whole life.'

'That was nice of him,' her mother observed.

Debby struggled to hide her surprise.

Did she just say something positive about my husband?

'Umm, yes. It was. But we got a really good price for the house in Exeter, so he figured he could splurge a bit. A bit of a 'now-or-never' moment, I think. He did it as a surprise because he knew I'd never have let him spend so much if I knew about it beforehand, even though it was what I really wanted.'

'Well, you've always watched the pennies, haven't you? Ever since you first started working. It's a good habit, but probably a hard one to break, even when you want something special.'

Debby nodded. 'Yeah, I got into the habit of saving early, and putting the time into finding what I wanted at a cheaper price, and I've never been too proud to have second-hand stuff, if its good quality. I'd rather have second hand quality than brand new rubbish. But having this incredible brand-new kitchen will be amazing! I can't wait for it all to go in.'

She laughed lightly. ‘I suppose it means you’re a grown-up when you find yourself getting excited about the quality of taps, and what kind of fridge you can put in a fitted kitchen!’

To her utter astonishment, Carole laughed. ‘You and Jayne were only little when we got the carpet in that house in Allenby Avenue. You probably don’t remember. We had bare floorboards before that, with rugs down. The carpet made such a difference, I still remember how thrilled I was.’

‘I’m sorry, Mum. For what I said the other day, at the hospital. I didn’t mean it.’

‘Yes, you did. Well, you meant the bit about how I treat your husband.’

‘Yes. That bit I *did* mean, but not the bit about stopping you from seeing your grandchild. I’d never be that mean, not unless you did something unimaginably awful. I was just so angry. Mum, I know you don’t want to accept it, but Darren really loves me, and he’s a good man. He made mistakes, like everyone does, but I really wish you could see how much more there is to him, beyond them. I wish you’d try, at least, because I absolutely adore him, and that isn’t going to change.’

Her mother poured the tea into the cups and sighed heavily as she set the teapot down. ‘I just wanted more for you.’

‘What, more than being happy? More than being cherished by a man who really loves me every bit as much as I love him, if not more? And more than us finally having a longed-for baby together after half a decade of crushing disappointment? What more could you want for me than that, Mum?’

She reached over and lightly touched her mother’s hand. ‘Dad told me a few things today, over lunch, about your father. Your childhood. It sounded horrible. Mum, why didn’t you tell us the truth? We could have helped.’

Her mother snatched her hand away, angrily, and something inside Debby quietly broke, all over again.

‘He had no right to tell you any of that! How dare he? And how could you have ‘helped’? You were children, for God’s sake!’

Caroles’ voice was waspish now, and Debby fought not to lose her temper.

‘We *were* children. And we deserved to be loved, Mum. Properly loved, not made to feel as if whatever we did, whoever we were, it was never going to be good enough for you. I never knew what your expectations were of me. All I *did* know was that whatever they were, I was never going to manage to meet them.'

She took a deep breath and carried on. 'I didn't come here to pick a fight. But I can't let that go, Mum. We weren't always children! We grew up, to a point where we could've handled the truth, but you still didn't tell us. If we'd understood, it might've made things easier for *you*. I don't know how, but it might've. And it certainly would've been easier for *us*, to know that you were in pain, so we didn't end up blaming and hating *ourselves* for the fact that you couldn't love us!'

Carole banged her hand on the kitchen table, making Debby jump. She started to cry, but Debby made no attempt to touch her again. Neither woman spoke for almost a full minute, and the ticking of the clock on the wall in the kitchen started to sound almost oppressive as the seconds slowly ticked by. Then Carole sniffed hard and spoke again.

'I have *always* loved you and Jayne, more than life itself. There was never a moment in my entire pathetic life where I wouldn't have laid it down, for either of you. What do you think this dislike of Darren is about? Hmm? I wanted better for you! Better than what my mother got saddled with, and better than what I settled for, with your father. He's a good man, Debby, don't get me wrong. But he's a doormat.' Carole shook her head, exasperated.

'I wanted you to not 'settle' too. I wanted you to have the best. I certainly didn't want you to end up shackled to some thug who robs decent people. God forbid.'

Debby was crying now, too; hot tears of anger and disbelief.

'Darren was never a thug, Mum. Yes, he used to be a petty thief and a criminal, and yes, he's done a few stints in jail. But that was a long time ago! He has never laid a hurtful hand on a living soul, and he has completely turned his life around! He's achieved the kind of things that a lot of people who *didn't* have a shit start in life are capable of doing. He's a really good man, in spite of what you think of him.

'And, by the way, Dad's a doormat because you turned him into one, Mum! You bullied us all, relentlessly, and I never understood what it was that drove you, but now I think I'm starting to, and I want us to talk about it.'

'Well, I don't want to talk about it, thank you very much. You can mind your own bloody business.'

'You need to mind yours too, then,' Debby retorted, 'and stop thinking you know enough about my husband to keep slagging him off to me. Because, as I said the other day, you might think you know who he was, but you don't know why, and you certainly don't know who he is now. I mean, it's not like you'd tolerate sitting down with him and allowing him the time and space to explain or defend himself, is it? *God forbid.*' She couldn't bring herself to leave the sarcasm out of her voice.

Here we go again. Why have I even tried, with her? It's just the same old hiding-to-nothing shit I always get when I try.

Carole simply rolled her eyes and changed tack. 'How are you, after the baby scare? Is everything alright now?'

Debby tried to ignore the surge of defeat that suddenly washed over her. When she spoke, her voice was weary.

'Yes, thank you. They said it was, and I have to take two weeks off, before I go back to work, which is annoying because I've only just started there. I'll only get statutory sick pay, so we might just have to put a few of the renovations on hold.'

'What?' Carole was clearly horrified. 'You really *would* be in that draughty old caravan with a brand-new baby?'

'Well, I'm surprised that you even care, to be honest, but hopefully we'll be far enough along with things to be in by Christmas, and I'm not due until March. I think the garden will have to wait a while, but maybe spring will be better for planting anyway. And all we need is one bedroom and the bathroom done, which it will be. The caravan's not draughty, by the way. Its amazingly cosy and comfortable. If we did have to be in there with the baby, it would all be perfectly fine.'

Silence settled again. Both women felt awkward talking about *anything*, since the conversational landscape felt like it was littered with landmines. Debby eventually broke the silence. She didn't feel quite ready to let her mother completely off the hook.

'Mum, you can always talk to me, about anything. I really do want to know what it was like for you, living with your father, the way he was. I want to understand.'

Debby *did* want to know more, to see if she could help her mother unpick some of the knots she was tied up in. Maybe, if she could, their relationship might be a little easier on both sides. She was convinced that her mother's failure to come to terms properly with her own childhood trauma was at the root of how she'd been with her own daughters. Carole's misguided idea of what was best for Debby and Jayne had created no end of problems for them. It was all very well wanting more for them, but she didn't need to be unkind with it. That was always a choice.

Carole's eyes clouded over with emotion. 'Okay, you want to know about your granddad? Well, I'll bloody tell you, then, and you can stick it in your pipe and bloody smoke it.'

Carole took a deep breath. 'He was a cruel, vicious man, Debby. He didn't have an ounce of goodness in him. One night, he threw my mother out of the house and wouldn't let her back in. He was in a drunken rage, more mean than I'd ever seen him. I was about six, I think, and your aunty Denise was about three. Your uncle Graham was still a baby. They were sound asleep, that night. They had no idea what was happening, thank God.

'Anyway, it was a freezing cold night. It was so cold there was ice on inside of the windows. Your nan was in her dressing gown, because she'd got up to me. I'd had a nightmare. I used to have a lot of nightmares,' she added, half to herself.

'Anyway, he woke up and told her to leave me alone to sort myself out, and she refused. So, he dragged her down the stairs by her hair, and threw her outside. She stayed out all night, on the lawn, in the freezing cold. I pushed my pillow and a blanket off my bed through the window to her, and she just stayed out there, under the tree, sheltering herself as best she could.

'I'd wet my bed, so I couldn't sleep in it, but I was too afraid to tell him. I knew I wouldn't sleep anyway. I made sure Denise and Graham were alright, and then I just stayed by the window all night watching her, watching me.'

Debby did reach out to Carole now, and held her hand tightly as she continued with her story. She was pleased when Carole didn't pull away as she'd expected.

'He went to work at half past six the following morning. It was still dark. As he walked past her, huddled and shivering in the garden, he told her to go in and get us ready for school. I ran her a bath and helped her get in it to warm up. I started to wash her, but she told me to leave her alone, and get myself ready for school, so I did. She made me promise not to tell anyone what had happened. I left her, in the bath, and when I came home from school in the afternoon she was cleaning the kitchen, and making supper, like she always did. She just pretended nothing had happened, and it was clear that she expected me to do the same.'

She looked up at Debby. '*That's* what it was like for me, living with my father, the way he was. Sometimes, we'd hear him beating her, throwing her around their bedroom. He often came home so drunk he could hardly stand, and he often just woke us all up so he could yell at us.

'It wasn't always that bad, though. He'd have weeks when he stayed sober. He wasn't very nice, in those times either, but at least he wasn't horrible. Just kind of aloof, like it didn't matter to him if we were there or not. We never knew how to talk to him, even in those times.

Carole stared into her half-empty teacup and shook her head softly.

'I was at your nan's with you, the day the police knocked on the door, to tell her he was dead. I'd taken you over there to visit. You were still a baby. They were separated by then, but they hadn't divorced. She was still listed as his next of kin.

'It was me who opened the door to them, two of them, standing on the doorstep with faces like smacked backsides. They asked for Mum, and I went and got her, and she told me to go back into the kitchen, but I didn't. It was like déjà vu, all over again, because they were always at the door when we were kids, telling her they had him in the cells. This time, I just knew it was worse, and I was right. He'd been blind drunk, again, and he'd been in a fight, and he'd been stabbed, and he was dead.' She laughed humourlessly. 'All I felt was relief, a) that he was dead, and b) that you were too tiny to know what was going on around you.'

'Oh, Mum!'

Carole shook her head. 'No. Don't feel sorry about it. I was glad! I still am. I'm *so* glad he isn't still around to hurt anyone. He was a horrible man. He never gave me the chance to love him, or even *like* him, come to that.'

'Tormented, by the sound of it,' Debby mused.

'Yeah, probably, and there's always a reason, isn't there, why people are such horrible human beings? Something made them that way. Something made *him* that way, but I never got to know what it was.'

Debby fought the urge to ask why her mother couldn't have applied the same logic to Darren, and wonder perhaps what might have sent *him* down the wrong path initially. At least Darren hadn't died a horrible man. He'd turned his life around and become an excellent one, dedicated to serving others. Perhaps the time would come to say all that, but it didn't feel appropriate right now.

'Did Nan know what made him like that?'

Carole shrugged. 'I've no idea. If she did, she never talked about it. We just didn't. You know, talk about it? Not even after he died. To the day *she* died, even in her lucid moments, she never talked about him. It was like he never existed.'

'Maybe it was better for her to think that, certainly in her final years. Easier. We just have to do what works, don't we, to get on in life, so our demons don't swallow us the way his swallowed him?'

'Yeah, maybe,' Carole conceded.

Debby ventured a question. 'Mum, is he still a demon for you? I mean, does what happened still upset you?'

Carole considered her daughter's question for a minute. Eventually, she nodded. 'Sometimes. Not often, because I don't think about it much. But now and then things remind me. The tone of someone's voice can upset me at times, and when I see some men who look a bit like he did, it can give me a case of the wobbles. It was all a long time ago now, though. It's not so sharp anymore, to think about it.'

'What did he look like, my grandad?' Debby was curious. 'Do I look like him at all?'

Carole softened, a little. 'Not really. He was dark. Tall, solid and dark-haired. You're a lot fairer, more like your nan.' Her face suddenly dropped and tears sprang to her eyes. Debby was instantly alarmed.

'What? What is it, Mum? Tell me!'

'Oh my God.' Carole looked stricken. 'Debby, I've just realised. Darren's dark, and tall, and he's got a lot of tattoos, hasn't he?'

'Yes, but what has that got to do with…'

Carole interrupted her. 'And he's the same build as my dad. Dad was dark with a moustache and a beard. The similarities… The same heavy tattoos and the same colouring and body shape...' She looked at Debby with horror, and she started shaking.

'Oh, Debby!' she wailed, as she covered her face with her hands. Her voice and her body were racked with anguish, and in that instant, Debby understood. Her mother had subconsciously felt the same way about Darren as she had about her own father. 'I didn't understand, I didn't, I didn't, I didn't understand,' Carole kept mumbling, and Debby knelt on the floor in front of her mother's chair and put her arms around her.

'*I* do! *I* understand. I understand, and it's okay, Mum. It's okay, you're okay. Nothing bad's going to happen to you. I'm right here.'

'Oh God, oh, God, I'm so sorry. I'm so sorry!' Carole slid off her chair and sank to the floor, and curled up into a ball. She just kept mumbling how sorry she was, and sobbing her heart out. Debby curled into her, from behind and kept her arms around her. She found herself crying too, and the two of them lay there for what felt like a long time, and probably really was, until their tears subsided and her mother stopped shaking.

Carole sat up first and propped herself up against the Aga. Debby had never seen her like this, distraught, stricken, and struggling for breath. She stood up and held out her hand, and Carole took it. She pulled her mother to her feet and guided her towards the living room sofa. Carole followed like a lamb.

'It's clearer to me now, why I've felt the way I have,' Carole explained, through her tears. 'I've been telling myself I wanted a better life for you, but I've deliberately ignored the fact that you've already got the life you want. I can see that you do. I've known it for a long time, that you're as happy as I ever hoped you could be, but I just couldn't let go of the fact that your choices were freaking me out. I couldn't convince myself that your happiness was real or would last. I've kept waiting for everything to fall apart, and secretly hoping it would…'

'Because on some level you thought Darren was your dad. A violent bully, a drunk, a fighter, an abuser.'

'Yes.' Carole's voice was barely above a whisper, now. 'There was never any evidence. You've never been anything but happy, and yet I couldn't let myself believe it, and I never understood why I couldn't, because you've always been strong, you've always known your own mind, and I've always been so proud of you for that.'

'Mum, I would never stay with a man who hurt me. I know a lot of women do, and I know *why* they do, but that's not me. If any man hurt me, no matter how much I loved him, I'd walk. I know that beyond all doubt. I must get that courage from you.'

Carole shook her head. 'No, Debby. I'm a coward, who's never wanted to face my past and understand what it did to my family, and what it's done to ours. You get your courage from your dad, believe it or not. He's got all the courage in the world, to stay with me.'

Debby snorted. 'Well, I can't say I disagree with *that* entirely, because you can be really mean to him. But it's not about courage, with him. He adores you. He's stuck around because he *gets* you! He understands everything, and he loves you. He always has and he always will.'

'I need to be kinder to him.'

'I'm not going to disagree with that, either.' Debby admitted.

'So, what, you've agreed with me twice in one day? That's got to be an all-time record!'

In spite of herself, and in spite of the gravity of the afternoon's revelations, Debby laughed. It was good of her mother, to try and lighten things up a bit, at the same time as she was still crying heavy tears. Carole Cameron was a lot braver than she believed herself to be.

'Dad might not have ticked all of your boxes Mum, but that's a big ask of anyone. He's given you everything he could, including the bloody trousers to wear, most of the time! I think that does deserve a bit more respect.'

'You're right, of course, as you usually are, and as annoying as it always is. Oh, Debby! I'm so sorry about how I've treated Darren. I don't even know him, do I? Not really. I just…..' Her voice trailed off, and the shame and bewilderment on her face made Debby's heart ache. She'd never seen *anyone* so vulnerable and raw.

'He wants you to know him, Mum. He'd love to talk to you properly. He *dearly* wants the chance to explain everything, about his past, about what happened to him, and to his friend who was killed. It's a very big story; the biggest ever, in fact. It's sad, and tragic, but its hopeful too, and completely extraordinary. It's certainly worthy of a listen. Maybe you could hear him out, whenever you might feel ready.'

Darren did want to explain his own difficult journey. It was tough, being continually condemned for past mistakes, and although he took it on the chin, it had to hurt, even though he always said it didn't, much.

Poor Darren. Debby had no idea how he'd react to being treated like a second-class citizen purely because of some bizarre subconscious case of mistaken identity. But childhood trauma is simply what it is, and it affected different people in different ways. Darren would understand, like Debby did herself, that Carole Cameron was only really guilty of fearing that her daughter would end up unhappy, or worse, at the hands of a man who couldn't be trusted. She expected him to harm or even decimate Debby, at some point in the relationship, and she'd been steeling herself against it, and trying to steel Debby against it too, from the moment they'd first met. She just couldn't have understood or explained it, before today.

'Maybe I *could* talk to him. Not now, though. I really don't feel ready for that. I don't feel brave enough, yet. But something inside me feels like it's starting to unlock itself, and I really can't explain why or how. All I know now, is that I have to try and find the courage you think I have, because if you believe I have it, maybe I can believe it too.' Carole was still crying, but her tears were quiet now. The wracking sobs had ended.

Debby was aware of the magnitude of today's breakthrough, and her own role in pushing her mother to talk, which had opened the floodgates. Carole's epiphany had implications for *all* of her relationships, going forward, and she would need time to process everything that had come up for her. But she seemed to believe she would get there, and Debby believed it too.

There was still a long way to go. Untold years of hurt, anger, misunderstanding and frustration had left their mark on the entire family. None of that could be erased with just one revelation, no matter how big it was. None of that pain could be swept aside like it hadn't mattered, or hadn't adversely affected Debby and Darren's lives – or her mother's, come to that!

There were still some tough conversations to be had. Nobody could kid themselves about what they still had to face, as a family, if they *were* to get past their problems. But now, it seemed that Carole's unexpected internal earthquake had put a break the wall she'd put around herself. There was a crack in it now, big enough to walk through, and Debby felt hopeful, for the first time in her life, that the light flooding into her 'dark' mother could only bring her hurt to the surface, and allow it to heal. She wasn't alone in that terrible dark place anymore, and all Debby wanted now was for Carole to start to recover from her own wounds, and hopefully be happier for it.

After two more pots of tea, plenty more talk, and quite a few more tears on both sides, Debby heard her father's car pull up outside. It was perfect timing. She felt exhausted, and was happy to be handing her mother back over to Don. She hugged Carole, and tried to make sure she was feeling a bit less wobbly. She promised to call her the next day, and she quickly intercepted her dad, just as he was coming into the cottage.

'Dad, Mum's in a bit of a state, but I think she's alright. Just be whatever she needs, tonight. Let her talk if she wants to, and leave her be if she doesn't, but give her a bit of T.L.C. would you? She won't say she needs that, but she really does.'

Her father looked bewildered. 'What's happened? Have you two had another bloody row?'

'No. Far from it, but it's her story to tell you, when she's ready. Thanks, Dad.'

She gave her father a quick hug and got into her car. Checking her watch, she figured she would be home before Darren, and could cook him a decent supper. They could eat early, and then she could tell him exactly what the day had delivered.

Within the safe, nurturing walls of Teapot Cottage today, a seismic shake had occurred in Carole Cameron's life that stood to have an impact on her entire family and beyond. The opportunity to heal old wounds had presented itself for everyone.

Some people said that the night was darkest just before the dawn. Debby couldn't help feeling that if the crack of lightning that had split the past open tonight was anything to judge by, maybe a brighter and more settled sky was on the cards for them all.

Chapter Twenty-One

As the sun started to slide behind Appletree Cottage, Darren stood at the edge of the sunken front garden, laughing with delight and disbelief. The garden looked incredible. He wanted to pinch himself, at the absolute blinder Don Cameron had played.

The night before, after Debby had spent the most bizarre and revelatory afternoon with her mother, Carole had astonished her still further by ringing later in the evening to ask her if she'd like to go over to Carlisle in the morning, to do some shopping for baby clothes, have a nice lunch, and get their hair and nails done.

The intention was to get Debby away from the cottage for the whole day, so that Don could come in with a team of landscape gardeners and their various accoutrements, to overhaul the front garden. It was nothing short of a Herculean task, and Darren was still blown away by what Don had managed to put in place. In just a few short hours, after his lunch with Debby, he'd managed to hire and commission an absolute army of workers, to come *the very next day*, and overhaul the garden. It had been like something off a TV show! Darren couldn't even begin to imagine how much money Don must have had to throw at this, to achieve it in record time.

For Darren, who desperately wanted to be involved, getting the day off work in a new job, with zero notice, had taken some doing. Luckily, his new boss had a soft spot, for pretty pregnant ladies and surprises. David Thornley had given in, as good naturedly as anyone could be expected to, and told him to take the day, 'but don't let it happen again. We can't manage without you around here for long.'

A very bemused and confused Debby had been picked up by her mother, first thing, and taken to Carlisle, protesting at the fact that they were getting on the road at the ridiculously early time of 8.15. Carole had refused, point blank, to explain why she wanted to go so early. Debby had thrown up her hands in surrender, accepted her mother's rare overture of kinship, and gone along with her 'madcap' plan.

Don had got out of the car before Carole had turned into the driveway at Appletree Cottage to pick Debby up, and had hidden behind a tree until they'd safely driven off again. Shortly thereafter, two men had arrived with a bobcat, and they'd gone straight into the job of clearing the brambles and other overgrowth from the sunken quadrangle and the raised beds on all three sides, in front of the cottage.

Another truck waited for the bobcat to leave, then came straight in and offloaded several tonnes of topsoil. After that, six young landscape gardeners who had turned up in the meantime immediately started distributing it evenly across the ground and behind the raised brick edging of the sunken area, which had also been expertly cleared by the bobcat. They'd brought enough ready-lawn to fill the quadrangle, and said that towards the end of the day, when everything else had been finished off, they'd have it laid in less than two hours.

Two truckloads of trees, bushes and plants had then turned up, and the landscapers had set about planting everything in the way Debby and Darren had already proposed and drawn up a rudimentary plan for. More vans and trucks arrived with rocks, paving stones and some beautiful garden ornaments, including a stone bird bath and matching sundial, and a water feature. A beautiful, ready-made wooden arch, completed with trellised sides, was erected and cemented in, leading directly to a newly-laid square patio area in the bottom left-hand corner of the garden where a rustic wooden bench table and chairs had been set up, with some elegant potted palms in tall pots placed around the edges.

The guy who had set the wooden arch in concrete had been at great pains to point out that it shouldn't have any pressure put on it for at least 24 hours, while the concrete set, and the men who were planning to lay the ready-lawn told Darren, in no uncertain terms, that it wasn't to be walked on for at least three days. But Darren was so overwhelmed with gratitude and disbelief, he'd have agreed to almost anything.

By five thirty, after a straight eight-hour shift with barely a break to eat the pizzas Don had arranged to be delivered at midday, everyone who'd been involved was well and truly gone. All that could be heard now, was the light trickle of water, thanks to the wonderful woman who'd set up the water feature to provide much-appreciated refreshment for the bees and other insects the garden would eventually attract.

Don stood beside him now, and also surveyed the scene. 'Not bad, eh?' he chuckled.

'Not bad? Don, it's a fucking miracle!' Darren still couldn't believe what his eyes were telling him. 'How the hell did you manage to pull this off? You've only been up here, what, three days?'

'I threw a lot of money at it. And I mean, a *lot*. I'll never tell you how much, so please don't ask, but let's just say that my plan for buying the classic Jaguar car I've had my eye on, in time for Christmas, has gone on hold for at least three years.' Don pulled an easy-osey face and shrugged.

'But what's a pile of polished metal, compared to this? You can always get what you want if you're prepared to pay for it, Darren, and I was. Although I'm not in the habit of spending money on such a grand scale, in this case, I wanted to do it. I'm lucky that most of who I needed to come today was already available, and I paid an eye-watering amount to get the rest to rejig their other commitments and come at such short notice, but I was happy to do that. Debby's joy is worth every penny. I can't wait to see her face.'

'Neither can I, but holy shit, Don! That does equate to a *lot* of coin. Tens of thousands, I'm guessing – not that I'm fishing! I do respect your request not to ask. Does Carole know about this?'

Don nodded. 'Yes. She was all for it.' He turned to Darren. 'I know how much Debby wanted to have the garden done in time for the baby. We both know that wasn't going to happen though, don't we, because of timing, jobs, weather, and finances? Babies are expensive too, and so are renovations. What's left of your capital is all for the things you need right now. It would've taken years, to get this done the way you wanted, and I figured we should help.'

'But Don, I wish you'd asked me, before you spent all that money. I've no idea when I can pay you back for all this! It'll probably be a decade or more.'

His father-in-law grinned at him. 'It's not a loan. It's our gift to you both, Darren. I don't want repaying for this. In fact, I'll be insulted if you try. Carole and I are actually gifting this garden to our grandchild, so he or she can learn to crawl and then walk in it. It'll be 'the garden Grandad built,' and I'll look forward to playing croquet with him or her on that nice lawn, which I think will be rather splendid when it's all taken proper root.'

'It looks splendid even now! And I'll have to buy a lawnmower now,' Darren mused, stroking his chin. 'And a bloody croquet set, I suppose.'

'Yes, you will, but I suspect you'll be able to manage that without too much help.'

At that precise moment, Don's car drew up in the drive, and Carole and Debby got out of it. Debby initially looked confused at the sight of her father and her husband, evidently getting along very well together, standing outside the front door. It was only when she came closer to the house, carrying enough bulging bags to stock a small shop, that she saw the garden. She literally screamed, dropped her shopping, and burst into uncontrollable tears.

Darren sprang forward and gathered her into his arms. He was covered in soil, but most of it had dried, and she didn't seem to mind or even notice.

'Surprise! You can thank your dad for all this. He organised it. I just provided a bit of spadework.'

'Oh my God, it is *stunning!* Dad! How on *earth* did you manage to do all this, in just *one day*?' Debby and looked across the beautiful new garden. She was shaking, and crying, and laughing, all at the same time. Darren decided she looked like a completely adorable and slightly insane halfwit.

Her father just winked at her. He picked up her hand and led her down the path, created in the same shade of stones that the house itself was made with, that curved gently and diagonally across the newly laid lawn. 'Don't walk on the grass for a few days, give it time to bed in.

'Right, so, in line with your vision, your plan that you very kindly managed to leave on the dining table, you've got a new apple tree in each of the two bottom corners of this trench behind the stone steps to the sunken lawn. Ferns and flowering shrubs all across the back fence line here, in the raised bed, with a water feature in the middle.' He gestured off to the right.

'Lots of bee-bomb seeds in there at this side, for your wildflower mini-meadow. Across the other side you've got some fast-growing shrubs, with some fragrant herbs interspersed, close to the picnic area here, so it will be nice when you're eating out here, as you wanted. Bird table in the middle on that side, sundial in the middle on this side. Stone baby dragons at the sides of the little steps leading down to the law. You didn't have those in your plan, but they're my contribution. One of them's your mother, and the other one is me.

'There's another patio around by the back door for your hot tub, when you get it, and there's a pergola around it. That's just been concreted in too, so don't go swinging off it for a day or two.'

Debby's eyes were still streaming. 'Daddy, this is magnificent. Utterly mind-blowing. Please tell me I'm not dreaming, that I haven't just stumbled into someone else's magic life.'

'Well of course you haven't! Debby Davies, This Is Your Life.' Don took a bow, and handed his daughter an imaginary book. He was clearly thrilled with her reaction. She looked over at Carole.

'Did you know about this? Oh, you did, didn't you! Is *that* why we had to leave at the crack of dawn, this morning? I thought you were insane! Now I know you were just being devious and cunning.'

Carole's smile faltered, and Debby noticed. She swiftly sprang forward. 'Mum, I didn't mean that in a bad way. I love all this. Thank you so much! It's absolutely perfect! It's everything we wished for, and so much more.' She looked at Darren, and her grin was a mile wide. 'We have a bird table!'

Don nodded. 'Yes, you do, and see, it's a two-tier one. Water in the bowl-shaped bit, for a bath, and a flat shelf above for the food'.

Carole held up a small parcel that she'd rummaged around in her voluminous handbag, to find. 'Here! A contribution from me.' She actually handed it to Darren, which surprised him. He unwrapped it with curiosity. It was a beautiful little windchime. 'Windrush Chimes of Mars,' he read, on the label, and held it up. It tinkled with a surprising richness to the notes. 'Thanks, Carole, this is gorgeous.'

She gave a tentative smile. 'I thought you could choose a place for it together, in the garden. I don't suppose these new trees are strong enough yet, to hang it off one of those.'

'They'd better be,' growled Don. 'The price I've paid for the bloody things!'

Everyone laughed, but Darren's laugh was just a little less boisterous than everyone else's. He was feeling a bit overwhelmed by Carole's unexpected gesture.

Don was now talking about arranging to get the skip, which he'd organised on a 24-hour hire, picked up the following morning. It was out on the road, so getting it collected wouldn't be intrusive at the cottage itself.

'You've thought of everything, Dad! I can't believe I didn't even notice that skip when we pulled in. Now you've mentioned it, though, I can't *not* see it.'

'Nobody could fail to see it,' Darren interjected. 'Considering its bright yellow and ten feet long!'

Debby hit him playfully. 'Alright, smarty pants. I was actually looking for my key in my handbag when we pulled in. That's why I didn't see it.'

'Okay, I'll believe you. Thousands wouldn't!'

Don spoke up again. 'In about a year, this will all look a lot more established. I've got a lot of plants in that will grow quickly, and some of them are a decent size to start with, so by spring it might all feel like it's been here for longer than it actually has. I hope you like it, kiddo.'

'Oh, Dad! Mum! It's incredible. I still can't believe it. I can't believe I won't get up tomorrow morning and it'll still be like it was *this* morning! I can't believe I'm not dreaming!'

Carole looked at Don. 'I think we need to get going. We shouldn't be late.'

She smiled, self-consciously, and explained. 'We're going out to supper tonight, back in Carlisle. Don booked a table at an Italian restaurant without bothering to ask me, so I have no choice but to put a face on.' She turned to her husband.

'You need a long hot shower, you filthy thing. And I need a cup of tea. So, we'll head off, if you don't mind, just as soon as we get the rest of your things unloaded from the car.' She looked pointedly at Don, who shrugged and followed her, but he had a smile on his face, and didn't seem to mind being summoned as a packhorse. Or being told he was a 'filthy thing.'

They returned with what seemed to Darren to be a colossal amount of shopping for just one person and for just one baby, and just one day. Then, once they'd laid it all at the front door, Don and Carole said their goodbyes, and left.

Badger gently put his nose into the palm of Debby's hand. 'Hello, gorgeous boy,' she murmured. 'Have you been helping a lot here today? I bet you have!'

'He's been a bloody nuisance, actually. He took a shine to one of the blokes with the digger, first thing. You should've seen him, howling for a cuddle. It was pathetic.' Darren regarded his dog fondly.

'Well, I don't blame him!' Debby countered. 'I'm standing here wondering if I have to howl for a cuddle myself!'

Darren slipped his arms around her and pulled her close. 'D'you like it, the garden?' he murmured in her ear.

'Oh God, are you kidding? I *love* it! It's even better than what we planned! How the hell did he pull it all off, in one bloody day? It's almost unbelievable. I'm literally in shock!'

'He coordinated everything yesterday, apparently, after you'd had lunch with him, and he paid well over the odds for them all to come at short notice. And I do mean *well* over the odds. He refused to say how much all this has cost him, but I wouldn't be surprised if he's thrown twenty grand at it. I'm still in shock myself, and not just about that. About everything really, and hey, what about your mum, giving me this lovely chime?'

He held it up, and it tinkled.

'I know, right? If your mouth had been open any wider, I'd have fallen straight into it.'

'Well, I do wonder though… 'Chimes of Mars'… is this her way of telling me there's still a war on?'

Debby laughed heartily. 'No, I don't think so. I'm guessing it's a message of a different kind, but we'll have to wait and see.'

'Rome wasn't built in a day, was it?'

'No,' she laughed again, 'but then again, most gardens weren't either, so I dunno if I'd be surprised about *anything* that happens next, around here.'

Chapter Twenty-Two

The kitchen windowsill looked a little bare now, Adie decided. For weeks, she'd had a dozen different pots on it, of various sizes, while she grew cuttings for the garden Debby Davies had planned for her new house. Appletree Cottage had certainly been in need of some nice plants and flowers, and Adie hadn't envied Debby and Darren one bit, as they faced the prospect of tackling the old place and making it liveable. She hadn't been over there yet, to see it for herself but Peg, who lived next door, had told her what was involved.

'It's no task for the fainthearted,' she'd said, with a grimace. 'It'll be beautiful when it's done, but they've a very long road ahead of them, especially with a baby on the way.'

Happily though, the biggest helping hand imaginable had come to the couple by way of Debby's parents, Carole and Don. Thanks to them, the garden had been revolutionised overnight. It was almost impossible to believe what had been achieved there in just one day, but Don Cameron had pulled out every last stop, to ensure that the garden his daughter dreamed about was something she wouldn't have to slave to achieve.

Adie had seen the photos of what Don had managed to make happen in there, in a mere eight hours. It was worthy of a TV documentary, and she couldn't even begin to imagine what it had cost. Something had been mentioned about having to put the purchase of a very expensive classic car on hold, but she had no idea what that really equated to. Many thousands, certainly, but the man had been happy enough to spend it. Adie suspected it would be the talk of Torley town for a good while to come, how the garden of Appletree Cottage had been so quickly and thoroughly transformed. Debby and Darren probably needed to brace themselves for a barrage of curious visitors.

The cottage itself needed a mind-bending amount of work, but the couple weren't daunted. They were excited, and were already working hard, juggling new jobs and renovations, and doing it with the widest smiles Adie had ever seen. She resolved to help in whatever way she could. Growing a few paltry cuttings seemed like a small thing to offer, but she also managed to track down a few chickens that were already laying, and were needing a new home after their ageing owners had decided to sell up in town and move to Liverpool, to be closer to their sons and daughter.

Mark had never forgotten the kindness of the Torley community when, over thirty years ago, he'd first arrived at 'Down Farm' with a new wife, and very little money to rise to the challenge of converting the old place from its run-down state to something liveable and workable. An extraordinary amount of help had been offered, by strangers from far and wide, and Mark still talked about it often. It had left a lasting impression on him, and he never hesitated to pay it forward, whenever the chance came.

He had readily provided a coop for Adie's chickens, by simply converting a little unwanted shed from Bob Shalloe's farm and using a few flagstones that had been sitting around at the back of the barn for years. It hadn't taken long to nail a few bits of wood into the shed as laying boxes and throw some straw into them, find enough chicken wire to make a run, take the lot over on the back of Bob's flatbed truck to Appletree Cottage, and 'set everythin' up fer't chooks.' Bob had also contributed some straw for the laying boxes, in addition to his little old shed.

With Eric Tripper's help Mark had knocked it all together in an afternoon, and made it fox-proof. The newcomers would be off to a good start, in their goal of achieving whatever self-sufficiency they could.

'Well done, lass! That's crackin'! Not sure 'ow they'll get on wi't rooster, but if they let the bugger stop on, and fertilise a few o't eggs, Dee and Dee might find theirselves wi' a few more daft bloody chooks in't run, one mornin'.'

Adie laughed at him, calling their new friends 'Dee and Dee.' But she had to agree that it was easier.

Sheila Shalloe had a passion for good-quality linens, and after raiding her airing cupboard, and proclaiming that she had more spare curtains and duvet sets than she'd ever get around to using, she'd offered some of them to the Davies'. Debby had been thrilled, saying that they'd had to leave all their curtains behind in Exeter, after the buyer of their house had insisted. Sheila's taste wasn't the same as Adie's, but Debby had been ecstatic over two matching pairs of sand and chocolate Laura Ashley curtains that only needed a small amount of hemming, to fit both of her downstairs bay windows. She was all the more grateful that they came with matching cushion covers. Sometimes, small things made a big difference.

Adie stood now, and took the empty coffee cups that were sitting on the table, over to the kitchen sink. Carole and Don Cameron had not long left, after coming up to Ravensdown House for coffee. Carole had surprised Adie, earlier in the week, by showing up at the front door and apologising for being so rude to her when she'd first gone to check on them at Teapot Cottage. She'd been embarrassed and – in Adie's opinion – humble and sincere.

Adie hadn't struggled to forgive her. Everyone had their demons to wrestle with, and they didn't always cope well, in the process. She'd been a hot mess herself, at one time, so she was hardly in a position to judge where someone else was coming from, in their failure to manage even a simple social interaction successfully. Nobody knew what anyone else was dealing with, did they? It wasn't fair to judge.

Adie smiled now, remembering how frustrated she'd been by the other woman's lack of welcome. Once she'd processed her reaction she'd quickly realised that being annoyed was merely a symptom of her own exhaustion. Now that had been addressed, with her and Mark's holiday booked, Carole's rudeness no longer felt so important. It had clearly still been playing on Carole's mind though, and Adie hoped the fact that she'd accepted Carole's apology with charm, grace, a smile, and an invitation to coffee, had let the poor woman off the hook.

It was now only a week until Adie and Mark would be boarding a plane to Barbados. She'd managed to get Mark to agree to three weeks, despite his initial protests. It was a long way to go, she'd reasoned, but they could fly direct, and there wouldn't be any stopovers. He'd finally given in and agreed.

Trudie and Kevin were coming too, but later. They didn't want to be away so long, so they'd be joining Adie and Mark after a week, and just having two at the resort.

Everyone was looking forward to a good stretch of time just lying by a pool doing nothing. Adie was particularly excited at the thought of having something resembling a second mini-honeymoon with Mark. She intended to go shopping, in the next few days, for some pretty underwear and a nice nightdress. She adored her husband, and wanted to shower him with love. Away from the farm, they could enjoy some quality 'love-time', and she was going to make sure they got it, in Barbados.

Trudie had produced a couple more lovely sundresses for Adie, along with the much-needed black and white trousers, and advised her that she wouldn't need to pack much more.

'You'll be poolside, for most of the time. I've got some sarongs and I'll pack them all, but apart from these frocks and pants, unless you plan to go gallivanting away from the resort, you'll only need three or four tops; a couple with a bit of bling or sparkle, and a cardi or two, and a decent pair of sandals.'

Adie wasn't convinced. She'd laughed at Trudie.

'You're joking, aren't you? I'll struggle to keep it to one suitcase! When I go on holiday, I take things I *might* need!'

'And do you use or wear even half of them?'

'Um, well, no. I don't suppose I do, if I'm honest...'

'Okay, well, I'm your OAP, and I don't mean old-age pensioner. I'll be your Official Accountability Person. Give me the list of what you plan to pack, and I'll tell you whether you're deluded or not.'

Adie laughed. 'It's a deal. But I get to do the same for you.'

Chapter Twenty-Three

Debby stepped into the showroom of Carla's, in Torley town, and introduced herself to the owner.

'Hi. Are you Carla? I'm Debby Davies. My husband and I have fallen in love with that gorgeous antique cot you've got in the window. We saw it last night when we drove past. We adore it! My baby's not due until next March, but we're getting the nursery prepared now. Is the cot still for sale? If so, can I have it please?'

Carla nodded. 'Yeah, sure. It's only been in the window a couple of days. Someone rang about it yesterday and said they were coming down to take a closer look, but I haven't seen them yet. I don't hold stuff. I used to but so many people just don't bother to turn up for it.'

'It looks Victorian,' Debby observed, and Carla nodded.

'It is, yes; made of iron and brass. It's beautiful, isn't it? I only finished restoring it last week. It was a bit of a mess when it came in, and it took me a while. It was rusted in places, so I treated it, but I thought it looked a bit heavy in the black, so I painted it cream.'

'I like the fact that you've given it gold knobs and feet too! It's gorgeous.'

'A standard cot mattress will fit into it, and if I were you, I'd order one online. You'll get a much better price than going to any shop around here. Check the reviews first, and make sure you get the best you can afford.'

Debby paid for the cot and arranged for it to be delivered to Appletree Cottage at the weekend. Carla offered her a cup of coffee. 'Since you've just spent a small fortune,' she said, with a wink and what looked like half a grin.

Debby grinned back. 'What, you mean you wouldn't have offered if I'd just bought that little lamp over there, for tens instead of hundreds?'

Carla just looked at her, with her eyebrows raised, and with a smile playing around the edge of her mouth.

'Thanks, Carla, yes! A quick one would be lovely! I've got to run up to Teapot Cottage after that, and look in on my parents. It's a holiday house up on Ravensdown Farm. Do you know it?'

She was surprised when Carla laughed.

'Yes, I know it very well. I've stayed there myself, and so has my son. He married Feen Raven.'

'Oh! So he's Gavin! I've met him! And your grandchildren, what are their names again?'

'Willow and Alder. Personally, I don't know what would have been wrong with Ena and Frank, as nice names for babies, but my daughter in law has a thing about trees and Celtic moons.' She shrugged and rolled her eyes, and Debby wasn't sure whether or not she was joking.

'They're a nice family, aren't they? I like all of them, very much.'

Now that she knew they were mother and son, the resemblance between Carla and Gavin was clear. They both had the same flashing green eyes and almost-black hair. Gavin was easy and open, but Carla was less so. Debby had the feeling that nobody would ever find out much about her if she didn't want them to, and she wouldn't hesitate to slam the door on someone who really annoyed her.

'Have you just moved here?' Carla enquired. 'I haven't seen you around before.'

'Yes, we've more or less just arrived. My husband Darren is the new vet in town.'

Recognition passed across Carla's face. 'Ah, yes; didn't he sort out Bob Shalloe and Dave Holloway's rams, after a fight up at Bracefields Farm, back in the summer?'

Debby nodded. 'Yep, that was him.'

Carla pulled a face. 'Well fair play to him for that, and for scoring the job to replace Stan Biggar at the surgery. Those are big shoes to fill.'

'Yeah, Dr Biggar was very well liked around here, I think.'

While Debby leaned on the counter, drinking her coffee, a beautiful, long-haired black cat wandered in, and looked haughtily at her, before sauntering arrogantly across to his bed, at the edge of the east-facing window.

'Wow! He's gorgeous! How long have you had him?'

'About thirty-five years,' Carla answered, in a deadpan voice. 'At least, that's how long I feel I've been a slave to the little sod. He just showed up here, last year, and wouldn't leave, so I've accepted that I'm stuck with him. But I've had worse company. At least he doesn't pretend to like me for anything more than the food I give him. He's honest, if nothing else.'

Debby burst out laughing. 'Yes, that's really all we are to them, right? Staff. Food slaves. We've got one the same, at our place. Lindy-Lou. Lazy old lump, she is, but we wouldn't be without her.'

Carla nodded. 'Yeah. Marmite's a pain in the arse but I'm used to him now. We lurch along together. He's good company when it suits him, and when he's not trying to trample Dave clean out of the bed, or chew his ears all night.'

'Dave? Oh, you mean Dave Holloway? You go out with him? That's nice.'

Carla shrugged. 'It's a fairly new thing. We've both been on our own for a long time. Nothing heavy, we're just seeing how it goes.'

'Well I think that's great. I haven't met him, but I'm sure I will soon. Darren said he was a good sort, and a good neighbour to the Bracefields Farm people, who are related to the Ravens. Everyone seems to be connected, around here, in some way.'

'Well, you'll meet Dave on Saturday morning, actually, because he'll be delivering your cot. And yes, I may as well warn you that you haven't got a shit-show of keeping much private in Torley. Most people do have mutual connections. It's a small town. Nobody's mean, but there's a few that do like to gossip a bit, and you'll just have to take it on the chin. There's no point in being precious. It won't be long before they all know how often you wash your bed-sheets, what you put in your shopping cart, and whether or not your car passes its next MOT. But, if you ever need anything, someone in this town will make damn sure you don't do without it. They're a decent bunch, for the most part.'

Debby laughed. 'Thanks for the advice, and for the coffee, Carla. It's been lovely to meet you, and the very regal Marmite, of course. Saturday morning then, for delivery. I'll look forward to that.'

She left the shop smiling. Carla clearly had a very good eye for old furniture, and how to restore it beautifully, and she was certainly an interesting character. *Better to be on her good side than not, though*, she thought to herself.

Up at Teapot Cottage, she found her mother making a late breakfast, and said 'yes, please' to the offer of a steaming plateful of bacon and eggs. Don had popped out to the shop for some bread, butter and milk.

'I'm so glad we've managed to reconcile, Mum' Debby felt compelled to confess. 'I don't suppose we'll ever be truly close, like some other mothers and daughters, but the fact that we're now getting along better means *everything* to me. I can't tell you how special it feels. I've waited all my life for this.'

Carole smiled gently at her daughter as she set the plateful of food in front of her. She spoke quietly.

'I know, and I don't wish to offend you by saying it, but you've always been the emotional one, in the family. Don't get me wrong; that's not a bad thing at all, in fact I've always wished I could be more like you. But I can't. I'm just not built that way, Debby, and I've never known how to deal with you wearing your heart on your sleeve.'

She sat herself down, and took a deep breath, before continuing. 'I've always known you needed more than what I could give you, and it's always made me angry with myself for not knowing how to do better. But I've taken my frustrations at myself out on you – *all* of you – for a very long time. It's only now that you're finally going to become a mother yourself, and I can see how good you're going to be at that, that I can tell you how truly sorry I am, that I failed you for so long.

'I can't be like you, but you're not going to be like me, either, and I'm glad about that. You'll nurture your child properly, and you'll listen, as children should be nurtured and listened to. You'll easily give your child what you deserved, and so much more besides.'

Debby reached across and squeezed Carole's hand. It was hard to talk, hard to swallow the lump in her own throat. She understood what it had cost her mother, to admit to what she'd just said. Carole had carried so much shame, bewilderment and pain from her own childhood; forced to pretend that hurt didn't matter, that pain had to be endured with quiet dignity because shows of emotion were seen as 'soft,' and never tolerated.

She cleared her throat. 'Mum, have you ever wondered about timing? I mean, how things just kind of happen when they're meant to, and not before? How trying to force something to happen before its ready just creates more problems?'

'What, you mean like waiting for divine intervention?' Carole's chuckle was quiet. 'No, I don't think I ever believed in anything like that, or in a God; there wasn't one that ever saved *me*, that's for sure.'

Debby nodded. 'Yeah, I get that. You must've felt so alone, growing up. So abandoned, by the people you were supposed to be able to trust.'

Her mother shrugged. 'I just got on with things, Debby. I didn't have much of a choice. Do *you* believe in God, though? It's something I've never asked you.'

Debby considered the question. 'You know, I'm really not sure. For such a long time I was railing at God as if I did believe, you know, when I felt abandoned too, after I couldn't get pregnant. Then I got to where you did, I suppose, thinking there couldn't be a God who would be so cruel as to keep denying me the only thing I really wanted, that wasn't even an extraordinary thing! It was just something I was supposed to be able to naturally do, as a woman.

'Now, I'm not sure what to believe. Were my prayers or frustrations finally answered? This pregnancy, and finally connecting with you on a meaningful level for the first time in our lives; were they just random things? Were they things that needed to evolve with strategic timing, ordained from some higher power, when they were *meant* to happen? It all feels like too big a question. I'm not sure there's an answer.'

People had been telling Debby for years, that she would fall pregnant, ‘when it was meant to happen.’ Did that also mean that finally making a meaningful connection with her mother was meant to happen too, as the *result* of falling pregnant?

She said as much to her mother, who did laugh now, with some mirth. ‘I don’t know, Debby. Maybe, maybe not. Maybe things *are* preordained. But maybe it’s all just random, and maybe that means we do just get lucky sometimes. Just because you might lose a penny, it doesn’t mean you’ll never find a pound.’ Carole squeezed Debby’s hand in return, then let it go. She shrugged, lightly.

‘All I know is what I feel; that what I’ve told you over the last few days isn't something I could’ve said a month ago. I don’t know why, but maybe I don’t need to. I think sometimes it just muddies the water to overthink some of what happens to us in this life. Perhaps we should just accept and enjoy where we are now, instead of being preoccupied with how or why we got here.’

Debby was pensive. ‘This grandchild of yours, Mum. He or she is going to need you. And Dad too. Grandparents will be important.’

Carole smiled and nodded. We’ll be at the other end of the country, of course, but we do want to be involved in whatever way we can, if you let us.’

‘I do wonder sometimes, you know, whether we’ve done the right thing in moving up here. On so many levels it makes perfect sense, but on just as many others, it doesn’t at all.’

‘Oh, I think it’s a good move, for all the reasons you originally said. It’s good for your careers, you’ve managed to buy a lovely little cottage, that you’re mortgage free on already, and you really shouldn’t underestimate how well *that* sets you up financially, for the years to come. It’s going to be great for your little one to grow up in a more peaceful environment too. Don’t worry about us old crusties,’ she added. ‘We’re not too old to drive, or catch a bus or a train, and you’ll visit plenty, I’m sure?’

‘Of course we will! We know how important it is for our child to know its family. Distance isn’t what it used to be, and it’s easier than ever to stay in touch, these days. We’ll make sure nobody misses out.’

Carole smirked. 'Well, you never know. Once your Dad retires officially, I wouldn't rule *us* out of moving away from the city either. I'm not saying we'd move all the way up here, but we're not completely opposed to the idea of coming a *bit* closer. We could get a nice house cheaper, with a decent garden, a bit like what you two have done, and maybe have a bit of a nest-egg left over.'

Debby was astonished. 'But what about Jayne? And what about all your friends?'

'Oh, Jayne has no idea yet where she wants to be, or what she really wants to do. It could be years before she figures that out, if she *ever* does! We can't stay put, just because of her. And as for our friends, well the same logic applies! Social media, public transport and driving. It's not like we have the top end of social lives, for goodness sake! We probably only go out once or twice a month! We can't live our lives for other people, Debby. We have to make decisions that make us feel good about the way *we* want to live.'

Carole poured them both another cup of tea. 'And I'm well aware of the irony, by the way, after *you* said the exact same things to *me*, just a few months ago.'

She pushed the cup of tea towards Debby. 'But tell me, d'you remember a place called Lytham St Annes, by any chance? We passed through there, years ago, when we took you and Jayne to Blackpool for a long weekend.

Debby shook her head. 'I remember the fun park; the Pleasure Beach, was it called? And I remember the gaming arcades and the tower, and a Ferris wheel on a pier somewhere, but I don't remember the place you're talking about.'

'Well, it's quite nice. On the seafront, not far from Blackpool. Very well-established houses and gardens there. We passed through again the other day, on our way up here. We stopped overnight in a guesthouse, to get a feel for the place, and we're going to stop again on our way home to take a little look at amenities, house prices, that sort of thing. It might be a reasonable compromise.'

The front door of Teapot Cottage opened and Debby's dad stepped through it, with a small bag of groceries. He broke into a wide smile, as soon as he saw her.

'Twice in three days! We're honoured!' He gave her a cheeky wink.

'I'm making up for lost time, and I know you're heading off tomorrow. Mum tells me you're going house-hunting in Lytham St Annes! That's pretty exciting.'

'It's just an idea,' Carole interjected, anxiously, and Don laughed.

'Yes, just an idea at this stage, but it might not be a bad one. D'you want to come back later, for supper? He held up his bag of groceries. 'Spag Bol, with garlic bread and salad. I can stretch it out?'

'Sorry, Dad. Darren's on evening call-out duty tonight, and I'm desperate for an early night. My back's aching and I could sleep for a week! But why don't you both come for breakfast tomorrow morning, before you hit the road?'

'Yes, we can do that. We want an early start though. Want to be on the road before nine.'

'Come at eight, then, and I'll have it all ready. Darren has to go before nine anyway, so that should all be perfect.'

Debby stood and hugged her mother. Carole was still as stiff as an ironing board, but she did put an arm around Debby and pat her on the back. That was progress! Debby also hugged her dad, and he hugged her back quite tightly.

In the car on the way home, she reflected on how, in the space of just a few months, everything had completely changed. A year ago, she and her parents had been so very, very far, from where they'd managed to get to now. They had finally promised to try and accept Darren too, now, which was the most important thing of all.

The future felt like it might be a lot brighter for them all. The child they were bringing into the world deserved to have the best possible chance of a life enriched by grandparents on *both* sides of the family. For the first time, it looked like that might at last be possible.

Torley seemed to be full of interesting people, with good hearts. Debby had always been a private person, and she was a long way from being comfortable with the idea that people she hardly knew would probably end up knowing a lot more about her than she really wanted them to. Carla Walton had warned her, about how hard it might be to keep as much privacy as she'd like.

But she had to admit that the people she'd met so far seemed genuine, with their kindness and concern. Perhaps it wouldn't hurt to let people in, a little more. After all, she really didn't want to end up like her mother; guarded, suspicious, and intolerant.

You had to make conscious decisions to change, if you wanted those changes to serve you. It wasn't enough, to hope for the best; that you'd somehow simply 'evolve' into a completely different and better person. You had to work at it. In much the same way as Carole and Don had to work to stay together, and to be better parents to their daughters, Debby and Darren had to work too, to fit into a new community where expectations were different. They had made a conscious decision to turn their backs on a big, impersonal city, and move to a small town where connections were closer and stronger. To fit into that culture, they had to be at least a little more 'accessible' to the people around them. Gone was the time where they wouldn't know their neighbours, but maybe that was no bad thing.

Everybody had to adjust their sails, at some point in life, she mused, to keep clear of a battering head-wind. She resolved to be more accepting of the local people who wanted to know more about her and her family. As Carla, Adie and Feen had all said, nobody in Torley was mean. Most people genuinely cared, and Debby was looking forward to making new friendships with people who said what they meant, and meant what they said. That, she thought to herself, would be a welcome change!

One Year Later

Debby smiled gently to herself, as she sat in her favourite wicker chair on the patio outside the front door, and watched the sun dip below the roof of Appletree cottage. There was always so much peace in the garden. Whatever the season, whether lush in spring, or more skeletal in winter, it was a beautiful, tranquil space.

Autumn was here once again, and many of the leaves had fallen already, after a very pretty time when all the colours in the garden at Appletree Cottage had changed and put on a show that could rival the autumnal hues of any official arboretum. Don's planting had ensured an abundance of colour. Glorious golds and rich reds sat alongside warm tones of rust, and honeyed hues of amber, as autumn glided by.

The gorgeous garden had so much character, now. Everything was even more beautiful than he'd promised it would be, a year on from when he'd put it all together. All through the past year, Darren and Debby had tended it with reverent care, and they'd enjoyed it immensely throughout the spring and summer. Even now, as winter was fast approaching, the days could still be lovely, with enough warmth and sunshine to allow them to still sit outside.

Ruby-Ellen Davies had arrived safe and well in early April, ten days late, after a long but straightforward labour. She came into the world with a thick shock of blonde hair and bright blue eyes, which had stayed blue. She was shaping up to look more like her mother than her dad, but it was early days, so they couldn't assume anything yet.

Debby and Darren had cried like babies themselves, when they held her for the first time. She was their miracle, their longed-for child, and she was completely, beautifully perfect in every possible way. Debby's gynaecologist had declared that he could see no reason why she shouldn't have several more babies if she wanted them. She and Darren were both keen for that, but they were content for now with Ruby. They knew that if another baby did come along, it would arrive when it was meant to happen, in no one else's time but its own.

The cottage was finished now, too, complete with the gorgeous new kitchen. Darren's mother Barbara, who'd done a diploma in interior design, had an amazing eye for colours and textures that worked well together. She and Debby had come up with a creative combination of traditional fabrics and soft modern colours, and the end result was a fresh and bright but cosy and inviting home. The two women had often talked for hours, comparing swatches and styles, and one or the other would regularly yelp with delight at finding the perfect item online. They'd natter half a night away, sometimes. Sheila Shalloe had offered Debby some beautiful designer curtains too, in her chosen colours, and they'd come with matching cushion covers.

Darren still hadn't found out who'd cleared the driveway so beautifully for them when they first arrived, and it very much looked like he never would. Nobody would own up to knowing anything about it at all. All anyone would say, when he asked around, was that 'things like that just happen around here.' It seemed that if someone needed a helping hand, someone else would often pitch in and provide it, without feeling the need to shout about it.

The implication was that he should simply accept the anonymous gift, in the spirit in which it had been offered, thank you very much, and stop asking questions. So he resolved to do just that, and to pay the same sort of kindness forward to someone who might need it, whenever the chance arose.

The estate agent, Lance Martin, had recommended his brother, who ran a local renovation and retrofit business, to come and strip the cottage floors, and wax them back to their former glory. The cost had been surprisingly reasonable, and Debby and Darren had been delighted to learn that the floorboards were all made of pine. Most were in good condition, with only a few in the bathroom needing to be replaced because of water damage. The dust had been horrendous, during the reclamation process, but the end result was stunning. The floors, throughout the entire house, were absolutely beautiful. Darren had remarked that he could never go back to carpet, and Debby had agreed on the spot. Instead, they'd splurged on some sumptuous rugs, to take the chill off the floors in winter.

The stone stairs at Appletree Cottage had been highly polished and had also come up a treat, and an elegant modern wrought iron and wooden handrail had been added. A lovely little office space had been tucked in underneath the stairs.

A fair bit of dry rot had been found in a few of the rafters in the back left-hand corner of the cottage, and that had held things up by a few weeks, because it all had to be replaced. They'd been shocked by the cost but had no choice about getting it done. It had hurt their budget but they'd managed to make the repairs and press on with the rest of the renovations. Pat had also lined the floor in the loft so they could use it as storage for now, with an eye on the possibility of a full conversion sometime in the future.

After the bathroom had gone in, and the eye-wateringly expensive kitchen had been fitted, complete with its sparkling new and gorgeous bottle-green Aga, an impromptu decorating working bee had taken place. 'Egg and Peric' Tripper (as they seemed to be locally known!) had showed up at the front door early one Sunday morning, out of the blue, with a massive potful of vegetable soup, another of chicken stew, and enough bread rolls to feed an army. They'd grinned as they came in with everything, and when Debby asked Peg what on earth was happening, she'd just winked and said; 'wait and see, love.'

Withing fifteen minutes of that, Eric had let an army of people in (including the Ravens, and Lance Martin and his wife Maggie) who had had turned up wielding paint brushes and rollers, wallpaper pasting tables, plastering trowels, power tools, and all sorts of other paraphernalia, and had set to work getting the house decorated. Debby and Darren had both been gobsmacked, until Mark Raven had explained, with a gentle shrug.

'It's just summat that's done, fer't locals. It were done fer me and' me first wife, a long time ago, when we 'ad a lot to do at Ravensdown. And we didn't even 'ave a babbie on't way like you do! It's just what tends to 'appen around 'ere, lad.' He'd given Darren a wink.

'At some stage yer might fancy bein' part of a workin' bee yerself, for some new bugger who might need an 'and to get established.'

At the end of that day, as everyone sat around with a beer or a glass of wine in their hand, toasting the job well done, Debby had turned to Darren and seen the happy tears in his eyes that matched her own. Haltingly, they'd both stood up and made speeches of sorts, thanking their new friends for the help, the love, and the welcome they'd all given. It was a humbling thing, to be so supported by people who still didn't really know them but were willing to do all they could to make them welcome and help them settle in. Debby smiled now, remembering how profound that was.

Lance, and his wife Maggie and their kids, had gone on to become firm friends. The couples shared a handful of common interests, and regularly got together for a bite to eat. In summer it was usually a barbecue in the garden, and in the colder months they'd sometimes have supper in front of the fire, at the lovely round pine dining table Debby had also bought from Carla's. She and Darren went just as often to Fellview Lodge; Lance and Maggie's modern stone-and-timber bungalow, just a little further down the road.

Debby was slowly getting to know some of the other mums in the area too, as a result of finally having some 'social currency' of her own. She met up for coffee with Feen, whenever she was back from London, and she and Darren regularly saw Mark and Adie too. They had become good friends, and Debby had also become good friends with one of the vet nurses at the surgery where Darren worked, who was also currently on maternity leave with a newborn. Being so readily accepted into the new community, like she finally 'fitted in' somewhere, was the most amazing feeling.

She had also recently started an informal weekly drop-in chat group, in a church hall over in Carlisle, for women who were struggling with infertility. So far, the group was going – and growing – very well. After starting with just two other women, there were now seven who were meeting every Tuesday evening for an hour and a half, to share their stories of sadness, frustration and hope. Debby could see that the weekly meetings were helping a lot, to reduce the chronic isolation the women were feeling, that she understood all too well. The irony hadn't escaped her, that only eighteen months ago she'd been horrified beyond belief at the prospect of attending a group like the one she was running now!

Badger had a new friend now too, a five-year-old springer spaniel cross, called Dolly, who had managed to run away with Darren's heart after her ageing owner unexpectedly died. Her son had brought Dolly to the surgery to see if the vets knew anyone who might want an already housetrained, happy dog with no behavioural problems. Darren had 'bagged' her in a heartbeat.

Two more cats had also joined the Davies family, a feisty young male tabby called Denzel and a white long-haired imperious old female called Queenie. She had pink eyes and she was as deaf as a post, but she always had plenty to say. Their old cat, Lindy-Lou, wasn't sure what to make of either of the two new felines, and after a few days of hissing and growling at each one when they arrived, she finally decided to just ignore them both.

Darren was a definite sucker for the waifs and strays that occasionally turned up at the surgery. He didn't bring all of them home, but that was only because Debby had put her foot down. She knew that if her soft-as-butter husband had his way, they'd be overrun with cats, dogs, and heaven knew what else, in next to no time. Of course, it was a hazard of the job for any vet who was even *half* as soft as Darren, that their house would end up being overrun with pets of different kinds. Debby was dreading the day when he'd come home with a pair of orphaned piglets or his arms full of fox cubs or pheasants.

They had gratefully accepted Adie's hens though, who'd otherwise been threatened with slaughter. They'd come with a rooster, as an unconditional part of the deal, and it had taken a while, to get used to him crowing at the crack of dawn, and often well before. But, after managing to overcome the deep desire to wring the poor creature's neck, they eventually got used to him, and he became as much a part of the family as every other critter was.

A pair of ducks had started visiting regularly too, probably from the reservoir just outside of Torley town. They quickly worked out that they had to keep well out of Denzel's wily way, and dodge the odd swipe from the increasingly irritable Lindy-Lou, but they didn't have to worry so much about old Queenie, who considered herself well above being distracted by such a trivial matter as birdlife, and usually looked at them with a level of disdain that only a matriarch cat could muster.

It was quite an impressive little family, when you thought about it.

And the blessings hadn't stopped at that. Beyond the twenty-two legs and four tails (if you didn't count the chickens) that made up the Davies family at Appletree Cottage (so far), there had been some extraordinary developments with the in-laws.

Before Don and Carole Cameron had left for home after their stay at Teapot Cottage, they'd come to breakfast at Appletree Cottage as arranged. Over the sumptuous feast Debby had cooked, they'd invited Darren to tell them his life's journey.

He'd told them everything, no holds barred, and at the end of his story they'd been stunned. Neither Don nor Carole could deny what kind of man he had to be, to have turned his life so dramatically around after something so devastating, to become a successful veterinary surgeon with a wife, a baby on the way, a home of his own that was owned outright, and the possibility of one day become a partner in his practice.

It was an extraordinary triumph over adversity, and it's magnitude hadn't escaped the Camerons. Nor had the fact that Darren was the gentlest, most generous and tender-hearted man imaginable, to their daughter. He adored her, and they finally had to admit it. It got to the point where they simply couldn't find a single reason in the world not to like him.

Relations had become been far more cordial, since then, to the extent that Don and Carole had been to visit twice; once when Ruby was born, and again a couple of months after that. Ironically, they were very comfortable in the caravan, which had stayed in the driveway after the renovations to Appletree Cottage had been completed. It was a compromise, because – much to their annoyance – Teapot Cottage had already been booked, both times they'd wanted to come.

Although they might never be bosom buddies, Darren and Carole had found a new respect for one another. As far as he was concerned, his mother-in-law's earlier attitude was gone and forgotten, and as far as *she* was concerned, she felt fortunate to have been so easily forgiven.

Debby's sister Jayne had recently returned from travelling and taken up a new full-time job in Manchester, before moving in and getting settled with a woman she'd fallen head over heels in love with, who already lived there. They'd met in Tanzania, when they'd both arrived there for a safari tour aimed at single female travellers. It seemed that Jaye would now be staying put, having found someone 'worth hanging up her travel shoes for' as she'd put it. Don and Carole were now more actively considering relocating to their beloved Lytham St Annes, now that both of their daughters were living 'up North.'

Debby and Barbara had got closer too, initially thanks to their collaboration over decorating Appletree Cottage, and they now talked regularly on the phone. Debby found an ease of communication with Barbara that she'd never had with her own mother, and Barbara was thrilled to be so much closer to her son's wife. She and Pat had been frequent visitors, over the past year.

Darren and Debby had spent their first Christmas at Appletree Cottage by themselves, before Ruby was born. It was the last time it would ever be just the two of them, and although they were excited about Ruby's arrival, they wanted to cherish their very last time as a unit of two.

This Christmas was going to be very different. Barbara and Pat would be here, and staying in the caravan. Carole and Don would be here too, but they'd booked in at The Beeches for Christmas week. Yet again, Teapot Cottage was unavailable; Adie's family would be there. Jayne had also booked a few nights at the hotel, with her girlfriend Liss. It seemed that the whole family would be together, and Debby was excited about that. The distance had brought everyone closer, and the irony of that wasn't lost on her.

Everyone would be having Christmas lunch at Appletree Cottage. She was keen to show off her newly-acquired Aga skills, safe in the knowledge that Barbara and Pat would be pitching in, as would Darren himself, to make sure the Christmas lunch coming out of her kitchen would be just as perfect as the kitchen was itself.

After that, there would be time for the King's speech and probably an afternoon snooze, before they all headed off to the Christmas Night party that was held every year at Ravensdown House. It was, by all accounts, *the* event of the Christmas calendar for the Raven family's friends in the area, many of whom were farmers.

Darren and Debby's entire family had been invited this year, which was incredibly generous, but that was fairly typical of Mark and Adie. '*The more the merrier*' was always their motto, especially at Christmas. Feen and her husband Gavin would be there, and so would Carla and Dave. There would be kids running around too, and for the first time in many years, Debby was glad about that.

Her mum and dad had been to a handful of relationship counselling sessions, after they'd realised a need to re-evaluate their marriage and get it onto a more equal footing, if it were to survive. Don was finding the counselling helpful. Carole said she was on the fence, but although she could still be infuriatingly stubborn, critical to a fault, and pointlessly picky at times, Debby had sensed a softening around her mother's sharper edges. She was learning to listen, and to share her own thoughts in a more constructive way. The counselling process was helping her too, even if she didn't realise it.

Her parents still had a long way to go, to be truly happy together, with each of them feeling like their needs were being met, but they genuinely loved one another, and they wanted to try and make things better. With the changes she'd seen so far, Debby believed they'd succeed.

She looked down now at Ruby, who was asleep alongside her, in her cane bassinette. She would soon be ready for her proper cot, the one Debby and Darren had bought from Carla's furniture shop in the town.

When Dave Holloway had delivered it early on a Saturday morning, all those months ago, Darren had offered him a bacon sandwich and a coffee. Across the dining table, the two men had quickly become friends. Dave was fun to be around, and so was Carla, even as she was trying to pretend she wasn't. She was a very keen observer of other people, and while she never remarked on someone's habits in a nasty way, her sarcastic summations were usually quite clever, often very astute, and nearly always funny. She also had a wickedly sarcastic sense of humour, and a surprisingly generous heart. Debby liked her a lot, and always made time to drop in for a coffee with her at her shop, whenever she was in town.

She stood now, and lifted Ruby from the bassinette. The baby was getting heavy. She weighed more than a stone now, and in a month or so she'd actually be learning to crawl.

Darren came outside and stood behind her. She smiled as he slid his arms around her waist, and chuckled as Ruby reached out a fat little hand to grasp the collar of his shirt.

'I've just had a call to say the firewood we ordered will be arriving in about an hour, Debs. D'you want to come inside now babe, and close that door? It's cold out here, now the sun's gone.'

'Yeah, I was just thinking the same thing.'

He leaned forward and lightly murmured into her right ear.

'You can never get enough of being out here, and looking at this gorgeous English garden, can you?'

'No. I never get tired of it. I don't think I ever will. It's not quite the view from Teapot Cottage, but it's *our* view and it'll do very nicely, thank you very much.'

Darren squeezed her waist, gently. 'We've done okay, babe, haven't we?'

She felt the tears well up in her eyes as she felt his arms draw her closer, and she inhaled the sweet smell of Ruby's beautiful blonde hair.

'Yes,' she said softly. 'We've done okay. It's been a long, hard road, but we've got here, in the end. It's mad, when you think about it; all that roaring and screaming we went through, about getting pregnant, when all I ever had to do was stop panicking, relax, and let things happen when they were meant to. Getting onto a better footing with Mum and Dad has been amazing too, and this cottage? Well, if Ruby is the icing on our cake, this little house is the cherry on the top of it.'

'Yes. You know, I've been thinking a lot over the past few months, about what Feen Raven said, and I think she was right, Debs, when she said that nothing happens, cosmically, until it's *meant* to happen. I've never been one for all that weird bloody New-Age stuff, have I? But I do find myself wondering, how she always knew that things would fall into place when the time was right, and not before. She said everything would come together for us, and it has, just like she predicted. I dunno how she seems to understand what's out there, and how it all works, when most of us mere mortals don't.'

'I know! She was so serene about my life, when I told her what a mess I thought it was; how hopeless. She just shrugged and said that I shouldn't worry about *any* of it. She told me our lives would change, but it would all be good. And they *did* change, and it *is* good. In fact it's so much *better* than good, I can hardly believe it. What a difference a year makes.'

'A year, and a magic cottage.'

Debby chuckled. 'You know, I think you might be right about that. Teapot Cottage is pretty special, isn't it? Gavin Black might have been right, when he said there was magic there. Look at what's happened since we went there! It's not just Ruby, it's all the stuff with Mum and Dad too. I wonder if any of it would have happened if we hadn't all gone there.'

'Who's to say, babe? It's one of the great questions of our lives, I guess, that we'll probably never be able to answer. But it led us to this place, and to the job of my dreams, didn't it? Even if the other stuff would've happened anyway, down in Devon, we had to have been at Teapot Cottage, for *this* to have come together the way it has.' Darren's voice was pensive.

'You're right, and I do feel we've landed where we were always meant to. I hope that one day Appletree Cottage will feel just as special as Teapot Cottage does.'

'It already does, to me. It did from the minute I saw it. I *felt* something here, and I still do, and I can't describe it, but maybe there's magic here, too. But I have a more pressing question, Mrs Davies. My question right now is; have you worked out what might be magic about *me*?'

She shifted Ruby onto her other hip then turned to kiss him gently. 'Oh yes, I'm very clear indeed about *your* magic, Dr Davies. I have no confusion whatsoever, about that.'

'Does it have anything to do with making beautiful babies, by any chance?'

'Indeed it does, sir! It most *certainly* does and, of course, the all-important practice involved in the process.'

'D'you think you could show me how to make the most of my talent, then?'

'I'd be glad to. Let me put this baby down for a nap. Once I've done that, I think there might be something we can be getting on with, in a manner of speaking, before that firewood truck arrives.'

Note from the Author:

*If you enjoyed this, or any of my other books, I'd love you to leave a review on Amazon.
It would mean a lot!*

www.anniecookwriter.com

Facebook: Annie Cook Writer
Instagram: anniecookwriter

Acknowledgements

For their input and support in bringing this book to the reader, heartfelt thanks go to:

My husband and best friend, Kerry Purvis, for putting up with everything an author is, and says, and does, even when none of it makes sense.

Dr Valentina Mauro (Senior Consultant and specialist in Gynaecology and Reproductive Medicine) from the Bourn Hall Cinic In Cambridge, England, for her expert guidance on the IVF treatment process, and her valuable perspective on the effects of unexplained infertility, on mental health and relationships.

Matt Manolides, Geospatial Product Expert, and Head of Overhead Imagery Operations at Google, for reassuring me that nobody is crazy for believing that sat-nav maps have human gremlins as route designers.

John and Phil; two amazing men who wish to remain unidentified, but who were brave enough to share their innermost thoughts and feelings with me about how infertility has affected their lives.

My long-time friend, Ruth Fegan, who has always been a rock to me in every way that matters.

Also by Annie Cook...

No Small Change

A Teapot Cottage Tale (#1)

**The 'change of life' means menopause.
But what if it also means reinvention, with the help of a little bit of magic?**

Adie Bostock is a self-confessed 'basket-case.' She's fifty-two, at the mercy of her haphazard hormones, and struggling to face the end of her marriage. Alone for Christmas and fed up with family drama, she lands at Teapot Cottage where she plans to wallow in guilt and self-pity in private.

But the cottage, with its mysterious healing energy, has other plans for Adie and she soon finds out that it takes more than one person to make things fall apart, and more than one to put them back together.

Confirmed widower Mark Raven is a rough-edged farmer determined to hide his heart. He's battling with grief and ageing, and keeping his rather dreamy daughter at least partly in the real world. Romance is not on his radar.

Adie and Mark want to keep things purely platonic, but an unseen influence is nudging them in a different direction. Then Adie's husband decides he wants her back. It's what she's been praying for, but is it still what she really wants?

Escape to the Lakes District, with this magical, life-affirming story about overcoming adversity and finding love again later in life.

The Power of Notes and Spells
A Teapot Cottage Tale (#2)

Every woman dreams of finding the love of her life. But what do you do when yours brings baggage that can hurt you and your family?

Feen Raven is often described as more than just a little bit barmy. The young 'white witch' has finally found her soulmate, but old family wounds are opened again when she finds out who he's involved with.

Gavin Black is on an unhappy errand that forces him to reconnect with his estranged mother. All he wants is to claim what's his and go home again, without any complications.

Carla Walton can't let go of a grudge. After a lifetime of pushing everyone away, she is isolated, bitter, and blaming everyone else for her problems. She wants to be left alone so she can keep ignoring her demons.

But Teapot Cottage, with its mysterious ability to heal the broken-hearted, always has a more complicated agenda for people who don't want to rake up the past. Pretty soon, Gavin, Feen and Carla come to question everything they think they do and don't want in life.

Will love and a little bit of magic help them find a way forward? Or will old family fractures be too hard to heal?

Come to the Lake District, to a gentle place where a beautiful blend of music and magic can heal the hardest hearts.

A Moral Swerve

Nobody comes home expecting to find intruders -
But what would you do if you did?

Alison Jones is single, lives alone, and doesn't have a lot of self-awareness. But, after coming home to find burglars in her house, she does a terrible thing without thinking, and is forced to confront some ugly truths about herself.

Darren Davies is a petty thief, stuck in the revolving door between small-time crime and prison. After he makes the biggest mistake of his life, he is compelled to re-evaluate the path his life is taking, and deal with the demons that drive him.

When Darren and Alison's lives intersect, they each find themselves on a soul-searing journey, as they struggle to come to terms with the catastrophic impact of their acts and omissions. After stumbling through the wreckage, the future for them both becomes crystal clear, but it's not what either of them expected.

As one door opens and another slams shut, choices expand and diminish.

At the crossroads of Beginnings and Endings,
who decides to go where?

Coming soon…

Ruin, Reins and Redemption
A Teapot Cottage Tale (#4)

Everyone makes mistakes, and some of them are hard to come back from. When you've taken someone else's life, and destroyed your family in the process, where do you begin, to pull things back together?

Stuart Thomson is a disgraced lawyer whose catastrophic error of judgement has all but ruined his life. By the time he leaves prison, after six years, he no longer has a career, a home or a marriage, and his troubled teenage daughter is barely speaking to him.

Meghan Thomson is almost fifteen. She's a mixed-up mess of anger and confusion, and she has no idea how she feels about anything at all, especially her father. When he books a holiday to the Lake District together, to reconnect, it's the last thing she really wants to do with a man she doesn't trust.

On holiday, father and daughter both struggle to understand each other. But Teapot Cottage, with its enigmatic way of turning troubled lives around, reveals an amazing opportunity they once could never have imagined. The future on offer means a whole new level of faith and commitment from them both, to make it happen.

Stuart and Meghan desperately need a new start. Can they trust themselves and each other enough to make it happen? Or does the heartbreak of the past make the leap of faith too tough?

In Torley town, in a very special cottage, lives are often transformed with the help of 'a little bit of love and magic.'